PRAISE FO
The Woman at th.

"An adventurous woman ahead of her time. . . . A fascinating historical novel."
—*New York Times* bestselling author Natasha Lester

"A uniquely female perspective of World War I. . . . A beautiful, touching, romantic women's fiction novel that is sure to delight fans of *Outlander* and *Downton Abbey*."
—*New York Times* bestselling author Lori Nelson Spielman

"Realistic and emotionally engaging. You'll believe every word."
—*Toronto Star*

"An absorbing and immersive portrait of a woman whose courage, determination, and resolve would be exceptional in any age—but forged in the crucible of the Great War, tested again and again by a society riven by change, Dr. Eleanor Atherton is a heroine I will not soon forget."
—*USA Today* bestselling author Jennifer Robson

"A riveting tale of medicine, courage, and grace under fire during the Great War. . . . Compulsively readable!"
—*USA Today* bestselling author Stephanie Marie Thornton

"Cornwall's realistic depiction of the battlefield horrors is enhanced by her magnetic, multidimensional characters. This emotionally charged novel delivers the goods."
—*Publishers Weekly*

"Meticulously researched and deeply emotional—Cornwall has a gift for bringing history to life."
—Christine Wells, author of *Sisters of the Resistance*

"Cornwall's book is a spellbinding read. The gritty descriptions of the makeshift hospitals in the midst of battle ring true, and the dialogue is pitch perfect."
—Historical Novel Society

THAT SUMMER IN BERLIN

LECIA CORNWALL

BERKLEY

New York

BERKLEY
An imprint of Penguin Random House LLC
penguinrandomhouse.com

Copyright © 2022 by Lecia Cotton Cornwall
Readers Guide copyright © 2022 by Lecia Cotton Cornwall
Penguin Random House supports copyright. Copyright fuels creativity, encourages
diverse voices, promotes free speech, and creates a vibrant culture. Thank you for
buying an authorized edition of this book and for complying with copyright laws
by not reproducing, scanning, or distributing any part of it in any form without
permission. You are supporting writers and allowing Penguin Random House
to continue to publish books for every reader.

BERKLEY and the BERKLEY & B colophon are registered
trademarks of Penguin Random House LLC.

Library of Congress Cataloging-in-Publication Data

Names: Cornwall, Lecia, author.
Title: That summer in Berlin / Lecia Cornwall.
Description: First Edition. | New York: Berkley, 2022.
Identifiers: LCCN 2022001433 (print) | LCCN 2022001434 (ebook) |
ISBN 9780593197943 (trade paperback) | ISBN 9780593197950 (ebook) |
Subjects: LCGFT: Novels.
Classification: LCC PR9199.4.C673 T48 2022 (print) |
LCC PR9199.4.C673 (ebook) | DDC 813/.6—dc23
LC record available at https://lccn.loc.gov/2022001433
LC ebook record available at https://lccn.loc.gov/2022001434

First Edition: October 2022

Printed in the United States of America
1st Printing

To Alphonse,

soul mate, confidante,

North Star

THAT SUMMER
IN BERLIN

PART I

English Pastimes

CHAPTER ONE

South Coast of England
September 1935

THERE WAS A storm coming.

Viviane Alden stood on the shore, the round pebbles shifting under her feet. For a moment she clutched the thick robe close to her throat as she stared out across the English Channel. The air was already yellow and heavy, but the dark clouds remained distant, mounded on the horizon over France. The waves were starting to kick up, but for now they were still merely fretful rather than angry.

She could still go back, climb the cliff, and slip into the house before anyone knew she was missing. All was in chaos anyway, with everyone busy preparing for tonight's party at Halliwell Hall. Now there was a storm she'd gladly miss. Her stepsisters would barely notice her absence, though her mother would certainly fly into a rage if she knew where Viviane was at this moment.

She stayed put, staring out across the water. This day was a sacred annual ritual for her, and her mother was probably still in bed, sipping tea and complaining about having so many things to manage. There was Margaret's betrothal party tonight, to be followed by her wedding. Julia, her second stepdaughter, was due to make her London debut in the spring, and the fifteen-year-old twins, Felicity and Grace, were unruly, inquisitive creatures who thrived on mischief. Fortunately, Miles, her stepson and Lord Rutherford's heir, was away at Eton, and out from underfoot. There was also Viviane's own wedding to the Marquess of Medway to plan for.

Except there wasn't. Not anymore.

Viviane had called Phillip last night and broken it off, though she hadn't told her mother yet. There'd be time later, of course. Or possibly not, with all that was going on today. The conversation would have to happen eventually—another storm that would need to be weathered— but today was not a day for the kind of news that would lead only to disappointment, arguments, and questions she didn't want to answer, first from her mother, then her stepsisters. They'd join forces as a unified flock to peck Viviane to pieces over letting a prime catch like Phillip Medway go. Then she'd have to face her stepfather. She raised her chin against the wind. She had her reasons, and it was between her and Phillip alone.

Today she had other things to think about. Seven years ago, on this very day, at this very hour, Viviane's entire world had collapsed.

She didn't cry or turn to look west toward Cornwall and home—her old home, since Kellyn, where her father had died, was lost to her now. She'd been the one to find him that morning, in the lake, and this was how she chose to remember him. What better way to dispel the horror of a drowning than by defying the waters? She was the Lady of the Lake—or of the English Channel, now—and she was an excellent swimmer.

Her mother had forbidden her to go near the water after her father's death, fearing Viviane would drown, too.

Viviane took a breath, ran down the shingle, and plunged into the icy waves.

The cold water closed around her. It wasn't like the warm green waters of the Lady's Lake at Kellyn. The Channel was fast and dangerous, black and salty, like tears. She waited for the water to become benevolent around her body, buoy her up in a loose, cool grip. It was memory and torment and pleasure all in one.

She hadn't cried on the day of her father's funeral, or even when her mother had told her that Kellyn, the estate that had been home to the Alden family for hundreds of years, was to be sold because there was no money to pay the exorbitant death duties.

At fourteen, she'd been too young and too shattered to ask questions, and her mother was consumed by her own anguished grief, torn between anger and loss. Did she remember the anniversary? Would she have agreed to this date for Margaret's betrothal party if she did? In seven years, she'd never mentioned the events of that day, the way she'd found Viviane, white-faced and silent by the lake, next to the lifeless body of her father, his face turned to the sky, his eyes filled with water and nothing else. Her mother's anguished screams had scared the birds from the trees.

The waves were kicking up in earnest now, a tantrum against the bully wind. Seabirds swooped, fighting the gathering power of the gale to screech a warning to her.

She ignored them. She wasn't afraid of the waves or tricky currents, was sure of the strength in her body, the power of her whole, healthy lungs. She'd fallen and broken her left leg as a child, and was left with scars and a permanent limp. She was awkward and clumsy on land, so her father had taught her to rule the water. They swam together like fish, like diving birds, like swans, and then lay on the grassy bank beside the lake to dry in the sun. When he'd caught his breath, and the wheeze and crackle in his damaged lungs eased, he told her tales of King Arthur, the sword Excalibur, the first Sir Alden of Kellyn, and Viviane, the Lady of the Lake. "The Aldens are the true guardians of the great sword, lass. Don't ever forget that. It is our duty to be worthy of that honor, to right what wrongs we can and do our best for those who need us most." He'd rise from the grass, knowing he must get dry and warm and return to the house to take the medicine that helped his lungs, ruined by a gas attack during the war. "A vile and cowardly weapon," he said. He rarely said more, but she knew when he was in pain by the strain on his face, by the harsh sound of his breathing, the rasps and whistles and hacking coughs. She'd also known that it had been getting worse, and he had more bad days than good.

The whole village—the whole country—had mourned the death of Major Sir Arthur Alden of Kellyn. Soldiers who'd served with him came from all over the country for his funeral. Winston Churchill had been there, and Lloyd George, and the Earl of Rutherford, who would become Mama's second husband.

Viviane took another deep breath and kicked hard, fought the fierce shove of the waves, pushing back with every stroke. *She* would never drown. She felt the cold numb her, willing her to let go, to release the air in her straining lungs. Was this what her father had felt in his last moments? She held her breath until her chest ached and dark spots spun before her eyes. Only then did she kick for the surface, using her weaker leg, forcing it to take her upward. She drew a long breath just as a wave crashed over her, and she swallowed half of it, coughing, choking on the burning salt water as it filled her throat.

The storm tide spun her around, stronger now. The distant shore was all but obscured by the rising waves. She was being carried away from the beach, and safety.

She gasped for breath, began to swim, but she was tiring, pushed to her limit, her heart pounding, her scarred leg aching. She willed herself not to give in to panic, to endure, conquer, and be strong the way her father had taught her, but she felt the knife edge of fear.

"Ahoy!" The call was garbled by the water, and she couldn't tell if it was just the wind or a gull playing tricks on her.

"Ahoy, I say—is that a mermaid?"

Then she saw it, a small sailboat coming toward her, bounding across the waves. The *Kipper*, Reggie Farraday's boat. The sail was bowed outward, glutted to bursting with wild wind, and the wee craft bucked like a rodeo horse. It seemed a miracle that he'd come, good old Reggie, her friend, the boy—and the heir to the earldom—next door.

"Perhaps it's a selkie," another voice said, also male, Scots tinged, and unfamiliar. They came alongside and looked over the gunwale at her. She peered up into a pair of eyes as gray as the sea.

"Oho! I know this mermaid!" Reggie grinned, his teeth flashing as white as a gull's wing as he trimmed the sails to hold the boat still. "Vee! Is that really you? I thought you were forbidden to swim in the sea."

She sent him a sharp look that belied her predicament and her relief at seeing him. "I'm surprised to see you out here, too, Reggie, what with so much to do before the party tonight," she replied tartly. "How's the sailing?"

"There's a storm coming. We were just heading back, actually. There'll be thunder and lightning before the hour's out."

"Do you not see those clouds?" Reggie's companion asked her. She was surprised by the admonition in the stranger's tone. "Did no one ever tell you it's dangerous to swim in a tempest?"

Before Viviane could reply, Reggie did. "We'd best take charge. Pull her in, will you, Tom? I'll hold the boat steady."

"No need. I can swim back," Viviane said, stung by the scolding, but a hand reached over the side, the sleeve rolled up and the palm extended. She saw calluses and the smear of something dark on the tip of one finger. She could see his face now, the features even, his expression flat, even as his eyes snapped with irritation.

"Come on, give me your hand," he said, edging the command with impatience. She had no choice, of course, and he knew it. She took his hand and let him haul her over the side. She landed in the bottom of the boat like a flounder and quickly righted herself. He regarded her with curiosity and male interest. Her swimsuit clung to every curve, and she felt naked under his sharp gaze.

"Hello, darling," Reggie drawled. "You're very wet, aren't you?" He kept hold of the tiller and let her help herself up onto the seat. "Tom Graham, allow me to introduce the Honorable Miss Viviane Alden, a dear old friend of the family, and the woman I hoped I would one day marry, but alas, she is betrothed to a much better man than I." She sent him a quelling look, but he simply grinned and went on with the introductions. "Tom and Geoffrey were at Cambridge together, which is how he came to be chosen as my brother's best man. Tom's also a reporter, working at the London *Herald*, so watch what you say." He winked at Viviane, navigating the waves.

"*Alden*?" Something changed in Tom Graham's face, a slight tightening of his mouth. He gave a sharpness to her surname, almost an accusation. Had they met? She scanned his face, but he was indeed a stranger. He stared back, his brows furrowing slightly, as if he knew something suspect about her. Or perhaps he did not approve of women swimming. She felt her cheeks flushing despite the cold wind, and she looked away, raised her chin with aristocratic insouciance as she tucked her scarred left leg under her perfect right one. She pulled off her bathing cap, her eyes on the horizon. The wind was icy on her wet skin, and she clamped her teeth together to keep from shivering and wrapped her arms across her chest.

"I say, that breeze is kicking up fierce, isn't it?" Reggie said, hauling on the tiller as the little skiff bounced on the rising sea. He looked at

Viviane. "You're cold," he pronounced. "Tom, lend her your coat, would you?"

For a moment Tom Graham hesitated. "Well come on, old man. Consider it an act of chivalry. I'd give her my own if I was wearing one." Reggie was clad in a thick sweater. He might have given her that, but his friend was already removing his tweed jacket. He dropped it over her wet shoulders without a word, and without touching her.

"Thank you," Viviane said stiffly. The garment was warm from his body, and it smelled like shaving soap, and him, she supposed, different from Reggie's expensive cologne or the scent of tobacco and hair pomade that clung to her stepfather's clothes. She glanced at Tom Graham and wondered if he was cold without his jacket, but he was staring at the thick clouds barreling over the horizon, his eyes narrowed against the glare, dark hair blowing back from a wide, clear brow, his white shirt molding itself to his lean body. He looked like a pirate, especially when compared to Reggie's crisp appearance, his clipped hair, thin mustache, and tailored clothing, all of it bought at huge expense to ape the casual ease that Tom Graham had at what was likely a far lesser cost.

She scanned the shoreline, and realized she'd drifted quite a way from the small beach under Wrenwood House, her stepfather's estate. Goodness, she had been in danger, hadn't she? She cast a sidelong look at Tom Graham, who was staring at her again, a mix of puzzlement and censure in his sharp eyes. "Drop me back at the cove below Wrenwood," she said to Reggie. "You're probably as busy as I am—there's so much to do before the party tonight."

Reggie made a face. "Yes, shouldn't you be home making yourself beautiful? Not that you're not beautiful now, of course, but my sister has been trying to decide on which frock to wear all week. You'd think *she* was the bride. What time is Phillip arriving today?"

She lowered her gaze to her puckered fingertips. "He . . . can't make it."

She felt Reggie's eyes on her, knew his brows were rising and he was waiting for her to continue. If they were alone, she might have told him about her broken engagement, but she could hardly do that in front of a stranger, so she looked across the water and stayed silent. The square bulk of Wrenwood came into view, standing firm on the cliff top, its granite face unperturbed by this storm or any other. She realized Reggie was sailing straight past the cove. "Just set me down in Wrenwood Cove, Reggie," she said again.

He frowned. "If it's going to storm, I can hardly toss you back into the sea like an undersized flounder. Come back to Halliwell with us, and I'll drive you to Wrenwood."

Viviane considered the consequences if she arrived home in Reggie's car, clad only in her swimming costume and a strange man's coat.

"I can get back faster if I go the way I came," she said. She'd climb the cliff path, slip back into the house via the garden, and say that she'd been out doing laps in the swimming pool if anyone saw her.

But Reggie shook his head. "And risk you breaking your neck climbing that cliff path? I think not."

"I assume she climbed down the path," Tom said, regarding her as if she were a puzzle to be solved—or a fool, perhaps.

"Did you really?" Reggie asked.

"You know I did. It's too long to go along the road. I left my robe on the beach, and my camera." Still, he frowned. "Oh, *please*, Reggie—I can hardly arrive at Halliwell like this. What will *your* mother say if she sees me in nothing but my swimsuit and—and a man's coat? She'll have a houseful of guests, and she won't appreciate any unexpected antics today."

She cast a sideways glance at Tom Graham, saw the interest in his eyes, as if he wanted to hear more about unexpected antics. She held tight to the lapels of his coat and sent Reggie a warning look, silently commanding him to hold his tongue for once.

"Perhaps she'll think I rescued you," Reggie said, flashing a grin.

She sharpened her glare. "I wasn't in any need of rescue," she lied. "And there'd be awkward questions if I returned to Wrenwood in your car, soaking wet."

He sighed. "I suppose this isn't the day to unleash a scandal. Fine, then, back to the cove with you." He turned the boat, and she braced herself against the seat as the *Kipper* skipped over the waves.

"Do you swim often?" Tom Graham asked blandly, as if they were taking afternoon tea and making polite conversation.

"As often as possible," she replied in the same tone.

"Her mater doesn't like her to—she thinks it's dangerous, what with the currents here. I agree, but there's no stopping Vee," Reggie said, and winked at her. "She's as brave as a lion."

Tom Graham regarded her with flat speculation. She shrugged deeper into the battered tweed of his jacket and changed the subject. "What time is dinner tonight?" she asked Reggie, though she knew the answer.

"Drinks at eight, dinner at nine, dancing till dawn. Is your stepfather back from London?" Reggie asked.

"Not yet. He's expected this afternoon," Viviane replied. Tom Graham was looking at her legs—which one, the scarred one or the perfect one? Her belly tensed. She didn't like exposing her flaw, but there was no way to hide it now. There was no pity or disgust in his flat gaze, but it was impossible to tell what he *was* thinking. He seemed to have a remarkable way of hiding his thoughts. It left no way in, no way to make sense of him by little telltale details. She was good at that with most people, but not this man. His examination reached her face, and he met her eyes. She lifted her chin in warning, a dismissal, but he held her gaze, and she was the one who looked away first. "Is Geoffrey home yet?" she asked, her tone bland, at odds with the blush creeping over her cheeks.

"I'm collecting him at the station at half past ten. I rather thought under the circumstances he might travel down with your stepfather," Reggie said, unaware of her discomfiture. She plucked at the edges of Tom's jacket once again, arranging it, smoothing it, gathering her composure like a shield.

"No, Rutherford has meetings this morning, so he's driving down later. I understand he and Geoff met for dinner last night. Geoff telephoned Margaret after, but he wouldn't tell her a thing other than that the beef was excellent. She had visions of them poring over calendars and agendas, choosing the date for the wedding without her, just so it won't interfere with government business. They wouldn't dare set a date without Margaret and both mamas there."

Reggie laughed. "Poor old Geoff. If he thinks he's in control of a single thing about his life from here on out, he'll soon discover he's wrong—or so I've heard from married friends. Tonight should be fun— Geoff will probably thrill the guests by getting down on one knee and presenting a betrothal ring to Margaret at last. My mother will love it—she likes a grand spectacle as much as Geoff does. I wonder which ring he'll give her? Not great-grandmama's diamond of course—as heir, that's mine." He glanced at her own left hand, where Phillip's grandmother's magnificent ruby betrothal ring had been until yesterday. Now it was tucked away in her dresser drawer until she could return it to him.

"Always nice to see a fine society match, the blissful joining of old money to old estates and like politics," Tom Graham drawled, a whiff of disdain in his tone.

She turned, ready to demand to know what he meant by that, but Reggie spoke first. "It's how it's always been done in the upper classes, old chap. Geoffrey is a second son. He needs to marry a woman of fortune, and Lady Margaret is an earl's daughter with a rather eye-popping dowry and a small estate in Hampshire from her grandmother."

Tom looked at Viviane. "And you, Miss Alden? Do you have a dower estate in Hampshire as well? Will you bring a fortune to your husband? I daresay a wealthy marquess like Phillip Medway doesn't need the cash." His voice was bland with condescension. He didn't suggest it might be love, or that she was lovely or witty or charming. How could he? They knew nothing about each other, and yet it appeared he'd already decided about her and found her lacking.

She felt her hackles rise. No doubt he thought he was being clever, that she wouldn't notice the disdain in his comment. Wait. Had she mentioned Phillip by name? She didn't recall that she had, but Tom Graham seemed to know him. He wasn't the usual sort Phillip associated with, but then, she'd only recently discovered there were a lot of things she didn't know about her fiancé—*former* fiancé. He'd turned out to be full of secrets, and she wondered now if the same was true of Tom Graham. Phillip hid behind a smoke screen of charm, using his good looks, his money, and his title to lure those who might amuse him for a brief time. Phillip was a dazzling creature, but hollow, too easily led astray. And what lay behind Tom Graham's smoke screen? She studied him again, but he was a closed book. It made her suspect that he did not reveal himself to very many people. He stood aloof, apart, even here in a tiny sailboat, elbow to elbow with two other people. She longed to plunge her hands into the pockets of his coat, see what he kept there. She'd like to photograph him, expose him, see what secrets her camera brought out.

Reggie laughed at Tom's question. "Vee? She has a wee dowry and a few jewels that will come down to her through her mother—the Countess of Rutherford is a duke's daughter—but she married a poor baron,

Vee's father, for love. Isn't that so, sweetheart? Viviane may not be nearly as well-endowed as her stepsisters, but she's a prize in her own right. There's no one to compare with Viviane."

"I didn't think anyone in the aristocracy married for love. It must have been quite extraordinary," Tom drawled.

Reggie chuckled. "It's not entirely unheard of, or against the rules. Geoffrey and Margaret would say they're in love. They look it, if you ask me, all starry-eyed and sticky. It's quite sickening. Of course, a match between one of Lord Rutherford's daughters and a son of Lord Deerbourne's was always seen as inevitable. We're neighbors. It keeps the land in the family, so to speak. In the Middle Ages we would have been betrothed at birth, a joining of noble houses, something as expected and comfortable as a favorite tweed coat, say," Reggie said, nodding at Tom Graham's jacket draped over Viviane's slender body. "I suppose they once expected *me* to marry Margaret, the heir and the eldest daughter, but she and Geoffrey were meant to be, as they say in the movies. There are three other Rutherford beauties to choose from," he teased, though Viviane knew he had no interest in any of her stepsisters. "How about you, Graham? Ever been in love, or married?"

"No, just infatuated a time or two," he replied. Viviane wished he'd go on, but he didn't elaborate.

Reggie chuckled. "Well, if you're fortunate, you'll find a lady like Vee, who's fair of face, devilish clever, and the daughter of a war hero to boot."

"A war hero," Tom Graham echoed softly, his tone flat.

Viviane raised her chin. "My father was Major Sir Arthur Alden of Kellyn." It pleased her to see that her father's name brought a spark of recognition to his gaze. He looked her over again.

"Have you heard of him, Tom? He fought at Sainte Courcelle and a host of other places. Viviane can list them if you like," Reggie said.

Tom looked away. "No need. I've heard of him. He was awarded the Distinguished Service Order," Tom said.

"Yes," Viviane said, surprised.

"My uncle was one of the men under his command. Sergeant Archie Graham." He stared at her with a slight frown but said nothing else. She had the distinct feeling that he didn't approve. She bristled. What kind of person didn't approve of a war hero?

"Here's the cove," Reggie said before she could ask. He put in as close to the shore as he dared, and Tom dropped the anchor. "I suppose you want me to carry you ashore and see you safe home," Reggie said. He glanced at his wristwatch. "Blast it—I won't have time to go home and change before Geoffrey's train arrives. It'll be tight as it is."

"Don't worry—I can wade in from here," Viviane said, gripping the gunwale, ready to drop over the side.

Tom moved as well, removing his socks and shoes. "I don't have anywhere to be. I'll escort her up the cliff," he said. "Go on, Farraday, meet your train. I can walk back to Halliwell."

"It's three miles!" Reggie said.

Tom shrugged. "I used to walk four miles to visit my gran when I was a lad." He leaped over the side into the water, which came to his hips, and didn't even flinch at the cold. "Do you need a hand?" he asked, turning to offer her one. She wondered if he'd carry her to shore if she demanded it. Something in his expression warned her not to.

"I'm fine." She ignored his hand and dropped into the water beside him. The water came all the way to her waist. "I can also climb the path on my own."

He smiled acidly. "I don't doubt you can. I can assure you I haven't a chivalrous bone in my body."

"What does that mean?" She waded out of the water onto the pebbled shore, and he followed.

"It means I need my coat back. Unlike Reggie or Geoffrey or you—it's the only one I happen to have with me."

"Oh." She looked at the coat she still clung to, mostly wet now. She shrugged out of it and handed it to him, and he folded it over his arm and let it drip. His wet trousers clung to long, lean legs and she realized he was quite tall.

Reggie hauled up the anchor and waved. "See you at Halliwell this evening, Vee. Luncheon is at one thirty, Graham. Don't dawdle."

Viviane was aware of Tom Graham's eyes on her as she picked up her robe. She pulled the thick garment around her and belted it tightly, then shoved her feet into her shoes and turned toward the path. He'd perched on a rock to put on his own sensible leather brogues, not bothering with his socks. He'd get blisters if he walked three miles without them, but it wasn't her concern.

She picked up her Leica and slung it over her shoulder.

"Fine camera," he said, noticing it. "Do you know how to use it?"

She pierced him with a rapier-sharp glare. "Yes. My father taught me."

He held up a hand. "No offense. I've never met a debutante who was content *behind* the camera. They're usually too busy posing in front of the lens."

"Met a lot of debs, have you?" She raised the camera to her eye, her hand cupped under the lens, and pointed it at him. "Give us a smile, duckie," she teased.

He continued to regard her soberly, and she took the photo anyway, then turned to lead the way up the cliff path, her spine stiff.

"You must have been quite young when your father died," Tom said behind her. "My uncle and some of his mates traveled to Cornwall for his funeral. Took a day off work for it."

She recalled the soldiers who came to pay their respects, and the families of the men he'd saved. The tiny church had been full. Her mother had been confined to bed, too grief-stricken to rise even for the funeral. Viviane had been there alone, just fourteen, accompanied by the housekeeper and her husband. "Thank you," she said to Tom Graham now, not knowing what else to say.

"Gas is an insidious weapon."

"You seem to know the whole story." She didn't want to talk about her father, not today, not with a stranger who hadn't known the man behind the heroic tale, what the war had cost him, what it had cost *her*.

"I'm a journalist," Tom Graham said. "I tend to be curious. My uncle told me about your father, how he was what the ordinary men called a good soldier, even if—" He paused, and she stopped in the middle of the path and turned on him. The sloping ground of the path meant they were at eye level.

"Even if what?"

He looked away. "Even if most of your class made rather careless officers—the ones who said they won the war and came home to marry for money and land in a desperate attempt to hold on to power."

"My class," she murmured, repeating his assessment of her. She was hardly an aristocrat.

"I know Phillip Medway, your fiancé. A marquess, a duke's son and heir. Your class, Marchioness."

She didn't reply. It had been less than twenty-four hours since she'd broken her engagement. A stranger, and a journalist, was not the first person she intended to tell.

"And just how do you happen to know Phillip?"

"We rowed together at Cambridge."

She paused. She turned sharply, glanced at him over her shoulder, and stumbled. Did he share Phillip's politics as well? He caught her elbow, steadied her. "Careful, your ladyship."

She pulled away, ignoring the steep drop inches from the narrow path. "I am not your ladyship."

"Yet."

"Jealous?" she shot back at him.

He frowned and stared at her, nose to nose. He didn't step back. There was no deference to her class or her sex. Up close, there was a corona of copper around the pupils of his gray eyes, and he had impossibly long, dark lashes.

"Now what does that mean? Are you fishing for a compliment? Must every man find himself at your feet? Reggie is certainly smitten. Of course, he'll be a mere earl, not a duke, and as his father is in the pink of health, he'll have to wait a long while for *his* title."

Of all the rudeness! She turned away and kept walking, faster now. "You're wrong about me, Mr. Graham."

"Am I? Reggie said if you weren't betrothed to Medway, then he'd marry you."

"He was teasing—it's an old joke between us. Not that it's any of your business."

"Even if it's the kind of love one might hold for a cousin, or an old friend, surely it's better than—"

She let out a sharp cry of understanding that rivaled the squawk of the wheeling gulls. "Oh, I see. You *are* jealous then, but not of me. Did Phillip once steal the affections of a lady you had hopes of? One of your 'infatuations'? He's a notorious poacher."

He blinked at her for a moment, then threw back his head and laughed. "You have sharp claws, Miss Alden. That's a rather telling supposition—is that why Reggie has been left pining for you? Did Phillip poach you away from him? It's your turn to be wrong. I wonder what your father would think of your marrying a man like Medway. What *would* the major say?"

Be true to your heart, your principles, stand for what's right, even if it goes against the tide. She heard her father's advice in her mind. It was one of the reasons she'd broken her engagement to Phillip, but she wasn't about to admit that to a man who imagined he understood her heart and her morals and motives. Tom Graham had decided he had the right to judge her choice, her class, her whole life after knowing her less than an hour.

It was on the tip of her tongue to tell him it wasn't his business, but she didn't want to argue with an opinionated stranger. Not today.

She turned and took the last few strides to the top of the cliff, reached the grassy ledge. "I know the way from here. You can go," she said imperiously, pointing toward Halliwell. He ignored the dismissal.

"*Is* it a love match between your stepsister and Geoffrey? For his part, Geoff seems quite smitten."

She folded her arms over her chest. "Are you always so protective of your friends, or do you merely have a penchant for giving matrimonial advice? Do you pen advice to the lovelorn for the *Herald*?"

A half smile creased his cheeks, as if he appreciated her jab. "No. I simply have a great need to right the wrongs of this world, I suppose. That's why I became a journalist."

She understood. It was why she took photographs. People lied. The camera did not.

"Yes, Margaret loves Geoffrey," she said, answering his question.

It wasn't like that between herself and Phillip. He was precisely the kind of suitor who'd delight any social-minded mama, especially hers, a prime catch. He was rich, handsome, and his title was ancient and lofty. Viviane had been flattered by his attention, his charm, and his interest. She'd wondered from the start why he'd chosen her when he could have any other debutante, ladies with grand titles and vast fortunes. He was pleasant company, made her laugh, and yet he offered a kind of freedom during their courtship that gave her hope. She imagined that it would be a thoroughly modern match, an equal partnership, and Phillip would allow her to live her life as she pleased, to take photographs and use her position as a marchioness to do good. She would allow him to pursue his interests as well, and together they'd change the world for the better. They'd share like ideals, friendship, and a loving regard if not a passionate romance, and it would be enough.

Or so she'd thought.

But Phillip didn't want that kind of wife. They had nothing in common, especially politics. In return for a life of luxury and privilege, she'd be expected to remain faceless and mute unless required and stay out of his limelight. His life and ambitions would go on. Hers would end. For most women, it would have been enough, but she had other plans.

The wind gusted, flicking at Viviane's hair and the folds of her robe, and the first drops of rain spattered in the dust of the path.

"Here's the storm," he said in an I-told-you-so tone. She decided that Tom Graham was a man who liked to be right, especially against someone of a higher class, and a woman he quite obviously didn't like, no matter who her father was or what friends they had in common. "And just look at those waves—you might have been swept away and drowned if you'd stayed out in that," he said.

Drowned. She felt her very skin recoil. He didn't know everything about her father, then—or if he did, he was cruel indeed. She raised her chin, gave him a look of lofty superiority.

"You'd best hurry along. You're sure to get wet on your way back to Halliwell," she said in her best to-the-manor-born tone.

He raised one brow. "I'm already wet, and it's little more than a prolonged squall, and it won't last the day. It will blow itself out by teatime," he said. He didn't touch his forelock, or bow, or mark her in any way as his social superior. He simply turned and walked away, his stride long, easy, and infuriatingly confident. *Mannerless.*

"Mr. Graham," she called, and waited for him to turn. She squared her shoulders and looked along her nose the way her mother or her stepsisters looked at an insolent footman.

"Thank you for the loan of your coat. I do hope the salt comes out. Have your valet—oh, wait. Do you have a valet? Of course you don't. I hope you weren't planning to wear it to dinner this evening. You *are* invited to dinner, are you not?" His jaw tightened. *She'd hit a nerve.*

A muscle twitched in his jaw. "I am indeed, Miss Alden, and I assure you I will be appropriately costumed for the grand show."

"Glad to hear it. It won't do to embarrass your betters. That's not the way for a climber like you to get ahead." She didn't wait for his reply. Instead, she pivoted on her heel and began to cross the lawn.

"And I will *never* drown," she muttered to herself through gritted teeth. "Never."

CHAPTER TWO

THE STORM OUTSIDE caused a second tempest inside the walls of Wrenwood House.

Lord Rutherford's four lovely daughters were loudly voicing their concerns that the rain would ruin their coiffures and force them to wear mackintoshes and galoshes with their gowns. Such a tragedy would spoil the arrival of the beautiful Devellin sisters, each more lovely than the last, and all in silk and sequins. Instead of processing up the stone steps of Halliwell Hall like princesses, they'd have to run pell-mell through the downpour.

"Does rain ruin satin?" Julia asked, glaring out the window at the rain. In response a boom of thunder crashed overhead, and the girls shrieked and fluttered like anxious geese.

Viviane thought of Tom Graham, walking through the deluge, no doubt soaked to the skin. It was his own fault, of course, and it served him right for insisting upon rescuing someone who hadn't needed his assistance, and if asked, she'd never admit otherwise. Perhaps his insufferable arrogance would keep him warm and dry.

"What if we're forced to wear wool?" Felicity said. "It would have to be wool, wouldn't it? Linen would wrinkle in the wet."

Julia pinched her younger sister. "Don't be such a silly child. You're only coming to the party because it's a family affair. They'll probably make you wear a bib to dinner in case you splash your soup and ruin whatever baby frock you wear."

"We're not babies. We're almost fifteen, and that's only two years and seven months younger than you," Felicity's twin, Grace, said, coming to her sister's rescue.

"There's a world of difference between *fourteen* and eighteen. I'm a grown woman, and you two are—"

Grace's snort of disdain cut the comment short. "Not until you make your debut, you're not, and that isn't until next spring. Until then, you're still a child. Isn't that right, Vee?"

Viviane turned from the window and dragged her thoughts away from Tom Graham. "Hmm?"

The sisters exchanged "the Look," that silent, secret language the four of them shared, the one that didn't include Viviane but was usually about her. "We were discussing what we will wear if the rain doesn't stop," Grace said.

Viviane glanced again at the pewter sky, the knife slashes of rain, the white froth on the black waves of the Channel. "It will be over by teatime," she said. The Look made its way around the room once again.

"How do you know that?" Julia asked, coming to stand beside her at the window. "It looks like it will never end."

Tom Graham had said so. Viviane wondered how *he* knew. She pointed to the west. "See? There's a bit of blue sky between the clouds."

The door opened and her mother came into the room. "Where's Margaret?" she asked, looking around the salon. "Sit up straight, Felicity," she directed, and scanned Grace for any sign of mischief. "Your hair will frizz in this damp," she warned Julia. "Have your maid brush it out." Only then did she turn to Viviane. "What time is Phillip arriving?"

Viviane's throat dried. "He won't be coming," she said quickly. "He's . . . busy."

"Not coming?" Julia asked, her blue eyes popping.

"Not coming?" Felicity and Grace echoed, sitting up straight at last.

For a moment her mother was silent, regarding her without expression, analyzing the deeper meaning of "busy" and "not coming." "Margaret's betrothal dinner is an important family event. It's been planned for weeks."

Viviane felt her cheeks fill with traitorous telltale color under the sword point of her mother's scrutiny. The countess crossed the room. "*Why* isn't your fiancé coming?" she asked. She glanced down at Viviane's left hand. "Where's your ring?"

There was no point in hiding the truth. She raised her chin, looked at her mother. "It's upstairs in my drawer. I have decided . . ." She swallowed. "That is, Phillip and I realized that it was not . . ."

Her mother's face paled. She reached for the pearls around her neck and plucked at them, a nervous habit. "You've broken it off!" she cried. Two spots of rage rose over her perfect cheekbones and spread. She stared at Viviane, waited for her to deny it, then put a dismayed hand to her cheek when she did not. "You've broken your engagement."

She heard the disbelieving squeaks from her stepsisters, knew without looking that they were staring at her in astonishment.

"Yes," Viviane managed.

"Why?" Her mother's voice was low and breathy. "Why would you do such a thing?"

"I—we—discovered that we didn't suit after all," she said. She knew it wasn't adequate, not for her mother.

"Didn't suit? He's the Marquess of Medway, the heir to a dukedom."

"He's the most eligible bachelor in all England, and so handsome!" Grace chirped, earning a quelling glare from her stepmother.

"We will discuss this in private, Viviane," her mother said in clipped syllables, and spun on her heel, striding toward the door, leaving Viviane to follow her down the hall. A bolt of lightning lit the long gallery that led to the Countess of Rutherford's apartments, followed by a cannon boom of thunder. Her mother didn't so much as flinch. She opened the double doors and waited for Viviane to catch up and enter.

"What did you do?" The question pierced Viviane like an arrow as soon as the doors were firmly shut behind them.

"Why do you assume it's my fault?" Viviane asked.

"Phillip Medway might have chosen any woman in England, the daughter of a duke or an earl, even a princess, but he chose you, a woman without a fortune, the daughter of a baron."

"You make it sound like he made a terrible compromise."

Her mother glared along the length of her nose. "Don't be glib, Viviane. You are smarter and prettier than your stepsisters. I raised you to become the wife of a powerful man, a duke at the very least. I thought I'd succeeded." She crossed to pour water into a crystal glass. "Who broke it off, you or Phillip?"

Viviane clasped her hands at her waist and raised her chin. "I did."

The water splashed over the polished mahogany surface of the table as the glass was set down with a bump. "For heaven's sake, *why*?"

"We would have made each other miserable," Viviane said. Her mother blinked, waiting for more, but Viviane remained silent, her heart pounding in her throat. She hated to disappoint her mother, but this was her life to live. Her mother took her silence for stubborn disobedience, which Viviane supposed it was.

"That's all you have to say? This might have been your betrothal dinner. You might have become the Duchess of Chalfont one day, one of the oldest, richest titles in England—" She broke off in dismay and shook her head, as if the whole situation was still incomprehensible to her.

Viviane felt her skin grow hot, and her chest and stomach began to ache at the start of the old argument. "I don't want to be a duchess. Not Phillip's duchess, at least."

Her mother paled and gripped the edge of the table, and Viviane wondered if she'd put a hand to her forehead and plead a headache and retreat to rest alone in a dark room. That had started after Papa died, when the loss of him, of everything, was simply too devastating to bear. But her mother stood tall, as fierce as the storm outside.

"What *do* you want, Viviane? Love? I married your father for love. I am the daughter of a duke. I went against everything my parents wanted for me, and they never forgave me, or truly accepted your father. I was courted by a dozen young men during my debut Season. I was the belle of every ball . . . but your father smiled at me, beguiled me, charmed me, until I wanted no other." She sat down on the edge of the settee with a sigh. "How I loved him. I gave up everything for Arthur, including the good opinion of my parents and my friends. Arthur promised to make it up to me, impress my family, make them accept him, and I believed him." Her lips twisted with bitterness, and she shook her head. "What did love get me? A few happy years, perhaps. And when he died, I lost everything yet again—my home, my security, my status. I vowed that day that I would see that you married well, very well, to a man with a fortune and a title that would always protect you, no matter what."

Viviane sat down beside her mother and took her hand. The countess's fingers tightened on hers. "I am a dowerless baron's daughter, Mama, and I have a limp. When Margaret and I made our debut last year, no one looked at me when she was in the room. They courted her, the Earl of Rutherford's lovely daughter with ten thousand a year. It didn't matter a whit if I was prettier or smarter or the daughter of a war hero."

"Phillip wanted you."

Viviane looked down at their joined hands. "No, he didn't. Phillip likes to collect unusual things, including people, and I was most certainly that, a novelty. My heart isn't broken, and I'm better off. Truly I am."

Her mother snatched her hand away. "Then *my* heart is broken for you, for your foolish pride. Is there someone else? Is it Reggie?"

Viviane almost laughed at that. "Reggie likes tall brunettes with lush figures."

"Don't joke, Viviane. Not now." Estella rose and paced the room. "We must find you someone else to marry, someone as good or better than Phillip. There's another Season in the spring, another chance to meet someone who will see what a prize you are—"

"Oh, Mama, please. Julia's making her debut. Would you have me compete with her?"

"I'd have you *outdo* her! That's all I've ever wanted. Why do you think I married Rutherford? Did you know I knew him when I was a girl, that he was one of the young men who courted me? I could have married him all those years ago. He and Arthur were rivals. I chose your father, and Lionel chose another bride. She died after giving him an heir and four daughters. When we met again after your father's death, Rutherford was in need of a stepmother for his brood, not a wife to love." She raised her chin. "He married me for that, and I married him for security, and for the social position that would allow me to see you married well. What else could I do? Your father left us practically destitute, with nothing but his high ideals and his silly legends. You can't eat ideals or wear fairy tales."

"He was a hero," Viviane said, her jaw clenching. She remembered her mother smiling at Papa, holding his hand, a woman in love, content and happy. Did she not remember, even a little, what it felt like to make a daring choice for love, to be passionate and joyful instead of dutiful? She'd changed the day he died, became harder, sharper, fiercer. Viviane had lost both her parents that day.

"Arthur was a dreamer," her mother said, her face cold, even as she remembered the man she'd once loved. "If he'd had a fortune to leave us, that would have been all right, but there was nothing. Nothing at all." She fixed an eagle's glare on Viviane. "I *will not* allow you to make my mistakes, or his. When you marry—"

Viviane gripped the arm of the settee, her nails digging into the damask. "What if I don't marry? What if I choose another path, decide to make my own way in the world?" Her mother stopped pacing and spun.

"What, work for a living? No!" The word cracked like a whip. She went to the window, stood staring out at the storm, waning now, fretting with her pearls again. Viviane was sure the string would break. They'd been a wedding gift from her father, and she always wore them. "Your cousin Lucy is also making her debut next year, my brother's girl. She is another duke's daughter, like I was. You can use the family connection to move in her circle, to go where she goes, and take advantage of the chance to meet the eligible lords in her train. She can't marry them all."

"No!" It was Viviane's turn to say it. It would be too humiliating to play the poor relation, following her dazzling stepsister Julia and her wealthy cousin Lucy, hoping for a crumb or two, a scrap of attention or regard, the off chance that one of their suitors might stumble and fall into her lap by accident and find himself trapped.

The clock chimed, and her mother glanced at it, and confirmed the time against her own watch, the diamond bezel glinting like another flash of lightning. "How late it is. We must dress. This is a special night for Margaret. Don't think for a moment this conversation is over. We'll speak later. Go and get ready and be sure to wear something dazzling." She rang for her maid and strode toward her dressing room.

Viviane had been dismissed, and there was nothing to do but go. Outside the storm gave a final grumble, subsided, and slunk away eastward.

CHAPTER THREE

Halliwell Hall

REGGIE CAME ACROSS the room to kiss Viviane's cheek as she arrived at the party that evening with her stepsisters. "Hello, Vee—you look divine, darling girl." He squeezed her hand. "Any trouble about this morning?"

She shook her head. "No. Margaret had the whole house in an uproar, of course. She went through everyone's closet trying to find the perfect frock for tonight."

He glanced at Margaret, radiant in pink chiffon, then back at Viviane's pale green gown. "You outshine her, and every other lady here," he said gallantly.

She laughed and took his arm. "What a loyal friend you are. I chose this dress because I hoped to be invisible. I brought my camera. I wanted to take a few photos of the happy couple, something candid they can show their grandchildren someday." She paused. "Did Mr. Graham make it back safely?"

Reggie raised a speculative eyebrow. "Made an impression on you, did he?" He pointed across the room. "He's over there, talking to Winston Churchill. That's actually why Tom's here—aside from the fact that he's Geoffrey's best friend. He's on assignment for the London

Herald. He's supposed to be covering the guest list, the menu, and the betrothal ring, but I believe he's also trying to get a story about what's really going on with the Germans and anything else Winston cares to talk about."

Viviane looked across the room at the infamous politician with a fond smile. "Mr. Churchill commanded my father's regiment in France for a time. He came to visit Papa at Kellyn, and he sent a lovely letter after his death."

Around them the salon was filled with late summer flowers from the countess's gardens and greenhouses. The scent and color were heady, a compliment to the ladies in their satin gowns and glittering heirloom jewels.

She studied Tom Graham, tall and lean in a tuxedo that was slightly too tight across the shoulders. His height also made him stand out, and there was something unique about him she couldn't quite identify. Not of our class, her stepsisters might have said, dismissing him, but it wasn't only that. It was the way he held his head, perhaps, listening not just to Churchill but at the same time aware of everything around him. He looked like a drawn bow pulled taut, ready to fire, though his expression was placid enough. He looked up and caught her stare. He took her in with a sweeping glance that went from the top of her head to the hem of her gown. If he thought she looked divine, he gave no sign of it. Sharp-eyed Winston followed the direction of Tom's gaze and grinned.

"Ah, there she is! Come and join us, Viviane, my dear, and I shall introduce you to my young companion."

"This is where I leave you," Reggie murmured to her. "I intend to avoid any political discussions tonight." He glanced around for other company, found only politicians, and made a face. "It appears they've got us surrounded. Good luck with Winston. Perhaps Tom will protect you, but I'm going to get a drink."

Winston's orator's voice carried to the very ceiling, explaining her to Tom as she crossed the room. "I knew Miss Alden's father. We served in the same regiment in France when I was lieutenant colonel of the Sixth Royal Scots Fusiliers. Sir Arthur was a fine man, a hero, and I considered him a friend." He clasped her hands and kissed her cheek when she reached him. "Still taking photographs?" She was aware of Tom Graham's eyes on her and wondered what he was thinking.

"Yes. In fact, I brought my camera tonight," she said.

"Capital!" Winston boomed. "Take pictures of everything, I say. The world is changing, and we'll soon need evidence that these halcyon days ever existed at all."

"Then in your opinion there is a war coming?" Tom Graham asked, shifting slightly, his shoulder a wedge between Viviane and Winston. Winston's fond gaze sharpened at once, and he swung his attention away from Viviane, fixed it on Tom.

She wasn't offended. Far from it. She recognized that Tom was engaged, his attention focused on his work. Nothing else mattered. So was Winston, for that matter. It was exactly how she felt when she was composing a photo, seeing the world through her camera, letting everything else fade away. It was passion, and it told her a lot about Tom Graham.

"Without a doubt there's a war coming. I have proof of it. I know it for a fact, but that's all classified for the moment. Now, Miss Viviane Alden, meet Mr. Tom Graham. His uncle was a sergeant in the Scots Fusiliers. He's also a schoolmate of Geoffrey's and will stand as best man at the wedding."

"Actually, we met this morning," Tom said, and for a moment Viviane feared he'd mention the circumstances, but she was saved when the butler arrived in the doorway to ring a small bell. "Dinner is served, my lady," he announced to the countess, who set down her sherry glass and rose to her feet at once, taking the arm of Viviane's stepfather as the ranking gentleman in observation of precedence and etiquette. The rest of the guests fell into place based on their social rank. Everyone knew their place, where they belonged, a medieval cavalcade on the march. Tom extended his arm, and Viviane stared at it. "Shall we?" he asked, probably because she was still standing next to him. There was no polite way to say no, so she took it and let him lead her in to dinner.

She scanned the place cards for her name, found it, and he stopped beside her. She glanced to her right, saw that he'd been seated beside her. She looked up at him and he met the surprise in her eyes with a grin. "Since Medway is unable to join us this evening, there was a last-minute shuffle and the countess asked if I would mind taking his seat beside you. Do you think we can get along for the whole meal without stabbing each other with the fish forks?"

He held her chair, and she sat, ignoring the barb. She turned to smile at the person on her left, hoping she could engage him in discussion and ignore Tom Graham entirely. Unfortunately, it was Lord Edgeway, Reggie's elderly grandfather, who was quite deaf. Short of shouting in his ear, any conversation with him would be rather limited. He was a member of the House of Lords, a die-hard Tory, and he obviously didn't approve of Winston Churchill, since he was glaring across the table at him and muttering under his breath. Reggie winked at her from farther up the table, where he was seated next to Julia.

"This is exactly the kind of party Phillip enjoys, isn't it? Motoring down from London for a long weekend of sailing and shooting and games," Tom said, needling her. "I'm surprised he isn't here. Did you have a lovers' spat?"

She waited until the footman finished serving the soup to reply. "And what kind of party do you enjoy, Mr. Graham?"

"I say, what kind of soup is this?" Lord Edgeway bellowed at her.

"Crème du Barry," she said back.

He frowned. "Cranberry?"

"Cauliflower," Tom leaned over to say, touching his lordship's arm to get his attention, and the old man nodded with a grunt.

"Well, whatever it is, I like it. Her ladyship's cook knows her business," Lord Edgeway replied, and resumed eating.

Viviane regarded Tom curiously, and he shrugged. "My uncle is deaf from the war, and from long years at the shipyards on the Clyde. He refused to use an ear trumpet, so he learned to watch people's lips move as they speak. Lord Edgeway probably has a similar solution."

"Is this the same uncle who knew my father?" she asked.

"Yes."

"And is he . . ." She didn't finish the sentence.

He flashed a brief grin. It transformed his face from interesting to handsome. "He's very much alive. You know what they say about old soldiers never dying."

Her heart gave a twitch. If only that were true. She looked around at the other diners. Her mother was enjoying herself, exchanging conversation with Geoffrey on one side and Winston on the other. Her stepfather was deep in conversation with Lord Petrie, no doubt about some government matter judging by the seriousness of their expressions. She heard Grace giggle, sharing some joke with Felicity, both of them rolling their eyes in Tom Graham's direction.

Were they admiring his handsome profile or mocking the ill fit of his dinner jacket? She felt indignation for him, shame that her stepsisters dared to be so childishly rude. She sent the pair of them a reproving glare, then turned to distract Tom, hoping he hadn't noticed.

"What do you write about, Mr. Graham?"

He looked at her with faint suspicion, as if her question might be frivolous or mocking. She held his gaze with a sober and unwavering expression she hoped conveyed honest interest.

"I write whatever I'm assigned. Right now, I'm working on a story about the social event of the year, which I just happen to be attending this evening." He glanced at Churchill. "And I'm also writing a piece about the Anglo-German Naval Agreement and one about the election."

"Hence your interest in Winston," she said.

"Yes, he sees allowing Germany to build up their navy as dangerous." He paused, pinning her with a sharp look, and she wondered if this moment of serious discussion was some kind of test.

She sipped her wine and glanced at the politician. "There are also rumors he's working on a clandestine committee to gather information for the prime minister's office."

His brows rose for an instant and she braced herself for sarcasm, something cutting about being surprised a woman—a *debutante*— would know or care about such things.

Instead, he nodded. "It seems Mr. Churchill has his fingers in many pies. He believes there's another war coming, and we're not ready. He's against appeasing Adolf Hitler, and he doesn't admire the German chancellor the way some in England do." He glanced toward her stepfather. She knew that Rutherford looked with favor on the improvements that the Nazi government had made in Germany, the renewed prosperity and efficiency, the restored pride of the nation defeated in the war and crushed by the peace treaty. He wasn't alone, of course. Many Britons favored finding a way—any way—to keep the peace and avoid another terrible war. They wanted jobs and relief from the crushing hopelessness brought on by the Depression that had held the nation in a death grip for five long years.

"This is hardly the kind of conversation for a dinner party," Tom Graham murmured. "Shall we change the subject to something more appropriate? Lady Deerbourne has a magnificent garden, and I understand that Lord Deerbourne is master of the local hunt. Do you hunt, Miss Alden?"

It was precisely the kind of conversation one was expected to have at such a dinner party, the banal, the pleasant, the things that interested the languid rich. Around the table, everyone else was speaking of such things, discussing flowers and the effect of an early autumn on roses. She resisted the urge to roll her eyes out of sheer boredom. Only Winston was speaking of war, using his dessert fork and a set of silver salt cellars to describe a crucial moment in the siege of Mafeking during the Boer War. She turned to Tom Graham, found his eyes on her, his brows raised, waiting for her reply. "Roses bore me. I'd much rather discuss politics or religion or even . . ." She bit her lip. She could flippantly mention the first two taboo topics for any dinner party, but not the last. She felt herself blush and sipped her wine.

"Sex?" he filled in, looking amused.

She raised her chin. "If you like," she said in her best bored, upper-class drawl. He merely grinned.

"We'd shock poor Lord Edgeway if he happened to read our lips. Perhaps we should speak of photography instead? What do you take pictures of? The rose garden, perhaps, or the hunt? Or do you prefer portraits of relatives or society friends?"

"Of course," she said blandly, a noncommittal reply, though her teeth were gritted. She didn't correct him or bother to elaborate. Tom Graham looked disappointed by her glib answer.

"Reggie told me you even have your own darkroom at Wrenwood, tucked away in a wee closet behind the scullery," he prodded. "Don't the chemicals wreak havoc on a manicure? Or do you have the servants do that part?"

She gave him an acid smile. "I develop my own film. How well do you know Phillip?" she asked, changing the subject yet again.

He sipped his wine. She watched his throat move as he swallowed, and she instinctively reached for her own glass. "He numbered among my acquaintances at Cambridge. We were both on the rowing team, and we spent a number of nights in pubs getting foxed with other friends—Geoffrey included." He paused, passing another searching look over her. "I understand he's become a supporter of Sir Oswald Mosley and the British Union of Fascists, Adolf Hitler's most ardent English admirers. Do you support Fascism as well, Miss Alden? Will you hold rallies at your London home or at Chalfont after you wed?"

The guards had come off the rapiers, rendering the blades lethal. She gave him an icy smile.

"I see we've moved back to politics. Is this still polite dinner conversation, or are you trying to ferret out a story for your paper?" Viviane asked. She could imagine the scandal of her broken engagement making the paper, the miss who threw over a marquess, complete with speculation as to why. Well, he wouldn't hear about it from her. She toyed with the ancient gold coin that hung from a chain around her neck, her lucky piece. She'd found the coin in the lake at Kellyn. One side of the coin showed King Arthur in profile, the other, his famous sword. Her father said it proved the legend of the lake was most certainly true. Knowing that, holding the coin between her fingers, calmed her, reminded her of her legacy, gave her confidence. She smiled at Tom, keeping her secret, as enigmatic as Mona Lisa. He raised one brow and grinned back with appreciation in his eyes, enjoying their sparring match. So was she. She could drown in that look, those gray eyes.

Winston chose that moment to lean across the table toward her. "Oh, my dear, it just occurred to me—today is the anniversary of your father's death, is it not? How callous of me not to offer my condolences. I had not forgotten, of course, never that." He raised a toast. "Here's to brave men and fallen comrades."

Viviane's chest caved inward as everyone solemnly drank. Her dinner gathered itself into a churning ball in her belly. "Fallen comrades? Who's dead?" Lord Edgeway demanded. Viviane glanced at her mother. Estella had set her fork down carefully on the edge of her plate, was staring at it, her expression bland. She clutched her wineglass but did not raise it to drink.

"Let's raise a toast to our happy couple!" Lady Deerbourne said, rising to her feet, her voice overbright as she sought to banish the pall that had fallen upon the party. Everyone got to their feet and drank. Margaret blushed and simpered, and Geoffrey grinned proudly.

"I'm sorry," Tom said to Viviane amid the renewed din of laughter and congratulations. "I didn't realize—"

She turned on him. "Why should you? You didn't know my father. Or me."

"He drowned, didn't he? They say—"

"I know what they say," she said through gritted teeth. "It was an accident. He was an expert swimmer."

"That's why you were out there today, isn't it? Swimming in a storm, defying the waves, trying to vanquish all that water, to prove—"

She stopped him with a fierce frown. She looked for mockery in his gaze. There wasn't any, but still she felt fury rise. She didn't want his understanding or his condolences, or Winston's or anyone else's. She wanted to kick off the ridiculous satin pumps with the special sole that hid her limp, run back to Wrenwood barefoot, and plunge down the cliff to dive back into the ocean, rail at the waves, since she couldn't scream at the lake at Kellyn anymore, where the Lady of the Lake had taken back Viviane's knight, her hero, her sword.

Instead, she held all of it inside, a storm under a placid surface. No one had ever seen her turmoil, her fear that it was true, that it hadn't been an accident, but it appeared that Tom Graham, a virtual stranger, had. That rattled her, and she had to get away from his all-seeing gaze. She glanced at her mother again, saw the warning in Estella's eyes, silently holding her daughter in place, ordering her to sit up straight, to find a more pleasant topic of conversation, and to deflect any talk of death or toasts to absent friends. The admonition was unnecessary.

She forced a smile and laughed at comments she really didn't hear. Tom Graham was silent now, and she was aware of his eyes on her, knew he was waiting for her to look at him, willing it, but she avoided him. She felt as brittle as glass. Pity would shatter her.

When the time came for the ladies to withdraw, she found Julia. "Please tell mother that I've got a slight headache and I'm going home." She didn't wait for her stepsister's reply but hurried through the library to the French doors that led to the garden. She'd go through the rose garden, slip across the park and the meadow, and find the path that led along the cliff top and back to Wrenwood.

At the end of the garden, in the shadow of a sculpted yew, she stopped to take off her shoes, flexing her cramped toes and easing the ache in her damaged leg. The grass was soft and familiar under her bare feet.

"Hold up, Miss Alden." He came along the path, the moon illuminating his evening clothes, his dark hair, his white tie, the lean height of him, like a black-and-white portrait.

She stiffened, caught, like an errant child. "Mr. Graham. Wherever did you come from? Did I neglect to bid you good night?" she said sharply.

"I was smoking on the terrace when you charged past me at a dead run. For a moment I thought the house might be on fire. If you're going back to Wrenwood, I'll walk with you," he said, leaning on the yew next to her. "I assume you are, since this is the route I took this morning."

"How chivalrous of you, but I know the way. I wouldn't dream of inconveniencing you. There will be dancing later."

"Still," he said, not moving.

She sighed. "It really isn't necessary. There's a moon."

"Which makes it pleasant for an evening stroll."

"Three miles there and three back. Some stroll."

"I could go and speak to the chauffeur if you prefer, beg a ride for you. I have a way with the servant class," he said drolly.

She started walking. "I am not a snob."

He shoved his hands in his pockets and walked with her, his stride long. She was aware of his height, his easy gait, and her own limp. "You, a snob? Of course not," he said with the slimmest edge of sarcasm in his tone. She picked up her pace, and he matched it easily. "Look, I made an unwitting comment about drowning this morning when we met. I didn't realize that your father—"

"It was an accident," she insisted again. "He was a good swimmer, but his lungs were damaged during the war. He mistook the depth, swam out too far."

"Was it here, in the Channel?"

"It was in Cornwall, at Kellyn, our estate. He taught me to swim in the lake there."

He didn't reply, and she felt the need to fill the silence. "He told me that Kellyn was the very lake from which the Lady of the Lake raised Excalibur to give to King Arthur."

"I thought that was Dozmary Pool."

"No. Dozmary Pool was where legend says Sir Bedivere returned the sword after Arthur's death. My father said that it was the wrong lake, too shallow to be the home of a water goddess. Our lake is bottomless, you see. Dozmary was a feint to keep just anyone from finding the sword's true home, to keep it safe."

"Do you believe that?" His comment was merely interested, not disbelieving or mocking.

"Of course. Well, I did when I was a child. It was my favorite place. I would go there with my father, and we'd read in the shade or swim. We'd dive deep, see if we could spot the glimmer of Excalibur among the weeds." She reached for the coin around her neck again. "I found this one day. It proves without a doubt that Arthur existed. I was so excited that I knocked my father's camera into the water—" She gasped and stopped walking. "My camera! I forgot it at Halliwell."

"If you're suggesting I go back for it, I'd rather bring it to you tomorrow," he said. "This is my second rather long walk today."

She considered. "Reggie and Geoffrey are coming for luncheon. I suppose you could come as well."

"I'm already invited, thank you. I trust yours is not the same camera you dropped in the lake?"

"No, he bought a new one."

"And you've used it ever since."

"I replaced it with a newer model a few years ago, when I got serious about photography. Are you shocked? Perhaps you agree with my mother and think it's not a ladylike pursuit. She despairs because I am not good at any of the usual feminine skills like watercolors or embroidery. I take good photographs, though. Photographs stop time, you see, preserve a moment or a person or a place so it can never be lost or forgotten. The camera shows exactly what's in front of it, and therefore it cannot lie. Each picture should tell a story, but a true one."

"And do your photographs tell stories?"

She turned to him. "Have you seen the photos taken by Margaret Bourke-White, or Dorothea Lange? Bourke-White traveled to the Soviet Union to photograph factories there, and Dorothea Lange's photographs of the people of the American dust bowl certainly convey the suffering, the hopelessness, the terrible loss caused by the Depression. That's truth—and story."

"Interesting. And I was thinking you'd be more interested in society portraits and candid snaps of your friends mugging for the camera."

"You say it as if it's impossible to combine the two. Madame Yevonde is very innovative. Have you heard of her? She has her own studio in London, a lady born, and yet she earns her living as a photographer. Her latest project is photographing society ladies cast as goddesses. She's asked Margaret to be Leda." The rain-wet grass brushed against her skirts, soaking them, making them heavy, slowing her pace. If she was alone, she'd kilt her skirts high, walk fast, and enjoy the slap of the cool grass on her bare legs.

"And you? Who would you be?" he asked her. "Athena? Artemis, perhaps, or Nike, the goddess of victory? Or Guinevere, perhaps?"

She snorted a laugh, an unladylike sound, but he didn't seem to notice. "Never Guinevere! She was fickle and faithless. She gave in to pleasure and seduction when she should have stuck to duty and honor."

"Who, then?" he asked again.

She laughed softly. "Why, the Lady of the Lake, of course, the guardian of the sword that protects a kingdom."

He stopped walking, and she paused to look at him. His face was in shadow, while the moon shone in her eyes. "Yes," he said slowly. "I can picture that."

Was he making fun of her again? What if he wasn't, what if he could truly see inside her head the way no one else had in seven years? It was a disconcerting thought, an intimacy she wasn't ready for. She needed to know him before she could trust him. She turned away and kept walking.

"And will photography still be your hobby once you're married to Phillip?" he called after her. "You'll be a marchioness. Perhaps you will be Guinevere after all. Will Reggie be your Lancelot, or will you keep your honor and leave him forever panting for your charms?"

It was an audacious question, and it stopped her in her tracks for a moment. She felt heat rise in her cheeks, was glad he couldn't see the blush. He didn't know she'd never be a marchioness. She could tell him, she supposed, even tell him why, confess the secret here in the wild dark, but it stuck in her throat like a bone. "No one has ever panted for my charms," she said instead, surprised at the bitterness in her tone.

"You underestimate yourself."

"Is that a compliment?"

"Are you fishing for one? From me?" He'd caught up to her, stood close enough that she caught the faint scent of his shaving soap, something plain and old-fashioned like her father had used. She closed her eyes and breathed it in, felt longing, and not just for her father. She was surprised that she wanted to know Tom's opinion of her—rather badly, in fact. She suspected that any compliment from him would be an honest one, true as a photograph. But what did it matter? She'd likely never see him again once this weekend—and the wedding—was over. "I'm not your type," she said as she turned and continued walking.

"And what type is that?"

"Someone you don't consider a snob, I suppose."

"You can't help it. You are simply a product of your class," he said flatly, stating it as a fact, a flaw that couldn't be fixed. So much for compliments.

"Aren't you?" she shot back.

He barked a laugh. "Hardly. I'm not of any class, really."

"A self-made man."

"If you like."

They reached the stile in the fence that separated Halliwell from Wrenwood. She climbed it, and the hem of her gown caught on a nail. "Hold on, I'll get it," he said.

The gown was lace, and sweetly ruffled along the bodice, one she'd worn for her debut in London last year. She hated it. Her mother had chosen it because "it might remind a gentleman of a wedding dress, make him see you as a potential bride." Viviane had asked the seamstress to make it up in green instead of virginal white, but it hadn't helped much. She wrenched free now, heard the fabric tear.

"Och, now it's torn. Perhaps your maid can stitch it up," he said in a light tone, as if he knew she'd done it on purpose, that she hated the damned dress and all it represented.

She grinned, glad it was ruined. It made her feel free, somehow, a burden lifted. She slipped over the stile and into the meadow and headed across the moonlit expanse of wildflowers toward the cliff path. The air was soft and sweet with the crushed scent of the blossoms as she passed. A fox, surprised by their presence, jumped out of the grass and fled, barking. Tom caught her arm for an instant, ready to leap to her defense, and his hand was warm on her skin. She didn't need his protection. She pulled away and kept walking.

When she reached the cliff, the sea below was inky black, the moonlight a silver inlay on the incoming tide, and the wind was fresh after the day's storm.

"Not thinking of another swim, are you?" he asked.

"The tide is wrong," she said. "Do you swim?"

"Me? No. I had a few lessons as a boy, but they didn't take. I rowed at Cambridge, and I fish on occasion, but I do not swim."

They walked on, and the black bulk of Wrenwood came into view, the ivy-shrouded walls absorbing the moonlight. "You've missed your chance to discuss things with Winston," she said.

"He'll be here tomorrow."

She crossed the lawn to the side door, and he followed. On the step, she turned to face him. "Good night, Mr. Graham," she said, offering her hand. She wondered if he'd kiss it or shake it. He stared at her outstretched palm for a moment as if he was wondering the same. In the end he did neither. He reached into his pocket and took out a cigarette case. For a moment the flare of the match lit up his features, then the smoke was a ghost between them. He stepped back, his expression amused as he held her eyes for a moment. "Good night, Miss Alden."

She watched him walk away, that long, easy stride of his carrying him out of the moonlight and into the shadows, and she wondered what might have happened if he had stayed a few minutes longer.

HE DIDN'T COME to luncheon the following day. Winston Churchill had left early for a campaign speech and Tom Graham went with him.

Reggie was the one who returned her camera. She spent the afternoon taking snapshots of Reggie and Geoffrey and her stepsisters romping in the sun, playing silly games on the lawn, and pulling faces for the camera. She wondered if Tom Graham would have joined in the fun if he'd been here.

But then, he hardly seemed the type.

CHAPTER FOUR

London
Fall 1935

"HUNGER MARCHES. BLACKSHIRTS. The election. The fall social Season. Whatever it is the Prince of Wales is up to. Weddings—and the Marquess of Medway's broken betrothal," Sir Maudesley Grainger said, calling out a list of the most important news stories of the day to the reporters seated around the scarred table. The editor in chief of the London *Herald* puffed on his cigar and blew a cloud of smoke into the air. It wreathed him like a shroud, then drifted up toward the dingy light fixture above his head.

"There are the usual sporting events to cover and the debates surrounding the possibility of our boycotting the German Olympics next year," Sir Maudesley continued. "Readers want to know what Mr. Hitler is doing and what the king has on his agenda. And scandals, gentlemen—our readers want scandals to liven up their dull little lives."

The reporters were silent. No one wanted to be assigned to cover the guest lists of balls and parties when there was real news to report, and that included Tom.

"Tom has friends in high places," Simon Bell suggested, raising his nose and his thick pinkie finger and faking—badly—an upper-class accent. "He probably gets invited to most of the better parties. He can get the scoop straight from the horses' mouths, so to speak, while waltzing or dining out or making his curtsy to the king."

Tom held his tongue and smirked as if he shared the joke. He'd heard it a hundred—a thousand—times before. Sir Maudesley squinted at Tom as another thick puff of smoke shrouded him like some mystical mage. "Friends in high places," he mused, squinting at Tom. "Isn't your friend Lord Geoffrey Farraday getting married in the spring? It's a love match, ain't it? Readers will eat that up with a spoon."

Simon chuckled, and Tom cringed inwardly. As Geoff's best man, of course he'd be at the wedding, and it was logical that he should report on the event for the *Herald*. He'd offer to do so later, closer to the wedding. "I have a contact in Oswald Mosley's inner circle," he said instead. Mentioning the name of the infamous leader of the British Union of Fascists always got the keen attention of editors and readers. "They're planning a march. I'd like to cover that."

That wiped the smirk off Bell's face, but he recovered fast enough. He was a good reporter, the only one as good as Tom. Almost. It was Tom's turn to smirk.

Simon pretended to yawn. "Another Fascist march? They march every week, don't they? Must wear out a fortune in shoe leather."

"Who's your contact?" Sir Maudesley asked around the cigar, squinting at Tom.

"The Marquess of Medway."

He saw the keen kindle of interest in the editor's eyes, a flare as bright as the end of his cigar as he inhaled.

"Isn't he a friend of the Prince of Wales?" someone farther down the table asked.

"He's also a new member of the British Union of Fascists, and cousin to Mosley's mistress, Diana Guinness, née Mitford," Tom said.

Simon whistled softly. "You'll want a senior reporter on this, sir. If I might offer to—"

Tom unfolded the newspaper that sat in front of him, laid it open to a spread of photographs. The first showed a group of men marching through the East End of London as the police looked on. The photographs were close-up, alive, visceral, showed faces and emotions, anger, and dignity.

"Phillip Medway can get me close to Mosley for an interview." He tapped the photographs with his finger. "I'm hoping that you'll assign the photographer who took these to work with me," he said, as if the assignment was already his. He could feel Simon's indignation rising in waves. *Young upstart*, Bell was thinking, but Tom wanted this chance to prove himself.

The editor leaned across the table toward Tom. "Anything special about this particular march?"

"There's a workers' march scheduled for the same day. Trade unionists, unemployed miners, hungry women and children who've come from all over the country, on foot. When they wear out *their* shoes, there's naught for it but to line them with newspaper or go barefoot," he said in reference to Bell's comment. "They want to see the king, and Mosley's lads intend to keep that from happening. Things could get interesting."

The editor's eyes widened, and his nostrils flared. He pointed his cigar at Tom. "Yes, cover it." He turned to Simon. "Bell, there's a football match coming up, the English national team versus the German equivalent. It's meant to be a practice match for the Olympics next year. The German minister for sport will be coming over, and I hear Hitler's pet diplomat and that darling of British society fascists, Joachim von Ribbentrop, will also be attending the game. He's invited a few of his closest upper-class English friends and admirers. I want to know who accepts that invitation." Simon scribbled in his notebook, pleased enough with the assignment.

"Carrey, you'll cover the meeting of the British Olympic Association. They're set to debate a potential British boycott of the games." Carrey nodded.

"The photographer?" Tom reminded his boss.

Sir Maudesley gazed at the photos and grunted. "Bloody marvelous work, isn't it? This photographer submits anonymously."

"Can we find out who it is? Offer him an assignment?" Tom asked.

Sir Maudesley shook his head. "You'll have to make do with one of our staffers." He rose to his feet. "That's all, gentlemen," he said, dismissing them. He turned back. "And, Tom? See if you can find some time to cover the fall Season while you're out and about, will you? Just a few odds and sods to delight our female readership."

Tom ignored the stony looks of his colleagues as he left the room. It was a familiar feeling—too high-and-mighty for the working class he sprang from, and too lowborn for his father's class, an earl's bastard but a very well-educated one. That didn't play well when he went home to visit his mother's kin in Clydebank, Scotland, where the men worked hard in the shipyards, drank hard, fought hard, and talked tough. They knew what they knew, worked at the same jobs as their fathers, and hated the English and the bloody aristocracy. Not that his mother's kin weren't proud of him, being such a smart lad and all—it's just that they didn't want to be seen with him down at the pub. On his father's side, the blood of one of England's noblest families ran in his veins, and they didn't want anything to do with him, either.

His mother swore his father had wanted to recognize him, but his lady wife had refused to stand for it. The best his lordship could do was to provide his former maidservant a house of her own near her kin in Glasgow and ensure Tom had a first-class education. Still, as the by-blow of an English earl, he was beaten up regularly at school until he learned to get along, use his wits, and play the game, finding just the right balance between humble, friendly, and smart. He refused to be deferential, and perhaps that helped. He still stuck out like blight on a rose, whether he was in Clydebank or Mayfair. He intended to change that, to take the opportunities afforded him and make a life out of all the disparate parts of himself, to change the lot of his mother's class, and his country. He was a good journalist, and he meant to be the best.

"Posh friends, eh?" Simon Bell said, shouldering past Tom as they left the room. "Wish I had 'em." Tom smiled at his colleague's broad back as he strode down the hall. Yes, he might have said if Bell had waited. Posh friends were useful indeed, but in the end it came down to brains, guts, and determination, and those qualities were all his own.

CHAPTER FIVE

Camberwell, London
November 1935

VIVIANE LEFT LADY Dunbar's Mayfair house early. She left a note telling her chaperone, Lord Rutherford's sister, that she was going to visit an old friend from boarding school. Instead, she went out through the mews and hailed a cab. She was quite happily going to miss joining Margaret and Julia for yet another wedding dress fitting, followed by another luncheon at the Dorchester, and yet more shopping afterward.

"Camberwell," she said, and the driver looked at her in surprise.

She wore trousers, and in the back seat, she shrugged into an old hunting jacket, an oversized men's garment that enveloped her from chin to knee. She bundled her hair into a knot and squashed a boy's cap on top of it, hiding every strand. The driver glanced at her curiously but held his tongue.

She patted her pockets, counted again the extra rolls of film, and adjusted the strap of her camera around her neck as they crossed Vauxhall Bridge, leaving the pristine, polite streets north of the river behind. On the south bank, another world existed, full of narrow lanes and crumbling buildings and the dank smells of poverty. Men pushed barrows here, scrabbled for an hour's paid work, or a day's, or a week's, if they were lucky. Otherwise, they gathered on corners, their faces drawn with worry and anger. Children ran in the streets without very much in their bellies. It had shocked her the first time she'd come to this part of London as a child with her father. They were paying a visit to a soldier from her father's regiment who'd lost his leg in the war. Her father often visited his men, to cheer them or to offer what assistance he could.

"Why aren't those children wearing any shoes?" she'd asked.

"They don't have any," he'd told her grimly.

"Why?"

"They're poor."

"But why?" she'd persisted.

He'd sighed. "It's the way things work. Some people have money, some don't." She'd scanned the people on the streets, who stared right back as they drove past. "It's not fair, but that's the way of it. Some of my men joined the army never having had new boots before," he'd murmured.

"What can we do to help them?"

"They need better living conditions, jobs," he'd said. "Education, good food, and hope." She had all those things, couldn't imagine life without them. At least until she saw the children who couldn't imagine life *with* them.

"Never lose sight of how lucky you are," her father told her then. "Always fight for what's right."

"Uh-oh, looks like the road is blocked, miss," the cabdriver said to her now. She saw a crowd of people ahead, a single-colored mass, gray and somber, like ghosts. "They're marching to the palace today to see the king. Much good it'll do them. I hear the Fascists intend to stop them. I'll take you back, shall I?"

"I'll get out here," she said, and handed him the fare. The crowd quickly thickened around Viviane as she got out of the cab, absorbing her in the tide. Men and women and even children were walking back the way she'd come, toward Vauxhall Bridge and on to Buckingham Palace, intent on standing outside the king's windows to ask for food and jobs and relief from the economic woes that plagued the country. They'd come from all over England, many on foot, hoping that this time they'd find someone who'd listen, that their king would make the men who governed in his name *do something*.

Some among them believed that Communism and trade unions were the answer to their problems, the best chance for a fair deal for the workingman. Others had come because they were hungry and cold and desperate, and another winter was coming.

Viviane studied the faces, taking in the details of the scene before her.

The stone-faced police were alert for trouble as they rode on horseback along the edges of the crowds.

The careworn faces of the women in the crowd were gray, seamed with worry as they walked forward, singing hymns and chanting for bread. They carried babies and held the hands of their littlest ones. Older children raced around the legs of the stalwart police horses, seeing the whole event as a kind of holiday, a chance to get a look at the king.

Viviane raised her camera. She composed each shot and concentrated on telling the story unfolding before her.

The shutter clicked on a woman wrapped in a tattered shawl, her fierce eyes raised to a policeman who stared back at her with cool indifference.

Viviane captured a workingman, his cheeks thin, his eyes burning like brands as he raised his fist and cried out for employment and dignity. He carried the tools of his trade with him in a canvas bag, ready and eager to work.

She photographed a sallow child in clothes that were too worn and too small, with old eyes in a sharp little face that should have been round and rosy.

Viviane's body thrummed as she moved with calm precision, lining up each shot and pressing the shutter, over and over again. The camera fired in a rapid series of tiny explosions, each click preserving a moment, an individual, one face, one story, out of the many that made up the crowd. It was why she was here. The process thrilled her, absorbed her like nothing else. She was one with the camera, focused, sharp, and precise.

No one spoke to her to object or ask what she was doing. The crowd shuffled forward, orderly but determined, their eyes on the London landmarks across the river, the spire of Big Ben, the white dome of St. Paul's.

Then came the cadence of drums in the distance, matched by the sound of hard-soled boots on the cobbles and the shouts of men chanting a different cry. The Fascists came around the corner in lockstep, black clad, orderly, and militant, their red-and-blue banners writhing in the sluggish breeze. They fanned out across the road, feet wide on the pavement, blocking the way forward.

For an instant the workers faltered, and mothers grabbed their children and held them close.

Viviane looked at the hard face of Sir Oswald Mosley, the leader of the British Union of Fascists. His black uniform was custom-tailored, his expensive boots bespoke. He looked down his nose at the workers before him, all aristocratic arrogance and disdain. Behind him, his men were still and cold, standing to perfect attention, eyes forward, their faces utterly merciless. A shiver raced up her spine as she glanced around, saw her own fear and uncertainty reflected in the faces around her. She drew an anxious breath—everyone did—and for a moment, everything was quiet, and the air crackled with tension.

In the uncertain silence, Mosley raised his arm in something akin to the Nazi salute. "You shall go no farther," he said, his voice ringing out.

That's all it took.

The first missile flew, a broken brick that hit one of the Fascists on the cheek and drew blood. He staggered back in stunned surprise, his hand clasped to his face, and Viviane took the picture. Enraged, the Fascists advanced, truncheons raised, and more bricks flew. And screams of rage and fear and dismay filled the air.

The violence surged around her, rising, fueled by rage and frustration and hatred. "Stop," Viviane said to a man who stumbled against the wall beside her, but he righted himself and rushed back into the fray without hearing, a brick clutched in his fist.

Viviane found a safe space in a doorway and took pictures as fast as she could aim, focus, and shoot. She captured tears, panic, rage, and pain, felt all of it in her own breast. Her knees shook, but her hands were steady.

Children were shrieking in terror, torn from their mothers, lost in the melee, and in danger of being trampled. She saw a small girl in the middle of the road, paralyzed by fear among the tall bodies. A dozen yards away, a mounted policeman spurred his horse to a gallop, riding down on the protesters, baton raised. He didn't see the child in his path.

Viviane didn't stop to think. She raced into the street, grabbed the girl, and kept running, ignoring the objection of her weak leg. She felt the horse's hot breath and the graze of the stirrup across her cheek. She lost her cap, but there was no time to stop. She shoved through bodies and sidestepped debris with the child in her arms, trying to find another doorway, another safe place. The child clung to her, mute with terror. A bottle hit the wall beside her head, spraying both of them with liquid and glass, and the child shrieked. Viviane crouched low, checking the girl's face for cuts. There weren't any, and relief made her limp. "Safe," she said in the child's ear, her own heart pounding against her ribs. "You're safe." She held the child as the sky fell around them, protected what she could amid the chaos, and waited for it all to be over.

TOM STOOD WITH the other reporters. He scribbled notes about the crowd, the weather, the arrogant faces of the Fascists as they marched behind Oswald Mosley.

"Look at him. Bloody marvelous, isn't he?" Terrance Milbury, the star reporter with the *Times*, said, following Tom's gaze to Mosley. "Do you know he can make his eyes flash? It brings women to their knees." He grinned. "Brings everyone to their knees, apparently. I interviewed him last week. He thinks communism and unions will ruin this country. We need pride, industry, and order. Britain must be governed by strong leaders. I can't say I disagree."

"Sounds like something the German chancellor might say," Tom said.

Milbury frowned. "He'll make short work of this rabble. They won't stand against a real show of might and authority. You'll see."

Oswald Mosley raised his baton, nodded to his drummers, and motioned his men forward. Tom felt the drumbeats in his chest. It stirred something primal, instinctively male, even if he didn't agree with the politics. He stood on the curb and watched the Fascists march past, fifty men under a red banner with a dark blue circle and white lightning bolt. As the breeze folded and shifted the image, it looked almost like the German swastika. Or a snake. Tom followed the marchers with several other reporters.

"Grim, this is," one muttered. "This isn't Germany."

"About time, I say," the *Observer* reporter replied, nodding to Milbury.

Then the drums stopped, and the Fascists fanned out across the road and waited. The sudden silence was filled by the murmur of feet on the cobbles, the sound of voices raised in an old hymn as the workers approached. They stopped at the sight of the Fascists blocking the road, and they, too, fell silent.

Tom glanced at the *Herald* photographer beside him. "Get ready," he murmured.

The first brick flew, and both sides erupted with rage, order forgotten as they rushed together. More bricks, bottles, and rocks filled the air, blood spurted.

"Here we go," the *Observer* man said, and hurried into the fray.

"Shite," Tom's photographer, Joe Kemp, muttered, and raised his camera.

Tom took notes as fast as he could write, used words to describe the violence, the shock, the fury. The police waded into the surging crowd, but it was too late to restore order. Women were shrieking, and children—why the hell were there children here?—wailed in terror. The Blackshirts used their truncheons brutally. The workers used sticks and bricks and even hammers. They tore boards from fences. Blood flowed across the cobbles.

The police were powerless, unable to do anything but blow their whistles or strike out randomly at the crowd that hemmed in their horses. No one paid them any mind. They'd need a hundred more police to end this, or the bloody army. Tom looked for Kemp, saw him engulfed in the crowd, cowering, buffeted, uselessly screaming, "I'm with the press!"

Tom dodged a bottle, and it hit the pavement at his feet and shattered. He ran for shelter, a safer place to stand, holding tight to his hat and his notebook. He threw himself into the scant protection of a narrow alley and peered out. He caught a glint of light on glass farther up the road and saw another photographer, a chap in a doorway, shooting fast, focusing his camera on the faces around him, the screaming women, the injured writhing on the ground, the blood-streaked faces contracted in rage. The man had an excellent spot, safe yet in the very middle of the chaos. His photos would tell the story from an intimate perspective. He hoped the man was from the *Herald*.

Then he lowered his camera. Tom's breath caught in his throat as he watched the fool dart into the melee, right into the path of an oncoming police horse. Tom yelled a warning, but his voice was lost in the din. The photographer scooped up a bundle of rags from the pavement, dodged, and missed the onrushing hooves by a hairbreadth and kept running, losing nothing but his cap.

A spill of russet hair tumbled out, a shock of copper against the gray, and he saw wide eyes in a white face. It wasn't a man at all. The shock drove the breath from his lungs, and he stared at her. It couldn't be. Not her, not *here*. Surely she was at home in Mayfair, tucked up in bed under a satin coverlet waiting for her maid to bring her toast and tea.

She turned her head, and he saw blood on her cheek.

Then the crowd surged between them, and when he looked again, there was no one there.

CHAPTER SIX

"THERE AREN'T ANY photos. My camera got smashed," Kemp said miserably when Tom found him after the riot. The photographer was sitting on the curb with a cut on his forehead, staring at the broken remains of the camera in the gutter beside him.

"No photos?" Tom echoed in horror.

"They'll have to rely on your brilliant descriptions, I suppose."

Tom sat down on the curb next to his colleague. No photos. He'd have to write the hell out of the piece and hope that words were enough. He watched as the other journalists climbed into cabs and left with their photographers and the visual record of the riot intact. A car pulled alongside, and Terrance Milbury leaned out the window. "Everything all right, Graham?" Tom didn't bother to answer.

"Did you get pictures?" Tom's photographer asked, tossing his bloodied handkerchief in the gutter beside his broken camera.

"Loads," Milbury said with a bloated grin. "How about we give you a ride back? We can compare notes."

"No thanks," Tom said. "I have some interviews to do."

"You can take me," Kemp said to Milbury. "Can't do much without my gear, and I've got a headache. I'm done for the day."

Tom watched them drive away. He got to his feet and kicked at the carcass of the broken camera. He walked up the street, dodging bricks and glass and the injured still lying on the bloody cobbles. He found a trampled flat cap in the middle of the road, but there was no sign of Viviane Alden. It had been his imagination, he decided. Anything else was utterly impossible, and he had a story to file. He stuffed the cap into his pocket and turned to go.

LATE THAT EVENING, Sir Maudesley came to find Tom as he was hunched over his typewriter, working from his notes, trying use words alone to paint a vivid picture that would allow readers to see the whole riot in their minds.

The small stack of photographs landed on his desk. The face of a woman looked up at him, her face bloody, her eyes wide with fear, a crying child clutched in her arms. You could see the sinews in those arms, the roughness of her work-worn knuckles, the lines of hopelessness and desperation on her face. Her eyes were haunted, and they conveyed all the futility and senselessness of the riot. Tom felt his breath catch. No number of words could capture what this single image did.

The next photograph showed a man shouting with rage, his lips peeled back from broken teeth, his face smudged, a brick flying from his outthrust hand.

Another chilling image showed a Blackshirt, his mouth a thin slash of white-lipped hatred as he met the eye of the camera with a menacing glare.

Every single photograph was brilliant and told a story of its own. The story Tom had to tell made sense now, with the right pictures to go with the prose. Tom looked up at the editor.

"Bloody marvelous, ain't they? Our freelancer came through," Sir Maudesley said around his cigar as he stalked away. "Use the best ones."

Tom flipped through the stack again. They were all good, and it was hard to pick the best. He frowned as he studied them, considered the vantage point. The photographer had obviously been standing right between the two sides as they met and clashed.

It must have been very near to the spot where he saw—or *thought* he saw—Viviane Alden.

"No," he whispered. "It can't be. She couldn't have . . ."

"Talking to yourself?" Simon Bell asked, passing Tom's desk. He picked up the photos and flipped through them, then whistled. "Joe Kemp outdid himself on these," he said.

Tom rose, took the photos back. "Not Kemp. A freelancer."

He crossed the newsroom to knock on Sir Maudesley's door. "Sir, the freelancer who shot these—is it a woman?"

Maudesley Grainger didn't blink. Most of the staff wondered if he was even capable of blinking. "Why do you think that?"

"I saw a woman with a camera today. The position of the photos . . ."

Sir Maudesley sat back in his chair. "There must have been a dozen people there with cameras—or a hundred."

"This photographer deserves credit."

Sir Maudesley shook his head. "No. As I told you, this one prefers to remain anonymous."

"Then you know who it is?" Tom asked, but the editor bit down on his cigar and waved Tom out.

"You've got a deadline to meet. Have the story on my desk within the hour."

Tom turned to go.

"Graham?" the editor barked his name, stopping him, and Tom

paused in the doorway. "Not a word about this. We got lucky and bought some pictures from an anonymous source when our own didn't turn out. Do you understand?"

He thought of Viviane Alden's family, her connections, her place in society. Of course, she wouldn't want it known she'd been out on the street, unchaperoned, in the middle of a riot. Wellborn ladies didn't do such things. Perhaps he'd underestimated this particular society miss.

"Can we expect more from this photographer in future?"

Sir Maudesley tapped the ash from the cigar into an overflowing ashtray. "I believe so. This particular person doesn't know when to quit."

Tom went back to his desk, matching the photos to his words. He recalled seeing the charging horse bearing down on her, knocking off her cap, releasing a spill of red curls. She'd put herself in great danger, might have been injured, or even killed, getting these. He wasn't sure if he admired her talent or thought her the most foolhardy woman on earth.

THE NEXT MORNING, as he was looking at the front-page spread of his report, Sir Maudesley passed his desk. "Graham, join me for lunch. One thirty, the Savoy." It wasn't an invitation—it was an order.

"Yes, sir," Tom said to the editor's retreating back, and wondered why he'd been summoned.

CHAPTER SEVEN

RUTHERFORD WAS READING a copy of the *Herald* when Viviane entered the dining room at the Savoy. She slid into her seat and felt her toes curl. Her photographs graced the front page of the newspaper, uncredited, but hers nonetheless. This morning's edition was on every newsstand she'd passed on her way here to answer her stepfather's summons.

He didn't ask her what she wanted. He ordered the lamb for both of them, though she would have preferred the chicken, with whisky for himself and water for her. That was warning enough that she was about to receive a stern talking-to, undoubtedly at her mother's behest. Her stepfather rarely sought out her company alone, or that of any of his daughters, for that matter. He left all that to his wife unless there was a problem.

He took a sip of whisky. "Your mother is most concerned about you, Viviane," he began. "A broken engagement for no obvious reason makes a young lady prey to scandal, and what you do affects your stepsisters. I wouldn't interfere, of course, but I've heard rumors. One of my colleagues said you photographed his daughter. He wanted to know how much you charge to do formal sittings." He looked along his nose at her.

"I told him that you were not in *trade*, of course, that you were a respectable young lady."

She sipped her water.

"Was I right to do so?"

"Meaning am I in trade?" she asked.

"Don't be impertinent."

"I take photographs of things—and people," she said.

"Your mother is most concerned for your future. As am I, of course. She—we—were dismayed when you broke it off with Medway. It's been months, and still people are talking. Can you offer any reason for causing such upset?"

She set her fork down and clenched her hands in her lap. "Phillip and I simply didn't suit." It was the stock explanation she gave to anyone who asked, her version of "no comment."

"Then find someone else," Rutherford said, making it a terse command. He stabbed a forkful of lamb, dipped it in mint sauce, and devoured it.

She waited until his mouth was full and raised her chin. "There's no one else I want to marry." His frown deepened as he chewed. Rutherford disliked disturbance in his routine, and he abhorred scandal, and she'd brought both upon him. As her guardian, he had the power to stop her allowance or banish her to Wrenwood if he so chose.

"I mean, there isn't anyone at *present*," she said quickly. "Perhaps I'll meet someone here in London, or next Season," she said, doing her best to look contrite and dutiful, to meet his expectations of proper feminine behavior.

Rutherford swallowed, cut another piece of lamb, and pointed it at her on the end of his fork. "You can't simply drift around London as you've been doing."

"Oh, but I'm not—I've been helping Margaret buy her trousseau—

and Julia is getting ready for her debut in a few months. I've been help-ing her as well."

"That's her aunt Selena's job," he said.

She twisted the fine linen napkin in her lap. How to charm him, convince him? She mimicked Julia's enthusiastic gush. "I do love Lon-don! I enjoy seeing reliable friends like Geoffrey and Reggie. They know *everyone* worth knowing. Just last week we all went to the theater with their mother, the countess."

He blinked, looked unsure. He fell back on the script her mother had no doubt provided. "Your mother wants you home at Wrenwood. I'm going down this weekend. You can accompany me."

Viviane's stomach flipped. She bit her lip and played the Ace of Feminine Vanity, a card any man with four daughters understood well. It trumped any king. "But I've accepted an invitation to a party. Mar-garet and Geoffrey are going, and I have a new dress for the occasion."

The earl, such a powerful force in the politics of the country, had no idea how to manage his daughters. It was why he'd married again. Fe-male emotions baffled him. Each and every one of his girls knew he could be easily managed when he was faced with what he considered "female problems," which included everything from tears to romance. Even logic, if it came from one of his daughters, upset the earl.

Rutherford looked utterly discombobulated now.

"And there's a gallery opening next week, and a fundraising tea at the British Museum on Thursday," Viviane rushed on. *And a Fascist rally to photograph on Wednesday.* "Would it not make more sense for me to stay in London, where I am likely to meet another eligible gentleman?"

He blinked. "Perhaps that is a sensible course of action. But there's to be no taking photographs of anyone for payment, is that clear?"

"Yes, of course, but—"

"I will stop your allowance if I hear any more tales. Do you want to make your mother ill, cause her worry and grief?" No doubt her mother had suggested those threats.

Rutherford regarded her, and his frown eased. "Then we have an agreement," he said, as if he were negotiating a treaty in the cabinet.

Viviane demurely lowered her eyes to her plate and hid a triumphant grin.

He glanced at his watch. "I must get back. There's a debate in the House this afternoon. I'll put you in a cab back to Selena's."

"Thank you," she said with a sweet smile, the one they taught debutantes and made them practice until their cheeks ached. She folded her napkin and tucked it beside her plate, her meal barely touched, and let him escort her out.

She waved goodbye and waited until the cab pulled away from the curb. She wasn't going back to Selena's just yet. There was a demonstration planned, a march of widows and mothers who'd lost husbands and sons in the Great War and favored appeasing the Germans to prevent another conflict. "Whitehall," she ordered the driver as she took her camera out of her bag and slung it around her neck.

CHAPTER EIGHT

THE SAVOY DINING room was not the usual place Tom ate lunch. Unless he was invited by someone important—his employer, for example.

Or his father.

He was surprised to see the Earl of Strathwood seated at Sir Maudesley's table when he walked in, but he carefully schooled his face to blankness.

The earl watched him cross the room, his expression equally devoid of emotion.

In the twenty-five years of Tom's life, he'd only met the man who'd fathered him twice, and they'd been brief, unsentimental encounters.

The first time had been when Tom was seven, and his father had come to Glasgow. He'd been in the park with his mother when a tall stranger approached them. "This is your father," she'd said simply. The earl offered his hand and Tom shook it while his mother held tight to his other hand as if the earl might try to snatch him away from her, but he let go and made no further attempt to touch Tom.

"He's a fine lad," he'd said, his eyes lingering on her, not him. Tom had squared his shoulders and stood between the man and his mother.

"He's smart," his mother said. "He deserves a better life than workin' in the shipyards, but he'll need schoolin' for that."

The earl had simply nodded. "I'll arrange it."

His mother had given him a push, sent him off to play, but Tom stood by a tree a little way off and watched them. The earl's fingers brushed his mother's hand, and for an instant she held on. Then the stranger who was his father had walked away without looking back.

It had been made clear to Tom that while the earl wasn't precisely ashamed of him, there was no possibility of a closer relationship, or any relationship at all, for that would embarrass the earl's legitimate family. In that moment, young as he was, Tom understood the scorn his mother faced for bearing a child out of wedlock, a shame he refused to share.

He learned he had half siblings who wanted nothing to do with him. When he went to Cambridge and began to travel in Geoffrey's social circle, he saw his half brother from time to time, usually across a room, but they never met. Tom didn't force the issue. The earl provided his bastard son with a gentleman's education, but otherwise Tom asked for nothing.

His father had been at his commencement ceremony at Cambridge, seated on the dais among the notable guests. He'd watched Tom graduate with a first-class degree, offered brief congratulations, and pressed an envelope into Tom's hand.

Inside was fifty pounds and a letter of introduction to an engineering firm in Glasgow, describing Tom as an intelligent young man with keen wits and a determination to make something of himself. Tom had used the money to travel to London instead, and he got the job at the *Herald* on his own merit.

It had been four years since Tom had last seen his father. He knew Strathwood didn't often come to London, and rarely ventured out among society, though his countess and children were part of the most prestigious social sets. If Tom wanted to see his half siblings, all he had to do was open the *Tatler*.

"You wished to see me?" he said to Sir Maudesley as he sat down. The editor showed not a whit of guilt for the surprise. He simply shifted his gaze to the earl, deferring the meeting to him.

"How are you?" Strathwood asked. "How's your mother?"

"She's fine. She took up painting a few years ago. She's very good. She paints the shipyards and the workers, the truly noble folk who run the world with their sweat and blood."

The earl quirked one eyebrow at Tom's acid comment but said nothing. He unfolded a copy of the morning edition of the *Herald* and laid it on the table between them.

"I didn't know you read the *Herald*," Tom said.

"I read everything you write," the earl replied. He didn't add anything beyond that, certainly not praise. For a moment there was silence. "Look, there's an important job I—we—wished to discuss with you," the earl said, glancing at Sir Maudesley.

Tom pointed at the newspaper. "I already have a job."

"There's another war coming." It was a statement, not a question.

"So they say," Tom replied.

"There are men in England who believe our best policy is to keep the Germans happy, to make concessions, overlook Hitler's transgressions against the treaty made at the end of the last war. What's your opinion?" Strathmore asked.

"Some say the French were too hard on the Germans," Tom said. "Perhaps it's our fault. Peace should be fair since war is not." He wasn't a Fascist by any means, didn't want to see what was happening in Germany come to Britain, but he said it to goad the earl, to make him blink.

Strathwood frowned. "Are you one of the appeasers, then?"

"Not at the *Herald* he's not!" Sir Maudesley said before Tom could make his own denial.

Tom folded his arms. "I'm a journalist. I look at both sides of a story," he said stubbornly.

"Yes, but where do you stand, in your heart, when you are not a journalist?" the earl persisted.

"You wish to know my politics?"

"Yes."

"For this job you mentioned? What kind of job is it?"

Food arrived. Sir Maudesley had ordered for all of them, roast chicken with tiny potatoes and peas. Tom would have preferred the lamb, but he stayed silent as the waiter presented the meal with a flourish. White wine splashed into crystal glasses—something sweet and German.

Strathwood sipped the wine. "The job?" Tom reminded him.

"It would involve fact-finding, reporting on a story of international interest."

Tom glanced at his boss, who was tucking into his meal with gusto. "I don't set my own assignments at the *Herald*. There's a dozen reporters, and Sir Maudesley decides—"

The editor waved his fork. "Consider yourself on special assignment."

The earl had yet to touch his own meal. Nor had Tom. "This job is . . . different. You'd be working for a new government agency."

"You expect me to leave the *Herald*?" Tom asked.

"Bite your tongue, lad!" Sir Maudesley said.

"No, not at all. In fact, it's most important that you keep your press credentials," the earl said, picking up his fork at last. He took a bite of the chicken. "I understand you speak German. You took a number of language classes at Cambridge, in fact—French as well." He smiled at the look of surprise Tom couldn't quite hide. "You're surprised that I know. Do eat before it gets cold. The sauce is excellent." He sounded almost paternal. "I know all about your studies. You scored top marks in everything. You rowed, played cricket."

"Now that's a rather fatherly thing, isn't it? Taking interest in a son who is essentially a stranger," Tom said acidly.

The earl ignored the comment. "I rather expected you to go into engineering, given your uncle's profession."

"Shipyard supervisor? You thought I'd follow in his footsteps, keep my place? I have cousins in the coal mines as well. I might ha' joined 'em doon the pit." He let his accent broaden into his mother's Scots.

The earl raised one brow. "That's not what I meant, actually. No work is undignified. No, I meant my younger brother, also your uncle. He's an engineer. He designs aircraft."

Tom had never even heard of the uncle the earl was speaking of. He'd made it a point to show as little interest in the MacCann family as they showed in him.

"Alexander has always been the smartest of all of us—until you," the earl said. "I hoped that you'd become an engineer, build things, fix things, and Alex would take you under his wing."

"So to speak," Tom quipped.

The earl smiled. "That's just the kind of jest Alex would make. You're very like him, you know. A true MacCann."

"I'm my own man, a reporter." He pointed at his byline on the newspaper.

"Yes. Alex had some ideas about that, too. He's part of this new committee, you see, and we think you can play a part."

"How? We've determined that engineering is not my area of expertise," Tom said, intrigued.

"How'd you like to be the *Herald*'s correspondent in Berlin?" Sir Maudesley asked.

Tom's brows shot up. "Me?" There were other, more senior writers on staff ahead of him for promotion. He glanced at his father, wondering if this was some kind of bribe, and just what strings might be attached, but Strathwood's face remained closed.

"Yes, you," Sir Maudesley said impatiently. "You're a good reporter, you're discreet, and you're smart. A foreign posting is a plum assignment, and is there anywhere more dynamic, more interesting than Germany now? Journalists from all over the world would give their eyeteeth to be there. The Winter Olympics are in February, and the Summer Games in Berlin next August. There'll be plenty to report on, and not just the athletics. This is an opportunity for the Germans to show everyone how clever they are, how very bloody superior. Hitler is a braggart. He'll want to show off his latest marvels of engineering, human and mechanical, supermen and super factories."

"They're already boasting about superior production capacity, the tonnage of steel they make, new inventions," Strathwood added. "They swear that it's all for perfectly innocent uses, but is it? Some think they're testing the waters, muttering about how unfair the Versailles Treaty was, waiting to see if anyone objects. Some believe that if they aren't stopped now—"

"Who?" Tom asked. "Who would I really be working for?"

Sir Maudesley shifted in his chair, and Strathwood ignored the question. "If the Germans aren't stopped, they'll take the next step, rearm in contravention of the treaty, and see what we're willing to do about it. But by then it will be too late," the earl said. "We know they're already designing faster planes, bigger warships, and new weapons, all while they swear that they want nothing but peace. They've created a police state, and I for one am curious to see how they'll hide all that from the tourists next year, aren't you?"

Sir Maudesley stabbed his finger into the tablecloth. "As journalists, we must expose his dirty secrets, provide proof that all is not as Herr Hitler would have us believe it is, d'you see, Graham? The bastards think the Olympics will buy them time, offer a distraction, a glorious spectacle to keep the world's gaze away from what's really going on. They'll smile and show how magnificently they've risen from the ashes of war in less than two decades to become the world leaders in technology, industry, and science. That's true enough, but why?" Sir Maudesley leaned closer to Tom, lowered his voice. "They want another war, that's why. We need someone who knows how to look and what to look for, has the brains to get the story behind the story. How I want to be the one to publish that exposé!" He slid his eyes away from Tom's to look at the earl. "This job isn't just for the *Herald*, but that would be your cover."

"My *cover*?"

"You'd be more than a reporter," Strathwood said.

"What, a spy? You want me to *spy*?"

Sir Maudesley winced and looked around to see if Tom's voice had carried, but Strathwood simply nodded. "In a manner of speaking."

"In a manner of speaking," Tom murmured, his mouth dry. He pinned the earl with a sharp look. "Why me?" he asked again. "Because I'm your bastard son, because you think I owe you something?"

Strathwood didn't even flinch. "Because you're smart, and you see what lies beneath the surface, beyond what's obvious. It was someone else who suggested you'd be right for this."

"It seems you made quite an impression on Mr. Churchill when last you met," Sir Maudesley said.

Churchill. The wheels turned in Tom's brain. That meant secret committees, the gathering of the kind of information and facts that went well beyond journalism. He realized that while he was interviewing Churchill at Halliwell, the politician was interviewing *him*.

"We want someone who knows how to fit in, someone who can read people and play their game. You've had to do that all your life, haven't you?" Strathwood said, offering no apology for that. Tom wondered how closely his father had watched him over the years.

"Are you willing or not?" Sir Maudesley demanded, editing the conversation, cutting to the heart of the unfolding tale.

He looked at his father. "Would I be working for you?"

"You'll be reporting to someone in Berlin, a discreet contact. He'll pass on anything of interest to the London office."

"The *Herald* will assign you to the British Press Corps covering the preparations for the Berlin Olympics, but you'll take your orders from—well, let's say Whitehall for now. You'll file reports with them," Sir Maudesley said. He looked away.

"What else?" Tom said. "There is more to this, isn't there?"

Sir Maudesley grinned. "Smart lad. The tricky bit is that you'll have to—let's say *encourage*—the Germans to trust you. You'll have to appear to be sympathetic to the Fascist cause. It helps that you are acquainted with men like Phillip Medway and Oswald Mosley here in England. You'll need to pass muster when the Germans check, y'see. They investigate the credentials and political leanings of all new members of the foreign press corps," Sir Maudesley said. "If you appear to be sympathetic to the Nazi cause, you'll be granted special privileges, given top interviews and exclusive press tours to enable you to write the kind of stories that could convince others back home of the power, glory, and rightness of Mr. Hitler's policies. You'll have to appear to be a willing cog in their propaganda machine, someone they can count on to write about the regime in glowing terms. Can you do that?"

"Be something I'm not?" Tom asked, glancing at his father.

Strathwood scanned his son's face. "Precisely."

"I understand Lady Janet's in town," Tom said, mentioning his half sister. "Her husband is up for election. Why not ask him? Surely there will be politicians attending the games."

"Wouldn't do," the earl said.

"Too good to get his hands dirty?" Tom asked.

"No. He's not a journalist, and Duncan is likely to see what he wishes to, not what's actually there," the earl replied.

"Poor quality in a lawyer," Tom said. "He favors appeasement, I take it?"

Strathmore's lips tightened, but he didn't reply. "Do you have any other questions?"

"How much time do I have to consider this?" Tom asked. Any journalist would give his right arm—if he wrote left-handed—for this kind of foreign posting. A certain degree of espionage always came with effective reporting. So did scrupulous honesty, in Tom's opinion. For this assignment he'd have to give up honesty entirely, write lies, and pretend to be something he was most certainly not.

"I'll need your decision at once, I'm afraid," the earl said.

"How soon? A week?" Tom asked. The earl's face suggested that would be too long. "A few days?"

"Now, lad. Here," Sir Maudesley said. "You'd leave for Berlin within the week."

Surprise coursed through Tom's body. He wondered what it would mean to refuse. He was tongue-tied.

Strathwood folded his napkin and set it next to his half-finished meal. "I'll be in at the Dorchester until tomorrow morning. My train leaves at eleven. I'll need an answer by then." He finished his wine and set the glass down. "I suppose I shall have to drink French wine from now on, I think, though I do love a good German Auslese." He rose. "It was good to see you."

Was it? Tom scanned the Savoy's busy dining room, filled with the who's who of London, lords and ladies, artists and writers being treated to a lunch they could never afford on their own, diplomats and rich Americans.

His gaze fell on a halo of russet curls, and he recognized Viviane Alden, and the sight of her caused an odd little jump in his chest, a jolt of electricity. She wore a blue dress with a ruffled collar today, and she was lunching with her stepfather, every inch the respectable lady. This was where she belonged, not in London's rough streets during a riot.

He'd thought a lot about her, the evocative images she captured with her camera and the risks she'd taken to get those shots. Scorn had turned to a surge of admiration. She was daring, clever, and it was clear she understood the plight of the people she photographed. She also pretended to be something she wasn't, and she was as expert at that as she was at wielding her camera.

Rutherford was leaning forward, emphasizing whatever point he was making with jabs of his index finger on the white linen tablecloth. Viviane had her hands in her lap. A lecture, then, or a reprimand. Had the earl found out about his stepdaughter's dangerous hobby? She'd give it up now, he supposed, disappointed. But she looked up at Rutherford, and Tom saw something flash in her eyes, a momentary look of stubborn pride, or determination, perhaps, and then it was gone. It made Tom smile. She enjoyed it, he realized. She *liked* the element of danger, the challenge of having a secret life.

Tom rose and hurried into the foyer where Strathwood was putting on his coat.

His father paused. "Yes?"

"I'll do it."

CHAPTER NINE

April 1936

MARGARET'S WEDDING DAY arrived on a bright April morning that was remarkably warm for the time of year, and the bride was radiant with anticipation as her sisters helped her dress.

There was a knock at the door, and the countess's maid entered. "His lordship would like a word, my lady. He was wondering if he could come in for just a moment."

"Of course, Hemmings," Estella said.

"Uh-oh," Grace said. "Just when you said nothing could go wrong, here it comes. What if Geoffrey's backed out?"

Margaret looked stricken.

"Of course he hasn't," Julia said, sending Grace a scorching glare.

The earl entered, looking ill at ease in a boudoir filled with women, flowers, and lace.

"Is anything amiss?" the countess asked, her hands on her pearls.

The earl's nose wrinkled at the thick scent of perfume. "Amiss? No, not at all. It's good news, as a matter of fact, and I wished to share it with you at once." He held up a telegram. "This is from an old friend in Germany—Count Georg von Schroeder." He glanced at Margaret. "He offers his congratulations to you and Geoffrey, but the telegram concerns Julia most of all." He looked at his second daughter. "As your godfather, Georg has invited you to come to Germany and stay with his family this summer. He promises a trip to the Olympic Games, and—"

"Me? Germany?" Julia jumped to her feet. "Oh, how wonderful! When do I leave?"

Felicity and Grace also leaped up and began to squawk and flap like geese, full of questions and comments and exclamations, and Rutherford sent a pleading glance at his wife.

"Sit down and let your father speak," she commanded, and the twins fell silent at once.

Viviane looked away. Of all the countries on earth, Germany was the last place she'd ever go. It was the homeland of her father's enemies, the belligerent foes that had started the war that killed and maimed so many. They'd invented and used the deadly gas that had ruined her father's health, an insidious weapon that kept on killing even long after the conflict was over. Surely Rutherford would not send Julia there. She waited for him to say no.

"But Julia is to make her debut in a few weeks," Estella said. "There are stories about what's going on in Germany, the violence and hateful speeches. I'm not sure it's entirely safe."

The earl frowned. "Safe? Georg is one of my oldest friends, and Julia is his goddaughter. He'll care for her as if she were his own. We were at Oxford together, and his family is one of the most ancient and noble in Germany. Georg has three sons and a castle in the German Alps—"

"A castle?" Julia cried. "Oh, Papa, I must go, I simply must!"

Rutherford kept his attention on his wife. "Other young ladies are going to Germany, girls from the finest English families. They get a bit of international polish, visit music festivals, see the mountains, and come home with a greater understanding of how the world works. Surely that can only forge closer social ties and peace between our two nations. I believe many of the stories we hear are exaggerated for dramatic effect by the press."

To Viviane, he sounded like he was making a speech in the House of Lords. Her mother looked thoughtful, not horrified. She crossed and took the telegram from her husband, scanned it.

"It says a longer letter will follow with more details," she murmured. "She'll need a chaperone, of course." She glanced at Selena. But her sister-in-law shook her head. "No, don't look at me, Estella. I'll be in Scotland in July and August. I go every year, and I couldn't possibly change my plans."

The trip would fall through, Viviane thought with relief. Julia could not go alone.

"Perhaps Julia could take Viviane," Rutherford suggested.

"Me? But I don't want to go to Germany!" Viviane blurted, and every eye in the room turned on her.

Her mother regarded her for a long moment before she handed the telegram back to the earl. "This is obviously not the time to discuss this," she pronounced. "It's Margaret's wedding day, and we must concentrate on that before we turn to other matters."

From the mantel, the antique porcelain clock chimed ten in a delicate but firm little voice. Margaret let out a small gasp.

"We've only an hour," she murmured, turning back to the mirror to apply the powder puff to her perfect nose yet again.

Viviane could feel her mother's eyes upon her like pins left in her gown by the dressmaker. Estella had something on her mind, and Viviane dreaded the conversation. It came as Margaret descended the stairs on her father's arm, when her mother caught Viviane's arm.

"I want a word with you."

"Margaret looks so lovely, don't you think?" Viviane said.

"Of course. She *is* lovely, but this should be your wedding day, Viviane. Phillip should be waiting for *you* at the altar."

"Mother."

"The scandal of your broken betrothal hasn't gone away. Phillip hasn't chosen anyone else, nor have you. People are *talking*," her mother whispered, her hand a claw on Viviane's arm, holding her in place as the rest of the bridal party descended the stairs. "I fear if you spend another Season in London with so much dreadful gossip hanging over your head, you will never attract a decent husband."

Her mother reached up to fix an errant curl in Viviane's coiffure. "I just want you to be happy. There's someone I want you to meet. The Duke of Bellshire is single, wealthy, and he wants a closer political connection to Rutherford's set. You are the granddaughter of a duke yourself, practically a perfect match."

"Practically?" Viviane murmured. "Oh, but this is Margaret's big day. We can discuss it tomorrow."

Her mother's eyes shone. "He's here today! I invited him to the wedding. It's my little surprise for you. You'll have him all to yourself, have the chance to charm him. There's no reason why you couldn't be married by June if you apply yourself. You won't have to endure another Season."

Viviane felt as if a trap were about to close on her. "Shall I simply announce my betrothal this evening?" Viviane asked sarcastically.

Her mother's smile was sharp, knife-edged, and determined. "Tomorrow will do. Or you could go to Germany until the scandal dies down. It can't last forever, and the count does have three sons."

"Mother, I—"

"Are you coming?" Rutherford called up to them, and Estella waved.

"I'll introduce you to Bellshire after the ceremony, and I've arranged for you to be seated next to him at supper," she whispered as they descended the steps.

Viviane's fingers shook as she helped her stepsister into the car, being careful to pleat the long yards of the heirloom lace train so it wouldn't crease. Her mother would be insistent this time. She had a duke in hand, and she wasn't going take Viviane's no for an answer. If she refused Bellshire, there'd be another duke after that, or an earl or a marquis, until she'd run through the whole list of eligible peers.

Viviane had hoped that after one more Season, her mother would relent and realize that Viviane did not wish to marry. Estella would never forgive her, of course. Rutherford would cut off her allowance, and she'd be on her own. It was what she wanted, just not yet, not until she could afford it on her own, and she'd eased her mother into the idea of her daughter making her own living as a professional photographer. She didn't want to be someone's wife for the sake of being married, to fit in with someone else's politics or ideals and opinions. She had her own. She wanted an authentic, genuine life of her own design.

Her mother would never understand that. Estella hadn't been raised to be independent. She needed to be married, to belong to someone who'd keep her safe and make decisions for her. Her husband's death had left her alone for the first time in her life. It had destroyed all the sweetness and joy her father had so loved about her, broken her, and left her bitter and afraid. Viviane had learned to depend on herself and to guard her mother's fragile feelings. Someday she hoped she would fall in love, but it would be a relationship of equals, built on trust and honesty, someone she *liked* as much as loved.

Until then, she would rely on herself.

She stood with her stepsisters and waved as Rutherford's car drove away with Margaret and their parents inside, and the next car pulled up to carry the bridesmaids.

There had to be a way out, a way to buy time. She just had to find it.

CHAPTER TEN

Halliwell

THE BRIDEGROOM BELLOWED as he launched himself into the air, stark naked, and hit the icy water of the lake. He came up gasping and whooping, only to be hit by another splash of green water as his brother dove beside him.

Tom waded in gingerly. The water was cold, and he was a poor swimmer, but this was a wedding day tradition among Farraday men. They'd race to the island in the middle of Halliwell's man-made lake where they would drink a toast to the groom, then swim back again to dress for the ceremony.

Tom suspected it had much to do with the other Farraday tradition of getting utterly pissed the night before and needing a bracing swim in icy water to clear one's head for the vows. He'd offered to row across to the island, perhaps to carry the flask and the glasses for the toast, but he was told a servant had already ensured those items were in place. He'd have to swim.

At least it wasn't deep, just cold enough to shrivel his balls into his throat. He kept one foot on the muddy bottom all the way.

Reggie won. He pulled himself out onto the shore and flopped down on the grass, naked, absorbing the warmth of the April sunshine. Geoffrey arrived next, and they hooted encouragement to Tom, laughing as he pulled himself out of the water at last and dropped down beside them.

"I take it none of your ancestors married in winter," Tom said. "What would you have done if the wedding had taken place in January?"

Reggie grinned. "Worn socks to keep our feet warm," he quipped. "Do the honors, will you, Tom, since you're the best man." Tom opened the waiting hamper, pulled the cork on a dusty bottle, and filled three cups with single malt whisky that was older than any of them, or perhaps all three of them combined.

He raised the toast and drank. Blessed heat flowed through Tom's icy limbs.

They lay back, staring at the cloudless sky. "Ready to be a married man?" Tom asked. "Can't imagine it myself."

Reggie grinned. "That's because you're ugly. Who'd marry you?" he joked.

Tom glanced at Geoff. He was truly in love, and Tom wondered what that felt like.

For a fleeting moment Viviane Alden came to mind. She'd be part of the bridal party. He'd been in Germany for five months and had only returned for the wedding. She was still taking chances—he'd seen photographs in the *Herald* that only she could have taken, daring images that captured her subjects with breathtaking clarity.

"How's the new job?" he asked Geoffrey. "Enjoying being a proper solicitor?"

Geoffrey glanced at him and turned serious, a rare thing for Geoffrey Farraday. "I am. It's an old firm, and a prestigious one. One of the partners is a new member of parliament. They say he'll have a cabinet post before long." He glanced at Tom. "Look, I had a telephone call this morning from him. I take it you know Duncan Chapman?"

Tom held his breath for a moment, then nodded crisply.

"The Honorable Duncan Chapman is married to Lady Janet Chapman," Geoffrey said to Reggie. "She's the Earl of Strathwood's daughter, and Strathwood is Tom's father."

Tom felt his throat tighten.

"Duncan fears things might be awkward today with you as my best man," Geoffrey said.

Tom braced himself. The usual warmth and good humor in his best friend's gaze had turned to doubt. "Are you asking me to back out?" He knew well enough that if Geoffrey wished to rise in his firm he'd have to choose Chapman over Tom. Nothing personal, of course, but with the right connections, Geoff might be up for a cabinet post himself one day.

Geoffrey had always known Tom was the earl's bastard son, but it never mattered before. Now it did. He waited for Geoffrey to answer his question.

Geoffrey sighed and looked away. "No. I only hope there won't be any difficulties. For Margaret's sake."

"Not from me," Tom said. "I am—estranged, I suppose is the polite term—from Strathwood's family. We've never even been formally introduced." He sensed Geoffrey was waiting for more than that, some promise, or perhaps a gentlemanly offer to withdraw from the wedding party and leave. Tom stubbornly held his tongue. He saw hesitation, a strangeness in Geoff's eyes that had never been there before, and he realized the whole yawning chasm of the difference in their classes had opened between them and would never close again. Geoffrey had chosen ambition and snobbery over friendship.

Perhaps that was unfair. Geoff had to make his way in the world just as Tom did.

Still, Tom wasn't going to make it easy. If Geoffrey wanted him gone, then he'd have to say it directly. Now that would be awkward, given that they were lying naked beside a lake, equals in that at least. Getting up and striding into the water to swim back would hardly qualify as a dignified exit.

"You're going to write a story about the wedding, aren't you?" Geoffrey asked.

"I promised my editor I would," Tom replied.

Geoff's jaw tightened, and he looked away.

Reggie slapped his brother on the back of the head. "Don't be such a prig, Geoff."

Geoffrey forced a laugh but didn't meet Tom's eyes. He got to his feet and hurried back to the water. "Bet you both a shilling I'll win this time."

They watched him go, cleaving the green water, swimming away from them and toward his future.

"These are his last moments of freedom. I suppose we should let him win," Reggie said. "Don't mind him. This job is going to make him a frightful snob. Marrying Lady Margaret Devellin is just the first step up for my little brother, and everyone expects him to go far. He's had so much advice, I doubt he knows what he really wants anymore." He drained his cup and got to his feet. "I think that's enough of a head start. We'd best go. My mother will be a dragon if we're late." He said no more than that, but his support was clear in his eyes. They waded into the water.

"Damn, but it's cold. I don't know why Vee loves swimming so much. It's sheer torture," Reggie said.

The icy water chilled Tom's sun-warmed flesh again. His best friend—former best friend—was climbing the far bank now, pulling on his clothes. He didn't bother to look for Tom, to make sure he hadn't drowned. Tom kept his head above the water, his gut tight with regret, anger, and pride.

HOURS LATER, AS the wedding guests danced the night away, Tom sat alone in the silken darkness, hidden by a friendly tree at the bottom of the garden, sipping whisky from a flask, silently toasting the end of an era.

The wedding had been perfect, the weather fine, the bride blushing and beautiful, the groom proud. The celebration that followed was grand indeed. The band was excellent, the champagne plentiful, and everyone was having a marvelous time.

Tom's part in it was over.

Geoffrey had been as tight as a drawn bow beside Tom all day, expecting a scene between Tom and the Chapmans, some snide remark, a snub that would spoil the day.

Tom had encountered Janet Chapman in the receiving line. His half sister had looked him over with eyes the same gray as his own. He saw her note the family resemblance and pinch her lips. She didn't say a word. Sir Duncan shook his hand with a politician's instinctive, impersonal grip before moving on.

That should have been the end of it, but Geoffrey remained tense and aloof. After today, this last duty born of long friendship, they would be strangers.

In a few days, he'd be back in Berlin, fighting to prove himself worthy there as well.

He hated it. Not journalism but the need to impress the bloody Nazis, to smile at them, write about them as if he admired them, stood with them, understood their twisted, hateful philosophy and approved

of it. Every word dragged at his soul. When the first of his German articles had appeared, his mother had written to him, asking what had
gotten into him. If he were home in Glasgow, she would have insisted
on a double dose of cod-liver oil. His uncle would have taken him out
behind the pub and knocked some sense back into him.

Tom had covered the Winter Olympics in February, a glorious, generous, friendly event. Everyone had been impressed by the gracious-
ness and good manners of the German people. Reporters with years of
experience were taken in, found themselves admiring Germany, and
Hitler.

Not a month after those games were done, Hitler had marched
troops into the Rhineland, reclaiming territory forfeited to France
under the Treaty of Versailles at the end of the war as punishment for
starting the fight.

The world had held its breath. There'd been a flurry of diplomatic
notes, but no direct action from France or Britain. The prevailing view
seemed to be that if Germany was allowed to have the territory, and
their pride, back again, then perhaps Hitler would be satisfied. So the
Germans stayed in the Rhineland, and preparations for the Summer
Games continued, another campaign to conquer the hearts and minds
of international tourists and athletes, an invitation to join with the Germans, to come and celebrate the peace and beauty of the Olympic ideal
in Berlin.

Hitler had demanded that the 1936 Olympics—*his* Olympics—be
bigger, better, and grander than any others. And as with the Winter
Olympics, anti-Semitism, violence, and talk of war would be hidden
away from foreigners, replaced by a few weeks of flowers and fun.

In Germany, newsreels and newspapers were already reminding
German citizens that they must welcome the world with a smile, show
hospitality to all, no matter who they were, for the duration of the

games. Travel posters, brochures, and guidebooks had been updated for the Berlin Games. Charming photographs of mountains and forests, rivers and lakes, quaint villages, and happy, rosy-cheeked, blond and blue-eyed folk graced the windows of tourist offices around the world. International journalists had been invited to tour the Olympic facilities as they were constructed, provided with fact sheets and stock images of strong, salt-of-the-earth workmen beaming with pride at a hard job well done as they built the massive stadium or the athletes' village. There were no photographs of storm troopers beating old men on the streets or Nazi parades or Gestapo agents arresting terrified citizens. Taking such photos could result in one's press pass being revoked. Tom had only words to describe the situation. He did what he could to get the truth out, even as he wrote lies. He passed the legitimate stories he uncovered to a Canadian journalist named Charlie Ellis, a correspondent who wrote for a number of Canadian, American, and British papers. Ellis got credit and praise for writing the truth, Tom's truth. It was a terrible risk for both of them, of course, and if either of them were caught . . . He put that terrifying thought out of his mind.

He'd expected this little trip home for the wedding to be relaxing and fun, a chance to be himself again, among friends. *Friends.* He tipped the flask to his lips again.

His ears pricked at the snap of a twig, the crunch of feet on the cinder path that ran behind the tree. He stayed still, expected whoever it was to stroll past and not even notice he was there.

"Damn it," Reggie cursed. "Look, it's too dark for a ramble in the wood. Wouldn't you rather dance? That will be difficult now I've broken my bloody foot on a tree root. What's this all about? You've never tried to drag me in the wicked darkness before."

Just Reggie on a tryst, Tom thought. Now he'd have to make his presence known . . .

"I need your help." The sound of Viviane's voice stopped him cold. What the devil was she doing in the woods with Reggie?

Curious, Tom stayed where he was.

"I have a problem. My mother wants me to marry the Duke of Bellshire, and Julia wants me to go to Germany with her for the summer."

Germany? Tom's ears pricked. Nothing would move him now.

"You've always said you'd never set foot in Germany, so should I offer my congratulations on your nuptials?" Reggie asked.

"No!" The word conveyed frustration and agony.

"Good. Bellshire's a dreadful bore, Vee. You can do better."

"Oh, Reggie, I was hoping you'd say that. I was also hoping that you might . . . that is, I was hoping that you and I might become engaged."

Tom felt his belly hollow out with surprise. For an instant the crickets chirped, loud in the silence.

"You want to marry *me*?" Reggie finally sputtered. "I proposed to you once and you said you wouldn't have me for a husband if I were the last man on earth."

"We were fifteen at the time," Viviane said. "No offense, but I still don't actually want to marry you—or anyone else. I just need to be engaged for a little while, to buy some time, throw my mother—and Bellshire—off the scent. It would be for a few months at best, until the end of the summer, perhaps."

Reggie groaned. "Oh, sweetheart. If you'd asked me a month ago, even a week ago, I would have jumped at the chance to help you out, but I can't do it."

"You . . . you can't?" she said in a dismayed whisper.

"I've been courting someone myself, Susan Chesterton-Barton. We have an agreement, you see. I wanted to wait until Geoffrey's big day was over. We plan to announce our engagement next week. No one else knows but Susan and me—and now you."

And me, Tom thought.

"Oh, this is a disaster!" Viviane said.

"I thought you'd wish me happy!" Reggie protested.

"Oh, of course I do. Susan is very . . ."

Her word, "charming," came out at the same time Reggie said "rich."

Viviane didn't correct him. "I just thought— Oh, what am I to do? Either choice is impossible. I don't want to marry. Nor do I want to go to Germany. My mother thinks if I'm tainted here by the scandal of my broken betrothal, and if Bellshire doesn't suit, I might find a husband there. Rutherford's German friend is a count, and he has a castle in the Alps, and three eligible sons—"

"Three? This is beginning to sound like the start of a fairy tale," Reggie quipped.

"Don't joke, Reggie. This is serious. My mother is quite desperate."

"The evil queen, determined to bend the lovely princess to her will."

"She's not evil. She's just . . ."

"Germany might not be so bad."

She was pacing now. Tom heard the crunch of her uneven gait on the path. "Not so bad? How can you say that? They were my father's enemies!"

"Must that mean they are yours as well?"

"They're trying to start another war, Reggie!" she said passionately.

"Can't you just refuse to marry Bellshire and say no to going to Germany?"

"If only it could be that simple. My mother would never forgive me."

"What about what *you* want, Vee? You said you wanted to have a career as a professional photographer."

"I do. Eventually. I just need time to convince her," Viviane said dully.

Reggie sighed. "Poor Vee. What will you do?"

"There's a way out of this. There must be."

"That's the spirit! You're the bravest woman—the bravest person—I know. And the cleverest. Damn. I'm out of champagne. Come on—shall I walk you back? I don't think my toes are broken after all, the night is still young, and I believe they're playing our song. At least we can still dance the night away."

"We don't have a song," Viviane said.

"Well, it's somebody's song, and romance is thick in the air. Isn't that good enough?"

Tom heard the smack of lips on skin and imagined Reggie bestowing a kiss on her cheek.

When they'd gone, he tipped his head back against the rough bark of the tree and grinned. He had an idea, something that might help Viviane out of her plight. Of course his intentions were purely selfish. It would help him immeasurably.

All he had to do was convince her to do the very thing she didn't want to do.

CHAPTER ELEVEN

VIVIANE EDGED AROUND the dance floor, trying to avoid Bellshire. It was silly and childish, and it only delayed things. She should march right out there, tell the duke she wasn't interested, and inform her mother and Julia that she couldn't go to Germany because she planned to spend the summer in Wales to photograph the plight of the coal miners.

Her mother would faint, need to be carried to her bed, where she'd remain for days, moaning about the ingratitude of her only daughter.

She bit her lip and stayed where she was, hiding behind an archway of flowers.

A hand on her elbow startled her, and she spun with a gasp.

Tom Graham stood behind her. "Dance with me," he said, his gaze insistent instead of inviting, firmly leading her onto the floor.

"I don't dance," she said, but he ignored her objection and took her into his arms. She glared at him for his audacity. He smiled, and it transformed his serious features into something boyish and playful and handsome.

He was an excellent dancer. He guided her easily. If he was compensating for her limp, it didn't show.

"You have a problem," he said, speaking close to her ear.

She tried to pull away, missed a step, wondered if he was mocking her limp after all, but he led her smoothly onward without slowing.

"What do you know of my problems? Is this another lecture, Mr. Graham?"

He smiled again, a beguiling grin that crinkled the corners of his eyes. "No, not a lecture. It's a proposition, in fact."

She blinked at him. "A proposition?"

Before he could answer, Bellshire tapped him on the shoulder. "May I cut in?"

Politeness demanded that Tom bow out, put her hand in the duke's extended palm.

Instead, Tom's hand tightened on her waist. "No," he said, and whirled her away, leaving the duke empty-handed and frowning. She wanted to laugh at Tom's presumption, but her manners were better than his perhaps, and she bit her lip to hold back the smile that threatened to break through.

"Now where were we?" he said.

"You were about to make an indecent proposal," she said.

One eyebrow flexed upward, and his lips rippled with amusement. "A *proposition*, Miss Alden—and not the sexual kind. I mean the kind that states an idea, a suggestion. An offer."

She glanced Bellshire, who was still standing on the edge of the dance floor, frowning at them.

"Come to Germany," Tom said softly as the violins crooned a passionate chorus.

Her eyes flew back to Tom's. "How do you know—"

He shrugged. "I overheard your conversation with Reggie in the woods."

A flush of heat filled her face. "You were eavesdropping?"

"I just happened to be in earshot. I didn't want to interrupt what appeared to be a tender moment. Did you drop to one knee when you proposed to him? I didn't actually see that part."

She glared at him, tried to pull away, but he held her fast. "Are you drunk? Do you think for one minute that I'd enter into a betrothal with you, even a false one?" she demanded.

"I got the idea you weren't happy about having yet another smitten lord in your nets. I can't imagine why not. Bellshire's very rich, has an ancient title, and even if he's not as handsome as Phillip, he's not unpleasant to look at. Isn't that every debutante's dream? So what if he's forty?"

"Don't mock me. Not now," she said, feeling her stomach tilt.

"I'm not mocking you, Viviane. I'm rescuing you," he whispered in her ear.

The song ended, and still he kept dancing, whirling her away from the impatient duke, who was making his way across the crowded floor once again to claim her. They were still dancing when the next song began. People were staring. *Her mother was staring.*

"Agree to go to Germany," he said.

She raised her chin. "I have no desire to go there. Ever."

"Not even if you can use your talents, expose terrible wrongs with your photographs, possibly even prevent another war? I thought you liked that sort of thing."

She gaped at him in surprise. He leaned close to her ear again.

"Yes, I know your secret, Viviane. I saw you at the Camberwell riot. Actually, you saved my bacon that day. My photographer broke his camera. Your photographs came through at the last moment. They were excellent, by the way, far better than his would have been. We made a good team, even if you didn't know it. It's only right, is it not, that I return the favor now and rescue you?"

Her legs turned to liquid, and his arm tightened around her waist, holding her up. "Don't faint," he whispered.

"I never faint," she said fiercely. "Is this blackmail? I won't allow you to—"

He met her eyes. "Interesting. It bothers you more that I know *that*, rather than any of your other, more salacious secrets. I know you proposed to Reggie, and I understand better than you know why you broke it off with Medway. He ruined a dear friend of yours, a Jewish gentleman, at Mosley's suggestion, made sure that man would never be accepted in polite society again. You found it cruel and unbearable. Am I right? That kind of secret sells newspapers, yet it's the fact that I know all about your greatest talent that upsets you."

She felt her cheeks heating again. They'd met briefly a handful of times, exchanged barbs, and parted again. Yet he knew all about her—or he thought he did. His praise of her work surprised her as much as his recognition of her hidden life. She didn't bother to deny any of it. She regarded him fiercely, a creature cornered by a cat, refusing to give up without a fight.

"Don't look at me like that," he said sharply, tightening his hand on hers for a moment. "I'm not blackmailing you. I want to help you with your dilemma—" He slid a subtle glance toward Bellshire, who was still frowning at them. "And I want to use your talents as a photographer."

Her mouth dried. It was what she wanted, and what she feared. "My mother—and my stepfather—would never agree to allow me to take a job."

"I understand that. It's why you take photographs anonymously, isn't it? It's a passion, a hobby, but you'd like it to be a career." She stared at him. He really did know all about her.

"What does this have to do with going to Germany?"

He whirled her away from Bellshire, who was once again coming toward them. "I've been working in Berlin for several months. I'm only back for the wedding. Officially, I'm a correspondent for the British Press Corps. I've written about everything from Hitler's speeches to women's rallies and the Winter Olympics. At present I'm covering the preparations for the Summer Games." He scanned her face, perhaps looking for any sign of surprise, or to gauge how impressed she might be.

She kept her face as placid as a pond. "Are you enjoying it?"

He didn't answer, but something telling passed through his eyes before he looked away—a moment of irritation, perhaps.

"I've heard rumors of what's going on in Germany. Rutherford says most of them are exaggerated, or outright lies," she pressed.

His eyes snapped back to hers. "Do you believe him?"

She glanced over at her stepfather, holding court with several other powerful politicians at a table on the edge of the dance floor, over champagne and cigars. "I'm not sure," she said.

"Then use your camera to expose the truth."

She looked at him, saw he was perfectly serious. "How? If I go, I won't have the—freedom—I have here. I'll be a guest in a foreign country with my stepsister. We'll be chaperoned. I can hardly slip away to take photographs of Nazi marches and beatings in the streets."

"Oh, there won't be any of that. At least, not while the world is looking. Still, as a visitor, the guest of a man of rank, you'll have access to many places I'd never be allowed to go. No one would question a pretty English tourist taking snapshots for her photo album."

Her mother was now standing beside Bellshire, glaring daggers at Tom Graham. She launched herself across the crowded dance floor like a ship setting sail. "My mother's coming," she warned Tom.

"Will you do it?" he asked, his eyes fixed on her.

But there was no time to answer.

"There you are," her mother said, giving Tom an imperious glare. "His Grace is waiting to dance with you."

Tom didn't immediately let go. She felt his hand tighten on hers for a moment, and he kept his eyes fixed on her. She had seconds to politely excuse herself and let Bellshire lead her away.

Or . . .

She stepped back from Tom and stood on her own, her shoulders back, her body drawn to full height.

"Mother, I've decided to go to Germany with Julia after all."

CHAPTER TWELVE

TOM SAT ON the fence that marked the boundary between Wrenwood and Halliwell, the world still sleepy and fragrant in the early morning light, and wondered if he'd made a mistake. He'd been tipsy, if not outright drunk. He'd said too much, revealed a secret operation he had no business speaking of, much less recruiting for. He wasn't usually an impetuous man, but Viviane Alden brought out something in him that he didn't recognize. She intrigued him, did the unexpected, *was* the unexpected.

He checked his watch, saw that she was late. Perhaps she wouldn't come, had forgotten about his proposition, been tipsy as well. He could leave now, *should* leave, since his train for London departed in an hour.

She appeared at the edge of the meadow, her russet hair bright in the rising sun. She wore trousers and a hacking jacket and her camera was slung around her neck. He stayed where he was, trying to imagine the conversation she must have had with her mother last night. And had Bellshire taken her decision lightly and quit the field? Surely there were dozens of other ladies ready and eager to marry a duke.

"Hello," she said, hauling herself up onto the fence beside him.

"Look, about what I said last night. You can change your mind," he said, not bothering with niceties.

She turned her head to look at him. "Why would I want to do that?"

"It could be dangerous."

Something kindled in her eyes, something akin to desire, he thought. She *liked* the idea of an adventure, a mission, a bit of something daring. It was why she swam in storms and walked into riots armed only with a camera. Was she so confident in her abilities, or did arrogance make her careless?

This wasn't a joke or a dare. The danger was real. He faced it every day, walked a fine line. He considered feigning a laugh, telling her it *was* a joke, and walking away. But as avid as she looked, there was a seriousness in her as well, courage and intelligence, and she was waiting for him to speak.

"My job in Germany is not quite as it appears," he said. He scanned the peaceful English meadow. "The stories I've been filing— Have you read them, by the way?"

She nodded crisply, her jaw tightening. "Some of them." She scanned his face. "Do you truly believe what you write? Your stories are different than they used to be."

"I'm not a Fascist." It felt good to be able to say it out loud to someone.

"Then why—"

"It's my damned job," he snapped. "Those stories are all pretense to impress the Nazis, gain their trust, worm my way into their confidence so I can uncover the real secrets. I am a favored correspondent, one who can be counted on to write approvingly, glowingly, about everything they do, no matter how underhanded or downright evil. I smile and nod and do as they bid me. It gets me into places I couldn't go otherwise."

"Just like a debutante." She plucked a stem of grass and ran it between her fingers.

He felt a swell of disappointment at her glib comparison. It was hardly the in-depth understanding he'd hoped for. "Look, perhaps this is a bad idea—"

"I mean that debutantes are primped and promoted and taught how to pose, preen, bow, and even smile correctly. Our personal opinions, ideas, and desires are kept hidden. Our chaperones deposit us at a ball, tell us which gentlemen to encourage, and steer us away from the ones we are to avoid. We are expected to flirt and coo and enchant a man— the *right* man—into a marriage proposal, all without him knowing what we're up to until it's too late and the spell is cast. Is that an apt comparison?"

"Yes," he said, realizing she understood after all. It rather amused him to be compared to a debutante, and he grinned.

"Did you enjoy being a debutante?" he asked her.

She tossed her head. "Not for a moment. I craved intelligent conversation, which was strictly forbidden. It's hard being that shallow."

"You'll have to do precisely that in Germany. Do you speak German?" he asked her.

"No, but I'm about to learn. My stepfather has decided that Julia and I must have a German tutor."

"And when will you leave for Germany?"

"A month before the games. Julia's godfather is the Count von Schroeder, an old school friend of Rutherford's. Have you heard of him?"

His trepidation rose. The Schroeders were Nazi socialites, high-ranking party members, ardent supporters of the new regime.

"The count has a castle in Bavaria," she said. "We'll stay there before we go up to Berlin."

Bavaria. Hitler's alpine retreat was in Bavaria. He wondered if the Schroeders would introduce Viviane to the führer. He liked English ladies. Oswald Mosley's young sister-in-law Unity Mitford was Hitler's constant companion, his pet English debutante. Would Viviane take her place? He shuddered.

"You can still change your mind," he said again. "You should."

She turned to look at him, searching his face for the reason why he was trying to dissuade her now. Their eyes locked. There were a million reasons he might have given her, but his throat closed, and good sense and all the warnings and cautions went unspoken. He was being selfish. He had told her his secret because he wanted someone to know the truth, to see behind the mask he wore, despite what others thought of him. It meant she'd share the danger, join him in trying to stop a war that was bigger than both of them. A breath of wind blew a lock of her hair across her face, breaking the spell between them. She tucked it behind her ear and looked away.

"Oh, Julia would kill me if I changed my mind now. She's very anxious to go. She was already planning her wardrobe last night after the wedding. She left a note asking Rutherford's secretary to order all the latest guidebooks first thing this morning."

She was holding on to the fence beside her hips, her knuckles white, her fingernails piercing the old boards, every line of her body anxious, even as she leaned forward, eager—or nervous.

"What are you thinking?" he asked.

"I'm not sure what to expect," she said. "I have only my father's stories to go by. The Germans were his enemies. I have a reason to go now, thanks to you, a kind of quest for the truth, not his but my own. I—" She hesitated. "How will I manage to look them in the eyes and smile, knowing they were responsible for the war and my father's death?"

His first thought was to reassure her, to tell her it was different now, that the Germans weren't enemies anymore, but that would be a lie. "The Germans want their visitors to enjoy themselves," he said instead. "I can say from experience that the beer is excellent and the pastries are delicious. Berlin is a vibrant and fascinating city, very modern." It sounded like a line from one of his pro-Nazi articles, and he suppressed a wince.

"But that's not what I'll be photographing, is it?" she asked.

He felt like a cad asking her to dive into such dangerous, deadly currents. She was pretty, well-bred, and young. The camera around her neck looked entirely decorative, a fashion accessory, unless you knew Viviane Alden better than that. Surely no one would question a lovely tourist when she smiled and raised that camera. "You already capture what others don't see, all the personal and the intimate details. You make people think, offer a new perspective, an understanding. Do that."

She ran her fingers over the camera. "After my father died, taking pictures helped me make sense of the world in small manageable pieces. The camera preserved moments, showed the truth, and never lied to me." The vulnerability disappeared from her eyes, replaced by sharp certainty. "I can do this," she said, as much to herself as to him.

He looked away before he fell into her eyes and drowned there, and glanced at his watch instead. "I've got to go. My train leaves in an hour." He climbed off the fence and turned to offer her his hand in assistance, but she jumped to the ground on her own. For a moment they stood awkwardly, staring at each other.

"Will I see you in London?" she asked. "Julia and I will need clothes for the trip. She wants to go next week."

"Perhaps. I'm returning to Berlin on Thursday night," he said. He'd planned to go up to Glasgow to visit his mother before he left, but he'd change his plans, wait for Viviane instead.

"Then ring on Monday or Tuesday. We'll be staying at Lady Dunbar's in Mayfair," she said, as if they were friends or colleagues or coconspirators. He wondered how exactly to describe their new alliance.

He met her eyes, felt something click, settle, and hold for a long count of ten, and found himself caught in her gaze after all.

She looked away first, a bloom of color filling her cheeks. He wished he had time to ask her again what she was thinking, but she turned back toward Wrenwood. "Goodbye, Mr. Graham."

He watched her go, as slender as the blades of grass around her boots, the drops of dew sparkling like a fairy path before her.

PART II

German Revels

CHAPTER THIRTEEN

July 1936

"Oh, Vee, we'll be leaving tomorrow, and we'll arrive in Germany the day after that," Julia said as they oversaw the last-minute packing. The trunks would leave today, sent on ahead to Schloss Glücksstern, the Schroeder castle in Bavaria. "I'm so excited I can barely stand it." She held up her copy of the newest Baedeker's travel guide, revised and updated for the Olympic year. "I've memorized every detail of our itinerary. Geoffrey and Margaret will escort us as far as Hanover and deliver us safely into the hands of the Count and Countess von Schroeder. Then we'll go south to Bavaria by car with the Schroeders."

"Say all that again, but in German," Viviane teased. She refolded a sweater, though she'd done it twice already and it was fine the way it was. She counted her handkerchiefs as well, and rearranged the other garments in the case, until Julia caught her hand.

"Just look at this picture," Julia said, pointing to a photograph of the Alps in the guidebook. "If it's this magnificent in black and white, I can't wait to see it in real life, in color," she said. "You will take lots of photos, won't you? I promised the twins I'd send them dozens and dozens of postcards and pictures and souvenirs."

"Of course," Viviane said. Dozens and dozens of photos indeed. She counted the rolls of film as she packed them. She'd bought out the supplies of every camera shop in Mayfair. Would it be enough? She swallowed the anxious knot in her throat.

"I intend to enjoy every moment," Julia said, "and I want to remember this trip forever." She jumped up. "I'd better remind Selena's maid to pack the Fortnum's hamper. She ran out of the room, leaving Viviane in peace. It had been at Fortnum's that she'd met Tom a few days after Margaret's wedding, offering to order the hamper on her stepfather's behalf, packed with all Georg von Schroeder's favorite English comestibles.

Viviane and Tom had walked together for a few blocks, and he gave her a verbal list of things to photograph. She was to keep an eye open for signs of military installations and soldiers. Factories were of interest, especially those making parts that could be used to make planes or guns or even ships. If she saw any violence taking place, and she could safely photograph it without risk to herself—and that point was emphasized— she should have her camera ready.

"What will I see?" she asked. "I've heard they beat people in the streets. I don't think I could stand by while someone was being hurt for their race or religion."

"You won't see any of that. Not during the Olympics. Everything will look calm, normal, happy, just like Mayfair. They've scrubbed the anti-Semitic signs off the walls and windows for now."

"And later?" she asked. He didn't reply, but she could see by his expression it would be bad, made worse, perhaps, by the interlude. Her stomach turned, and she felt her lips twist with disgust. "How can I pretend to like them?"

"Because you must," he said. "You don't have to approve, just make them think you do. You can tell the world the truth, expose them, but you are one person."

"Sometimes one person is enough. My father was one person and he saved twenty men in a gas attack, men who would have died otherwise."

He frowned. "One person can save twenty people and still sacrifice a hundred others."

"What's that supposed to mean?" she asked.

He looked away. "It means that being a hero is a matter of perspective." They had reached the corner where they were to part, and they would not see each other until they met again in Berlin.

"You will be careful," he said. It was a command.

"Aye, sir," she said, giving him a mocking salute. "Do you have further orders, sir?"

He frowned. "It isn't a game."

"Isn't it?" she asked him lightly. "I will be on holiday. Surely I must appear to be a typical tourist enjoying a gay excursion to a marvelous country I simply adore. Should I not do as Julia does and look dazzled and giddy and impressed by simply everything?" Tom looked as if he couldn't imagine her giddy and giggling.

"Just don't take unnecessary risks." A car backfired, and he spun, looking for trouble, casting sideways glances at the faces of people passing by. She watched him for a moment, and he caught her staring. "My apologies. I've gotten used to being watched, you see, in Berlin. There are eyes everywhere."

She felt a shiver rush through her and glanced around, but this was London, and no one was interested in two people standing on a street corner. He looked worried, not for himself, she realized, but for her.

She tilted her head and smiled at him. She wasn't usually a flirt, and she didn't believe in using feminine wiles to get her way, but she'd been practicing, watching Julia and even Grace and Felicity. If she was ever questioned in Germany, she'd pretend she spoke no German, didn't understand the rules, and she'd smile sweetly and bat her lashes. She tested that smile on Tom now, hoping to look brave and mysterious, *intrepid*. "I'll be the guest of a very important man. No one will question a camera-mad girl on holiday."

"Just be careful," he muttered again, regarding her dubiously.

"Should I tell you the same?" she asked. She offered him her hand, and he shook it, held tight for a moment as if he had more to say. She waited, but he let her go and walked away.

THE NEXT DAY a small package from a used book shop arrived. Inside was a 1932 guidebook for tourists visiting Germany, now four years out of date. The note that came with the book simply said, "Enjoy your trip," and was signed with Tom's initials.

Inside, he'd marked several places he recommended in Berlin—parks, cafés, and beer gardens.

Julia wasn't impressed with the cheap little book. "Why would Tom Graham send you a present? He hardly knows us."

"He knows Margaret and Geoff, and he's posted in Berlin for the *Herald*. No doubt Geoffrey mentioned we're coming," Viviane said. "He's simply being polite."

"We will be under the wing of Count von Schroeder. We won't need Mr. Graham's help." Julia flipped through the guidebook and took note of the marked pages. "The Hotel am Zoo, the Tiergarten, the museum. These are very ordinary places. Oh, but look—he's marked some nightclubs in Berlin. Perhaps he isn't so dull after all."

Viviane took the book back, tucked the terse little note between the pages, and placed it in her hand luggage.

CHAPTER FOURTEEN

Hanover

"THERE THEY ARE!" Julia cried, leaning half out of the window of the train as it pulled into the station at Hanover. "I recognize Count von Schroeder from his photograph."

"Do sit down, Julia. It isn't seemly to be so eager," Margaret said, though she was craning her neck as well, her bottom barely on the edge of the plush first-class seat. Geoffrey looked up from the *Times* and smiled at his bride indulgently. Viviane wasn't sure what she expected to see, but at first glance, Hanover looked like any busy train station at home in England. People milled on the platform, waiting or rushing for their trains. Mothers dragged children by the hand. Businessmen checked their watches with an impatient flick of the wrist, and country folk sat on benches, the women in kerchiefs and men in sturdy work clothes, and watched their fellow passengers with an interest that suggested they rarely came to the city.

But there were men in uniform, too, wearing brown shirts with swastika armbands, granite faces shaded under forage caps. As they swaggered along the platform the crowd parted instantly to let them through. They were polite—too polite—but no one seemed fooled. People kept their eyes downcast as they passed, and smiles faded to blankness.

Count Georg von Schroeder stood out in the crowd. He was tall, his dark hair touched with silver, his bearing proud, aristocratic, and military. Although he wore a finely tailored suit and not a uniform, people stepped around him and tipped their hats with deference. He paid them no attention. He was unsmiling, a stern martinet, the very image of the harsh, iron-willed foe she imagined her father had faced in the war.

But then the count caught sight of Julia and his blue eyes lit with pleasure, and his smile transformed him into someone kindly and gracious.

The woman beside him must be his countess, Viviane thought, looking at the elegant beauty in a smart suit, her blond hair shining under a neat little hat. She regarded the waving, grinning Julia with a stiff expression as they stepped off the train, examined her guests with a critical eye before she smiled, a twitch of her lips that barely reached her eyes.

"Hello, my dear," the count said, embracing Julia, kissing her on both cheeks before stepping back to look at her. "How wonderful to meet you, and how pretty you are. I trust your journey was pleasant? Ah, and here are your lovely sisters," he said, looking at Margaret and Viviane as he reached to shake Geoffrey's hand. Welcome to Germany." His English was perfect.

A boy about twelve in a Hitler Youth uniform pushed between the count and countess and snapped to attention. "Heil Hitler," he said, and raised his arm.

The count gently pushed it down. "This is Klaus, my youngest son." He rested his hand on the boy's shoulder and turned to the woman beside him. "And this is my wife, Countess Ilsa von Schroeder."

Klaus looked like his mother, and for all the world like an English Boy Scout. There was open curiosity on his face as he scanned the visitors. He clicked his heels together and bowed crisply. "Good day, fräuleins. May I inquire which of you is Julia and which is Viviane?" he asked in accented English.

"This is Julia," the count said, winking playfully at Viviane.

Julia giggled. "No, Godfather, I'm Julia!"

He chuckled. "Of course you are. I was teasing you. Your father has sent me pictures of you and your sisters since you were little girls. I would have known you anywhere."

The count turned to Viviane. "And you are Viviane," he said, reaching out to take her hand. His grip was gentle, but she couldn't help but imagine him in uniform, facing her father across a battlefield, giving the heartless order to release the gas . . .

Her reaction must have shown. His smile faded, and he let go at once and scanned her face for a moment as he stepped back and turned to the newlyweds.

"And here is Margaret and her very lucky bridegroom," he said. "Congratulations to you both and thank you for escorting our guests safely to us. I know you must return to England, but you've had a long journey and I hope you will join us for dinner this evening. Our hotel is nearby. We will stay the night, and then travel on tomorrow. Let's get you settled and find something cool to drink."

He extended his arm to his wife, who took it. The countess had yet to say a word, though her eyes darted like busy sparrows over her guests. "Come along, Klaus," she said to her son, who was now watching the trains and the troopers with keen delight. "Take Miss Viviane's case for her."

But Viviane held tight. "Oh, no, that's not necessary." The countess's sculpted brows rose toward her hat. "It's my camera, you see."

"Ah, you are a shutterbug!" the count said. "You will find beautiful scenery to photograph while you are with us."

"What make of camera is it?" Klaus asked.

"A Leica," she said, and he grinned.

"A fine German camera. Most superior."

"Vee takes the most wonderful pictures," Julia said brightly. "She captures the very essence of a person, and her scenic shots are truly breathtaking."

"Our Alps are most photogenic. All of Germany is beautiful. You will be pleased," Klaus said in his careful schoolboy English. "I will show you the best vistas."

As they walked along the platform, men tipped their hats and women regarded them curiously. Did they truly stand out so much as foreigners? Viviane wondered.

She looked around with a photographer's eye, past the smiling faces. A man in a storm trooper's uniform was searching the bag of a woman standing in front of him. Her eyes were downcast, and she wasn't objecting the way an Englishwoman certainly would as he rifled carelessly through her belongings. She held the hand of a young girl with enormous dark eyes, her grip so tight her knuckles were white. The girl looked up and met Viviane's eyes for a moment, her gaze full of fear. The storm trooper tucked something into his pocket and the woman swallowed hard but held her tongue. He threw her papers on the ground at her feet and turned on his heel to stride away. Viviane moved to help, but Geoffrey grasped her elbow. "This way," he said through tight lips. The child scrambled to pick up the papers as her mother closed the suitcase with shaking hands.

"But they need help," Viviane said.

"Don't get involved, Viviane. Do you hear me? This isn't England. You are on holiday. Enjoy yourself, and don't make a fuss, no matter what you see." She looked at him with horror, and he shrugged. "I come to Hamburg on business frequently. It is . . ." He shook his head, his face grim. "Just be careful." She felt chilled by the warning. The woman and the girl hurried past them, still white-faced and frightened, and boarded a train under the sour gazes of the storm troopers. Geoff looked away. "Look, they've cleaned things up, and they want visitors to be comfortable and happy. I doubt you'll see anything else like that. Now come along. I'm dying for a cold drink."

At the exit, a uniformed railway employee with a swastika armband nodded to them, his flat gaze traveling over Viviane and her stepsisters as they passed. When she noticed, he smiled at once, like a light bulb flicking on.

A liveried servant waited at the car. He snapped to attention when he saw the count. "All is in order, sir," he said in German. "I have sent the baggage on to the hotel." The count nodded crisply and turned to his guests.

"We have a long journey tomorrow, so we must get a good night's rest. We will travel at a leisurely pace, so you will have an opportunity to see the countryside. Tomorrow we'll stop in Leipzig, one of my favorite cities," the count explained.

Julia smiled. "I have all the newest guidebooks, including the updated Baedeker. There's so much I want to see."

"Then we shall make a list," the count said graciously, and helped his wife and goddaughter into the car. He glanced at Viviane and offered his hand, his expression speculative but patient. She stared at the black glove for an instant. It would be rude not to accept this small courtesy. She swallowed and placed her hand in his, and he smiled. "There now," he murmured, as if he was gentling a wild creature.

Viviane slid into the car, and the count followed, taking his place across from her, next to his son. He regarded her for a moment with a thoughtful expression, his eyes kind. She clutched her camera case on her lap and forced a bright smile to rival Julia's, though it tasted bitter on her lips.

She had to pretend, Tom had said, make them believe she was utterly, absolutely delighted to be here, play the game.

And sugar fooled more flies than vinegar.

CHAPTER FIFTEEN

As they traveled south, Viviane's first impression of Germany was how different it was from England. An English summer was soft and lush, the shapes and shadows gentle, meandering lanes edged with mossy stone fences and bird-filled hedgerows. Ivy softened old walls, and wildflowers hemmed paths and stitched embroidered borders on wind-rippled fields.

Germany's summer was sharper, hard gold fields set against black and unknowable forests of tall pine and fir. The sky was a crisper blue, framing dramatic, angular vistas. Man-made structures were square and efficient, built for function, villages laid out in tidy perfection. There were bright flowers everywhere, waving gaily from window boxes and pots or planted in orderly rows at the entrances of towns. German roads were straight, paved, and wide, designed for swift movement, for getting to one's destination with efficiency rather than for the slow pleasure of the journey. Even the farmers working in the fields were strong and handsome, models of wholesome perfection and the joy of life on the land. Their bronze muscles rippled under the hot sun, and their blond heads glowed.

Klaus played tour guide along the way. "Do you see those orchards?

The finest plums and apples in the world grow in abundance in Germany. Our cook makes the best apfelkuchen. It is my favorite."

"What about Black Forest cake?" Julia said. "Or strudel?"

Klaus's blue eyes lit up. "Of course! We grow cherries in Germany that are also unsurpassed anywhere in the world! Everything here is superior—"

The count ruffled his son's hair. "Klaus has a sweet tooth," he said. "And pastries are a weakness of my own. I remember English scones with clotted cream very fondly."

"There's some in the hamper we brought you," Julia assured him, and he smiled at her and put a hand to his heart in delight.

As they traveled, it struck Viviane that there wasn't anything out of place or sinister. There were Nazi flags, of course, and they passed groups of Hitler Youth, marching with backpacks, but English Boy Scouts did the same in the summer. Klaus saluted them as they passed, and they saluted back. There was nothing at all to suggest that another war was coming, or indeed that the last one had ever touched this bucolic paradise.

Viviane wondered if perhaps the British were mistaken in their impressions.

They stopped for luncheon at a picturesque inn beside the Elbe River. The door opened as they reached it, and a pair of storm troopers came out, dressed in the brown shirts and black caps. Viviane held her breath, but the soldiers smiled politely, and one of them held the door and waved them inside with a swastika-clad arm.

"Heil Hitler," he said, noticing Klaus's Hitler Youth uniform. The boy instantly snapped to attention and returned the salute. The pair went on their way, bootheels ringing on the ancient cobbles of the village street.

"I want to be a storm trooper when I am older," Klaus said, watching them go.

"You will join the SS like your brother," the countess said.

"My eldest brother, Otto, is an Obersturmführer," Klaus told Viviane. "I shall be as well."

"What the British call a lieutenant," the count translated.

"Otto has arranged a period of leave to come and meet you," the countess said with pride in her voice. "He will meet us at Glücksstern and accompany us to Berlin. He is posted there with the SS security service, the SD."

"Felix, our second son, will also be coming home to meet you," the count said. "He's a research chemist."

Viviane looked up with interest.

"Felix is the assistant director in the agricultural laboratory of his company," Klaus added, tapping his forehead. "He is very smart."

"I can't wait to meet them," Julia gushed, and the countess smiled at her eagerness.

After lunch, they strolled through a park along the Elbe River, enjoying the sun and the birds. Others did the same, and the scene was peaceful and ordinary.

Julia opened her Baedeker's guide. "It says that Leipzig is a famous center for music and industry, home to Bach and Mendelssohn," she read to Viviane. "It boasts the oldest railway station in all of Europe. It is a hub of industry and trade and coal, making use of the river system for transport. It also says it is a lovely city, which is most decidedly true." She pointed. "Oh, look—roses!"

"These gardens are quite famous," the count said, offering his arm. "Come and see them—the scent of the blossoms on a sunny afternoon is beyond compare."

Viviane lingered as they strolled away, raising her camera to photograph the river. The place was as peaceful and lovely as any English waterway. Around her, people were relaxed and ordinary, and they nodded politely as they passed by. She lined up another shot, walking backward to frame it.

She bumped into someone and turned.

"Your pardon," he said quickly in German, briefly catching her elbow to steady her and letting go at once, stepping back.

"No," she said. "I should have looked where I was going."

"My fault entirely. I was wondering what you were photographing. Do I detect an accent? You are not German?"

"No, I'm English," she said. "Is my German as bad as that?"

He switched to English. "Not at all. I was a professor of languages at the university. I have an ear for accents."

"What languages do you teach?"

He gazed at the river. "Oh, I do not teach anything anymore. I was relieved of my post. I am playing tourist myself today." He looked around with a sad smile. "This is one of my favorite places in all the world. I proposed to my wife at this very spot, and I could not leave without coming one last time."

"Are you on holiday as well?" she asked.

He scanned her face. "No, madam. I am leaving Germany. Not by choice, but of necessity. I am Jewish, and you may have heard that things are not so pleasant for Jews in Germany now. I am going to the United States. We are among the lucky ones with family there."

She stared at him, her stomach knotting. "You're Jewish!"

"Have I said too much? Are you among those who despise me?"

"No, of course not," she murmured. "I have heard, in England, that . . ." She could not describe it, the terrible images she'd seen, the brutality. She looked at this man, ordinary, respectable, charming. How could anyone hate someone for how they were born, raised, what they believed? "Is it truly so bad then?" she dared to ask.

He tilted his head and offered her a sad smile. "You have not been in this country very long, I think, or perhaps you do not wish to see what's truly happening." He leaned closer. "If I were to be caught in this park, I would be arrested or beaten or worse." He sighed. "Leipzig is my home. I was born here, but I am no longer welcome. I would not leave, but I have a wife and a son to protect. We must go while there is a chance, leave everything behind, and make a new life in America." He looked around him, drew a deep breath. "Ah, but I am sad to leave this spot. I wish I still had a camera to capture this place. Mine was confiscated, you see."

Viviane took another dozen shots of different vistas. She rewound the film quickly and removed it from the camera. She pressed it into his hand. "Take this. You can have it developed in America, and then you will have pictures to remember this place." He stared at the film in his hand in surprise.

"You are too kind," he said.

"I wish I could do more," she said.

He wrapped the film in his handkerchief and put it in his pocket. "Then when you return to England, tell them not to indulge Hitler. Tell them he is bent on the destruction of—"

"Miss Alden!" the countess called sharply, her tone a rifle crack. "Come here at once."

Her companion turned away without another word and hurried down the path.

"Who is that man? Was he bothering you?" the countess demanded, her eyes full of suspicion under her jaunty little hat.

"No, not at all. It was simply a chance conversation," Viviane said quickly. "He's leaving the country, you see, and he was visiting this lovely place for the last time, and—"

"He is a *Jew*!" The countess's mouth twisted on the word. She looked so utterly repulsed that Viviane's breath caught in her throat. "What did he say to you? What did he want?"

"Why, nothing," Viviane said. Her fingers tightened on her camera, and she held it close to her chest like a shield. "It was just . . . We spoke of the weather and how lovely the park is at this time of year." She raised her chin. "It was the kind of polite conversation one might have in England at a chance meeting."

The countess colored. "You are not in England now, and you are under our protection. You must be careful who you speak to."

Careful. Another warning to be careful. The beauty of the park suddenly felt oppressive, sinister.

Klaus stood beside his mother, glaring down the path at the retreating stranger. "If Otto were here, that dirty Jew wouldn't have dared to accost you!" he said. He put his hand on the Hitler Youth dagger on his belt. "If I'd been faster, I would have shown him what we do with Jews." He bent and picked up a stone, weighed it in his hand, then took aim.

"No!" Viviane said quickly.

"That's enough, Klaus," the count said sternly, approaching with Julia. His son dropped the rock but stuck his chin out mutinously. The count glanced at Viviane. "I trust you are unhurt, my dear?"

Her heart was pounding in her chest, but she forced a smile, clutched the camera hard. "Yes, thank you," she murmured.

"Then let us continue on with our journey."

"You must both be careful who you choose to speak to," the countess repeated for Julia's benefit. "We promised your parents we would take good care of you," the countess said, and shuddered as if the weather had turned suddenly cold, or a snake had slithered out from under the roses to ruin the day. Julia looked at Viviane with dismay, as if *she*'d done something unforgivably wrong.

"Let us continue our journey," the count repeated, guiding them back into the car. "We shall visit one of my favorite towns. What does your guidebook tell you about Zwickau, Julia?"

Julia looked it up, but Klaus jumped in before she reached the right page.

"There are many factories in Zwickau," Klaus said. "We have learned in school that it is a great center for German industry."

Julia reached the right section. "Yes, indeed. Castles, coal, and cars," she said with a smile.

"They have factories for everything," Klaus said proudly. "My brother Felix has promised to show me the chemical works someday." He grinned at Julia like a conspirator. "Colditz Castle used to be a hospital for madmen, but now it is a prison for those who foolishly dare to oppose the state."

"Klaus," the count said sharply, and earned a cold look from his wife.

"He is a clever boy. You should be very proud of him," she said mildly, stroking the back of her son's head. "He will be a fine man, and a loyal Nazi."

The count regarded his wife with a bland expression for a moment, and the only sound was the purr of the engine. Then he forced a smile and turned to Julia. "What else does your guidebook recommend?"

OVER THE NEXT few days, they drove southward, visited Zwickau and Bayreuth, Nurnberg and Munich.

Viviane took pictures of everything, the beauty of the pretty villages and—more subtly—the hectic industry of busy factories, belching steam and smoke into the sky. She posed Julia in front of them so the shot looked innocent enough, then shifted the focus to capture what lay behind her stepsister. No one—not even Klaus, playing director now—questioned her choice of background.

The landscape turned to rising green hills, and the peaks of the Alps appeared on the horizon, blue and white, their soaring crowns topped with mist.

"How breathtaking," Julia gushed. Her enthusiasm was infectious, and Klaus gazed out with an identical look of wonderment on his face, as if he, too, were seeing the mountains for the first time. The count smiled indulgently, and the countess read a book.

"Do you see why we are so proud to be German, Julia?" Klaus asked her. "Is it not the most majestic country in the world?"

"Yes," Julia said on a dazzled breath. "The guidebooks do not even begin to describe it!"

"The Germans are a magnificent race, stronger and smarter than anyone else. Our strength and superiority come from our land. We are the master race, and it is our destiny to rule over inferior—"

"Enough, Klaus," his father said sharply, and the boy stopped at once.

Viviane stared at the boy. Klaus's young face was hard as he spoke, his tone shrill with arrogant pride.

"Tell the young ladies the story of the goatherd and the old man of the mountain," the count instructed his son more gently. The countess looked on but said nothing.

AT LAST, THEY turned off the main road and climbed a narrower road that hugged the side of a steep hill. The road curved, and a wide valley opened below, surrounded by mountains. Around the next curve, the pointed fairy-tale turrets of a castle rose against the Alps behind. Julia gasped, and the count chuckled proudly.

"Welcome to Schloss Glücksstern, my family home. I have lived my life here, but still I am delighted when I return, and I love to see the same delight in the eyes of visitors," the count said, his eyes twinkling. "It was built by a prince as a hunting lodge more than a hundred years ago. My grandmother told me the schloss was gifted to my ancestors for heroism and services to the royal family, but my grandfather said his father had won it from the crown prince in a game of cards—hence the name, which translates to *lucky star* in English." His eyes remained on the still-distant castle as he spoke, full of pride and joy. "Whatever the truth of how Glücksstern became ours, it is our home, and I hope you will make it yours for the next few weeks."

The car swung between granite gateposts carved with the Schroeder family crest, and they drove into a wide graveled courtyard and pulled up in front of a stone staircase that led up to the arched doorway. The castle rose high above them, a collection of tall, narrow turrets that looked almost fragile against the brooding bulk of the mountains.

The servants appeared in the courtyard as if by magic, coming from some hidden doorway to line up at attention on the driveway, just the way an English household might do when important guests came to visit, giving their arrival a sense of formality, grace, and tradition. Viviane glanced at Julia, who was grinning with wonder, holding on to her hat as she peered out the car window at the mountains. She hadn't stopped smiling since they left London. She was ecstatic, delighted, and giddy with joy. It was certainly contagious. The count watched his guests, gauging their reactions to his home. Viviane met his eyes, unable to contain her awed impression of the lovely castle, and he smiled warmly. "Welcome," he said again.

The car door was opened, and a gloved hand appeared to help them out of the vehicle. The count regarded his staff and nodded crisply, and the butler stepped forward and bowed smartly, like a soldier before a commander. "This is Holcroft, my butler and head of staff. He's as English as you are," the count said.

"Welcome to Glücksstern," the butler said in round English tones. "If you'll come inside, we have tea ready in the east salon."

"What part of England are you from, Holcroft?" Julia asked.

"I was born in Birmingham, my lady. My father was English, but my mother was German." He drew himself up to his full height, a little over five feet. "I have lived here for six years, and I consider myself German."

"Come, I will show you the way," Klaus said eagerly, dodging around the butler to run up the steps two at a time. He pushed the door open and grinned, and Julia looped her arm through Viviane's and followed.

"Isn't it wonderful?" she whispered. "I knew it would be." She looked at her stepsister, her eyes shining. "I love everything about Germany, Vee. Don't you?"

Viviane felt her heart pound in her chest. It was the thin, fresh mountain air, no doubt, but it felt like exhilaration.

They stepped through the door into a magnificent entry hall before she could reply. Klaus rushed upstairs to the gallery that overlooked the space below. He unfurled a massive swastika banner, and it billowed down from the wrought iron railing. Viviane and Julia stopped in their tracks, and even Julia fell silent for a moment.

Klaus grinned down at them. "Welcome to Germany, dear ladies. Heil Hitler!"

CHAPTER SIXTEEN

ILSA VON SCHROEDER regarded her visitors over the delicate lip of her Meissen teacup. She preferred coffee, but Georg had insisted on serving tea to make his English guests feel more at home. Was not the point of this visit to show them Germany and the German ways of doing things? At least there was strudel on the tray and spice cookies, and not those dreadful English scones her husband adored.

She assessed the girls' impression of the schloss. Julia was as excited as a puppy, exclaiming over everything. Viviane was harder to read, a puzzle. Perhaps she was simply overawed by the trip or the beauty of Germany and now the castle. She had a slight limp. Perhaps that made her reticent.

Ilsa watched as Viviane took in the salon now, her eyes darting over every detail behind her own teacup. She followed the young woman's gaze, wanting to understand her, to pry her open like a clam and know what she was thinking. For once Viviane wasn't hidden behind her camera, and yet she looked at the room as if she were framing shots she might take if manners permitted.

This was Ilsa's favorite room in the schloss, timber framed, a vast and imposing space that proudly displayed the castle's origins as a hunting retreat. The walls were covered with the skulls and antlers of deer, and there were thick pelts on the stone floors by the massive fireplace as well. By contrast, the furnishings were entirely modern, a collection of low, comfortable settees placed around Persian rugs and polished oak tables. The antiques were family heirlooms of course, from the delicate Dresden figurines to the exquisite clocks. Fine portraits of Georg's ancestors hung in ornate gold leaf frames, regarding their English guests with stern Teutonic pride. Silver-framed photographs of her sons sat on the piano.

She looked up at the portrait of Count Otto von Schroeder, the ancestor her eldest son was named for, a soldier who fought with Frederick the Great and stood by the king's side at many great victories. He was painted with a small portrait of his commander pinned to his breast, over his heart. The führer admired Frederick the Great as an example of the greatest elements of German culture—superiority and courage.

Ilsa imagined her eldest son serving at the führer's right hand just the way his ancestor had served Frederick, rising in power and importance to the very pinnacles of the great leader's inner circle. Otto may be a mere lieutenant at present, but he had everything he needed to climb to the top—he was wellborn, fully Aryan, clever, ruthless, and determined to succeed. He had attended military school and then went on to study law at university. He was making a name for himself in Berlin already, was on the staff of Reinhard Heydrich, chief of the state Security Services, which included the Gestapo.

Ilsa worked hard to advance her son's reputation and career behind the scenes, though Otto may not know it. Georg certainly didn't. Men might think they ruled the world and made the important decisions, but in Ilsa's opinion it was always women who exerted subtle sway, applied tender influence over great leaders and bold events to get what they wanted. Nazi Germany was no different.

She looked at the English girls again. Lady Julia Devellin, her husband's goddaughter, was a trifle silly, but she was very young. She was blond and blue-eyed with good bones, a pretty girl who would blossom into a beautiful woman. Her father's family line went back to the Electors of Hanover, from whence came the Georgian kings of England, which meant she had royal blood. German blood.

Viviane Alden was very different from her stepsister. Her father was a soldier, which suggested a military heritage, an understanding of duty and honor. She was obviously intelligent, thinking more than she spoke. She wasn't Aryan in appearance—her hair was red, her eyes hazel, which was a mark against her as a breeder of Aryan sons. It was too bad about her limp, but at least it was not a defect of birth but the remnant of a childhood accident. Therefore, the flaw was a pity but not an insurmountable problem. Joseph Goebbels had a clubfoot. He was a brilliant politician and orator, almost as great a genius as the führer. He claimed his limp was a war wound, though Ilsa's dear friend Magda, Joseph's glamorous wife, had whispered the truth to Ilsa, that he'd been rejected by the army because of the birth defect. People overlooked the falsehood because his nimble intellectual abilities more than made up for a limp, and because he—and Magda—held a privileged place within the führer's closest circle.

Magda had been intrigued when Ilsa had told her they were expecting two English guests. Hitler adored the English aristocracy and desired a greater connection between the upper classes of their two nations. Marrying a nobly born English wife would be a feather in Otto's cap.

Ilsa set her teacup down and watched her husband. He loved the English almost as much as the führer did. If Georg had not been forced by the responsibilities to his homeland and his title to stay in Germany, he would probably have spent much more time in England. His student days there were among the happiest of his life, he always said. That connection had made the war harder for him, but he'd done his duty and valiantly led his men against the foe without flinching, even knowing they had once been his dearest friends.

Georg sat at ease now, beaming at the young ladies, conversing in flawless English about flower gardens and horse races and the summer weather in Scotland, where he fondly remembered fly-fishing with Julia's father in his youth. The girls were charmed, of course, because Georg was a charming man.

It was a pity he was not more supportive of the new order. He had not joined the Nazi party or offered his services to the new regime. He could do so much to help Otto if he wanted. Instead, he stood on his title and his past glories, and spent his days tucked away here at Glücksstern, pottering in the gardens, listening to music, or reading English books.

The führer's own mountain retreat at Berchtesgaden was close by, and she'd encouraged Georg to do the neighborly thing and offer his support and friendship to Hitler, but he refused, claiming he was simply a retired soldier with no part to play in modern politics.

While he did not strenuously object to Otto's joining the Nazi party or the SS, neither did he support his son with the kind of fervor Ilsa felt. He'd tried to convince her to send Klaus to school in England, but she refused to even consider it—Klaus would be educated in the elite SS school system and raised as a loyal German and a proper Nazi. He might rise even higher than Otto, though she pictured her youngest son as his brother's loyal lieutenant.

And then there was Felix, her middle son, the scientist, the intellectual. He wasn't a soldier, had no desire to be. He preferred the laboratory, saw the future in test tubes and chemical formulas. Georg was proud of him, loved him best, hoped that men like Felix, men of science and deep thought, would be the future of Germany and the world.

She looked again at Julia and Viviane and wondered anew if they were indeed suitable consorts for such great men, and if they could be brought to espouse Nazi doctrines and take their places as model German wives and mothers.

Her maid appeared in the doorway and nodded to Ilsa. She rose to her feet at once. "Your rooms are ready for you," she said to her guests. "Perhaps you'd like to rest before dinner."

Her husband also rose, setting his teacup down and clasping his hands behind his back. "Yes, you must be tired after such a long journey. Ilsa will escort you up, since it's easy to get lost in so many rooms and corridors. Perhaps we should scatter bread crumbs like Hansel and Gretel did to mark the way." He chuckled at his own joke, and Ilsa offered a pallid smile. "I'll give you a grand tour of the schloss tomorrow, so you'll know where you're going," he added.

"Otto will be home tomorrow." Ilsa made it a statement, a reminder to her husband that nothing could be more important than their son's homecoming. His smile slipped a little.

"Yes, of course. And Felix has promised to do his best to take a few days away from his work to come and meet you, but his work is important, you see, and he may not be able to get away. If he cannot, you'll see him when we go to Berlin." Did he have to make his pride in Felix quite so evident? Ilsa saw interest kindle in Julia's eyes, while Viviane's expression remained closed.

Julia wanted romance, then, and Viviane . . . well, Ilsa wondered why she'd come at all. What was it she was looking for? There'd be time enough to discover that.

"Come then," Ilsa said. "Let us go up."

CHAPTER SEVENTEEN

THEIR ROOMS ADJOINED, a lovely suite with two magnificent bedrooms, a modern bathroom, and a sitting room with wide windows that offered dramatic views of the Alps. If they needed anything at all, they need only pick up the telephone by the bed to connect with the kitchen.

There were chocolates, fresh flowers, and plenty of extra pillows and luxurious eiderdowns against the mountain chill, which was hard to imagine on a day with so much sunshine pouring through the windows.

On the bedside table in each bedroom, next to a crystal carafe of water drawn from a mountain spring, lay a copy of *Mein Kampf*, Adolf Hitler's memoir. There was another copy in the sitting room.

"Isn't it marvelous, Vee? I can hardly believe I'm here. I've pinched myself so often I'm surprised I'm not a mass of bruises. Look at the view!" Julia flopped into a comfortable armchair and gazed out the window.

Viviane came to stand beside her. "It is breathtaking, isn't it?"

"Did you see the photograph in the salon? The one of Otto in uniform? How handsome he looks. I can hardly wait to meet him."

Viviane thought of her father, of the portrait of him in his uniform, a soldier by necessity and duty, not for the swagger of a uniform, or any strong sense of pleasure in wearing it. "I find the SS uniforms a little sinister."

"Sinister?" Julia said. "I think they look so manly, so powerful. I've always been rather partial to men in uniform—all those proud portraits of my father and uncles in *their* uniforms, I suppose. I know they were all posted at HQ in London, but it's still so thrilling to imagine them on the battlefield, shouting commands, taking charge, vanquishing—" She put her hand over her mouth. "Oh, I'm sorry, Vee. I forgot about your papa. I don't suppose we should be talking about the war at all, not here. It's all in the past, and we're all friends again now."

"Are we?" Viviane asked through tight lips at the reminder of her father, here, of all places. Her enjoyment made her feel disloyal.

"Of course we are. Everyone we've met has been so charming, so kind. Have you not noticed?"

"Germany's not quite what I expected," Viviane admitted. Not at all like the photographs she'd seen in England, of storm troopers and riots, and hateful images of brutal anti-Semitism. She also thought of the stranger she'd met in the park. The friendly, charming people she'd met hardly seemed capable of such hatred, and yet Ilsa's reaction had been instant and vitriolic. Was it simply a case of a chaperone being overprotective? If she had photographed Ilsa's face in that moment, would the picture have shown that or revealed malevolent hatred? It had been gone in an instant, and the countess's lovely face had returned to placid politeness, her blue eyes as calm and flat as a lake after a storm. Viviane felt a chill and wrapped her arms across her body, looked at Julia, and wished she could ask her stepsister what she thought, what she'd seen that day, but she knew the answer to that well enough. Julia saw what she wanted to see, made up her mind from moment to moment, a pretty bird flitting from light to light and ignoring the shadows. She didn't like unpleasantness and refused to allow it to mar her happiness. She'd always been like that. It was endearing at home, but here . . . A warning hovered on her lips, but Julia smiled at her.

"I know some people say there's another war coming, but I really can't see how that's possible," Julia said, taking a chocolate from the crystal dish and popping it into her mouth. "I've seen no signs of it. I wish people at home could forget that dreadful war and move ahead. There is so much we could learn from the Germans—they are not the brutes we faced then. That's in the past, and now, if we can find a way to be friends, to learn from each other, and forgive, then we simply cannot have another war, d'you see? I think we should forget all that and enjoy ourselves, don't you? Not just you and I, here in this glorious place, but everyone, everywhere. Live and let live, as they say. Isn't that the surest way forward, to see the best in each other, to forgive our enemies their trespasses?"

"That's quite a sermon," Viviane murmured.

Julia rolled her eyes. "Oh, Vee. You've always been so serious. This is your chance to kick up your heels and enjoy yourself. In my experience, you see what you expect to see, so you might as well look for the good things. Imagine if people in England were as happy and openhearted as the Germans are. I am so glad to be here—I love the mountains and the castle, and we still have Berlin and the Olympic Games to look forward to. Count von Schroeder is so charming, and Klaus reminds me of Miles, coming down from school on holidays with his friends and playing soldier in the rose garden. Boys love that, don't they? I'm sure he means no harm. It's just a game."

Viviane blinked at Julia's insight. Her stepsister picked up the copy of *Mein Kampf* and glanced at the picture of the author on the cover. "I can hardly wait to meet Otto and Felix. Do you suppose they're very different from English gentlemen?" She dropped the book again. "We have so much to look forward to, and I intend to enjoy every minute!"

Was Julia right? Viviane looked out the window again, at the craggy, snowcapped peaks of the mountains, at the green meadows below. It *was* beautiful, and, yes, the count had been as kind and charming as she remembered her father being. Was he truly her enemy? What if everything in Germany really was as peaceable as it seemed?

She let her shoulders drop, releasing the tension in her body. Perhaps she *could* relax, simply enjoy herself, and take things at face value. Her father had taught her that peace and understanding were the antidotes to war. Would he mind terribly if she liked Germany and German people? The whole idea that there was something dangerous hidden behind the friendly smiles of the ordinary people suddenly seemed impossible.

She looked again at Julia, her face flushed with pleasure and anticipation. Her stepsister was free of her parents for the first time, an adult with the ability to choose her own activities, and she was reveling in it. Perhaps she should do the same, and simply enjoy the adventure. She could tell Tom that there was nothing to find, nothing wrong in Germany after all. Her photographs could very well provide a different truth than the one he expected.

And photographs didn't lie.

"What shall we do tomorrow?" Julia said. "Count Georg says the wildflowers in the Alpine meadows are magnificent at this time of year, and the guidebook says there's a waterfall nearby that simply must be seen. I shall ask about it at dinner, I think."

Viviane grinned at that and crossed the room to sit in the armchair beside Julia's. Perhaps Julia was right.

She landed on the book Julia had tossed aside. She picked it up and looked at the face on the cover. Above the Charlie Chaplin mustache, the führer's gaze was cold, hard, and proud, and Viviane bit her lip.

Photographs didn't lie.

CHAPTER EIGHTEEN

GEORG VON SCHROEDER sat in the comfortable solitude of his study with a glass of excellent Scotch whisky in his hand and the glorious sound of Wagner filling the room. He watched an eagle soaring across the face of the familiar, beloved mountain. He knew every crag and col and crest of that peak, had spent a lifetime climbing over every inch. He'd looked at this view in sun and storm, winter and summer and golden autumn, and never tired of it.

He sipped the fine Highland whisky, let the smoky peat taste of another land, another love, fill his mouth and his nose and warm a path all the way down to his belly.

He remembered a carefree month spent in Scotland in his youth and longed for the simplicity of that time. That powerful yearning for better times happened more often as he got older. Or perhaps it was regret. Not regret for anything in the past, but a feeling that the future would never live up to what once was, that all that was good in the world was being supplanted by darkness.

He loved his country, considered himself a proud and loyal German, but he had no love for Adolf Hitler or the Nazis. As an aristocrat and a senior military officer, decorated with the Iron Cross for bravery, he'd been among a group of men, army officers and aristocrats, mostly, who thought that it would be simple to control Adolf Hitler. They would let him rouse the people and restore the pride of Germany. He was good at that, had a gift for saying exactly what the masses wanted to hear. And when the little Austrian corporal got too big for his jackboots, they would simply dismiss him, use their power and position to flick him away like a pesky fly.

What fools they'd been.

They'd miscalculated, and now it was too late. Hitler controlled *them*, and every other aspect of German life. Georg's eldest and youngest sons were devoted to the führer and everything he preached, lost to reason. His wife as well. He still had hope for Felix. His middle son was devoted only to his work, followed science and innovation the way the others followed the Nazis. Men like Felix, intellectuals, would surely see through a mystic, a charlatan. They'd break his spell, restore order and balance and good sense to the world again.

It was why he'd arranged for the daughters of his English friend to visit. He hoped their pretty faces would lure his sons away from political dogma, charm them onto a more reasonable path, show them another way. He stared into the whisky in his glass, seeking a vision of the future in the golden liquid. Perhaps his sons would go to England, make a life there.

He smiled at the idea. Dear Julia, his goddaughter, was charming. She looked like her mother, blond and blue-eyed, Aryan-looking enough even for Ilsa. Lionel would provide his daughter with an excellent dowry and make her a wedding present of one of his English manors—one in Scotland, Georg hoped, so he could visit.

Julia's stepsister was another matter. Viviane was quiet and thoughtful.

Her eyes tracked the landscape. She looked deeper into things, sought hidden meanings. She was reserved, and he'd seen her recoil when she looked at the portraits on the piano in the salon—the ones of him in his Great War uniform, and of Otto in his SS uniform, a garment designed to exude power and menace, to make the man inside look bigger. Even Georg hardly recognized the boy his son had once been in that photograph, with all the kindness and innocence stripped away and replaced with hard suspicion and towering pride. It was Ilsa's favorite photograph of Otto, and the one Georg hated most. For him, it showed in one image all that Germany had become, all that it had lost since Adolf Hitler had come to power, the twisting and warping of the next generation to hate without reason. Georg didn't understand the hatred of the Jews, but when the war had been lost, the people wanted someone to blame, and Hitler had given them a scapegoat—Germans who were different, a community unto themselves. They'd been stripped of citizenship because they weren't German at all, according to the Nazis. He frowned, considered the terrible cruelty, the terror that was being perpetrated by lies. But what could he do? He was only one man, clinging to sanity and sense as the men around him were swept into the maelstrom that would drag them all into another war. This one, he knew, would be even more terrible than the last, and that had been devastating enough.

There was a knock at the door and Georg frowned at the interruption. He lifted the needle of the recording, and Siegfried ceased his impassioned song. "Yes?" he called out, and Holcroft entered. "Obersturmführer von Schroeder is arriving, sir. He's just passed the gate."

Otto was home.

Georg turned away, put the record into the sleeve, and switched off the machine. It gave him a moment to compose himself, to hide his frown from Holcroft. "I assume the countess knows?"

"Yes, sir. She has been waiting eagerly all morning. The staff are already lined up to welcome him."

"Then I shall be down directly."

He finished his whisky and waited until Holcroft left the room before going to the window to watch his son's motorcycle approaching the castle at breakneck speed.

CHAPTER NINETEEN

THE HARSH BUZZ of the motorcycle's engine echoed across the mountains and bounced off the castle until it was overwhelming, the sound coming from everywhere at once, growing louder as the vehicle got closer, and Viviane winced at the noise. The motorcycle was black, and the rider wore black as well, darkness hurtling toward them at a dangerous speed. He didn't slow as he approached the castle. Polished metal sparked in the sunlight, hitting the eye like bullets. At the last possible moment, the rider turned, braking hard, and a shower of gravel sprayed Holcroft's pant legs like shrapnel. If it hurt, the steadfast butler gave no sign of it. He stood at attention and raised his arm in a Nazi salute.

The rider dismounted and raised his own hand in a laconic salute, as if the full effort wasn't worth making for a mere servant. He wore goggles and an SS officer's cap, and a long black leather coat and dusty boots. For a moment he stood still, catching his breath, perhaps, and looking up at the castle's façade towering above him. The sun glinted off his goggles as he lowered his gaze to look at the two strangers on the stairs, standing with his mother and brother.

Before anyone could speak, Klaus launched himself down the steps and straight into the tall black figure of his brother, hugging him around the waist. One black-gloved hand cupped the boy's blond head affectionately as he took off his cap with the other.

"Hold this for me," Otto von Schroeder said in a deep, genial tone, and handed it to Klaus, who immediately put it on. Otto reached for the strap on his goggles and took those off, too, and tossed them to the boy.

Viviane felt a frisson of surprise. Otto von Schroeder was young and handsome under the black garb, an older version of Klaus. His hair was as blond as a wheat field, his eyes as brilliantly blue as the sky. Julia gave a little gasp and clasped Viviane's arm. "He's even better than his photograph," she whispered.

The countess descended the steps and touched her son's face. "How well you look," she said.

"You as well," he replied, bending to kiss her cheek. "Where is father?"

"In his study. He'll be right out."

Viviane didn't miss the slight tightening of Otto's jaw as his smile faded. "Never mind. Come and meet our English guests," the countess said, turning to present Viviane and Julia with an elegant gesture. Julia didn't wait for him to come to her—she went forward eagerly.

She tripped on the stone steps and would have fallen if not for Otto. He stepped forward and caught her in his arms. For an instant they stood nose to nose, staring at each other before he set Julia on her feet and stepped back. "You must be careful, fraülein. These steps have claimed victims before. I fell here as a boy." He tilted his head back and pointed to his chin. "It took six stitches to close the wound."

"I'll bet you didn't even cry," Klaus said, looking at his brother adoringly.

Otto grinned. "Of course not." He sent Julia a broad wink, and she blushed.

"This is Lady Julia Devellin," the countess said, "your father's god-daughter. And this is Miss Viviane Alden, her stepsister."

Otto bowed crisply, clicking his heels together. "How nice to meet you both. Are you enjoying your stay in Germany thus far?" His English was only slightly accented.

Julia, who usually had so much to say, was dumbstruck. Viviane glanced at her before she replied, but she was staring at Otto in surprise. "Yes. We've only been here a few days, but the mountains are beautiful."

"You have never seen anything like them, I assume, since there are no such mountains in Britain. I wish I had been here to see your faces the very first instant you spotted them on the horizon." He looked at Klaus. "Were they awestruck?"

His young brother nodded eagerly.

"Otto." The count stood at the top of the steps, regarding his son, their kind, jovial host now a stiff-backed and stern Prussian officer, his hands clasped behind his back, his face granite.

"Good day, Father," Otto said, equally unsmiling. He turned away to hand his gloves to Holcroft. There was no affectionate greeting between father and son, and Viviane wondered if that was because they were both soldiers. A cloud sailed over the sun, and the air felt the way it did before a storm, electrified, crackling with tension, waiting for a peal of thunder to shatter the sky.

The countess laughed gaily and took her eldest son's arm. "Come, you must be starving. Helga has made apfelkuchen and raisin cake."

Otto patted her hand. "I'll go to my room first. I am very dusty, and I need a bath."

He unbuttoned his leather coat, and Holcroft helped him out of it, the butler's diminutive frame nearly collapsing under the size and weight of the garment. Underneath, Otto wore a gray SS uniform. His shoulders were broad, his waist narrow, his legs long. The insignias on his collar and the diamond-shaped patch on his sleeve identified him as a member of the intelligence police, the SD.

"Oh," Julia breathed. If Otto heard, he gave no indication of it.

Klaus still wore his brother's cap and was marching around the foyer with his arm raised, humming a military tune.

Otto smiled charmingly at Viviane and Julia. "I hope you will excuse me while I make myself presentable for such lovely company." His grin deepened, showing dimples in his cheeks. "I have brought presents to welcome you to Germany and to my family home. I will retrieve them from my kit and bring them down."

He bowed again and walked smartly to the staircase, his bootheels ringing. Klaus scampered after him eagerly. "What did you bring me?" he demanded.

Julia put one hand to her cheek and the other to her hair, patting her curls as Otto disappeared up the stairs. "I'd better freshen up as well. I must look a fright," she said, though she looked lovely with her color high and her eyes sparkling. She grabbed Viviane's hand and hurried up to their rooms.

Once they were inside with the door shut, Julia threw herself onto the bed. "Did you see him?" she asked Viviane.

"Yes, of course I did. I was standing right beside you," Viviane teased.

"He's so handsome, and so charming, and so . . . Oh, I think I might be in love!"

Viviane laughed. "You've only just met him! He might have bowlegs or hammertoes for all you know."

Julia sobered. "No, he's perfect, I just know it. Every inch of him—oh, he probably thinks I'm a clumsy oaf, tripping like that. I shall have to make up for it by wearing something dazzling to tea." She rushed across to the armoire, threw the doors open, and rifled through the garments inside. "The pink dress? The green one?" She turned. "Oh, Vee, you choose. I simply can't. What do you suppose is his favorite color?"

Gray. Or black, perhaps, came to Viviane's mind. Instead, she reached past her frantic stepsister and picked out a pretty dress with a floral pattern. "Here, wear this one. It's lovely on you, and it has all the colors he could wish for. One of them is bound to be his favorite."

But Julia was at the dressing table now, brushing her hair. Viviane crossed and took the brush from her. "You look beautiful," she said, pulling the bristles through Julia's curls. "You looked beautiful earlier, too, in your yellow frock."

"Oh, but he's seen this one now," Julia said. She pinched her already-rosy cheeks, picked up a tube of lipstick, then paused, staring at it. "German men don't like women using makeup, do they?"

She'd worn lipstick, powder, and mascara every day they'd been here, stubbornly refusing to give it up after years of waiting to wear it.

Now she opened the drawer, dropped the lipstick in, and shut it again. She bit her lips to redden them and rose to change her dress, tossing the yellow one aside. She stepped into the floral frock and did up the buttons with nervous fingers.

"Will I do?" she asked Viviane. She looked beautiful, her cheeks glowing, her eyes as bright as stars.

"You'll do," Viviane said, turning the brush on her russet curls, fluffing them a little. She didn't bother to change her dress. She was wearing a simple pale blue frock with navy piping around the collar and pockets. It was sophisticated, comfortable, and it suited her well. She was more practical than Julia. They'd be staying in Germany for three months, and if they changed clothes for every meal, they'd soon run out of things to wear.

She picked up Julia's yellow frock and laid it carefully over the back of a chair.

Julia bounded toward the door, looking as eager as Klaus.

In the drawing room, they found Otto at the piano with his mother and brother standing by, watching him adoringly. The count was seated in a chair near the fireplace, as far from the tender family scene as he could possibly be. He and Otto both rose as Viviane and Julia entered the room.

The uniform was gone, and Otto wore a white shirt, tweed slacks, and a blue sweater that matched his eyes. His hair was still damp from his quick bath, and he looked relaxed and genial. Viviane saw the countess glance at Julia's altered dress, and Viviane's unchanged outfit. It was the kind of look her own mother would have cast at them, an inspection, a judgment. It was always easy to tell what Estella was thinking, but Ilsa's face remained placid, her opinion unreadable. "I have just ordered coffee," she said. "Otto prefers it to tea."

Julia glanced at the piano. "Do you play?" she asked Otto.

"He has a great talent," the countess interrupted, sending her son a fond smile.

Otto laughed lightly at his mother's outburst. "She is exaggerating. I play a little," he said. Across the room, the count looked on silently, pensive.

"Play the 'Horst-Wessel-Lied' for her," Klaus suggested, smiling at his brother.

"For pretty young ladies? No, of course not. I might play Wagner, or Beethoven."

"Do you know any show tunes?" Julia asked. "Fred Astaire's 'Cheek to Cheek' is all the rage in England just now. Shall I sing it for you?"

Otto's smile melted away, and silence fell like a thick blanket over the room. "It is not appropriate," the countess said coolly. "The composer is a Jew."

"Oh." Julia turned as red as a peony.

"There are several local festivals you must attend, so you may see what good music truly is, true German music." Otto's tone was a shade darker now, and the comment felt like a command, not an invitation. Then, just as suddenly, Otto's expression softened again, and his smile was back. "We shall arrange for tickets."

"How kind," Julia murmured, batting her lashes at him.

"I'd almost forgotten—here are the gifts I brought from Berlin for you," he said, and turned to take a pair of identical books off the top of the piano.

He held them out, one for Julia and one for Viviane. "No doubt even in England you have heard of *Mein Kampf*, our führer's great work?"

This edition was slightly different from the one upstairs—this one was bound in red leather and had the eagle rune of the SS embossed in gold on the cover. "The Reichsführer-SS had this edition printed specially for his officers," Otto said proudly. "I do hope you will enjoy reading it. It is most enlightening, and I will be most pleased to help you to understand the führer's words—and the language—if you require assistance."

"Thank you," Julia said, not even looking at the book. She clasped it to her chest as if it were the most precious gift in the world and beamed at Otto.

Viviane managed a tight smile. What on earth would she ever do with two copies of *Mein Kampf*? This book was heavier than the one upstairs, the pages thicker, the paper finer, as if the führer's words had added weight and importance for the SS. She glanced at Otto, standing at attention in just the presence of Adolf Hitler's book, and wondered if he was even aware of his military stance.

"Shall we play a little Beethoven?" the countess said, sitting down at the piano, and the soothing, universal sounds of the *Moonlight Sonata* filled the room.

Across the room, the count looked on silently, his expression unreadable.

CHAPTER TWENTY

VIVIANE AND JULIA had been at Schloss Glücksstern for a fortnight when Felix von Schroeder arrived home.

Unlike Otto, he arrived quietly—soundlessly, in fact.

Viviane was in the rose garden, photographing the heavy blossoms, while Julia sat in the shade, struggling with her German as she read *Mein Kampf*—the leather-bound version Otto had given her—with a determined expression. Viviane lined up a shot of a fat bumblebee, slow and heavy with a cargo of pollen. Before she could take the picture, a shadow fell over the rose, and the bee departed. She looked up to find a young man close beside her, peering intently down at what she was doing. He was road dusty, his hair wind ruffled around a sunburned face. He wore a short Alpine jacket and sturdy hiking boots, and carried a rucksack on his back.

He pushed his wire-rimmed glasses up his nose with one finger and grinned at her. "It appears that I've spoiled your picture," he said in German, then nudged her shoulder and pointed. A black butterfly with red-spotted wings rested on the shaggy head of a wildflower a few feet away.

"A New Forest burnet," he murmured. "Lovely, isn't it?"

For a moment she watched the graceful creature, dazzled. When she looked up, she found the stranger was staring at her, not the butterfly, and he was only inches away.

Viviane rose at once and stepped back, holding her camera in front of her chest like a shield. He glanced at it, then back at her.

"Are you going to shoot me?" he quipped lightly, switching to English, raising his hands. "My father might object, though my mother would probably have me pinned to a board and framed for display in the library with all the other butterfly specimens. Have you seen the collection? I used to study them as a boy, and I made her a gift of the best ones. I'm Felix von Schroeder, by the way. I usually come through the front door, but I thought I'd avail myself of the pump in the kitchen yard before I encountered anyone today. I'm rather thirsty."

"You're Felix?" Julia said, dropping the book beside her chair and coming across the grass. She wore shorts and a form-fitting sweater, and she looked like a movie star. Felix's brows rose toward the thatch of his hair. "Did you *walk* here, all the way from . . ." She trailed off. "I am Lady Julia Devellin, and this is my stepsister, Miss Viviane Alden."

Felix wiped his palm on his trousers and offered his hand, first to Julia, then to Viviane. His grip was light, gentle, almost tentative. "I surmised that you must be our English guests. I am very pleased to know you, and, no, Lady Julia, I didn't walk all the way from Berlin. I took the train from Berlin to Munich, and from Munich to Garmisch. From there I hiked through the mountains."

"But that must have taken days!" Julia said. There was no dazzlement in her stepsister's eyes for this Schroeder son, Viviane noted, only a slight, baffled distaste at his disheveled state.

"I enjoyed the fresh air after being in the city for so long." He flicked a glance over Julia's trim figure. "We Germans like to be in nature as often as we can, to restore our spirits." He quirked a wicked little smile. "There is nothing so unfortunate as a drooping spirit, especially before such lovely ladies. You are as—reviving?—as a hike in the morning mist, and I am—"

"Felix!" Klaus barreled across the lawn and stopped in front of his brother before he could continue his teasing little speech. There was no hero worship in Klaus's eyes for this brother. "Father will be pleased you're home at last."

"And are you also pleased?" Felix asked, regarding his little brother's Hitler Youth uniform.

Klaus grinned at once. "Yes, of course. Did you hike up the mountain?"

Felix nodded. "I camped by the lake last night, under the stars. I saw an eagle this morning, so I climbed the rockfall and followed her to her nest. She had three eaglets, just like Mutti."

Klaus grinned. "What did you bring me?"

"Something new I'm working on, but you'll have to wait to see it. I need a bath and a change of clothes, and I've interrupted what looks like a very pleasant afternoon among the roses. I shall go in and make myself presentable and see you both later." Viviane watched him walk across the lawn in an easy lope, a climber's stride. Klaus followed him only as far as the nearest tree, where he climbed up into the branches and disappeared.

Felix looked back over his shoulder, caught Viviane's gaze, and grinned. "Welcome to Germany, Miss Alden," he said, and was gone as silently as he'd arrived.

"How different he is from Otto," Julia said, picking up her book again, brushing an ant off the leather cover. "And what a way to arrive. What do you think of him?"

"I daresay he didn't expect to find us in the garden," Viviane said. "And I haven't had time to decide what I think of him."

"Every family has a black sheep. I suspect he just might be the Schroeder version," Julia pronounced with a toss of her head. "I'm going inside to change. Otto promised to take me for a ride on his motorcycle."

CHAPTER TWENTY-ONE

FELIX VON SCHROEDER was funny, observant, intellectual, and interesting. He listened more than he spoke, asked questions, and, unlike Otto, he did not correct the opinions of others based on Nazi doctrine. Viviane found him good company and a refreshing change from the intensity of his mother and brothers. Felix had read many books beyond *Mein Kampf.* He also admitted that he loved jazz, though he warned her not to tell his parents or he'd be disowned on the spot. "Then I would never see you again," he said charmingly. He was also an irredeemable flirt, quick with teasing comments she suspected were meant solely to make her blush.

He poured two glasses of pear cider as they sat on the terrace after luncheon.

"So how do you like Germany?" Felix asked.

"It's beautiful. The mountains are unlike anything in Britain."

"Yes, we are fortunate in that. And yet I think it will be the destruction of us in the end."

Viviane frowned. "What do you mean?" she asked.

He sat back in his chair and studied her. "We've become arrogant in Germany. Perhaps you don't see it, but it's quite true. All this majesty, this beauty, it is our birthright, what makes us strong and pure and bold. Does not such a race of supermen deserve to rule the world?"

Was this a test? Viviane regarded him without speaking, sipped her cider, and kept her face carefully blank.

He laughed and leaned closer. "You need not fear me. I am not a Nazi. My mother is horrified of course, and if Klaus knew, my little brother would report me to my older brother, and Otto would happily arrest me and commit me to a camp for reeducation."

He peered at her over his glasses as if he were gauging her opinion on that.

"Surely they wouldn't," Viviane murmured, since he seemed to be waiting for some kind of comment.

He sat back and folded his arms, looking at her skeptically. "You do not believe that loyalty to the führer is stronger and far more important than even ties to family and friends? Have you not read *Mein Kampf*, our führer's masterpiece?"

"I have two copies of it," Viviane said, looking away.

"But have you *read* it?" Felix asked.

"I will, of course," she said, a false promise. She should read it, she supposed, to understand Germany's leader and his theories. She'd managed to skim only a few pages so far and found it dull.

He shook his head. "No, you won't, and you shouldn't. Most of the people in Germany who say they've read it have not. They buy it for show, display it in a conspicuous place, but never even open it."

"Have *you* read it?" she asked.

He laughed. "*Mein Kampf* is not meant to be read. It is like one of Hitler's speeches, intended as a performance, not a book. It's those lectures that mesmerize people, skillful bits of theater to draw them in, whip them to a frenzy of adoration and hatred in equal measure." He leaned closer. "All the pageantry is meant to confuse the common man, to dazzle him until he does not know what is real or true anymore. It is euphoric, like cocaine or heroin, and one craves more after just one taste. He's a magician, our Herr Hitler, a mystical prophet. He appeals to everyone, tells them exactly what they need, and they believe him. Our young people crave the bright future he promises, the chance to feel they are superior to the rest of the world. Our old people want revenge, someone to blame for Germany's defeat and for all they lost in the war—sons, husbands, fathers—and a peace that was worse than the war, shameful. Hitler has cleverly made them believe that the Jews and the Communists and the French all cruelly collaborated to inflict immeasurable suffering on the German people. It's brilliant, even if it's all lies. One scapegoat is as good as any other, don't you think?" He smiled grimly. "No, don't answer that. You are British. You cannot possibly know what it was like here after the war."

Viviane felt a flare of anger. "My father was a soldier in that war, just as yours was. He fought with honor and courage. His regiment was caught in the gas attack, a new invention, more deadly than previous types. He went out onto the field, endangered himself, to bring his men back, soldiers too blinded and incapacitated by the poison to save themselves. It took six years, but the damage to his own lungs eventually killed him. When he died, my mother and I lost our home, our heritage, everything. I know plenty about the suffering caused by the war."

He regarded her with sympathy. "I am sorry. And here I am, a man who works with chemicals and gases for a living. Do you hate me for that?"

She was wary of the question. "Should I?"

He wet his finger, ran it around the edge of his glass until it squealed. "Perhaps you should. The chemical I'm working on right now can kill. It reacts with air, and the victims have no chance at all. Within a few minutes they die. Then the gas disperses, and the air is clear and clean again. Children could run through the same space a few hours later, completely unharmed."

She gaped at him in horror, numb. "How can you do such a thing?"

He threw back his head and laughed. "Your face, Viviane—you are as pale as the snow on the mountain! The stuff I'm working on is an agricultural chemical. It kills pests in the fields, protects food crops to improve the harvests and feed more people. It is not sinister unless you are an insect, a parasite. Then it is very deadly indeed."

He grinned as if it was a fine joke, to make her think of death, to make her remember. She stared at him, shaken, and wondered if he was ever serious. He joked about everything, even poison and death. She got to her feet. "I think I'll go upstairs. I have some letters to write."

"Viviane, wait—" he called after her, but she didn't stop. She hurried up to her room and locked the door.

CHAPTER TWENTY-TWO

"YOU CANNOT SAY you've experienced Germany without taking the chance to camp in the mountains," Otto said at dinner, smiling across the table at Julia. "I propose we leave tomorrow, do some hiking, and sleep under the stars for a few nights. You will see things that I doubt are in that guidebook of yours."

"But we're leaving for Berlin at the end of the week," the countess said to her son. "I simply haven't time to go camping."

Felix grinned. "I don't think he was inviting you, Mutti—just Julia and Viviane and me."

The countess frowned at him and set her fork down. "Without a chaperone?"

"Would six other people be enough supervision? There's a youth group going," Otto said. "There will be hiking, swimming, and camping— wholesome exercise in nature."

"Is Otto not a suitable chaperone? He is an esteemed lieutenant in the SD—his word is his bond," Felix said around a mouthful of food. "He will be too busy leading everyone in song and races and climbing challenges for any— What's that charming English phrase, Father?"

"Hanky-panky?" the count said.

"Yes, that's it," Felix said, laughing. "There will be no hanky-panky."

"Would you like to go?" Georg asked Julia and Viviane.

"Of course she would," Otto said, answering for Julia. He turned to Viviane. "Would you prefer to stay behind? The terrain will be quite rugged."

He meant her limp, of course, feared it would slow the progress of the rest of the group. She lifted her chin. "I wouldn't miss it. I'm sure the scenery is magnificent, and I can't wait to photograph it." She'd keep up if it killed her, she decided.

"Very well. There is nothing that strengthens the body, mind, and spirit like time spent in nature, hiking," Otto said.

Julia giggled. "That's exactly what my guidebook says—that Germans can be characterized by their love of hiking and singing."

"And what characterizes the English?" Felix asked.

"Good manners, perhaps?" Julia said, looking along her nose at Otto's younger brother, her smile fading to aristocratic haughtiness. Julia didn't appreciate his sense of humor.

"We'll start our trek from Garmisch-Partenkirchen, where the Winter Olympics were held. It's quite close by and very charming," Otto said. "I can show you on a map, and—"

"What's for dessert?" Felix interrupted.

"Kirschtorte," the countess replied. "How long will you be away?"

Otto shrugged. "Three days, more or less."

"Again?" Felix asked.

The countess sighed. "Kirschtorte is your brother's favorite. I suppose we could delay our trip to Berlin by a day, then."

"Three days of song, sun, and fun," Felix said. He raised his glass toward Julia in an exaggerated toast and winked at Viviane. "We shall watch for butterflies and be on our very best behavior."

————

THE NEXT DAY, they joined a group of seven young men and women, all fit, robust, and glowing with health, joy, and vitality. Every one of them could walk all day, singing as they went, climb mountains, swim in icy mountain lakes, and still have the energy to make camp and tell stories around the campfire until late into the night.

Viviane couldn't help but compare them to the youth in Britain, poor and dissolute, weighed down by the cares of their parents and the hopelessness of the future. They were dull-eyed, hollow-chested, malnourished versions of their German counterparts.

The young Germans spoke happily of their future—the men at university or in the military or as civil servants. The girls were expected to become wives and mothers.

Without exception, they all embraced Nazi philosophy, adored their führer, and celebrated the purity and superiority of the German race. It crept into everything they did or said. Even keeping fit and healthy was a duty to Hitler. They laughed and joked and sang the "Horst-Wessel-Lied" and other patriotic songs. The women deferred to the men in all things and spoke glowingly about home and hearth and having babies.

"Don't any of you want a career?" Viviane asked. One of the young women had been at university with Felix, had studied chemistry, was considered brilliant, but she'd had to give up her place for a male student of lesser caliber. She showed no signs of regret. The others looked at Viviane blankly.

"We *will* have a career," a woman named Hedda told her. "There is no higher honor than bearing and raising the next generation of Germans. Mothers are revered in Germany. It is how we can best serve the führer. It is our duty to choose the best, strongest man, and find joy through family."

It sounded like a prepared speech to Viviane, but Hedda's face was alight with conviction. "My sister had her first child last year, a sturdy boy. She is not married, but there is no shame in that. My parents are old-fashioned, and they were unhappy, but the father is an SS man, and even they soon realized what a high honor that was. Her son is named Adolf after the führer."

Viviane glanced at Julia, but her stepsister's eyes were on Otto, who was discussing military training with the men. She looked smitten.

"Julia," Viviane said, barely realizing she'd spoken until she heard the tension in her own voice, the fear for her stepsister. Julia looked at her sharply. They communicated volumes without saying a word. Julia resented Viviane's interference, her wordless plea to be cautious. She felt capable of making her own choices, knew what she wanted. *Wait*, Viviane said silently, *think* . . . but Julia rose and crossed to Otto, who grinned at her, basking in her adoring attention.

"We are going to swim," he said to Julia.

Julia gave a dramatic shiver. "Too chilly for me, but I shall watch from the shore."

The men laughed, and Julia's eyes widened. "What's funny?"

"We swim naked. I doubt Englishwomen could bear the magnificent sight of that," one of the other men said. "You are more—repressed, perhaps—than German women?"

Julia frowned. "Viviane swims."

The men laughed. "The lame one?" one asked in German, perhaps thinking she didn't understand his language. Julia still struggled with German, but Viviane understood—if not the precise word he used, she knew what he meant when he cast a disdainful look at her leg, encased in warm trousers against the evening chill. She saw Otto follow his friend's stare, then look away as if it meant nothing—not the insult or her limp, or her, for that matter.

"The girls will stay here and tend the fire. The water is cold, and we'll need hot coffee when we get back," Otto said, an offhand, casual order, but an order nonetheless.

"Then why swim at all if it's so cold?" Julia asked.

"It is a test of their fortitude, their strength," Felix said, still lounging with the women by the fire. "Do you really swim?" he asked Viviane.

"Of course she does," Julia said sharply. "She is descended from the Lady of the Lake."

Everyone looked confused.

"As in King Arthur's Lady of the Lake?" Felix asked.

"That's right," Julia said, raising her chin.

"What a little spitfire you are, Julia. I meant no offense. Many Germans believe they are descended from Siegfried and Brunhilde, Valkyries, gods, and warriors. Am I not correct, Otto?" Felix said, laughing. His brother sent him a sharp and silent warning, a command to hold his tongue. Instead Felix turned to grin at Viviane. "And Viviane is obviously of similar ancestry, a lady of unknown depths, a sword-wielding goddess to rival our Valkyries. I'm most intrigued."

"Are you coming with us, little brother?" Otto said impatiently.

"When I can stay by the fire and sing songs with so many lovely young ladies? The delights of an icy lake pale by comparison."

Otto's expression hardened to disdain for a moment, and his eyes narrowed as he glared down at Felix. They, too, were having an unspoken conversation, and Viviane felt the tension between the brothers. She wondered if Otto would order Felix to his feet, force him into the water. For a moment the silence stretched, then Otto turned to the other men. "Come on, my friends, let us challenge ourselves. Whoever stays in longest and swims farthest wins." He turned and ran down toward the lake, tossing off his shirt as he ran, and his friends followed, doffing their clothes and whooping with joy. The girls cast frank and admiring looks at the naked men racing through the darkness toward the lake. They didn't turn away or giggle nervously the way English girls might have done.

Viviane heard the splash of the water as they dove, the curses at the coldness, and her limbs flexed, knowing how it felt to feel the chill, the tingle, the lightness of being in the water. She longed to dive deep, to know what secrets lay hidden beneath the dark surface of this mountain lake. She touched the coin around her neck, rubbed the smooth surface absently.

"Come and help with the coffee, Vee," Julia said, touching Viviane's arm as she rose to her feet, and the spell was broken. She turned to find Felix watching her, his gaze speculative. She could sense the tension around her, the eyes of the German girls upon her, wondering what she would do, what she *could* do.

She smiled at Julia. "I suppose we'd better get blankets ready as well," she said, and turned away from the sight of the lake.

CHAPTER TWENTY-THREE

AFTER A LONG morning of hiking—the third day of it—the sound of
church bells echoing through the clear air from a tiny village and the
sight of small houses and farms was pure joy. Viviane had kept pace with
everyone else, even with her limp. Felix had walked beside her, keeping
up a stream of cheery conversation, making jokes, and gossiping. Julia—
who did not hike at home—also kept up the grueling pace, just to impress Otto. She was starting to flag, her cheeks glowing with effort as
much as sun. She looked as relieved as Viviane was to see civilization.

"See that square tower? It's a convent, and it has been here since the
sixteenth century," Felix told her as they descended along a steep goat
track. "Apparently a young shepherdess, looking for a lost goat, wandered into this valley. She found her missing goat by a spring and
brought the rest of the herd down to drink. The water was so pure and
sweet, the milk they gave was dramatically improved in both quality
and quantity," Felix told her. "It made her family rich, and in thanks for
such a miracle, they built a shrine, which became a convent in 1532." He
told the story like a scientist, full of time lines and facts, and Viviane
smiled at him.

She liked Felix very much, his quick wit and sense of humor. He was wiry and thin where his brother was strong and broad. He was dark haired like his father, not blond like his mother. When he spoke, his ideas were his own, not a direct quote of what the führer thought. He caught her arm and pointed out the wildflowers they passed, named them, described their chemical constituents while she enjoyed the color, the way the light caught the folds of the petals and leaves. Bolder blossoms stood in the sun, posing for the camera, while other flowers avoided it, nestling shyly in rocky crevices. Around them, the others marched with their packs on their backs and their eyes on the sky, their heavy hiking boots treading on the marvelous flowers without even noticing.

As they neared the village, Viviane could see a cobbled square below, dominated by a gasthaus. The little hotel had tables set outside, covered with checkered cloths. Viviane thought of lemonade, and tea, and a chance to rest her aching feet.

She took Julia's arm. "I want a cold drink and a proper toilet," she whispered in English.

Julia let out a long breath. "I want a slice of cake. No, two slices."

"A tall glass of beer," Felix said, eavesdropping, also switching to English. "And a plate of schnitzel. This village is famous for schnitzel."

"I thought it was famous for the convent," Viviane said. "And the miracle of the goats."

"Oh, it is." He grinned at Julia. "You must have a glass of goat's milk with your cake, Julia. It will fortify you to walk another hundred miles."

Julia gaped at him. "Is that how far we still have to go?" she asked, trying to keep the dismay out of her voice and failing.

Felix laughed. "Otto arranged for father's car to meet us here. You won't have any more hiking to do."

Julia looked giddy with relief. "Really? How long will it take to reach Glücksstern? Will we be home by tomorrow?"

Felix pointed to the mountain behind the village, a graceful green and blue giant with its snowy head in the clouds. "Do you see that peak?"

"Of course," Julia said.

"Glücksstern is on the far side, a short drive away."

"But we've been walking for three days!" Julia said. "How can that be?"

"We've done a circle," Felix said, shrugging.

"D'you hear that, Vee? We'll be back at the castle soon. We can have a hot bath, sleep in a proper bed—"

"You do not enjoy sleeping under the stars, breathing the brisk mountain air, bathing in an icy stream fed by an ancient glacier?" Felix asked her. And Julia bit her lip.

"Don't tell Otto, but I think I hate hiking," she whispered, glancing ahead at the object of her affection, who was leading the group, setting a breakneck pace.

"My lips are sealed," Felix said. "Now, what kind of cake will you have? Will you have whipped cream on top of it?"

Julia sighed. "Kirschtorte, with a whole bowl of whipped cream. Do you think they have apple cake as well, and strudel?"

"And gingerbread, and the most excellent beer," Felix said.

They were approaching the stone arch that marked the entrance to the village.

A large sign welcomed visitors. Unless you were Jewish. The village, the sign declared, was proudly Jew free.

Viviane stopped in surprise. Felix followed her gaze and stopped talking, his smile fading. Otto and the rest of the group also stood before the sign.

"Finally," one of the young men said.

"How marvelous! The citizens are to be congratulated," Hedda said.

Otto was silent. His gaze slid over the exhausted Julia and met Viviane's eyes. She didn't say a word.

"Come," he said, and led the way across the town square to the gasthaus.

A man in an apron hurried out of the little inn and welcomed them with a broad smile and waved them to seats at the tables, chatting ebulliently in German. His grin faded when Otto said something in his ear. He nodded soberly and led Otto inside. The rest of the group scarcely noticed. A moment later a young woman came out to take their orders.

"Let's go and freshen up," Viviane whispered to Julia, and followed Otto inside.

She waited outside the ladies' convenience while Julia washed her face, just around the corner from the spot where Otto was speaking to the owner.

"I'm SS Obersturmführer von Schroeder, SD," she heard Otto say.

She heard the click of the gasthaus proprietor's shoes, knew he must be bowing or saluting Otto. "I'm honored, Obersturmführer. Heil Hitler. I'm Herr Wachter. I know your father, of course. I am the mayor of our little village, as well as the proprietor of this inn. On behalf of our citizens, I welcome you. Is there anything I can do to make your visit more pleasant?"

"The sign at the entrance to the village—was that your idea?"

Herr Wachter chuckled. "Why, yes, it was." There was a warble of pride in his voice.

"Take it down at once." Otto's command cut through the mayor's good humor like a stiletto.

"Take it down?" the man parroted, his tone slow with bafflement. "But I thought—"

"There is a directive from Berlin. All such signs are forbidden. The Olympic Games will bring in many foreign tourists. We do not want any misunderstandings about Germany, now do we?" The coldness of Otto's voice sent a shiver up Viviane's spine.

"Why, no, Obersturmführer, certainly not. I hadn't thought . . . that is, we do not get many foreign tourists here."

"There are two young ladies from England in my party today. They are guests of my family. *They* are foreign tourists."

"Oh. Oh, I see. We meant no offense, of course. We are proud people, and—" He stopped. "I shall order the sign taken down at once."

"Good." The single word came out like the purr from a tiger. "Between us, I commend your achievement. The führer would be most pleased. I shall see that your dedication is noted in Berlin and that you receive a citation in due course. More towns should take such initiative, but not until after the Olympics."

"Yes, of course, Obersturmführer von Schroeder. Thank you."

"Bring some beer for my party," Otto said, and the pair moved off.

Julia came out, her face washed, her hair combed to order. Her sun-pinked cheeks made her look like a goddess. Viviane walked back to the table with her. Within minutes, a pair of young men scurried past the gasthaus, carrying the sign. They ducked into an open doorway across the square and disappeared. A few minutes later, they returned with another sign, the paint still wet. "Welcome English Visitors!" was written in German. They paraded past at a more sedate pace, smiling and nodding and making sure everyone seated at the tables in front of the gasthaus had time to see it.

Viviane's throat closed, but Felix barked a laugh. "Much more democratic. More—*gemütlich*. Do you know the term? It means pleasant and happy and congenial." He raised his glass of beer to the men, who grinned. "I assume Otto had a word with someone. He's very important, and the SD is more terrifying than the Spanish Inquisition."

Viviane watched as the sign was raised, nailed up in place of the other one. She wondered how they had made the village Jew free, what they'd done, if there was blood on their hands that was as bright as the wet red paint. Herr Wachter set a slice of cake in front of her with a broad grin and gave a speech of welcome in German, bowing repeatedly, like a windup toy.

Julia nodded when he was finished. "What did he say?" she asked Felix.

"In essence? Welcome to you, most beautiful English ladies," Felix translated.

Julia took a forkful of cake and sighed. "I'm learning more German every day, but he spoke so fast. What was all the fuss about the sign— what did the first one say?"

"Could you not read it?" Felix asked, his smile fading to a surprised gape.

"Not a word after '*willkommen*,'" Julia admitted. She took a forkful of kirschtorte. "Oh, this is delicious!"

Felix studied Viviane. "And you, Viviane—did you also not understand the sign?"

Viviane considered for a moment. Should she admit she knew more German than Julia and had understood perfectly? "No, not a word," she said, and looked away.

Above them, veils of cloud flew across the face of the mountain in long streamers to block the sun. "Looks like we're in for some rain," Felix said. He looked at the untouched slice of cake in front of her. "Are you going to eat that?"

She slid it toward him. "All yours," she said with false brightness. She shivered as the storm clouds gathered and dark shadows formed under the charming eaves and in the doorways of the pretty village, turning it sinister.

CHAPTER TWENTY-FOUR

Hotel am Zoo, Berlin

THERE WAS A knock on the door of his hotel room, and Tom looked up from his typewriter.

He opened the door to find a tall man standing there, twirling his hat in his hand. He was a stranger, and yet he looked familiar. He regarded Tom with frank interest. "Alex MacCann. Mind if I come in?" he said tersely.

His uncle on his father's side.

"I'm just on my way out," Tom lied.

MacCann looked at him with eyes that were the same as his own and his father's. "Pity. I've been looking forward to meeting you." Instead of leaving, he stepped past Tom, tossed his hat on the desk.

He looked around, took in the battered typewriter, the half-empty glass of whisky, and the open door that led to the small bedroom. Tom waited silently while MacCann looked his fill, then shut the door to the suite when MacCann showed no signs of leaving. He recognized the stubbornness in his uncle's closed expression, another family trait. He also shared Tom's lean height, his dark hair, and even the line of his jaw. His eyes returned at last to Tom, and he took him in, too, from top to toe before he smiled. "You're a true MacCann," he said.

"My name is Graham."

"Still," Alex MacCann said with an easy shrug.

Tom waited for him to say why he was in Berlin and why he'd come here today. Instead, he crossed to pour himself a glass of whisky when Tom didn't offer. He sipped and grimaced. "I'll send ye something better. This rot is worse than bloody schnapps."

"I like it well enough."

"You're like your da in that, too—a man of few words. Why use three when one will do? He said you were stubborn—*independent* was the word he used, actually."

"Is he checking up on me?"

"No. I'm your contact, so I suppose *I'm* checking up on you. The gentlemen in London thought it would look less suspicious if a relative dropped in to call on you from time to time, since we're both in Berlin and the Nazis have their eye on you. I wasn't unhappy with the assignment. I've wanted to meet you for some time. Do you have any questions?"

"About you or this job?" Tom asked.

Alex MacCann grinned. "Aye, *independent*," he muttered. He reached into his breast pocket and pulled out a tourist guidebook for Tom. "There are a few places we'd like you to get to during the Olympics if you can manage. We think the Germans will be a bit distracted with so many people to keep an eye on. You've already done well, earned a reputation with the Nazis as a reliably sympathetic correspondent."

Tom couldn't see it as a compliment.

"Now we want you to ask to do more. There's a list of places in the guidebook, mostly factories. They're building airplanes, you see, better than anything we have, and we need to know more about them."

"You're an aircraft engineer, are you not?" Tom asked. "Wouldn't you know better what you're looking at than I would?"

"Oh, I've been on all the tourist junkets. They proudly show visitors modern assembly lines turning out perfectly innocent steel widgets or the kind of parts most people wouldn't recognize. If they're told it's a radiator or a new motor for an automobile or a housing for a household appliance, why wouldn't they believe it?"

"But?"

"They aren't automobile parts or appliances. They're airplane components. They're building hundreds of airplanes, even thousands, hiding them in plain sight, so to speak. Each factory makes a single part, then those parts are shipped to another factory and put together until there's a whole fleet of airplanes. They're doing it with other things, too, like tanks and guns. And they're training pilots. Most recently they've been sending pilots and planes to Spain to support the Fascists and to test their designs."

Tom had read about the brewing civil war in Spain. The Russians supported one side, the Fascists the other, and ordinary people were caught in the middle.

"The Nazis can't resist showing off. Charles Lindbergh, the American flyer, is coming to Germany. He's a sympathizer as well, a real one, unlike you. They'll welcome him with open arms, take him around, and show him their latest aircraft designs just to thumb their noses at the Americans. They're counting on Lindbergh to go home and gush about the marvels of German engineering, let everyone know just how formidable the new German war machine will be. They'll likely take their favorite journalists along on the tour. Ask to be assigned to cover his visit. Keep your eyes open. There's a list of the kind of parts we want you to look for in that guidebook." He reached into his pocket and pulled out a piece of sheer fabric, decorated with a random spray of embroidered dots and tiny flowers. "Looks like a lady's hankie, doesn't it? It's even perfumed. No one will question a romantic keepsake carried close to your heart." He opened the guidebook and folded out the enclosed map of Germany and laid the sheer silk over it. "The wee dots and flowers correspond to the important places we want a look at. If you go to any of these places, pay close attention. We're trying to get a photographer assigned to work with you, but so far the Nazis haven't approved our choices. You can't by chance use a camera, can you? We'd rather you didn't. It's too risky to do everything, and it's hard to hide a camera if you're not supposed to have one." He handed Tom a German phrasebook designed for tourists. "There's the code for communications so you can include sensitive information in a newspaper piece, and make it look like nothing more than a glowing report on the magnificence of the Third Reich."

Tom left the phrase book on the desk. "There's a young woman in Germany now, a photographer. I asked her to take pictures."

Alex frowned. "A woman? Who is she?"

"Miss Viviane Alden. Her father was Sir Arthur Alden of Kellyn."

Alex stared at him. "And her stepfather is the Earl of Rutherford. He's an appeaser at best, a sympathizer at worst. Are you sure you can trust her?"

"Yes. She's in Germany with her stepsister. I asked her to take pictures of exactly what you're looking for. The Germans might wonder why *I'm* taking photographs, but they're not likely to question a girl tourist, the guest of a well-connected German family."

"Is this sex or duty?" Alex asked baldly.

"She's smart, and she wants to stop a war as badly as anyone else."

"Aye, well, young debs have been coming over to Germany in droves, hoping to find husbands. Quite a number go home smitten with Hitler. Will she?"

"She blames the Germans for her father's death. He was gassed during the war, died after a number of years as an invalid," Tom said. She may have changed her mind, he thought. She'd been in Germany for almost a month, and they hadn't spoken, had agreed not to until she arrived in Berlin with her hosts.

"Aye, I know the story. They trotted poor Major Lord Kellyn out at parades and unveilings as a hero for a short while after the war."

"My uncle—my maternal uncle—was at the battle. He knows the truth, what really happened," Tom murmured. A kernel of doubt suddenly lodged itself in his throat. What if Viviane Alden failed and was caught? What if she did fall for the German illusion of peace and joy, or was lured astray by the charms of a handsome Nazi? Would she give Tom up to her new friends? The possibilities for disaster, things he hadn't considered before, loomed large now. He'd assumed he knew her back in England, what she wanted, what she'd do. Being in Berlin, amid spies and subterfuge and shifting loyalties, had made him realize he didn't really know anyone. He regarded Alex, wondered how far he could trust his uncle, this new and unknown relative.

The game was more dangerous now, very dangerous. The Nazis didn't want anything to spoil the illusion of the Olympic idyll, break the spell. They'd be even more watchful now, the stakes higher. Anyone who dared question the German regime simply disappeared without a trace, was arrested on a pretext, or was bustled off in the night to one of the new concentration camps.

Tom was diving into a bottomless pool of intrigue and suspicion. He was working for the shadowy men behind men like Alex, and he was doing his damndest to convince the Nazis he was on their side.

Tom was also playing his own game, because his conscience wouldn't allow him to lie, not without finding a way to tell the truth at the same time. Doing that was complicated and dangerous, a bit of subterfuge all his own.

Independent, his uncle said. He had no idea.

His uncle stood, waiting for an explanation or assurance that Tom was truly on board. There was flat concern in his gray eyes—not for Tom but for the mission. Tom raised his chin and frowned back.

"My kin in Glasgow are convinced I'm a Fascist. They don't like it. I may never be able to go home again," he said.

Alex's brow cleared. "Is that all? *I* know the truth. So does your father, and there are others—"

"Not family," Tom said sharply. "The kith and kin who have always welcomed me, the ones I care about."

Alex raised one brow at the rebuke. "Can you do the job or not?"

For a moment they stared at each other. Tom picked up the map, then crossed to the desk and took out a label and a pen. "Darling, think of me while you're away." He wrote it in a slanting script. He wrapped the sheer fabric around the label and tucked it between the pages of the phrase book. He met Alex's bemused look. "Best give them a reason why a bloke is carrying a perfumed silk hankie in his pocket."

His uncle laughed out loud. "I think ye'll be good at this."

He'd better be. The alternative was deadly. "I'll get the information you want." He paused. "I want something in return."

Alex's brows rose. "Oh? And what is that?"

Tom set his jaw, hating to ask for a favor but needing to all the same. "If something happens to me, I want someone to go and see my mother, tell her the truth. Tell her . . ." What? That he was leading a double life, lying and telling the truth, and trying his damndest not to slip on the knife edge he was walking on? He didn't want her to be ashamed of him. He settled for "Just tell her."

Alex merely nodded. "I'll see to it. In the meantime, I'm at the Eden. Like it or not, I'm your favorite uncle for the next few weeks, your nearest and dearest kith and kin. I'm not your father, so take the chip off your shoulder." He looked at Tom again, noting the family resemblance, perhaps, or wondering if he could trust this offshoot of illegitimacy, but his carefully guarded expression revealed nothing concrete. Now that was another family trait Tom was familiar with. He knew his own face mirrored that same canny look, his thoughts closed and private.

"I'll leave you to it, then." Alexander MacCann picked up his hat without another word and left as suddenly as he'd arrived.

CHAPTER TWENTY-FIVE

Dresden

VIVIANE ALDEN WAS a fascinating puzzle, Felix decided as they traveled to Berlin.

He'd wondered since the day in the village if she might be something other than what she seemed, a pretty foreigner on holiday. She was so serious at times, and even when she was smiling, there was a controlled edge to her gaiety. She'd said she spoke very little German, though she conversed with his mother in Ilsa's native tongue.

And ever and always, there was the constant click of her camera.

She was interested in everything she saw—mountains and flower gardens, castles and countryside, and even factories, trucks, and swastikas. She posed her lovely sister by mountain lakes and against the backdrop of a convoy of lorries loaded with crates. She seemed fascinated by rail hubs and factories. If Klaus were here, he'd be able to recite all the facts about Germany's industrial capacity, steel production, and assembly-line output, and all the rest of the lessons and indoctrinations he'd learned at school. But Klaus had gone to join his Hitler Youth troop for a summer rally. His little brother had just been made some kind of junior leader, which meant he could order his playmates around, and he got to carry the flag when they marched. It would make the little pest an even bigger prig than Otto. Ilsa was so proud of her sons—her youngest and her oldest, at least. Felix had always perplexed her.

She couldn't understand why he was content in a laboratory, closeted away out of the limelight, researching pesticides. Vermin, he might have told her, came in so many forms, but she wouldn't listen. He remembered the horror on her lovely face when as a child he'd made her the gift of a mounted display of butterflies. It had taken him weeks to gather them, gas them, and pin them so they were as vivid and lifelike as possible, even in death.

She didn't understand how important his work was. She simply hated the fact that he worked with the great Nobel Prize–winning chemist Solomon Hitzig, his boss, his teacher, his mentor, and a friend—and also a Jew.

Felix quirked a smile. Sometimes he'd tease poor Mutti with "Heil Hitzig," just to annoy her.

Hitzig was the top man in his field, a genius, his work worldrenowned, but Ilsa saw only that her son was subordinate to a Jew.

The Reich wasn't so picky. They might detest Jews enough to remove them from positions of responsibility or power—stripping great minds from the universities, sciences, and the arts—but they knew when someone was irreplaceable. Even the Nazis could not deny that Solomon Hitzig was one brilliant mind they could not do without. There were a scant handful of such rare birds. Those useful Jews were given special status, and the honor and privilege of working for Hitler, whether they wanted to or not.

He looked out the window of the car and saw that they were approaching Dresden, an ancient and lovely old city. Viviane was also gazing out the window at the ancient spires and domes, her eyes darting over the vista, pausing as if she was framing a photograph, then moving on. His mother had insisted that they bring both cars on the trip north so they'd have more space, and Otto and Julia were with Mutti in the other Daimler, while Felix and his father traveled with Viviane. Georg smiled at her rapt expression. "You are impressed, I see. We call Dresden Florence on the Elbe," his father said to her. His smile faded a little, and he turned to look at the old city, looking at it the way a man might look at a woman he'd once loved, changed now, and no longer charming in his eyes. "It used to be a place of culture, learning, and modern art."

"And now?" Viviane asked.

His mouth tightened, and his expression hardened. "And now our government has no love for modern art, and so they made it disappear. Many things have disappeared of late. Stop near the bridge," he ordered the driver. He smiled at Viviane as he helped her out of the car and pointed out the perfect vantage for a photograph—a purely tourist photo, of course, Felix noted. She dutifully raised the Leica to her eye. "This is one of my favorite views of the city, looking across the spans of this bridge, gazing at the spires. It reminds me of Oxford. Have you been to Oxford?" Georg said.

"Yes. It still holds a fond place in my stepfather's heart."

"Like all graduates." Georg smiled.

"What is this bridge called?" she asked, pointing.

"This is the Augustus Bridge. It has been here since the twelfth century. Napoleon crossed it with his armies in 1813. Shall we walk across it?"

"Yes, please," she said, and took the count's arm. Felix walked on her other side, admired her shapely, delicate limbs, her pretty summer frock and her fashionable hat, the stylish shoes with one ever-so-slightly raised sole on one side, designed to even her gait. Her cheeks were flushed by the sun, her eyes keen on the river, the birds, the people strolling past. Still her eyes flicked over every detail, paused, and moved on, as if she had a second camera in her brain. She did not look like a happy tourist.

To Felix, she looked like a spy.

Ah, but the day was sunny, and the Elbe flowed with gamboling gaiety, brightly blue under the summer sky. The golden sandstone of the city gleamed, and a surge of patriotic pride went through his breast at the beauty of his country, the history, the dignity. His father's face reflected the same emotion.

It was time, Felix thought, for a little scientific experiment. He nudged Viviane. "Now we've seen the old architecture, perhaps we should see the new. There are a number of new industrial plants near the rail station, and the modern, efficient design of those buildings is quite marvelous," he said.

He watched a spark of intense interest kindle in her eyes, and he let his smile widen.

He had her.

PART III

Berlin Games

CHAPTER TWENTY-SIX

Berlin

"WE COULD SPEND the day at Wannsee. We could go to the beach."

Tom watched the lovely Trude Unger, model and aspiring actress, pace his hotel room with restless impatience. She went to the window, flicked aside the curtain, and looked out at the Kurfürstendamm, one of Berlin's liveliest streets, frowning at the view. "Or we could find you a better hotel."

"I like this one just fine," he replied through the open door of the bathroom as he lathered his face to shave.

"You could choose whatever you like, short of the Adlon, of course."

"I doubt my paper would pay for that."

She came to lean on the doorframe, posing, to watch him. Her expression suggested impatience; her folded arms confirmed it. "You need not concern yourself over that. You have friends here. Very important friends."

"Other than you?" he asked lightly.

"Oh, but I am just your faithful interpreter and guide," she said, though they both knew she was more than that. She worked for the Gestapo, and he was her assignment. She'd probably been told to seduce him, to engage him in a little pillow talk, find out if he had any secrets and help him spill them. He'd resisted her charms, but he played along with her, and they'd come to an unspoken agreement. He didn't want to risk losing her and being reassigned to a more determined operative, so he fed her harmless gossip from the press corps, things she could report to her bosses to let them think she had Tom Graham in her pocket, that if anything truly important came up, that she'd be the first person he shared it with. In return, Tom behaved himself for the most part, didn't give her any trouble, and gave her time to pursue her true ambition, which was to become an actress, no, a *star*. He was an easy job for her, if a trifle dull. He suspected she found trying to charm him a challenge she couldn't resist. She liked being adored.

There was a knock on the door. "I ordered coffee," she said as she went to answer it. He heard her speaking in German to the waiter who wheeled the cart into the room. He could smell eggs and sausage, a good, hearty breakfast, as if he were going to work a full day on the Glasgow docks instead of doing nothing more strenuous than conducting a few interviews arranged for him by Trude. She was urging him to write a few lighthearted pieces about the beauty of Germany, the thoroughly modern and carefully ordered gaiety. That meant, of course, that someone had ordered her to steer him toward such stories, see that he wrote them, told the world how much he liked Germany and how marvelous every bloody thing about it was.

Trude had been introduced—assigned—to him when he returned to Berlin after Geoffrey's wedding. She was tall, blond, blue-eyed, and beautiful, a Valkyrie in the latest Paris fashions. She liked champagne and schnapps served together, one chilled, the other slightly warm. She was gay and bright, and she told him she was an actress at Joseph Goebbels's UFA studios. She'd fallen hard for Tom at very first sight—or pretended to—despite no encouragement from him. She wasn't his type. Her handlers would have known that if they'd bothered to look into it. He liked serious women, more intellectual and less showy. A redhead, perhaps, one who preferred to be behind the camera instead of in front of it.

He and Trude had become friends of a sort. She had simply arrived this morning, early, clad in an elegant pale-yellow suit and a saucy little hat, and walked into his hotel room. A swastika brooch formed of gold and garnets glittered in the silken folds of her artfully tied scarf. That was new. He wondered if she'd gotten a promotion since he'd last seen her—or a generous lover. She probably wasn't a true Nazi. She wasn't rabid enough for that. She simply acted the part to survive and thrive. She probably kept a photograph of Adolf Hitler inside the lid of her compact for show, in case anyone checked.

There was no point in objecting to her visit now, since she obviously wasn't going to go away. She'd be by his side for the day, watching over him.

"Orange juice or grapefruit?" she called from the main room where breakfast was being set out.

"Just coffee," he said, pressing the blade of his razor against his throat and drawing it through the thick soap. She murmured something to the waiter, and he heard the door open then close as the man left. He heard the splash of coffee as she poured a cup.

A moment later the cup rattled on the saucer. "Pah! This isn't coffee. Come, I know a charming little café on the Unter den Linden. Let's go there."

"Can't," he said, wiping the last remnants of soap from his face.

She appeared in the doorway, a frown marring her perfect face. "What? Why?"

"Press briefing. They're to tell us what there is to see during the Olympics. I understand Mr. Goebbels will be there, and Richard Strauss, the composer."

"But I arranged a visit to see a children's choir rehearsing for the opening ceremonies," she said.

He sent her a level look, one that spoke volumes. She gave in and rolled her eyes.

"All right. I shall come with you to the press briefing instead," she said. She crossed and swiped a bit of missed shaving soap off his neck with her fingertip, lingering just a second too long. He stepped away from the intimate gesture and rubbed at the spot with the towel. She stood between him and the door, her lips pursed in invitation, unable to resist one more attempt to break through his armor. Unlike ordinary German women, she wore lipstick, a blood-and-roses shade of swastika red. She was waiting for him to kiss her, to lead her into the bedroom. How many women had he known who were exactly like Trude? At home, he was a novelty for upper-class English ladies and honorable misses, an intriguing man of a lesser class with acceptable looks and suitable manners, someone to practice their wiles and their powers of seduction on, a man who didn't matter. They looked at him and wondered if they could breach the walls he put up around himself. They gave up easily enough—none had ever wanted to work that hard. Trude was more determined, of course, but she had more to lose if she failed and everything to gain if he gave in.

He stepped around her and went into the bedroom to dress. He might have closed the door, but he suspected she'd only open it again, so he didn't bother. He shrugged out of his robe and chose a clean shirt from the wardrobe and one of the two suits he owned. He left that door open, too, expecting she'd want to know what was in his closet.

She ran her manicured fingertips over the keys of his typewriter and glanced into the open armoire before she reclined on the bed, watching him. "Oh, not that tie! Have you nothing better than that? I shall have to take you shopping."

He knotted the tie anyway, ignoring her offer, and shrugged into his coat. He tucked his notebook into the inner pocket and left her in the bedroom. Breakfast had been laid out in the small sitting room, and he noted his reflection in the domed metal covers that kept the food warm. He grabbed a cup of coffee and downed it in one gulp, then glanced at his watch.

She looked less certain as she picked up her purse and followed him to the door.

"Aren't you glad to see me?" she asked as they got into the lift.

"Of course," he said. "How have you been? Any new movies?"

Those red lips pursed, and her lashes swept down to cover her eyes. "I am waiting for the results of a few auditions," she said. "Everything is shut down for the Olympics, except Leni Riefenstahl's production, and that will feature athletes, not actresses. It will be quite an extravagant thing, filming the games. The budget is huge."

He regarded her with interest but didn't bother to reply. She straightened her hat as they stepped out of the hotel into the sunlight, making herself camera ready.

It was the day before the official opening ceremonies of the 1936 Olympic Games, and Berlin was crowded with international tourists. The city had been reimagined, a movie set designed to delight the masses—clean, green, flower and flag bedecked. The German people were perfect caricatures of joy and discipline. They were, after all, as Nazi propaganda described, the true descendants of the ancient Greek Olympians—bold, intellectual, and physically perfect. They'd scientifically researched it, proven it. At center stage, the imposing sports stadium stood tall, looking as if it had been created by a race of giants— or supermen. The German people played jolly and gracious hosts. On every corner, a stalwart yet cherubic Hitler Youth stood ready to help visitors across the busy thoroughfares. The confused or lost were pointed in the right direction by kindly policemen with broad smiles.

But there were flaws in the image, too, visible to anyone who cared enough to look for them.

There were no newspapers to be had, at least not the notorious anti-Semitic ones that had been so prevalent only a month or two earlier. The newspaper boxes now held flowers or tourist pamphlets. The hateful signs painted on the windows of Jewish businesses had been scrubbed clean—everything had been scrubbed clean. The city was immaculate. Crisp Nazi pennants and banners hung from every lamppost and window, the red background sparkling like blood in the summer sunlight and the jagged black swastika crisp and cruel and spiderlike. The flags reminded visitors that all this magnificence and celebration had been brought to you by the mastermind Adolf Hitler. And with the Depression raging everywhere else in the world, the visitors were only too delighted to accept everything at face value, happy to be somewhere prosperous and pleasant. If there was something sinister behind the scenes, they didn't want to know about it. They were on holiday.

He liked Kurfürstendamm because it still felt somewhat honest. It wasn't quite as stuffy as the Unter den Linden or as tony as Friedrichstrasse. It had good cafés, simple restaurants, and shops and bars for ordinary folk. Still, he could not get past the idea that he was on a movie set, everything carefully staged to offer the director's view of perfection, complete with a glamorous starlet on his arm. He could smell the cloying sweetness of Trude's perfume. It didn't suit her. It was the scent an ingenue might wear, an innocent lass of tender years who loved flowers and hadn't been long out of the schoolroom. Trude was a woman of experience and subterfuge. He let her cling to his arm, fully aware that her Baltic-blue eyes made note of every person he spoke to, from his brief nod toward the doorman at his hotel to the man who bumped into Tom on the crowded street, murmured his pardon, scooped his fallen hat up off the pavement, and hurried on.

"He spoke to you in English!" Trude said, swiveling on her high heels to assess the man as he went on his way. It had been two words, just "My apologies." Tom's stomach clenched. It had been a mistake. If the poor chap was investigated, and the accidental encounter analyzed for anything suspicious, they'd find out that Tom knew him after all, that his name was Charlie Ellis, that he was Canadian and a journalist. The Nazis didn't like Charlie's aggressive anti-Nazi reports. They'd taken him to the border and kicked him over the line more than once. He'd simply come back.

"Do you know him?" Trude asked.

Tom shook his head. "No. I suppose I must look like a tourist," he said lightly.

"But I don't!" she replied.

He laughed. There were times when his little Nazi minder could be rather delightful in her vanity. It was the only truly honest thing about her.

He paused to look in the window of a bookstore, both to peruse the books on display and to check the reflection in the glass to see who was behind him. Charlie was standing across the street, smoking a cigarette now and watching him, his usually open expression pensive. Tom swallowed. One of them was in trouble.

The North American journalists, men like Charlie Ellis, were among the most determined to show the world the truth at any price, bugger the risks. Charlie Ellis was brutally honest in his reports. He showed the ugliness, the violence, and the plight of those who didn't agree with Germany's new order in brilliant language, and the papers that picked up his stories loved him and didn't question where he got his facts. But the Nazis did. Tom let his gaze slide over Ellis's reflection, their eyes meeting in the glass before Charlie looked away.

"*Mein Kampf,*" Trude murmured, her eyes flicking over multiple copies of the only book displayed in the window. "It's as if there are no other books in all the world."

"At least in all of Germany," Tom said. "Have you read it?"

Her eyes glazed over as she lied, an unfortunate thing for an actress. "Of course, cover to cover, twice."

They walked past a cinema that was showing a film with Hans Albers, Germany's most popular leading man. He felt Trude's hand tighten on his arm. "What I wouldn't do to work with Hans," she said. "He's filming a new picture with Lotte Lang now. How fortunate for her, but it's Lída Baarová who gets all the best parts. It's who you know as much as how talented you are. Lída's lucky—she lives right next door to Herr Goebbels on lake Wannsee." And if rumors were true, the Czech actress was the propaganda minister's mistress. The Nazis saw beauty and either took it for themselves and distorted it to fit their own ideals, or they destroyed it if they could not.

AN HOUR LATER, he stood with other handpicked journalists, taking notes, while Joseph Goebbels spoke, his smile sly, the SS guards by his side stalwart and watchful.

And faithful Trude stood by his side, smiling for the cameras, the little swastika brooch on her breast glinting in the explosion of flashbulbs. And all the while, she kept one hand on Tom's sleeve and one eye on every scribbled word he wrote.

CHAPTER TWENTY-SEVEN

JULIA WAS ALMOST beside herself with delight at the sights of Berlin. Viviane joined her in staring out the windows of the car as they drove through the city and Felix and Otto pointed out the marvels of Berlin's busy streets, the Unter den Linden and Friedrichstrasse and noisy, hectic Kurfürstendamm, lined with shops and cafés, clubs and bars. The count and countess were in the second car and had gone directly to the Hotel Adlon to ensure their reservations were in order and their rooms were ready.

"Kurfürstendamm is my favorite street in all Berlin," Felix said. "No matter what time of day or night it is, there's excitement here and so much to see and do. Look, there's the Quartier Latin, which is one of the best clubs in Berlin. I saw the actress Pola Negri there once."

"You did?" Julia said, her eyes widening. "I saw her film *Mazurka* in London last autumn. It was wonderful. She is so glamorous, so talented."

"I understand that *Mazurka* is one of the führer's favorite films," Otto said, approving Julia's enthusiasm with a fond smile, and she blushed with pleasure.

"Is there any chance we might see her in person while we're here?"

Julia asked him. "At that club Felix mentioned, perhaps? Maybe she'll bring Charlie Chaplin. I've read that they're very good friends."

Otto's brow furrowed, and Felix laughed. "Oh, you won't see the Little Tramp in Berlin. His latest film, *Modern Times*, has been banned by Herr Goebbels."

"Why?" Julia asked.

"It wrongly promotes Communism," Otto said sharply, his mouth a flat line of disapproval now. "We shall see other films if you like, suitable ones."

Julia batted her lashes at him. "I have so much to learn about music and movies. I am glad I have you to teach me," she simpered, and it was Viviane's turn to frown. Felix nudged Viviane's arm and rolled his eyes.

"*May* we go to the Quartier Latin?" Julia persisted.

Otto offered a thin smile. "Perhaps. But only if my mother approves."

"Oh, but with you by my side, then surely—" Julia's pretty plea was interrupted as the car came to a halt, surrounded by a jam of other vehicles and pedestrians.

"What's happening?" Julia asked, looking out the window.

"Go and find out," Otto ordered the driver in a far sterner tone than the one he used to coo at Julia.

They watched as the driver approached the policeman, who pointed to a knot of people at the side of the road. The policeman tried to dismiss him, but the driver said something that made the officer's jaw drop. He turned to look at the Schroeders' Daimler. He hurried over at once, and Otto rolled down the window.

"What is the reason for this delay?" Otto said coldly.

The policeman removed his cap. "Good afternoon, Obersturmführer von Schroeder. A man was knocked down in an accident, a foreign journalist. We are awaiting the ambulance."

Viviane's stomach knotted, and Julia gasped. "A foreign journalist? Vee, isn't that friend of Geoffrey's here in Berlin?"

Both Otto and Felix turned to look at her.

"You have a friend who is a journalist?" Felix asked.

Viviane didn't reply, busy looking out the window, trying to see past the crowd. Was that blood on the pavement? Her stomach turned.

"He's not a friend, precisely," Julia replied. "Just an acquaintance, someone my brother-in-law knows."

Viviane glanced at her, saw the faint concern on Julia's pretty face. No, he wasn't a friend exactly. He was more than that, or less. She realized how little she knew about him. Who could she send word to if the victim was indeed Tom Graham? Who would mourn him? She felt desperation rise like a bubble in her throat, and she reached for the door handle.

Otto's hand clasped her wrist. His fingers were cold and dry despite the heat of the day, and she glanced at him. "I must insist you stay in the car. Crowds can be . . . unpredictable," he said. There was curiosity in his eyes as he scanned her face, and Felix was looking at her with the same expression.

I know him, she wanted to say, considering pushing Otto's hand away to get out anyway, but his grip tightened subtly, as if he'd guessed her intention. *Berlin is dangerous.* Tom had warned her. She'd thought he meant for her. She pulled her hand back, clasped it with the other one in her lap.

"We don't even know if it is Geoff's friend," Julia said. "Is he Scottish, with dark hair?" she asked the policeman, who still hovered by the open window, apparently waiting for any further instructions Otto might have. He looked confused and slid his gaze toward Otto.

"Is he *English*?" Otto rephrased in German, as if there was no difference, but the policeman shrugged. "I don't know, Obersturmführer.

All we know is that he is not German, and he has a press pass in his pocket. It is quite damaged and impossible to read."

Damaged. What if Tom was lying in the street? What if that was indeed his blood that bystanders were carefully avoiding stepping in as they ringed the victim, stared down at him with vague curiosity? The expressions were strangely guarded, dispassionate, as if scenes like this one were commonplace. Viviane's stomach churned. How could that be, that one could look at the scene of a tragic accident and show no pity?

Julia put a hand to her cheek. "What if we have to write to Margaret with the news that Mr. Graham is dead? It would quite ruin our holiday."

"*Is* he dead?" Otto asked the policeman, his lips tight, his tone cool as if it made no difference at all beyond the inconvenience of the delay.

"No, not dead, though his legs are badly broken," the policeman said quickly.

"Did the driver not see him?" Felix asked.

The policeman's brow furrowed. "Perhaps not. According to witnesses, the car was going very fast when it hit him." He looked at Otto again. "It appeared to be a government vehicle, black, with official—"

Otto silenced him with a gesture of his hand. "Wait here," he said to the rest of them as he got out. He shut the door and stepped away, looming over the policeman, speaking quietly. He followed him through the crowd, which automatically parted. Viviane held her breath, waiting for the shock of recognition. If it was Tom, if it was, what could she do? But they were too far away, and she couldn't see the victim. Otto was issuing orders, and others were jumping to obey. He returned to the car and got in.

"I have ensured that an ambulance is coming, and that he will be taken care of," he said to Viviane.

"His name?" Julia asked, and Otto glanced at her, irritated for a moment, as if he resented the impertinence of her question. He simply shook his head.

"What hospital?" Viviane asked, her mouth too dry to say more than that.

Otto's sharp expression softened itself into a grin. "Why, the closest one, of course. He will be well cared for, I assure you. The best thing we can do at the moment is to continue on to the hotel. My mother will be concerned if we are late. Drive on," he ordered, and the car moved forward.

Viviane scanned the faces of the crowd as they slid past. All that careful curiosity now turned to the Daimler and the people inside. A woman on the sidewalk held a handkerchief to her cheek, shocked by the accident, or perhaps she was just mopping away a bead of sweat in the heat of the day. How thoroughly Germans hid their emotions, cast their faces into blankness, as if human concern was dangerous. She held her breath as she tried to catch a glimpse of the victim—of Tom, if it was him—as the car edged past, but someone had tossed a coat over him. One leg was twisted at an impossible angle, and his hat lay in the gutter. She saw the notebook, like the one Tom used, crumpled and bloody in the gutter. Another policeman bent to pick it up, tucking it into his pocket. He smartly saluted Otto as the car passed, and others turned, regarded them more carefully before they, too, raised their arms.

"They probably thought you were the führer himself," Felix quipped as they moved past the scene and picked up speed. Otto ignored him.

The incident behind them, Otto grinned at Julia. "I think we must continue our tour another day," he said ruefully. "My mother will be waiting," he said again.

"And no one dares to keep Ilsa von Schroeder waiting," Felix added.

"Not even the Gestapo. She won't worry. She'll probably be delighted when she hears a foreign reporter was run down in the street." He earned a sharp glare from his brother, who smoothly changed the subject.

"The Olympics begin tomorrow," Otto said. "It will be a busy day, with so much to see. We shall settle you in at the hotel and get a good night's sleep."

"Will we see the führer tomorrow?" Julia asked, as if she, too, had forgotten about the accident, that Tom Graham—or someone, even if they didn't know him—might be badly hurt or dead. Viviane's fingers tightened until her knuckles were white, and she swallowed the lump in her throat, held herself still. There was nothing she could do now, not until they reached the hotel, and she could telephone the Hotel am Zoo, the place he'd marked in her travel guide. What if he didn't answer?

What if he did?

She turned to find Felix regarding her with naked interest. She smoothed her expression to placidity.

Otto smiled. "Yes, of course you'll see the führer," he told Julia, and Viviane's attention jerked to her stepsister. She was staring at Otto with utter delight.

"Then I shall practice my salute."

The car pulled up at the hotel, and the doorman reached in to help the ladies from the car. Viviane felt nausea roll in her belly, couldn't bring herself to touch the proffered hand behind the congenial smile of welcome. She slid out and stood as Julia alighted.

"We shall see you for dinner later," Otto said to her. "But now, I have an errand to take care of."

Felix clasped Viviane's hand, unfurling her tight fingers, smiling at her. "Don't worry. Tomorrow the blood will have been washed from the street, and all will be well." He leaned closer. "I think you intend to rush up to your room and call all the hospitals," he whispered. "Don't do that." He nodded toward Otto, "Let him do it." He scanned her face, serious for once. "This is Berlin, and everyone is anxious to see that everything is gay, bright, and glorious for our visitors. No shadow will be allowed to fall over these games, no hint of scandal or unhappiness. You must smile until your face aches, and simply enjoy yourself. Nothing else matters. Nothing else will be allowed to. If it is your . . . acquaintance . . . then it would be better not to make a fuss. It might make it worse for him. Do you understand?"

"And if it wasn't?" she asked through tight lips. Her body was so tense she felt as if she might shatter. She glanced around, saw the polite, welcoming smiles of the hotel staff, smiles that didn't quite reach their eyes.

"If it wasn't . . ." Felix looked at Otto again, then looked back at her. "Then the victim was merely a stranger. Does that make it easier?" he asked. "I think you have a soft heart for victims, and perhaps you see victims where there aren't any. Is that true? You probably pet stray dogs at home, wanting only to help. But here the dogs will turn on you."

"Are you coming, Felix?" Otto asked. "I can drop you at your apartment on my way."

"Yes, of course," Felix said, turning. He looked back at Viviane with a wink.

"Go inside, have a cup of tea, and tell Mutti we were wonderful tour guides. We shall see you later for dinner."

Viviane watched him go. It was her second warning of the danger, including Tom's. What would he want her to do? What did *she* want to do?

"You go up. I want to buy a postcard from the kiosk," she said to Julia in the lobby.

"Can't it wait?" Julia asked. "We must change for dinner."

Viviane forced a smile. "My mother is every bit as fierce as Ilsa, and I promised to write a card every day."

"All right, but don't be long," Julia said, and let the bellhop lead her toward the waiting elevator.

Viviane crossed to the telephones. "Hotel am Zoo," she said to the operator, and heard the call connect. "Mr. Graham's room," she told the desk clerk who answered.

She held the receiver in icy hands, her throat dry. She'd hang up when he answered, just needed to be sure he was safe.

It rang a dozen times with no answer. "Is there a message?" the desk clerk asked, coming back on the line.

She shut her eyes. "No," she said, and replaced the phone in the cradle.

CHAPTER TWENTY-EIGHT

Saturday, August 1, 1936

NO ONE EVEN mentioned the accident the next morning. Not Felix, who arrived at the Adlon to take breakfast with his family and their guests, or Julia, or even the newspaper that had been placed next to the count's plate. Viviane glanced at the headlines, but they were all about today's opening ceremonies. The count caught her frown and thought she was looking at the weather report, it seemed.

"How disappointing. This is not what Berlin is usually like in August," he said, frowning at the heavy gray clouds that squatted outside the arched windows of the Hotel Adlon's café. "There is a prediction of rain showers throughout the day."

"Will we need umbrellas?" Julia asked. Otto was busy with official duties all day, and they wouldn't see him until the opening ceremonies concluded this afternoon. Julia had carefully chosen her outfit for the grand event, a smart blue suit with red trim on the pockets and collar. The matching red hat was designed to make her stand out in the crowd, a beacon so Otto might see her from a distance. Viviane knew Julia feared he wouldn't be able to see her hat—or much else—if she was tucked away under an umbrella, lost in a sea of other umbrellas.

"I thought you English were used to rain," Felix said, winking at Viviane.

"Perhaps it will stop by this afternoon and the sun will come out," Viviane said, more for Julia than Felix. "We're used to that in England as well."

"It will not rain," the countess said firmly. "The führer will not permit it. This is an important day."

Her husband and son sent her dubious looks. "Even *he* cannot stop the rain from falling, Mutti," Felix said, and the countess glanced around her nervously.

"Lower your voice, Felix. You never know who's listening, or how they might interpret even a seemingly innocent comment made in jest. Your brother has warned you to watch your tongue."

Felix leaned toward his mother and whispered, "Surely no one could possibly doubt the loyalty of Otto von Schroeder's family, not with Otto in the honor guard and our little Klaus a flag bearer at the Hitler Youth rally this morning. We are the perfect modern German family, are we not? Why, we're even playing host to two lovely young foreigners of rank and beauty, both of whom are utterly dazzled by our country." He winked at Viviane. "Are you not dazzled, Fraülein Alden?"

"Stop whispering," the countess said sternly, countermanding her earlier order. "People will think we are plotting something." Felix grinned at her, and she glared another warning at him before she turned to her husband. "We have a busy day ahead. This morning we will attend the Hitler Youth rally in the Lustgarten. I promised Klaus we'd be there. I reserved places on the roof of the Old Museum, so he might look up and see us."

"But how will we see *him*?" the count asked, tucking into his breakfast with gusto. "There will be nearly thirty thousand children there, all dressed the same."

"He is a flag bearer and a squad leader," the countess reminded her husband, stirring her coffee with sharp little strokes of her spoon. "This afternoon, we must take our seats at the stadium early to avoid the crush." Her breakfast remained virtually untouched. Perhaps she was too excited or anxious about the day's events, or the hearty meal was too rich for her slim figure. Julia copied their hostess, barely nibbling on the edge of a bit of toast. Viviane toyed with the fruit and cheese and croissant that had arrived with her coffee. She glanced at the door of the elegant café and wondered if she could politely excuse herself and try telephoning Tom again.

"Have you plenty of film?" the countess asked Viviane, interrupting her thoughts. "I'd like a photograph of Klaus if he is fortunate enough to be chosen to meet the dignitaries. Otto is trying to arrange it."

"We could always stop on our way to the rally and load up on another dozen rolls of that new color Agfa film," Felix said. "D'you suppose that will be enough? We'll want to get Herr Göring's good side, and he's a large man. Goebbels is very short and thin by comparison, and the führer is larger than life, a spectacle in his own right. He will have hundreds, thousands, tens of thousands of cameras aimed at him at every moment. Be sure to capture that—our mighty leader at his best, proudest, and most triumphant."

The countess sent her middle son another quelling look, and he sent her a cheeky grin in return and tossed his napkin on the table. "I'm afraid I must take my leave. It might be a holiday today and Saturday, but I have an errand at the lab before the opening ceremonies this afternoon."

"We must be in our seats early. There will be a dreadful crush, and we must set an example and be punctual," the countess reminded him again. "You won't be late?"

"Of course not. No matter how dense the crowds, I shall wade though the terrible tide and find you." Felix leaned down close to his mother. "Now what is protocol today? Shall I give you the Hitler salute now, kiss your hand, or simply walk away?"

Ilsa's lips pinched in disapproval, and she sipped her coffee and ignored him. He came around the table and kissed Viviane's hand instead, then Julia's, with a resounding smack of his lips, then shook his father's hand and bowed slightly. "Enjoy the rally, and wave to Klaus for me," he said cheerily, and was gone.

"You really must speak to Felix," the countess said to her husband. "He'll get into trouble."

"One of Germany's best and brightest young chemists?" the count asked, his silver brows rising toward the severe line of his clipped hair.

Ilsa showed no pride. Her eyes were as hard as glass as she watched Felix walk away. "He should be in uniform, like his brothers."

"We've given two sons to the cause. I believe that we've done our duty. There must be a few free thinkers left," the count said.

A passing waiter overheard and sent him a sideways look but said nothing. The countess's cheeks flushed. "Our family is devoted to the führer and the Third Reich," she said loudly.

The count sent her a flat look as he folded his napkin with calm precision and laid it beside his plate. "I believe estimates of the crowds will prove to be quite correct. We'd best go to our rooms and get ready to leave," he said mildly.

A few drops of cranky rain flicked at the windows as they rose and filed out of the café, with the waiter watching them go with dull speculation.

But then, Viviane was growing used to being watched. Out of pure contrariness, she sent the man a bright smile, raised the Leica, and took his picture, the man watching her watching him watching her.

CHAPTER TWENTY-NINE

The Lustgarten

"WE SHOULD BE up there," Trude said to Tom as they made their way to the press area at the Old Museum for the youth rally. The flat roof of the building had been converted to a viewing platform, offering a bird's-eye view of the ceremony taking place below.

Tom scanned the battalions of Hitler Youth, proud, upright, sober young Germans in perfectly orderly lines. Not a single child was giggling or fidgeting or whispering. It was most unsettling. They stood row on row on row, some twenty-nine thousand of them, perfectly still, eyes front, spines stiff, boots polished, eyes gleaming with patriotic pride. Tom wanted to snap his fingers or shout "fire!" to see if they were real.

It was chilling to see this army of babies, but this was not merely a gathering of children for a ceremony. It was a calculated demonstration of the absolute power and control Hitler held over the hearts and minds and bodies of Germany's youth. They were being trained to do anything for their führer, to obey his orders without question, even give their lives if he asked it of them. Their older brothers had already been conscripted, were off drilling and marching and occupying the Rhineland.

Tom glanced around at the crowd. Did no one else see the menace of this? Proud mothers waved handkerchiefs embroidered with swastikas, fathers who'd fought in the Great War stood at attention with their sons, the next generation of soldiers. A band played, and a children's choir sang military songs and hymns of devotion to the führer, promising to serve him unto death. In a few years' time these fresh-faced boys would be men, soldiers who'd already trained for years.

Beside him Trude giggled and waggled her manicured fingertips at several young boys who were watching her pass by, their mouths hanging open at her beauty. They grinned back, and Tom relaxed. Perhaps they were just lads after all. Then their commander, a boy only a few years older than they were, sternly ordered them back into position, and they obeyed at once, snapping to attention with alarming precision.

Trude walked on, enjoying the appreciative looks from older men in the crowd instead. She may not be a movie star, but she knew how to act like one.

Tom took out his notebook, made note of the names of the men on the podium waiting to address the assembled youth. Baldur von Schirach, the Nazi Party's national youth leader, stood with an official for German sport and the minister for Science, Education, and National Culture. Under his direction, the educational system had been transformed. Teachers had been informed that their primary duty was to raise and educate good Nazis. He'd made the Nazi salute mandatory in classrooms across the nation and had dismissed the theories and discoveries of Jewish scientists like Albert Einstein as flawed and useless. They would no longer be taught.

Propaganda Minister Joseph Goebbels, the tiny, elegant, quick-eyed figure, was arrogant as he surveyed the youth arrayed before him, smug and satisfied at this, another triumph of propaganda, subterfuge, and sleight of hand. Tom swallowed the slick sourness that formed at the back of his throat, and the hair on the back of his neck rose as the propaganda minister's dark eyes swiveled in his direction, passed by him, then returned to hold his gaze. It was like staring into the eyes of a snake. Then Goebbels glanced at Trude, and one dark brow twitched, the tiniest acknowledgment of her. Tom heard Trude's sharp, pleased little intake of breath at the propaganda minister's notice.

Tom took his place among the press. Simon Bell, his colleague from the *Herald*, nodded to him. "Heard about Charlie Ellis?" he muttered behind his hand, his eyes forward.

Tom glanced at him. "Ellis? The *Toronto Star* correspondent?" he said, his voice as bland as he could make it, even as his skin prickled.

"Yes, that's him. He met with an accident yesterday while crossing the street. Hit by a car, both legs shattered. He might not walk again—yet is he concerned about that? Not a bit. He's more upset that they took his notebook. We warned him to be more careful, weeks ago. He was taking an awful risk. No one knows how he got access to the information he used. Bloody marvelous work, worthy of a spy, I'd say. Maybe the Nazis are right about him."

"Where did you hear this?" Tom asked, his heart pounding, a bead of icy sweat sliding down his spine. Simon smirked at him.

"Something Tom Graham doesn't know about? A story that slipped your notice while you were hobnobbing with the locals?" he said, and slid a look at Trude. "A friend of his, another Canadian reporter, was supposed to meet Ellis yesterday, but he didn't show up. The Gestapo came instead."

"Was Ellis arrested?" Tom asked. He pictured the bold reporter in a dank jail cell with an expert interrogator asking pointed questions.

"He's in the hospital," Simon said. He looked around. "I daresay if not for the new rules that apply during the Olympics—the kind and friendly treatment of foreigners—things might have been different."

"He'll be sent home, I take it, to Canada?" Tom asked, scanning the crowd.

Simon grunted. "If he lives, I suppose he will—if they don't pin some trumped-up crime on him. They'll make it something even his embassy can't get him out of."

"Is there anything they can use?" Tom asked, his jaw tight. "In his notebook, perhaps?"

Simon shrugged. "He didn't share his ideas with me. He had his own informant, I hear, someone well-placed. Any idea who that might be? That poor bastard should be warned, just in case."

Tom's belly rolled over. The message was loud and clear. A cheer went up as a runner entered the Lustgarten, carrying the Olympic torch. He moved between the assembled ranks of Hitler Youth and climbed the steps of the Old Museum, where he touched the flame to a cauldron, setting it alight. The roar of the delighted spectators was deafening.

"Bloody marvelous, isn't it?" Simon murmured. "What a spectacle they've created." He put his fist to his chest. "You can't help but feel it, can you?" He indicated the audience on the roof of the Old Museum. "The public, the tourists, everyone—they're eating it up."

"Blood and circuses," Tom said through tight lips.

"Aye," Simon said. "What will you write about this day, Graham?"

Tom regarded his colleague for a moment. He was living a lie. "The truth," he said.

Simon smiled, filling the gap between his front teeth with his tongue.

"But who's truth? Theirs or ours? Whose side are you on, Tommy? It's been a mite hard to tell lately."

Tom felt his stomach lurch again. He played the game he'd been assigned to and hated himself, felt dirty doing it, not heroic. He'd made up his own rules, found a way to live with himself, giving Charlie information on the sly. Perhaps they hadn't been sly enough. What would Charlie say if they questioned him? Would he give Tom up as his source?

He thought of the Canadian reporter's go-to-hell attitude toward the Nazi regime, their warnings and threats. He ignored all of it, wrote the truth. He'd been good at the subterfuge, liked it, considered it a game. It had been amusing, almost fun, and it seemed utterly foolproof. They found ways to meet without meeting, to exchange notes and information without appearing to even know each other. Yesterday morning, when he'd bumped into Charlie on the street, the blow had knocked both their hats to the pavement. Tom picked up Charlie's hat, and Charlie had taken Tom's, a clever bit of sleight of hand, an exchange of the information tucked under the lining. How many times had they exchanged hats as if by accident in cafés or on park benches? He wondered where Charlie's hat—*his* hat—was now. He glanced at Trude, made sure she wasn't listening before he replied to Simon.

Whose truth would he report? Simon had asked him. Charlie Ellis's truth.

"My truth," he said, and let Simon make of that what he wished.

CHAPTER THIRTY

THE LABORATORY WAS empty of scientists and assistants. The stainless steel worktables were clear, the gleaming equipment neatly covered against dust. The lights were off, the shades half closed, giving the huge room an abandoned look.

Only the corner office, framed with wide glass windows so the occupant could observe every workbench and table, was occupied. Felix saw the professor's gray head bent over the surface of the desk as he entered the lab.

"Professor Hitzig?" Felix called out so he wouldn't startle the old man. Hitzig cringed easily, had much to fear. Still, the chemist jerked back at the sound of the call, and Felix saw him hurriedly tuck the notebook he'd been writing in into his pocket as Felix approached. He pasted a reassuring smile on his face and held out a brown paper parcel. "I brought you a pretzel, still hot."

The man behind the desk, the great Nobel Prize winner, the unmatched genius, relaxed and smiled and pushed his glasses up his nose. He wasn't as old as he looked—the last few years had taken their toll. He lived in terror, sure the next visitor to this lab would be the Gestapo, coming to arrest him for the crime of being a Jew. He'd seen it happen to other colleagues, men as brilliant as he was. They were relieved of their posts at universities and laboratories, their life's work destroyed in front of them before they were thrown into the street, humiliated, made to disappear. Felix knew Hitzig feared he would suffer the same fate sooner or later, that his work would be left unfinished or misunderstood. To Solomon Hitzig, his work was everything. But the Nazis let him stay on, because no one else could do what Solomon Hitzig could. They had need of him and couldn't get rid of him. Not yet, at least.

Felix smiled brightly at the professor. Hitzig had no family now, and he loved Felix like the son who had disappeared from his life years ago. Felix was his assistant, his protégé, and his friend. Together they were working on a formula, not quite finished yet, that was of the utmost interest to the Nazis. They were eagerly awaiting the last details, the final, perfect version of the new gas, a deadly and more efficient fumigant for pests, or so they claimed. They told the world that the new chemical would improve farming, increase production, feed the world, but it had a darker purpose as well. Felix knew that, and so did the professor. He knew Hitzig feared that the Nazis might turn his pesticide into a weapon, turn it on people instead of locusts and caterpillars. The professor could not stop his work, plead moral grounds. Not only would the Nazis kill him if he did, but he was a proud man, a true scientist, and his mind would not allow him to stop before he had the answer, knew the secret, had battled nature one more time and won. The formula had become Hitzig's holy grail, his obsession, the pure, magnificent potion he was certain would save the world—and his own life—if used for peaceful means. He was fooling himself if he thought that's why Hitler's regime wanted it. Felix knew the great professor was under the spell of his own genius, his former power and prestige, and the sheer terror of what would happen if he failed.

Felix sat down and smiled across the desk at the man who'd once been so confident in himself and his work. He was now a shell, hollowed out by fear, thin and anxious. His hair had turned gray almost overnight, and his back was stooped from trying to look small and insignificant.

A car horn sounded outside, and Hitzig flinched and glanced anxiously at the window. "It's just a car. The traffic is quite impossible today, and tempers are fraying," Felix said soothingly.

The professor forced himself to relax. He folded his hands on the desk and peered at Felix.

"Yes, of course." He pushed his spectacles up his nose yet again. "Shouldn't you be out celebrating the start of the Olympics yourself, my boy?"

Felix shrugged. "I thought you might need help. I knew it would be quiet here today, good for getting some work done. I still have that compound to finish testing."

Hitzig scanned Felix's face, and Felix kept his expression soft, reassuring, adoring until the great chemist nodded. "Yes," he murmured. "Yes. Thank you, but it can wait until Monday."

"Why wait?" Felix said. "Have you finalized the formula? We could test it immediately."

Hitzig's eyes slid away. "No, not yet."

Felix regarded him. He knew the professor well, better than anyone else. He knew the whole story of his life, had helped him with his work for nearly five years, first as a student and now as his premier lab assistant, second in charge.

He glanced at the small, framed picture on the professor's desk, the portrait of himself with his late wife, taken during the war, when he'd been part of the team that developed gas weapons. Hitzig believed gas was humane because it killed or wounded quickly and did not cause the terrible destruction of traditional bombs and bullets.

His wife had not agreed.

"This gas will kill the pests that eat our crops. It will improve production and increase yields. We will share it with the world, and no one will ever go hungry," Hitzig murmured, a mantra, a spell he repeated over and over. Felix wondered if he was speaking to him or to the woman in the photograph, a plea for understanding.

"It would indeed be a great gift to mankind," Felix said, to remind the professor that he was still there. And it *would* be a gift if the world was truly good and Germany wasn't ruled by a madman.

Last year, the Italians had used poison gas in their conquest of Ethiopia, devastating the civilian population. The Germans had watched with great interest.

Once the Nazis had what they wanted from Hitzig, he'd simply disappear. Someone else, someone Aryan, would take the credit for Hitzig's work. Felix felt a morsel of pity for him, but he was an idealist in a world of hard practicalities, of hatred. Felix didn't hate anyone, or love them, either, with any kind of fervor. He didn't understand why the Nazis hated the Jews to the extent they did. Why not blame the French or the Communists? The Jews had become a political tool, a common foe, and Hitler held the magic wand to vanquish them. He waved that wand, cast his spells, murmured incantations, and roared curses to mesmerize the people, bring them to heel, give them a reason to join him, love him, obey him.

Order, bread, and pride. Felix swallowed a sneer at the stupidity of all of it and kept smiling for the professor's benefit.

Everyone thought they were united in a common cause, but it was every man for himself in the new regime. No one else understood that, saw the truth of it, but Felix did. Other fools would die for an illusion, a lie, but he was smarter than that, smarter than anyone knew, even Hitzig, the great genius, the fool.

Felix unwrapped the pretzel, still warm, and pushed it across the desk toward his mentor. The fragrance of warm bread filled the room. "There's another reason why I came today."

"What's that?" Hitzig asked, breaking the pretzel in half, passing some back to Felix.

Felix let his expression turn serious. "The time has come, Professor. I think we must get you out of Germany."

"Now? But I haven't finished—"

"No, but you will. You're almost done. The final compound is—"

But Hitzig was shaking, breathing fast, his eyes rolling in terror.

"How? They watch me night and day. They will never allow me to leave."

Felix leaned forward and took the old man's icy fingers in his own. "The Olympics will have everyone busy and distracted. I have an idea."

CHAPTER THIRTY-ONE

Olympic Stadium

"'THE GATES OF the Olympic Stadium will open at one o'clock, and spectators are instructed to make their way into the area in an orderly fashion and be in their seats by three thirty,'" Julia read from the Olympic program as the count's car pulled up at the gates of the massive sports complex. It was a breathtaking building that spoke of grandeur and glory as it dwarfed the human beings pouring into it. Viviane looked up at the imposing concrete structure, bold and modern and terrifying, square against the delicacy of the interlocking Olympic rings that adorned the entrance. How did one begin to photograph such a gargantuan building?

"Look at all these people," Julia said as the car slowly edged through the eager tide of visitors pouring around them. Uniforms—the SS in black, the storm troopers in brown, and army-in-field gray—were everywhere, standing steadfast and watchful, boulders in the stream as tourists in brightly colored clothes flowed around them.

"We shall be fine once we are inside," Ilsa said. "We have reserved seats to the left of the führer's box."

"She cannot wait to see the führer himself, in person, and all the men seated with him," the count said to Viviane and Julia, regarding his wife. "She brought binoculars for all of us."

Ilsa tipped her chin up. "And why not? This is a celebration of great historic importance, a gift from Germany and our führer to the entire world. The whole world is here to admire our leader, and it is our patriotic duty as Germans to salute him. He is a great man, and he has created a marvel."

She straightened her hat and pinched her cheeks as she got out, squared her shoulders as if she was going into battle. The crowds surged around them, and the count reached for Viviane and Julia, took their arms. "I think we'd best stay close so no one gets lost, don't you?" he said, and guided them into the stadium.

FROM THEIR SEATS inside, Julia took the binoculars and scanned the crowd for celebrities and people she knew. She carefully marked their names on her program. "Look, there's Charles Lindbergh, the American flier, seated next to Hermann Göring!" she said. "How pretty his wife is!" Her smile faded. "And there's Diana Guinness and her sister. How sick making! I can't stand Unity Mitford."

"I didn't know you'd met them," Viviane said, following Julia's narrowed gaze. The lovely and notorious English Mitford sisters were indeed ensconced in Hitler's private box. Diana was Oswald Mosley's mistress. Phillip knew her well and found her charming. Her younger sister Unity Mitford was Hitler's "particular friend."

"Of course I haven't met them," Julia said. "Margaret and Geoffrey know Diana."

She wrote Diana's name in her program but not Unity's.

Viviane scanned the crowd herself, the press box in particular, just a dozen feet or so below their seats, holding her breath, looking for

Tom. He wasn't there. Her heart constricted, and she was suddenly sure he'd been the reporter run down in the street. She swept the crowd again—and saw him.

He was seated among the most favored members of the press corps, separated from the other foreign journalists, closer to the dignitaries. He was alive and healthy. She gasped, pressed her hand against her racing heart, almost giddy with relief, and the count looked at her.

"Are you quite all right, my dear?" he asked in his perfect English. She looked into his eyes, saw the dignity and strength and dismay in the blue depths, the reflection of swastikas that waved around them. She tried to pull away, but his hand tightened. "Do you find the crowds overwhelming? Don't look at them." He pointed up toward the sky. "Look up. The sky is empty and clean and pure. I used to look up at the sky during the war, at the clouds or the stars. It made it bearable for a moment, allowed one to go on in the face of the impossible." She glanced at him, but his eyes were turned upward, his brow furrowed. Above the stadium, a huge zeppelin floated into view, decked out in swastika flags, the massive airship all but blotting out the cloudy sky. It seemed there was no place to look where there was not a pointed boast of the might of the German regime.

The sight reminded her, and no doubt Georg von Schroeder, that another war was coming, and looking away wouldn't stop it. What would he do? What would her father have done in this moment? Her breath caught in her chest, a hard, aching, bitter bubble of dismay.

She looked for Tom again, wanted the reassurance that he was still there, still safe. This time, he was looking back at her. His gaze, even half shadowed under the brim of his hat, was as powerful as a touch. It was reassurance, warning, and relief. She half rose from her seat, wanting to rush to him, to tell him how worried she'd been. Then a willowy blond beauty touched his arm, diverting his attention and breaking the spell, and he turned away, followed the woman's point to the west gate of the stadium. A deafening cheer rose, and the crowd was suddenly on their feet, and she lost sight of Tom.

Adolf Hitler entered the stadium with Olympic committee officials. Screams of adulation filled the stadium, reverberating through Viviane's chest, rising through the soles of her feet, taking all the air out of the vast space.

"There he is!" Julia cried, and Viviane looked at her, surprised by her gushing delight for the German leader, but she was pointing somewhere else. "There's Otto!" He must have been in the honor guard that flanked the delegation, a phalanx of identical men in identical uniforms, all tall and fair-haired. How Julia knew which one was Otto was a mystery to Viviane.

Her stepsister's exultation was drowned out by the frenzy of the crowd, a hundred thousand people on their feet chanting Hitler's name, arms raised, a human hedgehog of manic devotion. Close by, a woman fainted in a fit of rapture. Another was screaming with tears streaming down her cheeks.

Viviane had to remind herself for once to raise the camera, take pictures, her hands shaking as she clicked the shutter as fast as she could.

On the field, a blond child in a white dress ran to the führer, offered up a bouquet of flowers, saluted, then dipped a curtsy.

The orchestra played the double anthem, a combination of the German national anthem and the "Horst-Wessel-Lied," and it blared through the speakers, an accompaniment to the screams of the crowd.

Hitler arrived at the podium, a distant, tiny figure on the vast field, yet somehow larger than life, a colossus. Was anyone looking at anything else? He stood behind the microphone, silent for a moment, a perfect pause that focused the attention on himself, made everyone draw a breath and hold it in anticipation. He looked around, surveying the adoring crowds as they surveyed him, his shoulders squared, his expression smug, pleased by the adoration. He held up his hand, a salute, a command, a blessing, and the crowd fell silent. In the revered hush, he declared the games open. Only that, a few brief words that echoed through the loudspeakers, reverberated off the hard concrete of the stadium, filled the air, even as he stepped back to take his seat.

The great composer Richard Strauss stepped up to the conducting stand to perform his "Olympic Hymn," facing the Olympic Symphony Orchestra and a choir made up of three thousand singers.

There were cameras everywhere, evidenced by the click of thousands of shutters, the pop of flashbulbs. Movie cameras mounted on trucks on the field below followed the action, pointed in every direction. What did they see? Viviane wondered. What images of this day and this moment would they capture?

You see what you're looking for, Julia had told Viviane weeks ago, when they first arrived in Germany. Then, Julia had wanted mountains and waterfalls, parties and flirtation. Now, Viviane watched as her stepsister raised her arm and opened her throat and screamed "*heil*" in unison with the people around her, her eyes bright, caught in the moment. She saw Viviane watching her and grinned. "Come on, Vee—get into the spirit of things. People will think you're a stick!"

People *were* frowning at her, Viviane realized, wondering why her arm wasn't raised in the Hitler salute. With shaking hands, she put the camera to her eye and clicked the shutter at anything and everything. These shots wouldn't turn out. She wasn't concentrating on focus or composition.

But no one could expect her to salute Hitler while she was busy taking pictures.

More deafening cheers rose again as a runner entered the stadium carrying a torch. "'The flame came all the way from Greece. It symbolizes the connection between the first Olympics and these games,'" Julia said, leaning close to Viviane's ear, reading from the program. The runner climbed the steps and raised the torch high above a cauldron. He, too, paused for a dramatic instant, the moment choreographed, carefully staged for the greatest effect, before he touched the burning brand to the rim of the bronze bowl.

The flame leaped to life, and thousands of doves were released into the air, flying for the sky and freedom in hectic patterns, adding their panicked voices to the crowd's cries of delight. Then the guns fired a salute. The frightened birds released a storm of shit, and it rained down on the assembled athletes, spattering hats and jackets and hair, and the cadence of the crowd turned to horror or laughter or dismay.

With the games officially open, Hitler left the stadium to the triumphant strains of Handel's "Hallelujah Chorus."

"What did you think of that?" the count asked Viviane as they walked out, maneuvering through the crowds toward their waiting car. "Such spectacle. Everything the masses could want. You can see why he is so popular, can you not?"

There was no need to ask who he meant. Viviane glanced at her host.

"Hindenburg or Bismarck or the kaiser did not receive such accolades. I daresay even Frederick the Great did not raise the kind of frenzied passion Herr Hitler does. I'm afraid I am an old fossil in this country, a relic of a past I much preferred. I do not understand why others adore this man. He holds no charm for me."

He spoke softly, so only Viviane heard, but she glanced around, looking for anyone who might be eavesdropping. Otto had warned them before they arrived in Berlin that they must guard their words and opinion, that this wasn't England, and there were ears everywhere. "Not to catch you in a lie, of course," he said when Julia had frowned. "More because we Germans want to know what everyone thinks of our games, of this magnificent gift we are giving to the world."

"The führer is welcoming everyone with open arms, showing off his benevolent, peaceful intentions," the count continued now. "Are you convinced?"

Viviane looked around, saw people watching people, discussing opinions on the glory of the event, everyone flushed with pleasure. No one was looking directly at her, but still she guarded her opinion, that it had been both electrifying and terrifying. How easy it had been to feel mesmerized by such a grand event, all the pomp, power, and patriotism. "It was . . . thrilling," she replied. She scanned the crowds for Tom Graham but didn't see him. She had half expected he would find her, say hello, but he'd disappeared from his seat when she looked for him after the ceremony ended.

"There's Otto!" Julia cried, hurrying past Viviane, rushing down the last flight of stone steps to where Otto waited by the Daimler with the chauffeur. In uniform, his face in the shade of his cap, he towered over the driver, exuding power as he watched the crowds pass by, his gaze sharp, almost . . . *menacing*. It made Viviane shiver. Then he grinned when he saw Julia hurrying toward him, holding on to her red hat with one hand. He took Julia's elbow for a moment and looked into her eyes as if they'd been separated for weeks instead of hours.

"Do you think Julia can convince Otto to visit England?" the count asked Viviane.

Viviane looked at him in surprise. "You'd like him to go to England?"

A more senior officer passed Otto, and he released Julia at once, and snapped to attention, his expression hardening yet again. He raised his arm in a smart Hitler salute, clicking the heels of his polished boots.

"Yes," Georg said, watching Otto. "I want my son to leave Germany and go to England. That's exactly what I want."

CHAPTER THIRTY-TWO

THE QUARTIER LATIN was the hottest, most elegant, exciting, and expensive nightclub in Berlin. It sat on the exalted street corners of Nürnberger Strasse and Kurfürstendamm, and limousines glided up to the double doors, one after the other, disgorging lovely people in diamonds and satin. Uniformed doormen escorted guests inside with smiling deference.

Inside, the Quartier Latin was a world apart. Evening dress was strictly required, while military uniforms of any kind, no matter how high the rank or excellent the tailoring, were forbidden with equal strictness. Only money gave orders here.

Tom looked around the tony club as he entered with Trude on his arm, or rather, *he* was on *her* arm, since it had been her idea to come here tonight. She'd insisted on it, in fact. It was like walking onto a movie set. There were plenty of intimate conversations going on at the little tables around the dance floor, lips to ears, forehead to forehead, romantic trysts and discussions of all manner of plots, from movie scripts to political machinations. Tom had heard that the Quartier Latin was the place to come if one needed to get out of Germany fast and had deep pockets.

The advantage of arriving with Trude was that she rendered him invisible. People looked at her, not him, as she sashayed, smiled, and posed. She did all three as she tripped along in high heels, shoulders back, chin high. She batted her lashes as she looked around, each snapping glance like the flash of a camera, marking who was here and who was worth speaking to.

For his part, Tom took note of where the exits were and the less famous faces, the ones in the shadows on the fringes of the glamour, only their eyes gleaming through the smoke of their cigarettes. He recognized a few Gestapo officers, a handful of party officials, and one or two Soviet embassy staffers. There weren't many journalists, mostly due to the prices, but that meant that those with something to hide were freer, less careful without the presence of the press. Trude paid the tab when they came here, of course—or her bosses did. Tom's expense account didn't stretch to the kind of prices the Quartier Latin charged.

He watched the heavy-lidded stares of the security office members he recognized to see if anyone nodded to Trude or touched a finger to his nose or his earlobe in some secret sign. Tonight, with the Olympic Games so gloriously begun, the restaurant was mostly full of tourists and diplomats, writers and movie stars, and with so many people to watch, and the sheer pleasure of seeing such exalted idols in the flesh and at their most playful and indiscreet, the atmosphere was relaxed. A woman shrieked with the kind of carefree laugh that put the jazz trumpets to shame as they were shown to their table, instantly greeted by a smiling waiter who took Trude's order for champagne with a gratified nod. "May I suggest the 1934 Pol Roger?" he said smoothly, looking at Tom, who nodded. It was an excellent recommendation. He'd helped polish off a bottle of that at Geoff's wedding, a gift from Winston Churchill.

He scanned the crowded dance floor, watched the sequins sparkle on backless gowns as the women inside them swayed. The ladies wore full lipstick and mascara here, and dripped with diamonds, the scrubbed wholesomeness of German womanhood forgotten in favor of lush glamour.

A handsome couple swept past on the dance floor, and Tom recognized Julia Devellin. She looked beautiful in pale yellow silk—and utterly smitten with her handsome partner. Tom's heart checked hopefully. If Julia was here, then . . .

He found Viviane at a table with a man he didn't know. Her red hair was swept up in an elegant coiffure, and she was smiling, her head close to his in intimate conversation. She was wearing a blue satin evening gown that fit her to perfection, enhanced the delicate strength of her slim figure. She was in her element, confident, serene, and lovely.

He glanced again at her companion, noted his hand on Viviane's arm, his intimate smile, and the fact that he was sitting too close to her.

Trude grabbed his arm, and he nearly shook her off.

"Look—there's Willi Forst!" she gasped, indicating a sleekly handsome man leaning on the bar. "You know, the director. His movie *Allotria* premiered in June, and he's acted in movies with Marlene Dietrich and Pola Negi. When Willi Forst casts you in a movie, your success is completely assured!" she said, her eyes glowing.

"Why don't you go and say hello to him?" Tom said, his eyes returning to Viviane again. Her throat was a silver column when she laughed at something her companion said.

"Just walk up and speak to him?" Trude objected breathlessly. "I couldn't be so bold." But she was already taking her compact from her evening bag, examining her flawless face in the tiny mirror, practicing her pout, her pucker, and the seductive sweep of her lashes. She snapped it shut. "Perhaps I will, just for a moment. Do you mind terribly?"

He sipped his champagne. "Not at all."

She was on her feet before he'd finished speaking those three short words, her eyes fixed on her quarry, her smile bright, her stride languid yet purposeful. He saw the director's head turn, watched his eyes travel over Trude's magnificent figure. He didn't look away. The meeting would be a success—or a seduction.

Tom rose from his own chair and wove his way between the tables toward Viviane. She was watching the dancers and didn't immediately see him coming. Her friend did, and his grin faded. His eyes narrowed slightly behind his spectacles, as he warned Tom away with a glare, but Viviane turned. Her practiced smile fled, and her eyes widened in surprise. "Oh," she said softly. Her hand curled on the white tablecloth, made a nervous fist. Her eyes were so luminous that he could see his own reflection in them. It felt like the only right, sensible thing in the whole world, finding her here, being held in her eyes.

"Dance?" he asked her at the same time as her friend said, "And who is this?"

Before Viviane could reply to either question, Julia returned to the table, breathless and lovely, her cheeks pink. "Tom Graham!" she said. "How nice to see you. I heard you were in Berlin. I didn't think we'd see you, though." She kissed his cheek as if he was an old friend—or perhaps to make the man looming behind her jealous.

"Who is this?" Julia's gargantuan companion parroted the man at the table. Tom recognized Otto von Schroeder, of course, Reinhardt Heydrich's right-hand man, a rising star in the secret police. He'd heard that Schroeder's methods of interrogation were quite innovative. He was tall and broad, steel eyed and iron jawed, a granite statue of Hitler's perfect Aryan man in a tuxedo. The way he was looking at Tom now, he knew that tomorrow morning the file with his name on it—and he had no doubt he had one—would be pulled and scrutinized.

"This is a dear old friend from England," Julia said, though they barely knew each other, laying it on thick for Otto. "Tom was the best man at my sister Margaret's wedding." She put her hand on Schroeder's arm, smiled up at him, and the granite statue softened like sugar in the rain. "This is Otto von Schroeder," she said, almost breathless.

"Tom Graham—ah yes. Your name came up the other day," Viviane's companion said, rising, and without offering an explanation of that. He regarded Tom with open curiosity. "I am Otto's little brother Felix. They tend to forget I am here."

Felix, like the cartoon cat, Tom thought. For a moment he was just as inscrutable as a feline, too, scanning Tom's face, gauging him. He held out his hand for Tom to shake, his grip firm. He turned to Viviane. "You see, he has come to no harm after all. Shall I call for another chair?" The question was spoken in a light tone, but Tom heard the slight edge. *Don't stay*, he read in the undertone. He glanced at Viviane, found her cheeks flushed with hectic color. Just what was Felix von Schroeder to Viviane?

"I can't stay," he said, glancing at Trude, who was still busy charming Willi Forst. She'd forgotten all about him. He noted that Viviane's eyes followed his and took in the actress. Her brows jerked slightly, and he knew exactly what she was thinking. "Would you care to dance?" he asked her again.

"She can't—" Felix began, but Viviane had already risen to her feet and put her hand in his. Her fingertips were cool, and he instinctively closed his hand on them and squeezed slightly.

She let him lead her out, doing her best to hide her limp.

He gathered her into his arms, his hand warming the satin of her gown, the silkiness of the sleek fabric mimicking soft flesh. The band was playing something slow, the clarinet and the saxophone paired off in a romantic duet while the piano chaperoned. "How is your leg?" he asked.

"It's fine," she said quickly, dismissing the question. He felt her hand curl on his shoulder, and the faint touch shot through him. "You look well," she said. She bit her lip and looked up at him. "There was an accident the other day. A journalist was run over by a car. I was afraid—I thought—it was you."

He was lost in her eyes again. He managed to shake his head. "No. He was a colleague named Charlie Ellis." How to explain? "He . . . he asked too many questions," he said simply.

It didn't appear to comfort her. "You are . . . more careful, I hope?" He glanced at Otto von Schroeder again and wondered if he could ever be careful enough.

"Do you worry about me?" he asked, forcing a grin, teasing her, trying to lighten the mood. "Are you not enjoying your—*holiday*?" He flicked his gaze toward the table. Otto was gazing at Julia, but Felix von Schroeder was glaring holes in Tom's coat.

She followed his glance and blushed. "Felix is not a—" She stopped herself before she could say "Nazi." He watched her slam the word shut behind her lips, purse them. She'd learned to be discreet and careful. He wondered if something had happened to make her so. He longed to ask, but this wasn't the place. He tucked the question behind his own teeth.

"He's a chemist," she said instead, to describe Felix von Schroeder.

Tom's brows rose slightly.

She tossed her head at the sarcasm in his eyes, at the unspoken quip she obviously knew was lurking on the tip of his tongue. It was an imperious little gesture. "Your friend is very pretty," she said.

"Trude? She's on loan," he said. "She keeps an eye on me."

He was careful to support her weak leg without making it obvious as they moved through the steps. She looked up at him through her eyelashes, not believing for an instant that Trude was anything other than his lover. It was rather flattering, Tom decided, grinning at the little demonstration of jealousy.

"I like your dress," he said. "Blue suits you well, better than the green dress you wore to the betrothal dinner or that pinkish bridesmaid's dress."

She blinked. "You remember what I wore?"

He let the question slide. He remembered those dresses, and he recalled the way the strap of her swimsuit had caressed the sleek wet skin of her shoulder the day they met, and how she looked in his coat. He remembered her in a boy's cap and baggy trousers, standing in the middle of a riot with bottles and bricks flying around her, unperturbed, her camera raised. He'd remember her like this, too, in a glamorous club, dressed to the nines.

"Tell me about your trip," he said. "Are you enjoying Germany?"

She raised her chin. "I am," she said, as if he'd accused her of something. "It's been . . . very pleasant. Not entirely what I expected." There was a healthy, sun-kissed glow about her, as if she'd been romping outdoors. She looked magnificent. His thoughts must have shown in his eyes. She drew a quick breath, her lips parting as she stared back at him. The music changed moods as the trumpet joined the clarinet, drowning out the saxophone to wail its own passionate mating call. The tempo picked up, and he guided her into the new rhythm. "I've taken hundreds of photographs," she said, and glanced back at the table, where Felix was still watching. Did the man ever blink? Tom wondered. She tossed her head and smiled as if they were discussing something innocent. "I'd love to show them to you."

"I'd love to see them," he said, fixing his eyes on her, ignoring Schroeder. "Perhaps lunch? Tomorrow?"

The sudden grip on his shoulder surprised him, pulled him hard enough to jerk him back, out of step.

"Tom, darling, there you are," Trude said in a loud voice. "I've been looking everywhere for you, you naughty boy." Her painted lips pouted playfully and her tone was bright, but her eyes were sharp, taking in every detail of Viviane's person. He wondered if there was a file on Viviane as well, or if there'd be one started.

"I've been right here all along," he said. "I met an old friend from England. This is Miss Viviane Alden. She's in Berlin for the games, a guest of Count von Schroeder."

He saw Trude's eyes widen. She knew the Schroeder name and the reputation as surely as she knew Willi Forst's. To her credit, she simply broadened her smile and plunged ahead. "How wonderful," she drawled. "And are you enjoying your holiday, Miss Alden?" she asked, switching to accented English.

"Yes, thank you," Viviane said, regarding Trude with interest. She glanced at Tom, a frisson of uncertainty in her eyes now. She wondered how they'd meet if he had Trude by his side every day, and possibly every night. Viviane stiffened in his arms, stopped dancing, and tried to break away, but he held her in place, waiting until the song ended. Trude stood by and waited, the jealous, careful minder that she was. He wondered if her boss was here tonight, in this very room, watching. For a second, he wondered if it might be Otto von Schroeder, but the Obersturmführer was leading Julia back onto the dance floor for the next number. He didn't even glance at Trude, or Viviane, or anyone else.

Tom escorted Viviane back to the table, and Felix shot to his feet. Viviane took her seat. "Thank you," she said, her eyes on Tom, her gaze speaking volumes. "I shall ring you. Where are you staying?"

"He's at the Hotel am Zoo," Trude said, her red-tipped fingers closing on his sleeve. "Do you know it?"

"Everyone knows it," Felix quipped. "But hum a few bars to make sure."

For a moment Trude looked confused, then she got the joke. She shook out her hair as she threw her head back to laugh.

"Would you like to dance again?" Felix said to Viviane.

"I'm a little tired," she said. "But perhaps fraülein . . . ?"

"Trude Unger. Yes, I'll dance."

Felix had no choice but to lead her out, and Tom took his seat.

"A lovely couple," Tom murmured.

She looked at him sharply. "Your Trude is quite pretty," she said in a stilted tone.

"Jealous?" he asked. "Of Felix, of course, not me. She's not really my type."

She quirked one eyebrow. "I saw you with her at the opening ceremonies today. You had excellent seats."

"Yes. I'm a popular chap. Everyone wants to be my friend. Take Trude, for instance. She's an actress—and a spy," he said softly, leaning close to her ear, catching the tantalizingly subtle scent of her perfume. "Haven't you noticed? You can't breathe in Berlin without someone watching you. That's what happened to poor old Charlie. Sadly, he was on his way to meet me when he was struck down."

She sipped from her drink, her hand trembling slightly. "You? Is he—badly hurt?"

"Two severely broken legs. He'll limp for the rest of his life. They'll put him on the next boat back to Canada and suggest he may not wish to return to Germany."

She paled.

"Steady," he warned. "I told you this was dangerous."

"How are we going to meet?" she asked. "It seemed like a simple thing when we spoke in England. Does Trude *ever* leave your side?"

He followed Viviane's gaze to where Trude danced with Felix von Schroeder. Both partners were more focused on Viviane and Tom. Trude caught Tom's glance and waggled her fingers at him. "She's diligent," he replied. "We'll have to think of something. Is there anything incriminating on your film?"

"Vacation snaps, but it's what's in the background, I'm afraid. Felix helped me pose Julia at an aircraft factory, sitting in front of—"

He moved his hand to silence her. "Felix?"

She colored slightly. "As I said, he's not . . . what his brother is." He wondered if she'd gone mad, trusting Otto von Schroeder's brother. Had it gone beyond that?

"Does he ever leave your side?" he said, repeating her question back to her, only sharper, more pointed. He had the strangest desire to punch Felix von Schroeder. He wanted to ask Viviane if she'd fallen in love with her Not-a-Nazi, changed sides. The question was bitter on his tongue.

She ignored the question. "How will we manage to meet?" she asked again, obviously nervous.

He wondered that himself. A flash went off, and he saw Felix and Trude caught in the photographer's sights. The man would offer to print the photograph and sell it to them.

Tom had an idea. "Your society portraits. Trude is an actress, and no one loves having her picture taken more than she does. If she thought you were a professional portrait photographer, she might wish to pose for you."

Viviane's eyes lit, seeing the possibilities at once. The song ended, and Felix led the actress back to the table. "I saw that portrait of Diana Guinness you took," Tom said loudly. "She's never looked lovelier."

"You know Diana Guinness?" Trude said, her eyes kindling.

Viviane took up the game. "Yes, of course. She's an old friend. I took her portrait for a charity ball."

"Viviane is an excellent photographer and quite popular with the smart set in London," Tom said. "She brings out something in her subjects that's magical. Geoffrey—her stepsister's husband—says his very favorite photograph of Margaret is one that Viviane took. Everyone who's anyone in London wants Viviane Alden to take their picture."

Trude fixed her gaze on Viviane. "Then you simply must shoot me! I met Willi Forst tonight, the film director, and he's asked for some stills. He's considering me for his next film." She tilted her head as if she was already posing for the camera.

"She's on holiday, and a guest of—" Felix began, but Viviane kept her eyes on Trude.

"I'd be delighted to photograph you, Miss Unger. You'd make a lovely subject."

Trude grinned at Viviane. "Do call me Trude. I think we're going to be very good friends."

Otto and Julia returned to the table and Tom rose at once and held the chair for Julia. "Ring me tomorrow and we'll arrange something," Trude said, reaching into Tom's pocket for his notebook, tearing out a page. She jotted her telephone number on it and handed it to Viviane. Viviane turned to smile at Tom, looking like a cat that had a mouse caught between her teeth. Tom took Trude's arm. "I think they're playing our song, Trude. Shall we dance?"

He felt something warm kindle in his belly as he led Trude away and wondered what it was. Then he realized it was a sense of pleasure, something he hadn't felt for a long while.

It was the anticipation of seeing Viviane Alden again.

CHAPTER THIRTY-THREE

"WE HAVE RECEIVED invitations to all the finest parties that are taking place during the Olympics. We cannot accept them all, so we must choose the best," Ilsa told the girls at breakfast the next morning as they were seated at their usual table by the window in the Adlon's café. Julia looked delightedly at the thick stack of invitations in the countess's hand, all of them printed on expensive paper and all of them embossed with swastikas, which made Viviane shudder. "There's no party like a Nazi party," Felix might have quipped if he were here. She looked out the window at the weather, while Julia gushed over the dazzling array of exclusive society events. The cool, wet weather was unusual for August in Berlin, everyone said, and a terrible shame for the Olympic Games.

The games went on anyway, rain or shine. Each day, loudspeakers mounted in the trees along the Unter den Linden broadcast the sporting events taking place that day as they happened. People stopped on the busy street to listen to the broadcasts of the most popular events, or they visited the special viewing rooms that featured the new medium of television, a marvelous box that showed wavy black-and-white images of races and medal ceremonies.

Outside the Adlon and the Eden and other premium hotels, polished automobiles waited to whisk Olympic officials and guests of the very highest rank and importance to the day's events at the stadium. The city was crowded and chaotic with so many visitors.

"Which invitations shall we accept?" Julia asked eagerly. "How many can we accept?"

Ilsa smiled at her fondly, like a dear friend—or a daughter—and Julia smiled back. Viviane regarded her stepsister with a slight frown. She was growing very close not just to Otto but also to his mother. The two hardly seemed to even notice that Viviane was sitting beside them.

"We'll start with the most important ones, of course," Ilsa said, smiling. "Herr von Ribbentrop is hosting one, as is Hermann Göring, and the Goebbelses will be holding a very grand party at their lovely estate on Peacock Island."

"May we attend Herr von Ribbentrop's party? He knows my father," Julia said.

Ilsa nodded. "Of course, my dear—and it would be quite impossible to attend the Görings' party without attending the Goebbelses' affair. Do you both have suitable gowns for so many parties? You can't wear the same dress twice. You'll need to look your very best. Magda Goebbels is the head of the German Fashion Institute, and she will be watching." She smiled at Julia. "These are important events for Otto, and he must be seen. Having you on his arm will impress people."

Julia blushed with pleasure at the compliment.

"We shall visit the shops this afternoon." Ilsa made it a command, not an invitation.

"Oh, but I have plenty of gowns, and the count has invited me to attend today's events with him at the stadium," Viviane said quickly. "He is particularly interested in the hundred-meter race."

Ilsa's smile dimmed. "A race? My husband does not realize that looking beautiful is a race, the most important race of all." She turned back to Julia. "Then you and I will go, Julia. I know just the shop, Schulze-Bibernell. Herr Schulze designs beautiful evening gowns. Or we could go to Hilda Romatzki's salon."

Viviane watched her stepsister's face light up at the prospect of a new dress. Julia liked glamour and luxury above all things. She had bought every fashion magazine available at the newsstands at home, and copies of *Die Dame* littered the floor of their hotel room. She had adopted Berlin style with a British twist, sporty little jackets over floaty, summery, flowered dresses with saucy hats perched on her blond head. She used belts and scarves and bracelets to great effect, drawing admiring stares wherever she went.

The hotel's dapper concierge entered the café and peered around the room. His gaze stopped on the Schroeder table, and he came toward them. He bowed to Ilsa and beckoned a bellhop behind him, who bore a massive bouquet of flowers.

"Excuse me, Countess von Schroeder. We have received a special delivery for Lady Julia. I was instructed to present it to her at once, with this."

He proffered a small box on his flat palm, the way one might offer sugar to a horse.

Julia stared at the box for a moment before she took it and opened it. Her face blossomed as she gazed at the contents in rapt joy. The glitter of jewels reflected in her eyes.

"Oh, how wonderful! Vee—look at this! It's from Otto."

Viviane suspected a ring, but it was a brooch—a swastika picked out in rubies, set in gleaming jet and gold. Viviane stared at it for a moment, trying to think of something to say, something that wouldn't offend Julia, who was clearly delighted with the gift, but her stomach turned at the hateful symbol, presented as a token of love. She forced a smile and nodded, then turned to sip her coffee, now cold.

"How lovely," Ilsa gushed. She touched the gold swastika on her own collar and beamed at Julia. Julia wiped away a happy tear and bit her lip. She looked like a girl with a crush—or a woman in love. Surely she wouldn't wear the garish bauble. They'd laugh over it later, Viviane thought. Julia preferred pretty, delicate jewels. Diamonds and pearls were her favorites. Julia turned to the waiting concierge. She took one of the blossoms from the bouquet, a gardenia, and tucked it into the ribbon on her hat. "Would you take the rest of the flowers to my room, please?"

"At once, my lady," he said, his eyes glowing, and hurried away with the footman. Everyone was watching, waiting to see for themselves what treasure lay in the little box embossed with the logo of Berlin's most exclusive jeweler.

She took the brooch from the box and handed it to Ilsa. "Will you help me put it on?" she asked, and Ilsa pinned it to the lapel of her jacket, over her heart. There was a collective sigh from the Germans at the nearest tables, smiles of approval. Even the other foreigners looked impressed at the sheer size of the brooch. Julia put her hand over it for a moment. "I think I shall wear it always," she murmured in careful German, and Ilsa beamed.

Viviane stared at the happy tears in her stepsister's eyes and blinked. Was this more than a flirtation? It didn't matter. In less than a month they'd return home to England, to sense and sanity and ordinary English boys Julia could flirt with and discard before she married a lord her father approved of. Her crush on Otto von Schroeder would fade and be forgotten.

"Good morning," Felix said, appearing at the table. He had a way of silently coming and going that never failed to surprise Viviane. He smiled at her. "I thought I'd come early so we could walk along the Unter den Linden before we meet my father at the stadium. There's someone I'd very much like you to meet. Hurry and freshen up, and we'll go while the rain holds off."

In their room, Julia fondled Otto's gift, admiring it in the mirror. Viviane picked up the hairbrush and brushed her stepsister's blond curls.

"Julia, darling, things seem to be going awfully fast with Otto. We're going home at the end of the month. It wouldn't do to get too attached."

Julia's smile only broadened as she turned. "Oh, Vee, I'm *so* in love— and I think he's in love with me." She touched the brooch again. "No, I'm *sure* he loves me. Is that so bad?"

Viviane's stomach tensed. Her stepsister was barely eighteen. "Love takes time. Once we're home, and you have time to consider—"

Julia's smile faded to anger. "Home? Why would I go home?"

Viviane gaped at her. "What are you saying? You can't stay."

Julia glared at her in the mirror. "Isn't that precisely why we're here?" she said. "To find husbands? Do you doubt that's what Georg von Schroeder had in mind when he invited me, and why Papa agreed? I'm simply fortunate enough to be in love. No, I don't think my father would be surprised to hear I wish to stay in Germany. In fact, I think he'll be very pleased."

Viviane's fingers were numb on the hairbrush, and she set it down. "Things may change between England and Germany—they will. What if there's a war?"

Julia laughed. "Why should there be a war? Germany wants only peace." She picked up the brush herself and ran it through her hair. She looked beautiful and vibrant.

Viviane stared at her. "Don't be so naive, Julia. The Germans are not what they seem. This is a game, a charade. None of it is real. It's an enchantment, a spell. Under the shining surface it's rotten and ugly and hateful."

Julia rolled her eyes. "I love this country. I feel that more strongly here than I ever did in England. I feel alive, exhilarated, and happy. Things happen here, good things, and Otto is the best thing of all."

"It isn't real. It's . . . infatuation, not love!" Viviane said, desperate. "And it isn't patriotism, it's mania, based on hatred, not pride."

"What do you know of love, Viviane? You were engaged to Phillip, and you threw him over. Why should I take your advice?"

"Oh, Julia—take my advice *because* of Phillip. I thought he would make the perfect husband, but . . ."

Julia turned to look at her. "Because Phillip is a Fascist, you mean? Isn't that really why you ended your engagement? Why else would you do it? He's handsome, charming, and rich. He's the kind of man every woman dreams of marrying, but not you. Why should politics matter? What difference does it make if a man is a Whig or a Tory—or a Nazi, for that matter? Otto is everything I've ever dreamed of in a man, a husband. He's perfect, and he's perfect for me. How could it be wrong to love your country with complete and utter devotion?"

Viviane swallowed. "But where does that leave you? Do you come before or after his love for Germany, and Hitler?"

Julia reddened but didn't reply. She grabbed her hat and set it on her head. The swastika brooch cast bloodred sparks of light against her white throat. She turned, her eyes softer. "I don't want to argue. I'm too happy. Please don't spoil this for me. Find your own way to be happy, Viviane." Viviane gaped at her stepsister, her heart aching. What more could she say? "I'll see you later," Julia said brightly as she picked up her gloves. "Ilsa is waiting for me, and I don't want to be late."

CHAPTER THIRTY-FOUR

FELIX LOOKED UP at the sky as they walked along the Unter den Linden. "There's no rain today," he said. "At least not yet."

"It can't rain. You've brought an umbrella with you, so it will shine all day. If you had left it at home, it would have poured," Viviane replied with a smile.

"Is that some kind of English rule?" Felix asked. "Because if it is, it doesn't work very well. Does it not rain all the time in England?"

"That is a terrible exaggeration, I'm afraid. Sometimes there's mist or drizzle or damp fog," she said. "There are over three hundred words for rain in the English language."

"Is that true?" he said.

"Of course not. English summers are glorious. Saying it rains all the time is like saying Germany is dange—" She stopped herself, but he looked quickly at her.

"Is that how people feel? That Germans are dangerous?"

"I didn't mean that," she said, thinking of her conversation with Julia, not wanting another argument over politics and patriotism today. "Germany is lovely."

"But dangerous," he persisted. He stopped walking and took her arm. "You're not wrong, Viviane." He gestured at the flowers growing on a balcony above them; at a poster of a tanned and healthy German family growing wheat, pinned to a wall outside a shop; and at a newspaper box filled with geraniums instead of papers. "All of this is illusion. But you know that of course. You're clever enough to look behind all this to see what they're hiding." He pushed back the spill of flowers so she could read the name on the newspaper box, *Der Stürmer.* "Usually, there's a new edition of this hate-filled—and most dangerous—rag, published every week. It was ordered suspended for the duration of the Olympics so tourists wouldn't see the ugliness, hatred, the violence we've all come to believe in."

He tossed the geraniums onto the ground, breaking the pot, scattering dirt and blossoms on the pristine cobbles of the street, leaving the empty gaping hole and the ugly logo exposed to view.

Viviane looked around to see if anyone noticed, but passersby seemed to be going about their own affairs. Aside from annoyed glances as people skirted the mess, no one said anything.

"You see? You've learned to look over your shoulder, to watch the watchers. Who might see and report on you? Is it that man in the tobacconist's, casually looking out the window, the woman sitting on the bench across the street, or the man waiting on the corner?" He looked at a Hitler Youth standing under a tree, staring up at the loudspeaker mounted among the branches, broadcasting the events from Olympic Stadium. "Even children are taught to watch others and report anti-Nazi behavior to the authorities—even their own parents if they seem disloyal."

"Not Klaus," she said.

He frowned. "*Especially* Klaus. I heard him berating a maid for cursing God, the government, and the führer when she banged her thumb. He threatened to tell Otto and have her arrested. Arrested! Do children in England behave so, have that kind of power?" She shook her head, her mouth dry. "Of course not. Your country is civilized. It is not 'dangerous,' as Germany is. In England, you can speak up without fear. You do not hate others the way we've learned to."

She glanced around again as his voice rose, anxious now. "Oh, don't worry. I am a Schroeder. No one will dare touch me. My brother is an SD officer, my father was a hero of the Great War, and my mother is a dear friend of Magda Goebbels. And my little brother is a tool in Hitler's hand. He smiles sweetly at you now, but he will do as he's told, betray you, and fight you like a rabid little dog."

"You're angry," she said, keeping her voice low. She couldn't recall ever having seen him in anything but a jolly, teasing mood.

He scanned her face. "Yes." He took her hand, squeezed it in his earnestly. "That's why I asked you to come with me today, to meet an old friend. He's in great danger, and I need your help."

She swallowed. "My help?"

His smile was back, rueful and contrite. "I've frightened you, and I've said too much for the moment." The clock tower chimed eleven. "Come, we'll be late, and my friend will worry."

He took her arm and guided her along the busy street, smiling and nodding at passersby as if nothing had happened. The storm was over, and he was the old Felix again, lighthearted, never serious. They passed a loudspeaker and listened to the announcer describing a race.

"Jesse Owens, the American sprinter, is racing today," Felix said. "He has caused quite a tempest in the teapot. He's good, and people fear he just might be good enough to beat everyone else, even our superior Germans. Do you think he'll win?" he asked her.

"I don't know," she said, still shaken by his outburst. "Does it matter?"

He threw back his head and laughed. Now people glanced at him suspiciously, as if being happy was the most dangerous thing of all. "Of course it matters! He's American, and he's a Negro. Did you not know? Only Aryans are expected to win at these marvelous games. Plans have been made, you see. Somewhere, in some bureaucrat's office, there are schedules and lists, all stamped and sealed by the Nazi party. They don't like when things don't go as they wish." He grinned. "I hope Owens wins. I hope I'm there, and I get to see Hitler's face, and Goebbels's. Wouldn't that be a laugh?"

She didn't reply.

"Let's make a wager. I say Jesse Owens will not win. Hitler himself will rush down and trip him at the finish line if he must, but he won't be permitted to win."

"How can they do that with the world watching?" she asked.

"So you think he will win?" he pressed.

"Yes, why not? What do you want to wager?"

He scanned her face and raised a brow. "I don't know. A pfennig or two? Or shall we bet something more interesting, more exciting?"

"Like what?"

He considered. "A kiss?"

It was her turn to burst out laughing. He put a hand over his heart and frowned.

"You laugh. Do you not think me capable of tender feelings? You are beautiful, Viviane, and I've grown quite fond of you. Or is it something— or someone—else? The chap you danced with at the Quartier Latin, perhaps? Is he more to you than just a friend of your stepsister's husband?"

Her cheeks flamed. "Tom Graham?" she said, and looked away, down the street, at the flowers and the crowds and the bloodred Nazi flags. "He's an acquaintance. I barely know him at all."

"Oh, but what I'd give to have you look at me the way you looked at him last night!" he said, teasing. "There, that's what we'll wager—if Jesse Owens wins, you will grant me a long, smoldering look of desire."

Had she really looked at Tom like that? She felt the blush renew itself, stain her cheeks telltale scarlet as her heart turned a somersault in her breast. "Don't be silly, Felix. I have never looked at anyone that way." Felix was easy to like, easy to flirt with, knowing it meant nothing at all.

Perhaps it meant more to him than she'd thought.

He lifted her chin with the tip of his finger. "Then I will be the first." He grinned. "Now I have all the more reason to root for the American."

They walked on, and she stopped short. "What?" he asked innocently.

"You said you wanted to wager *against* him."

He grinned again and plucked a daisy from a flower box. "I changed my mind. I want to win as badly as Herr Owens does." He held out the flower, and when she moved to take it, he snatched it back and tucked it into his lapel.

FELIX LED HER through the streets of Berlin, from the grand tourist areas to a humbler neighborhood of old buildings. They passed a housewife arguing with a policeman.

"You are not permitted to hang your laundry out of the window until after the Olympic Games are over," the officer said sternly, pointing above him to the offending items on the windowsill. "It is not good for tourists to think—" He paused when he saw Felix and Viviane coming and tipped his hat. "Good morning," he said, and turned back to the woman. "If you please, take it down. It is only for a few days, *nein*?" he said in a more cajoling voice.

"Are you lost?" A man called to them from an open window where he was enjoying a cigarette.

"No, I know where I'm going," Felix replied. "Do you?"

"You don't look like you're from this neighborhood," the man continued, eyeing Viviane's summer dress and stylish hat.

"I'm not. Nonetheless, I know where I'm going," Felix said pleasantly. "There's a policeman coming along the street, by the way. You may want to put that cigarette out. It doesn't look good to foreigners, and the führer detests smoking."

The man ducked inside and closed the window.

They climbed the steps of a humble apartment building and entered a dark foyer. A circular staircase rose upward, the steps worn from use, the wrought iron railings sagging ever so slightly, like a genteel lady who has fallen upon hard times in her old age yet strives to maintain a certain standard as best she can. "My friend is on the third floor," Felix said with an apologetic smile. "There is no lift, I'm afraid."

She followed him up, her leg objecting, though she refused to let it show. At last, he stopped in front of a door and knocked. "It is Felix, Professor Hitzig," he said softly.

The door opened, and an older version of Felix stood there, peering over the top of his glasses at his visitors. He regarded Viviane with surprise.

"It's all right, there's nothing to fear. This is Miss Viviane Alden, from England. Viviane, this is Professor Solomon Hitzig, my supervisor and my friend. I am one of his research assistants. You may have heard of the professor, even in England. He won the Nobel Prize for chemistry."

"That was a very long time ago, before the war," the man muttered.

Viviane recognized his name. She felt her belly flip, then curl. "Hitzig?" she said, her lips tight.

He looked at her again, his dark eyes sharpening. "Yes."

"The man in charge of developing gas weapons during the war, of deploying them against the British and French—"

He was staring at her in horror. "I—"

She stopped on the doorstep, refusing to step over the threshold. Felix tugged her arm. "Come inside, Viviane. Yes, he's that Solomon Hitzig. It was another time."

"It was . . . war," the man said, stepping back, looking anxious.

Viviane balked, tried to flee. "Wait." Felix stopped her, his grip harder now, insistent. It hurt. She looked at him in alarm, and he let her go. "Please," he said. "There's a reason why I brought you together. You both lost someone dear to you, and many others died or were wounded. What if you could stop that from happening again? Would you do that?"

"He killed my father," she whispered, her throat closing. "It was his invention, his fault."

She couldn't look at the chemist. She kept her eyes on Felix, felt them sting, fill with tears until his face blurred.

Felix made a soft sound and stepped toward her, protective, sympathetic, kind. He held out a handkerchief, but she couldn't take it, couldn't touch anyone. She swiped furiously at her tears with the heel of her hand. "Take me back to the hotel, please," she said in clipped English. To speak German now would surely strangle her.

Hitzig shifted his stance uneasily. "I thought it would save lives, shorten the war. My wife begged me not to do it . . . but I was sure it was right. She could not even bear to look at me. She . . . died, and my son blamed me, just as you do. He has not spoken to me since her death," Hitzig said. "I am sorry for your suffering, fraülein." He looked at Felix. "It was cruel of you to bring her here, Felix."

"No, it was necessary," Felix insisted. "Come inside and sit down, Viviane. People are staring," he said, though the hall was empty. She glanced at the closed doors and wondered if listeners lurked behind them. "I will make coffee." He walked down the hall to the kitchen, left her in the open doorway of the flat. She heard the sound of cups clattering on saucers, the hiss of a kettle heating on the stove.

Neither she nor the professor moved. They stood a dozen feet apart, staring at each other. "Please come in," he murmured.

She made herself take a step inside, and he nervously moved around her and shut the door.

"How did your father die? Where did he fall?" he asked finally, his lips stiff.

She raised her chin. "At a place called Sainte Courcelle. There was a small wood there, or there once was. Most of the trees were blighted from bombardment. My father was in charge of a battalion of men."

Hitzig peered at her over his glasses, frowning.

"They were ordered to attack that morning. My father was going along the line, making sure everyone was alert, still at the ready. He could have sent a sergeant, but the men were tired, needing encouragement, a friendly word from their commander. He wanted them to know he was beside them." She told him the story just as her father had told her.

"I remember the way they looked, silhouetted against the first light of dawn as they came out of the trenches. We hadn't expected so many," Hitzig murmured. "They didn't run . . . They *walked* across no-man's-land. They looked so . . . easy, casual, so confident, as if they were out for a morning stroll. We didn't expect that."

"You were there?" she asked.

He shut his eyes. "Yes. The German commander in that sector wanted the scientists to be present when the gas was used for the first time. Then, if it needed improvements, we would know firsthand what needed to be done." He paused. "I think he did not want to take the responsibility himself for the outcome, did not approve of such methods of warfare. The old soldiers did not, you see. They felt using gas lacked honor, made us cowards. We scientists saw it as a way to save lives. When we saw the enemy coming, the order was given to release the gas, to stop the attack before we were wiped out." He stared at the wall above her head as if he could see the events of that day played out there. "I remember the way the gas cannisters exploded, the yellow fog that blotted them from view. I waited for them to walk right through it, to keep on coming. We didn't really know if it would work, you see. If the wind was wrong, or conditions were too wet or too dry . . ." He rubbed a shaking hand across his mouth. "But they didn't come. We hadn't fired a shot, and they were screaming, and the sound of those cries strangled in their throats, came out garbled, wrong. The commander couldn't stand it. He ordered our troops to fire, to cover that terrible sound, to end their suffering."

"My father went out after his men," Viviane said. "He carried back as many as he could before he was overcome himself. It permanently damaged his lungs. He had trouble breathing for the rest of his life, suffered terrible nightmares. He . . . drowned."

Hitzig looked at her sadly. "I am sorry for your loss, fräulein. There were many things in that war that should not have happened. So many useless deaths. And now—" His face crumpled, and he lifted his hand and stared at his palm. "I would cut off my own arm if I could call back my life's work, stop what's to come, but I cannot. And now my own life is in danger."

He stopped speaking as Felix came out of the kitchen carrying a tray. "Come into the sitting room," he said. The chemist indicated the way, and Viviane followed, her gait stiff. "Sit down, Viviane," Felix said again as he set the tray on a table already overburdened with papers and books. She perched on the edge of the settee, and the professor sat across from her. Felix pressed a mug of coffee into the old man's hands. "I've surprised you, Professor. Drink this while it's hot." He looked at Viviane, solemn for once. "Did he tell you?" he asked as he handed her a cup as well.

She took it, swallowed hard, and nodded. "He was there," she said, her jaw tight.

"And did he tell you he's tried to make amends since then? After the war the professor began to work on a new chemical gas, one that will help mankind. The uses are purely agricultural, designed to kill insects and thereby increase the harvest."

"I want only to save lives," the professor murmured.

Felix looked distraught. "A noble goal, but I'm afraid there are other ways to use his invention." He regarded Viviane with a searching look. "They—the Nazis—want to use the professor's simple agricultural product as a weapon, use it to kill people instead."

Viviane felt her stomach curl against her spine. She stared at the cup in her hand, into the depths of the coffee.

"Please believe that it is not what *I* intend, fraülein. Gas is my life's work. It is beautiful, mysterious, noble, the perfection of science, the most basic element of life."

"Then stop. Quit your job," Viviane said. "Refuse to do it."

Hitzig glanced at Felix, his brow furrowing, and Felix swallowed. "He can't quit, Viviane. He's a Jew. Surely you know what that means."

She did indeed. "Then leave Germany."

Felix frowned. "If you think it is so simple, then you don't understand at all. He cannot leave—his work is too important to them. They are forcing him to continue his research. He will work until they've decided he's given them everything he can," Felix said fervently. "And then . . ." He shrugged and glanced at his mentor. "They can never let him go. He would take his magnificent mind to another country, and then what? No, when they have no more need of him, they'll kill him, Viviane."

She blanched, looked at the old man in his chair, gray-haired and confused. Did he deserve that fate?

"The Nazis know the power of his work. They allowed the Italians to test gas for them in Ethiopia last year. Thousands died—women, children, innocents. When the professor finishes his work, then Germany will use his gas—stronger, more perfect than the stuff in the last war—to target their enemies and destroy them like vermin."

She stared at him, her body numb, her lungs unable to draw enough air, drowning.

"I've been searching for a way to get him out of Germany, to help him escape before it's too late. If he were simply to disappear, take his formulas with him, they could never use his invention." He looked at Hitzig. "I recently discovered that his son is in England. I hope that you will help him leave the country, you see, take him with you when you return home."

Viviane felt numb. "How can I do that?" She bit her lip. "I know Winston Churchill. He's a member of parliament, determined to stop another war. I could write to him. He could issue a formal protest—"

Felix leaned forward in his chair. "It is a noble idea, but it is too soon for that—or perhaps too late. We need to get the professor out of Germany as soon as we can. In England, his presence, his knowledge, would give the British a stronger negotiating position, you see. Hitler could not fight, wouldn't dare. Will you help us?"

What would her father say? Viviane wondered. Would he save the man who killed so many? Arthur Alden had crawled across no-man's-land that day, rescuing as many men as he could, risking his own life for them. It had been an act of sacrifice, of noble courage in the face of a cowardly weapon. She listened for the sound of his voice in her head, needing his advice, his opinion, but there was only silence. She met the professor's eyes, saw the blank fear, the regret.

She set her cup on the table, the tea unsipped, and studied her hands, clasped them so tightly in her lap that they hurt. "I need to think about it."

Felix was quiet for a moment, and she could feel his gaze on her without looking. What was *he* thinking? Then he sighed. "You see, Professor, it is not an outright refusal. I'll convince her yet, you'll see." He drained his own cup, drank every drop, set it down gently on the tray, and rose. "I think we'd better go. My father will be waiting for us at the stadium, and we don't want to miss Jesse Owens's race, now do we?"

He smiled at the professor and held out his hand to Viviane with a smile, as if nothing was amiss, as if he hadn't asked her to do the impossible for the man who'd killed her father. She looked at Hitzig again, met the resignation in his eyes, the fear. Was there regret as well? She couldn't tell. She turned her attention to Felix's extended hand, stared at the smooth white palm, the manicured nails. "Come," he coaxed her, and she took his hand and rose.

His fingers were cold.

CHAPTER THIRTY-FIVE

T OM SAT AT a small table outside a café and sipped his coffee, strong and black, and watched the crowds go by. Trude was upstairs in her small apartment, a space she shared with two roommates, selecting clothes, jewelry, hats, and fripperies for her photo shoot with Viviane Alden. He'd been a distraction and an obstacle to the process, and Trude had sent him out. He savored the time alone—though he doubted he was entirely unwatched. He glanced at his watch, saw it was a few minutes past ten, and Viviane was late. She would be bringing Julia, of course, and possibly the Countess von Schroeder as chaperone, he supposed, which might account for the delay, if they were also choosing clothes and hats and gloves for the day.

"Hello."

Viviane surprised him when she slipped into the chair across from him, all alone.

"I expected you'd be coming from the other direction, from the Adlon," he said. "Don't you have a chaperone today? Where's Julia?" He was babbling. He stopped talking and looked at her. She wore a blue and white dress and a darker blue jacket. Her wide-brimmed hat framed her face and those luminous eyes of hers.

"Julia had other plans, so I came alone," she said. "I told her I needed to buy more film."

It was on the tip of his tongue to rebuke her for being out by herself, for putting herself in danger, but there were other women strolling the street by themselves. He pointed to a window above the café. "Trude's apartment is upstairs. Do you want a cup of coffee before we go up?"

She slid a book across the table toward him, a battered copy of Dickens's *A Tale of Two Cities*, and he looked from the book to her. "I found a copy of your favorite book," she said, loud enough so that anyone watching or listening wouldn't have to strain to hear. He reached to open it, but she put her hand over his, and the shock of the light touch stopped him. "Don't open it here, in this wind. Some of the pages are loose." She looked at him with fierce intensity, and he read the warning in her eyes. He looked again at the book, and he wondered what actually lay between the battered covers. Not Dickens, apparently. A note perhaps? He met her gaze, his brows raised, the question in his eyes.

She grinned, a cocky, arch little smile. "It's a special edition. Read it later, when you're alone," she said.

Her coffee arrived and her hand fluttered back from his. She picked up the spoon and stirred it, though she added neither sugar nor cream. The book sat on the table between them.

"I'm not late, am I?" a voice said.

Tom looked up and saw Felix von Schroeder standing beside the table. Viviane's start of surprise, the way her cheeks flared into full rosy bloom, told Tom that Felix hadn't been expected. "Felix!" It was half breathless.

Viviane looked like a woman caught doing something she shouldn't. She made a terrible spy after all.

Felix looked at Tom. "Felix von Schroeder," he introduced himself. "We met briefly the other night at the club, but it was dark." He did not offer his hand but took a seat between Tom and Viviane. "I understand that you are an old friend of Viviane's—or the friend of her friend—the reporter," he said. "She was most distressed when she thought you might have been run down in the street. It was a dreadful accident, was it not? But with so many reporters in Berlin at the moment, I suppose it was bound to happen." He regarded Tom with speculation. "I do hope you are careful to look both ways when you cross the street." He glanced at Viviane's flushed cheeks. "Look at you, so surprised to see me."

"I am. How did you know where to find me?" she said. Her tone just missed being casual, came out breathless. Tom wondered if she was truly happy to see Felix von Schroeder. He certainly wasn't. Felix leaned closer still to Viviane. Tom clenched his teeth at the possessive gesture.

"It's not so very sinister. I met Julia in the hotel lobby this morning. She was on her way out with Mutti. She said you were heading to buy more film for your camera. Mutti, being a scrupulous chaperone, immediately made me promise to keep an eye on you today. I checked three shops before I saw you sitting here."

Tom suspected he'd been following Viviane all along. There was something about Felix's smug grin, as if he'd won some kind of game. How long had he been watching before he joined them at the table?

Felix indicated the café, the street, with a wave of his hand. "What made you choose this café? It's rather out of the way, isn't it? There are better ones. We could go and—"

She raised her chin, leaned back a little, away from Felix. Tom hid a smile behind his coffee cup. "Can't. I'm here to photograph Fraülein Unger today," she said.

Tom pointed skyward. "Trude lives above this café. Actually, it's not such a bad little place. It's usually quiet, and the strudel is good," he said. "Don't you think so, Viviane?" He said it as if they did this often, just to needle Schroeder.

He watched Felix's jaw tighten as he glanced at the windows above him for a moment before he fixed his eyes on Viviane, as if he couldn't bear to look at anything else.

Felix von Schroeder was jealous of him, Tom thought, amused for a moment—or perhaps it was suspicion, and Felix had been sent by his brother, not his mother, to watch Viviane. His amusement faded at that.

Felix's gaze fell on the book on the table. "*A Tale of Two Cities*. My father made me read that when I was a boy." He moved to pick it up, and Tom heard Viviane's quick little indrawn breath. Tom got to the book first.

"I was reading to pass the time before Viviane arrived," he said. He slipped it into the pocket of his raincoat. It was heavy, and he realized it held more than just a note. It burned against his chest like a guilty secret.

"Oh?" Felix said with a brittle smile. "I would have thought you would be reading newspapers, or perhaps a magazine, given your profession."

"Usually, but you know what they say about all work and no play," Tom replied.

Felix raised one eyebrow at the quip. "An apt description of reporting on the Olympic Games," he said. He turned to Viviane, and his smile thawed. "Do you have enough film?" he said to Viviane, and for a moment she looked tongue-tied, a bloom of color rising over her cheeks. Felix rolled his eyes. "Did you manage to purchase what you needed? I have no doubt the lovely Fraülein Unger will want dozens of shots. A pity you don't have a movie camera like Leni Riefenstahl."

He shifted his chair slightly closer to Viviane's and regarded Tom. "Speaking of moving pictures, what do you make of the new technology of television, old chap? Bloody marvelous, isn't it?" The mocking accented English cant set Tom's teeth on edge. "And have you received one of Miss Riefenstahl's sharp little notes yet?"

He turned to Viviane. "The great lady director Leni Riefenstahl hates to see reporters in the crowd at the stadium, especially photographers who might interfere with her filming. She's had little cards printed, and if anyone gets out of line, she has one of her errand boys race over to deliver one. 'Leni Riefenstahl calls upon you to remain in your spot when you take images. Do not move around. If you ignore these instructions, your press pass will be revoked.' No one would dare disobey. You might also warn your pretty paramour not to get too close to Hitler's box. I've heard Leni is a jealous goddess when it comes to the attention of her führer."

"My paramour? Oh, you mean Trude," Tom said. "She's my official government-appointed tour guide. She's more interested in Goebbels— he's the one who likes starlets, helps them rise to the heavens and shine."

Felix's lips quirked, and he chuckled, as if he knew exactly what Trude was to Tom, or thought he did. Perhaps he'd spoken to his brother. "Goebbels—with such connections to high places, what more would an ambitious reporter need?" he said. Tom didn't bother to correct him. He saw the veiled warning in Felix's eyes, as good as a slap across the cheek with a glove, an invitation to a duel over the favors of a lovely lady. Not Trude, Viviane.

"What do you write about, Mr. Graham?" he asked. "I must assume you do not take photographs, since your—Trude—asked Viviane to take her picture."

Tom smiled. "I work with words alone." He sent Viviane a quick look. "There are others who capture images so much better than I could."

"Indeed," Felix muttered. "Have you seen Viviane's work?"

Tom nodded. "A few portraits, in England, of family and friends, that sort of thing."

Felix sipped his coffee. "Family."

"Tom is a dear friend of my brother-in-law," Viviane said quickly. "We met last fall, when Geoffrey married my stepsister. Tom and I were both in the wedding party. He mentioned he was working in Germany when he heard Julia and I were coming over."

"How kind," Felix said. "He could not have known that the Schroeders are excellent hosts, careful chaperones, and also dear family friends."

The tension was thick, the warning clear. And Felix held Tom's eyes for a long moment. Viviane jumped as the window above them opened. "Trude's ready," a dark-haired woman called down. "Come up."

Viviane shot to her feet, tipping over her empty coffee cup as she did. "That could have been a disaster," Felix said. "Your camera might have been ruined in the deluge. Or Mr. Graham's book, if he hadn't been so quick to tuck it out of harm's way."

Viviane was busy with her camera and didn't notice the less-than-subtle warning. Felix was dangerous, Tom realized, astute and watchful. And jealousy made him more so.

"No harm done since the cup had nothing in it," Tom said lightly. He righted the cup and set it back on the saucer. For a moment, Felix frowned, then Viviane glanced at him, and that charming sunshine smile of his clicked back into place.

Felix took Viviane's arm, pulled her close to his side, and clasped her hand where it lay on his sleeve, an intimate, possessive little gesture. "This should be fun," he said. But Viviane was looking at *him*, not Felix, and he noticed that she didn't grip his hand in return. It was a dangerous game, one Tom had no interest in playing. The stakes were too high, both for him and for Viviane. All of Felix's affection couldn't save her if she was caught.

Tom looked away, cast his eyes up to Trude's window. "One mustn't keep a lady waiting."

"Or an official tour guide," Felix replied, sending Tom another cutting smile as he led Viviane inside.

CHAPTER THIRTY-SIX

IN MAGDA GOEBBELS'S elegant salon, Ilsa von Schroeder smiled at her companions over the delicate gold-rimmed edge of her cup. The cup was part of a tea service Magda had received as a wedding present, and like Magda herself, the porcelain was paper thin and adorned with Nazi symbols.

Ilsa had come to meet Diana Guinness, the blond British beauty, Sir Oswald Mosley's lover, and she'd brought her own English guest. Beside her, Lady Julia Devellin smiled shyly at the assembled women, the two English aristocrats elbow to elbow with the wives of the German elite, and Ilsa felt a surge of maternal pride for her young visitor. Julia wore the lovely pin Otto had given her over her heart on her pretty summer dress. Magda had admired the workmanship of the piece, and Diana Mosley said she intended to commission one just like it for Sir Oswald's birthday. Julia responded with a charming smile.

Ilsa couldn't be more delighted in Otto's interest in the girl. Julia was lovely, with blue eyes, pale skin, and blond hair, and she was English. Hitler liked English women. Diana's sister Unity Mitford was a great favorite of the führer's. She would visit him at his mountain retreat, sit at his feet, and allow the great man to stroke her hair. Not that

Hitler would ever marry her, of course, but he encouraged his men to wed English women. Such alliances would forge strong ties—silken ones—between England and Germany, and the French would be left out in the cold in the new European order.

"Are you enjoying the games?" Julia asked Diana.

Diana smiled. "Oh, very much. So exciting to watch, don't you think?" She leaned in like a conspirator, and Ilsa's ears pricked. "To tell the truth, I go more to watch the people than for the sport. Unity likes the events. She'll be at the stadium now, avidly goggling at the field through her binoculars. They were a gift from Adolf so she won't strain her eyes."

Julia laughed, the demure sound like the silver tinkle of a small bell. Ilsa met Magda's gaze, and Germany's First Lady of Style and Influence raised her brows in a subtle question. Ilsa smiled back in silent reply to the unspoken question. Yes, if she had anything to do with it, she would see her son married Lady Julia Devellin. She was gratified when Magda nodded her approval.

"Your father is the Earl of Rutherford, is he not?" Magda asked Julia.

"Yes. He and Count von Schroeder are very old friends. Papa would have liked to come to Germany himself, but my stepmother's health is delicate," Julia replied.

"Did you and Diana know each other in England?" Magda continued.

Julia glanced at her countrywoman, nearly a decade older than she was, once married to the heir to the Guinness brewing empire and now divorced. She was one of the fabulous Mitford girls, the belles of English society, each one of them more eccentric, outspoken, or high-flying than the last.

"Julia is closer in age to my youngest sister," Diana said. "Though I daresay she understands the trials of being one in a family of so many girls, since Lord Rutherford has a number of daughters of his own. We have that in common, among other things."

Magda's eyes lit. "Is your father an admirer of Germany?" she asked baldly.

Ilsa held her breath and waited for Julia to answer. Diana, too, regarded Ilsa's protégé with a heavy-lidded gaze and a half smile.

"Of course—he was most eager for us to come to visit," Julia said.

Ilsa's toes curled in her shoes. It was the perfect answer, not too long or detailed, nor too short as to be impolite. It gave Magda something and nothing. Magda would recognize the diplomacy, the subtlety of such a reply. As the wife of Hitler's friend and propaganda minister, Magda walked a fine line herself. She was powerful yet female. She'd used her wits and her charm to rise to where she was, and while the führer remained unmarried, she was his official hostess, his shining example of German womanhood—a successful wife, a prolific mother, an arbiter of taste and style, and a charming supporter of all things Nazi.

As it had been throughout all the history of all the world, it was Ilsa's opinion that women were the real power in Nazi Germany, working behind the scenes, whispering suggestions and advice in the ears of their men, influencing great events with a delicate lift of a perfectly manicured finger. Magda would know that, and so would Diana Guinness. She suspected that little Julia could easily be brought to understand it, groomed, as it were, trained and polished to be another jewel in the Nazi firmament. One day Lady Julia Devellin—Lady Julia von Schroeder—might even eclipse Magda.

For now, it was enough to encourage the blossoming romance between Otto and Julia, to bring her into the upper echelons of German society and wait.

"You are here with one of your sisters, I believe," Magda said to Julia, just so Ilsa would know that she knew all.

Julia smiled. "Viviane is my stepsister. She is helping a friend today. She takes marvelous photographs, you see. She captures something special about everyone. She agreed to take some pictures of an actress—Trude Unger. Perhaps you've heard of her?"

Magda's eyes glazed over, and Ilsa almost cringed. It was the first misstep Julia had made.

Magda's husband had a penchant for actresses, the younger and prettier the better. One glance from him, one night or afternoon in his bed, and they became stars—of gossip, if not on the silver screen.

Diana's brows shot up. "Not the Viviane Alden who was betrothed to Phillip Medway?" she said. "I should have recognized the name at once. Phillip is a dear friend of ours." She sipped her coffee, her eyes wide with curiosity. "Whatever happened to end their engagement? Phillip wouldn't say."

Julia's smile was forced. "A difference of opinion."

"A political difference?" Diana pressed, setting her cup down.

"Personal, I believe, though, like Phillip, Viviane has never said what precisely caused the end of their betrothal." Julia looked away, delicately signaling an end to the conversation.

"The Marquess of Medway is one of Oswald's lieutenants," Diana persisted, explaining to Magda.

"And obviously very high-ranking," Magda said with pleasure. "It is good to see so many supporters of the Fascist cause in the upper levels of English society." She glanced at Julia speculatively, and at Ilsa, as if she wondered if there was more to the story. Julia remained silent.

"You should have brought your stepsister with you today. We might have winkled the truth out of her, sympathized. There is nothing so tragic as an unhappy love affair," Magda said, feigning disappointment.

"Will our führer be attending your party, Magda?" Ilsa asked, changing the subject. How she would love to present Julia to Hitler on her son's arm. Out of the corner of her eye, she saw Diana's blue gaze turn crisp. Oh, yes—even she recognized Julia as a potential distraction from her sister Unity, a new British beauty to charm Adolf Hitler.

"The guest list has run to thousands!" Magda said, putting a dramatic hand to her chest, deftly avoiding Ilsa's question. "Joseph wants it staged like a movie production. He's designed sets and costumes for our guests, had the whole island made over into a Venetian fantasy."

Julia lit up. "How marvelous!"

Ilsa smiled as if the marvel of it was still to be seen, knowing Magda's party would have competition. "We will be attending all the important parties, of course—the Görings', and the Ribbentrops', and several of the embassy events," she said.

Diana grinned at Julia. "Oh, we simply *must* attend Ribbentrop's party—there's a rumor that he's about to be appointed as the new ambassador to Britain, and we must show our support." She put a languid hand to her cheek. "And the wine will most definitely be plentiful!" It was a sharp little reference to the new ambassador's roots as a wine merchant. The ladies laughed, enjoying the jab at the unpopular minister.

As they rose to leave, Magda touched a finger to Julia's brooch, admiring it once more. "It was very nice to meet you, my dear. Do give my regards to Otto. We shall see you both at the party."

It was a clear indication of Magda's approval, her blessing of the girl as "suitable." Ilsa beamed. It was as good as setting her son's polished boot on the next rung of the ladder of success.

CHAPTER THIRTY-SEVEN

TRUDE'S TINY APARTMENT resembled a henhouse after a fox attack. Trude and her roommates were squawking like chickens, flapping and fluttering and debating what the actress should wear for her photo shoot. The air was thick with cheap perfume and the smell of stale coffee and burned toast. Feather boas, satin gowns, and other, more subdued garments of every style and color were draped over every surface.

Viviane found a space to stand against the door, as out of the way as she could manage. Tom and Felix backed themselves into the tiny kitchen, merely a small hot plate on a minuscule table with a wobbly leg propped up with a copy of *Mein Kampf.*

"Best use of it I've ever seen," Felix said.

"I'm Lotte. Will you take my picture next?" asked the buxom brunette who'd called to them from the window, merely glancing at Felix before turning to flirt with Tom, who was taller and better looking. Felix frowned, noticing the slight, but Tom simply regarded the young woman blandly and pointed at Viviane. "Miss Alden is the photographer."

Lotte turned to cast an appraising glance over Viviane.

"I'm Berta," the other roommate said, poking her blond head out from behind the screen in the corner where Trude could be heard fretting that none of the clothes available exhibited her best qualities as an actress or a woman of grace and beauty.

"Where on earth am I going to take photos in here?" Viviane murmured, looking at the cramped space.

"There's a small balcony," Lotte said. "If Trude goes outside, and you stay inside and lean out, it might work."

Berta squeezed into the kitchen. "Pardon me, but I need some milk for my coffee," she said, her breasts pressed to Felix's chest, her nose inches from his.

"How do you *sleep* in here?" Felix murmured, shifting against the table, stumbling over *Mein Kampf.*

"Oh, we don't sleep here at the same time," Lotte said with a smile. "We're all actresses, you see. I work nights at the Sherbini Bar. Berta works by day at a tobacconist's shop, and Trude—" She smiled and shifted her eyes sideways to Tom. "Trude works sometimes by day, sometimes at night."

"Yes, I understand she's an official tour guide," Felix murmured, shooting Tom a sharp look. "Quaint name for it."

Berta reached to the highest shelf of the small cabinet for the milk jug, and her lush breasts were pressed to Felix's chin for a moment. In the crush, a hat box toppled off the top of the cabinet and spilled its contents. Tom caught a concoction of feathers and straw that looked like a dead game bird. Viviane suppressed a smile at his horror.

Berta giggled and took it from him. "It's one of Trude's hats."

"Perhaps we could go outside, take the photos in a park," Viviane suggested.

Trude stepped out from behind the screen, looking like a Hollywood screen goddess in a satin sheath, her eyes lined with kohl, her lips siren red.

"You can't go into a park looking like that," Felix said, dazzled by the delectable sight of Trude in full bloom. Tom said nothing at all.

"You're gorgeous, Trude, but Felix is right. We need a better setting to do you justice," Viviane said.

"My apartment has plenty of windows, lots of light, and a decent view of the city," Felix suggested.

Have you been to Felix's apartment before? Viviane glanced at Tom, reading the silent question in his gaze.

She lifted her chin. *What if I have?* She looked away and smiled at Felix. "I think that might do."

"Where is this place?" Trude asked.

"Near the Lustgarten," Felix said.

Trude's eyes lit up, a challenge considering the sheer weight of the cosmetics on her sultry lids. "The Lustgarten? It must be nice. How perfect!" she said. "I'll pack a few things so I can change my outfits, hmm?" she said, and began to toss the scattered clothing into the air. Berta and Lotte joined her, choosing and debating, keeping and discarding outfits and all of them clucking like chickens once again.

Viviane glanced at Tom. He wasn't watching the actress like Felix was, lost in the luscious sight of her, the way the gown clung to her hips, sculpted her breasts. He was looking at *her*, his arms folded across his chest, his hat askew. He looked like a reporter, like a spy, and yet so familiar, a bit of home, perhaps, of ordinary life and safety. She suppressed a smile and the desire to swipe an errant feather, shed from Trude's hat, from his shoulder.

But this wasn't home, and neither of them was truly safe. She looked at the outline of the book in his breast pocket. She'd found it at a bookshop and hollowed it out with nail scissors in the bathroom while Julia slept. It held ten rolls of film, packed tight. She might have chosen a bigger book, but she liked the irony of the title.

He shifted his eyes toward the door, then back. He was leaving. She felt a moment of panic, swallowed it, and nodded almost imperceptibly. Where would he go, what would he do with her photographs? She longed to ask.

"I think I'll head to the stadium, do some reporting," he said to no one in particular, and moved toward the door. He put his hands on Viviane's shoulders, moving her enough to slide behind her. She breathed him in, and for an instant, he squeezed slightly, the gesture a warning, a reassurance, or perhaps just a farewell.

"Tommy?" Trude called to him as he opened the door, and he turned to glance at her. Viviane saw the way his jaw tensed at the call, at the use of the pet name. She wondered again where he was really going.

"Don't forget the reception at the State Opera is tonight," Trude said, giving him permission to go yet reminding him she would expect him to behave and return promptly. Viviane looked up at him, just inches from her beside the door. He didn't reply to Trude. "Will you and Julia and the Schroeders be attending this evening's event?" he asked her.

"Of course," Felix answered for her. "As they say in England, everyone who is anyone is on the guest list, and the Schroeders are very important. It should be great fun. They've been making over the State Opera House for weeks just for this reception. Like everything else about these games, the glamour of it all will impress the world."

"Will the führer be there?" Berta asked.

Felix looked at her pityingly. "Of course not! He is a busy man. He will be hard at work, taking care of all of us, making sure the ship of state is smoothly on course. He has no time for fun or frivolity. He is sending Herr Goebbels and Herr Göring instead, the Laurel and Hardy of the Third Reich."

Lotte snorted a laugh, but Trude frowned. "Do you speak this way in front of your brother, Herr von Schroeder?"

Felix wasn't deterred. "Does anyone? My mother would wash my mouth out with soap if she heard me say such a thing, and I shudder to think what Otto might do to me. Don't worry, Fraülein Unger, I shall be on my best behavior tonight, suitably awed, properly deferential, and fiercely patriotic." He grinned at the actresses. "You see, we are all actors, clowns, heroes, lovely ladies, and dastardly gentlemen. The State Opera has seen worse performances than the ones we will play tonight, I daresay."

Berta threw back her head and laughed. "Obviously you will play the clown, *mein* Herr. You are very naughty."

"I have a clever flower for my lapel that squirts water. Will you be there?" Felix asked her.

"Me? Of course not. I don't have the kind of friends Trude has," Berta said, and glanced at her flatmate. "Will you wear that dress tonight, Trude? It will certainly impress."

"Ah, but who will you impress first, Göring or Goebbels?" Felix asked. "It is a difficult choice."

Trude flicked her chin skyward. "I shall impress them all."

She glanced at Tom. "Tommy will be with me, of course."

Felix sent him a vicious little smile. "Caught in front of the cameras for a change, on the arm of the glamorous Fraülein Unger, written up in the news instead of writing it."

Tom frowned, and Viviane knew he hated that idea.

Trude worked her way across the room, pushed between Tom and Viviane. "We shall enjoy ourselves tonight, *nein*?" She pressed her mouth to Tom's cheek, left a smear of lipstick, a red brand of ownership. She didn't bother to wipe it away.

"Go on, Tommy. Enjoy the games. I shall expect a full report on who pole-vaulted the best, or however you say it, and who ran the fastest. And don't forget to make note of what the ladies in the stands are wearing."

Viviane waited for him to look at her as he took his leave, wanted that glance, the nod of his head, perhaps, but he left without another word, and the door closed behind him.

CHAPTER THIRTY-EIGHT

Tom walked for a block before he hailed a cab and got in. "The Eden Hotel," he said, instead of directing the driver to the stadium. The thick bulk of *A Tale of Two Cities* burned a hole in his pocket. Some joke.

From the Eden's busy lobby, he sent a message up to room 408 and waited for a reply, reading a newspaper with his hat pulled low. He supposed he looked more like a spy than a journalist. He looked around, identifying the watchers, the too-casual, too-ordinary men in corners or by the newsstand or pretending to look out the window as if they were waiting for someone. They were all of a type, their eyes sharp, their faces instantly forgettable.

Guests flowed around them, everyone well dressed, for this was the Eden, home away from home for the well-heeled traveler. Diplomats and esteemed guests of the state were accommodated here in plush suites. Bellhops scurried like mice, carrying packages from Berlin's most exclusive shops or escorting small dogs on jeweled leashes. Secretaries and diplomatic assistants were dropped at the front door in cabs and rushed through the lobby, clutching briefcases full of reports and dossiers. The watchers regarded those men with interest until they disappeared into the elevator, and then they made note of which floor the lift stopped at.

Tom walked to the rack of postcards and tourist brochures, pretended to peruse them.

"Are you here for the games?" a young woman asked him with a smile, a guest perhaps, holding a handful of brochures and postcards in her hand. "There's so much to see, isn't there?" She pressed a pamphlet into his hand, and he read the title emblazoned over a lovely image of the mountains. *Get to Know Beautiful Germany: An Indispensable Guide for Every Visitor to the Olympic Games in Berlin.* "I've found this one particularly useful," she said helpfully.

Behind him, a bellhop cleared his throat. "If you'd like to go up, sir," he said in accented English.

Tom nodded and turned to wish his momentary companion a good day, only to find that she'd already gone.

In the elevator, he idly opened the brochure she'd handed him. It surprised him to see a map with the title "Concentration Camps, Penal Facilities, and Prisons." Red dots marked the locations across Germany. A starred notation remarked, "SA torture chambers not included, for they are too numerous."

He glanced at the elevator operator, a young man in a crisp hotel uniform, his smile as precise as the perfect crease in his trousers, as polished as his shoes, but he was watching the floor numbers tick past. At the fourth floor, he opened the doors with an efficiency borne of thousands of repetitions and bid Tom good day.

Alone in the hallway, Tom looked at the brochure again. The usual photos of castles and museums, parks and gardens were interspersed with images of SA men with dogs, beating people on the streets or posing in front of stores with anti-Semitic slogans painted on the windows. A photo of fresh-faced Hitler Youth hiking along a mountain track was printed next to an image of similar boys throwing books on a bonfire. Pictures of happy tourists pointing and smiling at the glorious Olympic Stadium were next to blurry images of concentration camps, guards with whips, and snarling dogs.

The door of room 408 opened, and Alexander MacCann stepped out, wiping shaving soap from his chin. "I thought I heard the elevator," he said, looking expectantly at Tom. "Are you coming in?"

Tom entered the room. The remains of breakfast sat on a tray on a small table. "I can send for fresh coffee. Or whisky, if you prefer," his uncle said.

"It's a mite early in the day," Tom said. He held up the brochure. "Have you seen this? Someone in the lobby gave it to me. A young woman."

Alexander took it and flipped through. "Yes, there are people printing them in other countries and smuggling them in. This one is particularly well-done, but don't get caught with it. There are newspapers as well that look for all the world like ordinary editions of the local rags but are anything but. What have you got for me?"

Tom took the book out of his pocket and handed it to his uncle, who regarded the spine. "*A Tale of Two Cities*?" He opened the cover and noted the film in the hollowed-out compartment. "Clever," he said. "I like the title. Was that your idea?"

"One must have some fun," Tom said, not bothering to mention Viviane.

Alexander raised an eyebrow at the quip. "So I see. You have lipstick on your cheek."

Tom grabbed the napkin off the breakfast tray and wiped at his face while Alex took the film out of the book and set it on the table.

"I take it your lady friend took these, one of the Earl of Rutherford's girls, the ones visiting the Schroeders? Which one is the photographer, the redhead or the blond?"

"You're watching them?" Tom asked.

"Keeping an eye on them. The blond is quite chummy with Otto von Schroeder."

"Not her. Her stepsister, the redhead." He didn't want to share Viviane with his uncle. He wanted her anonymous, invisible, and safe. "What do you know about Felix von Schroeder, Otto's younger brother?" Tom asked.

Alexander was quiet for a moment, his thoughts unreadable as he scanned Tom's face. "Why? What's this about?"

"He seems to be Viviane's constant companion."

"Jealous?" Alexander asked bluntly.

"No," Tom lied. "He made some rather interesting comments about the government," he said. "Things more in line with that brochure than *Mein Kampf*."

"So he might not share the dogged devotion of the rest of his family?" Alex asked.

"Yes. Or he may be playing a part, luring Viviane into a false sense of security, trying to get her to reveal herself. She's not a professional. She's simply doing this as a favor to me. I don't want to see her get hurt." He realized he was crushing the brim of his hat in his fist and forced himself to let go, to toss the hat on a chair before he ruined it. He resisted the urge to pace and thrust his hands into his pockets.

"Now how would we explain *that* to Rutherford?" Alexander drawled. "You might have thought this through before you got her involved, laddie. Have you seen any of her photographs? What if they're all crooked, blurry impressions of castles and mountains and pretty flowers?"

"They won't be," Tom said.

"I'll have them developed and printed, and we'll see." Alex picked up his jacket off the back of a chair and put it on. "Come on. I'm here as a tourist. Let's go out and do some sightseeing, just you showing a kinsman around Berlin, eh? Nothing clandestine."

"I think I'll pass on that," Tom said.

Alexander shook his head and sent Tom a bemused smile. "No, you won't. It's part of the mission, lad. Why do you think they chose me to be your contact? What's more ordinary than an uncle and his nephew spending time together, seeing the sights, having coffee. Family stuff."

Tom shook his head. "We're not family. We're strangers."

Alex's expression remained the same. "That we are, but that's going to change."

"Did Strathwood put you up to this?" Tom asked.

"No, not specifically. It simply makes sense to those in charge to use a connection that already exists. Blood being thicker, as they say. You can't disagree with that logic."

Tom remained stubbornly silent.

"Like it or not, you're stuck with me," Alex said. He scooped up the film, took it into the bedroom, and returned without it.

"What will you do with it—take it to a chemist?" Tom asked.

"Not necessary. The Eden is the home away from home for the most important foreign diplomats and businessmen—and others. The film will be picked up within the hour, printed, and evaluated, and we'll see if your Miss Alden has captured anything useful. If she has, it will find its way into the right hands in England." He walked to the door and opened it, waiting for Tom to go through before he shut it behind them. "No need to worry about it. Let's go and enjoy the day like two braw Scots on the loose."

"ARE YOU AN engineer or a full-time spy?" Tom asked bluntly as they walked through the zoo a short while later.

"Do you think the two careers incompatible?" Alexander asked him, tossing a peanut to a parrot. "I design aircraft. I want them to be the safest, fastest, most modern flying machines in the world. We learned after the last war that the one thing that will win a war, and win it fast, is airpower. Whoever owns the skies will be the victor, and I want to make damned sure it's my country, not this one. I need to know what my competitors are designing so I can build something better to counter it, d'you see?"

Tom nodded.

Alex tossed another peanut and grinned. "It's not very much different than what you do. You look behind the scenes, delve into secrets in order to get a story. You keep your eyes open and decide if you believe what you see. Like that tourist pamphlet—a good bit of journalism must be clever, readable, and informative, and expose the unpalatable truth if required, convince people. Once you read such an article, if you're a thinking man, you know better what you're dealing with. You know yourself that you have to present the hard news carefully, an iron rod in a velvet sleeve, and you need all the facts in order to write a truly good report. Am I correct in that? Is that how it works?"

Tom didn't reply. "Aren't you afraid of getting caught?" he asked instead.

Alexander pulled the tourist brochure out of his pocket. "This is a warning of just what happens to the ones who do get caught. Most people won't even understand it, let alone heed it. Look around you. See how happy the tourists are? The Nazis have done an excellent job of creating peace and perfection and justifying such extremes of patriotism. How could anyone believe in war or violence or hatred when there's music and flowers and a spectacle to divert their attention, soothe their worries, amuse them?"

They left the zoo and crossed a busy street. Alex pointed to a policeman directing traffic. "Watch this."

"Pardon me," he said in English, "but I seem to be somewhat lost.

Can you help me?" The policeman turned at once, beaming. Alexander held out the brochure to him, open to a map showing the zoo. Beside the photos of smiling people feeding the elephants, there were other photos of caged people in striped prison uniforms peering out at the camera, their eyes hollow with despair.

The policeman glanced at the pamphlet. "Ah, the zoo! Berlin's zoo is one of the finest in the world. If you go along this street and turn to your left, it's a short and pleasant walk to the gates."

"Thank you," Alexander said, and returned to Tom's side. "You see. He didn't look past the headline on the page or the jolly photo of children and elephants."

Tom held his breath, kept his eyes on the policeman, waited for him to blow his whistle and point at them, or give a secret nod to someone hidden in the crowd, and have them followed or arrested. Alexander chuckled.

"I can see why they chose you. You're good. You've taken in every possibility and kept your eyes open, but you show no fear. Just keep doing that."

They crossed the street, and the policeman smiled at them once more, then turned his attention to an unruly cabdriver.

"One thing," Alexander said as they reached the other side. "Your photographer, Miss Alden. Is she as careful as you are?"

"I hope so," he said. "She's . . . brave."

"She's also in the belly of the beast, so to speak. Otto von Schroeder is an up-and-coming man in the SD. He won't take kindly to any side adventures by a guest of his family. He won't hesitate to deal harshly with her. He'll do what it takes to keep his place, improve it. He had a university student arrested a few weeks ago for some comment she made about the regime. She was the sister of an old school chum of his, just a silly girl, young and pretty and incautious. She was tortured. Otto told her brother that she'd taken ill, had decided to go and spend a few months in the country at a rest camp, frolicking in the sun and singing patriotic little songs all day."

"How do you know about her fate?"

Alexander scanned the street, his eyes shadowed under his hat. "This isn't my first trip to Germany. I met her sister last year, and we had a relationship. Much like your photographer, I suspect. Otto arrested the wrong sister. Her family was shocked, of course—her father is a party member—and they blamed it on the influence of people outside the family, the students she associated with." He glanced at Tom. "Does that describe your Miss Alden? A fine family, her stepfather a senior member of parliament and an appeaser?"

Tom swallowed hard but didn't reply.

Alexander pointed to a café with music playing and an outdoor terrace filled with happy tourists. "Let's stop for a drink, shall we? Then we'll go to the stadium and cheer for circuses and spectacles."

CHAPTER THIRTY-NINE

"What a lovely apartment," Trude gushed as she looked around Felix's flat, took in the large and elegant room, the old wood and leather, and the floor-to-ceiling shelves overfilled with books in untidy stacks. "What is it that you do, Herr von Schroeder? Are you in the same line of work as your brother?"

Felix crossed to scoop a pile of papers off the sofa. "Not at all. I'm a chemist. I'm sorry about the mess. The maid comes in twice a week, and this is her day off."

"A chemist? Do you make up medicines and pills in a shop, then?" Trude asked, running her hand along the back of the leather sofa.

Felix quirked a smile. "Not that kind of chemist—I work in a laboratory, doing scientific research."

Viviane's gaze fell on a silver trophy proudly displayed on its own shelf. A gold medal was mounted in a frame beside that, as well as a number of framed certificates. Felix pointed to them. "I am the best and brightest chemist in Germany." He glanced at Viviane, smug with pride. "Well, save for the professor, of course, but no one else is as good as I am." He truly believed it, she thought, he looked sure and arrogant, peering through his spectacles and down the length of his nose.

"Have you invented anything I might know of?" Trude asked.

Felix laughed. "I very much doubt it, unless you make a habit of reading scientific journals."

Trude's eyes glazed with disinterest.

"Will this do?" Felix asked Viviane, indicating the room with a sweep of his hand.

"Perfectly," Viviane said. "The light is wonderful." She crossed to the window and looked out at the view of the city. The sky was clear today, the sun shining down on a perfect summer day. "Come over by the window," she said to Trude, and spent a few minutes composing the photograph. "Smile, but not too broadly."

"Like this?" Trude asked, pouting her lips and lowering her painted eyelids to half-mast, the typical pose of a sultry actress who traded on her looks rather than her talent.

"No, not quite," Viviane said. "Look out the window at the city," she directed. "How do you feel about Berlin?"

Trude shrugged. "I grew up in a small town. I dreamed of coming to Berlin. It is the most exciting city in the world, the most modern, the best in every way. I love it here."

Viviane nodded. "Then look at that view and think of how the city you love is spread out before you, tempting, full of delight and possibility."

Trude turned to the view, a softer smile on her curved lips, a look of determination on her lovely face. It made her intriguing, a woman with hidden depths.

Viviane took the picture.

"What is your favorite film?" she asked Trude.

Trude gave her a heavy-lidded look of amusement, as if the question was silly. "At the moment? Whichever is the most popular one, the one everyone is talking about."

"And why is it so popular, what are people saying? Why do they like it?"

"The actress plays a woman who loses her love and undertakes a journey to find another. She is sad but hopeful. She keeps her heart hidden, though she yearns for love, for understanding, for peace."

"How does she show all that without saying a word?" Viviane asked.

Trude slumped slightly against a bookshelf looking into the invisible mist of the future, her mouth soft, her jaw hard.

Viviane took the picture.

"If you were in love—" Viviane began.

"Who's to say I'm not?" Trude said, and Viviane thought of Tom, but Trude sent Felix a playful wink. Viviane took that picture, too.

"If you were in love and he made you very happy, brought you a gift or a surprise, how would you look at him?"

Trude crossed and stood in front of Felix, and Viviane moved so she was shooting over his shoulder. "Say something to make me deliriously happy," Trude said to Felix.

"You're very pretty," Felix said, and Trude frowned at him.

"*Nein*. Make it something you'd say to the woman you love, darling. This is acting, and you are my leading man. Isn't that correct, Miss Alden?" Felix glanced over his shoulder at Viviane.

"What should I say?" he asked.

"Tell her she's stubborn and dangerous and utterly thrilling," she said. "Make her try to read that in your face, make her mad, then smile at her, beguile her, make it impossible for her to forget you, or even look away when you're in the room. Make her long for you when you are not." She felt the metal of the camera in her grip, warmed by her hands, an extension of all she saw in her mind and heart. Felix was still staring at her.

"Now who was the man who made you feel that way?" he asked softly. She felt her face heat under Felix's earnest gaze.

"How's this?" Trude interrupted, posing again.

Felix spun, his expression changing in an instant to rage. "Don't be a cow!" he shouted at her. Trude's eyes widened, and her jaw dropped. He laughed, then turned to Viviane again, the fury gone. "No offense, Fraülein Unger. I simply wished to shock you, bring out something real for the camera. She looks utterly real now, don't you think, Viviane? Vulnerable, exposed, uncertain. Is that how you feel inside? It is a dissection of sorts, a way to lay you bare, so we might see what makes you tick."

Viviane took the picture, but her hands shook.

"You *are* like your brother," Trude murmured, looking vulnerable indeed.

CHAPTER FORTY

THAT EVENING, THE Schroeder family climbed the red-carpeted marble steps of the State Opera House. The grand space was crowded with international diplomats, senior government officials, actors, artists, and foreign guests of honor.

The countess was dazzling in gold satin, her hair piled high on her head and an heirloom diamond necklace clasped around her slender throat. The count looked wonderful in his tuxedo, proudly wearing his military medals and orders.

Behind them, Otto escorted Julia, who wore pink silk. She wore the pearls her parents had given her as a coming-out gift and a white fox fur stole with a diamond clasp.

Viviane followed behind her stepsister, on Felix's arm. She wore pale blue again, a different gown, the neckline draped, the bias-cut silk clinging to her slim curves.

When they arrived at the top of the stairs, Felix leaned close to her ear. "To the right, Herr Goebbels is holding court, representing the Reich government in the führer's absence. He has all the dazzling entertainers on his side of the room, the most brilliant writers, composers, and actors. And over there"—he pointed to the left side of the room—"Hermann Göring is representing the government of Prussia. Göring has gone for a more heroic guest list. That's Charles Lindbergh from America by his side, and the German ace pilot Ernst Udet. The presence of both is carefully staged to remind one that Göring was also a heroic flyer during the war. I wager my father will lead us to the left to start the evening, since he, too, was a warrior, and he doesn't like Goebbels. Still, he knows it is necessary to pretend to like everyone. So much subterfuge, and so much importance given to playing the game right. I have a great desire to snub everyone, just to be shocking. Shall we be shocking this evening?" he asked her.

Viviane sent him a quelling look, and he laughed. A photographer stepped in front of them and snapped a picture, the flashbulb exploding, blinding her for a moment. "You could teach him a thing or two about capturing a decent image. He might have given us warning so we could arrange ourselves in a proper pose or pull a face." He pointed to a famous actress, who was managing to hold a conversation, sip champagne, and pose for the hungry, circling cameras all at the same time.

There were speeches. The head of the German Olympic Committee thanked the government for its support. Hermann Göring raised a toast to the absent führer. Joseph Goebbels gave a stirring speech that praised the Olympics as a festival of peace and joy, a link to unite the peoples of Europe, and declared Adolf Hitler's Germany to be the driving force for peace in Europe. People leaped to their feet and applauded. A chorus of "Seig heil" burst forth from the loyal party members and the military men present. Goebbels's dark eyes scanned the room in a slow sweep, taking note of who was cheering and who was not.

Champagne and schnapps flowed.

Viviane watched as Otto presented Julia to everyone of importance. He stood stiffly as he was introduced to the people Julia knew, other British aristocrats, diplomats and celebrities on holiday, and political friends of her father's. Viviane noted that he led Julia away from her countrymen as quickly as he could, back to the German guests.

"She's surrounded. She might as well give up," Felix quipped to Viviane as they watched.

"We're going home in a few weeks," Viviane said.

"Yes," Felix agreed. "But perhaps arrangements will be made, a flurry of letters and cables and phone calls made, and there will be a wedding in the spring. Here or there. Would you like to wager on it?"

"Another wager?" Viviane said, forcing a light tone. "I don't think I can afford to play." She sipped her champagne. What if Julia was truly in love? If there was a war, Julia would be forced to choose sides. She looked at her starry-eyed stepsister and wondered whether she'd pick her homeland and her family or Otto von Schroeder. She wondered if Rutherford, or Estella, for that matter, would allow such a match. Julia was only eighteen. Viviane's heart ached, and she hoped Julia's first love affair wouldn't end with a broken heart. Or a war.

She knew the moment Tom Graham arrived. The rest of the press corps had been carefully contained, herded in before the speeches and herded out again when they were done. But Tom was with the beautiful Trude, his special pass. The starlet clung to him like a barnacle. Viviane watched him nod politely to the people Trude introduced him to, mostly on Goebbels's side of the room. That calm but keen expression of his told Viviane he was listening, making notes, even if his notebook was out of sight. How handsome he looked in his tuxedo, Viviane thought, sipping more champagne—she really did love champagne. Other women were casting admiring glances at Tom as well. Trude, she thought, was going to have competition.

A puff of air hit her ear, and she jumped. "Are you going to stare at him all night?" Felix asked.

"Who?" she managed.

"Trude's 'Tommy.' Your English friend," Felix said, rolling his eyes.

She sipped more champagne, let the bubbles tickle her tongue. "Oh, is he here? I was looking at Trude. Perhaps we should take a few more shots in the Lustgarten," she said quickly.

"Never play cards, Viviane. You are far too easy to read. You blush when you lie."

He rose and pushed through the crowds to Tom and Trude. Tom's eyes swung to hers, locked and held. He was also easy to read, if you knew him. He'd learned to keep his face carefully blank, not letting even a spark of light show behind his shutters, but a tiny muscle in his jaw ticked when something affected him. And there it was—the almost imperceptible little movement as he looked at her. Her heart—her whole body—thrilled as if she had champagne bubbles in her blood. And so she did. She sipped again to cover her smile. Felix leaned close to Trude's ear and pointed to their table.

The actress hurried over to kiss Viviane's cheeks, enveloping Viviane in a cloud of perfume. "I cannot thank you enough for taking my picture. When will they be ready?"

Felix chuckled. "I made arrangements this afternoon. The film is being developed as we speak. May I deliver the photos to you tomorrow?"

"I would love that!" Trude said, her eyes glittering.

Viviane saw Tom frown slightly. Jealousy? No. He was looking at her, not at Trude or Felix. With a sweeping glance he took in her blue dress, the diamond clips in her hair, the polish on her nails, and the champagne in front of her before he brought his eyes back up to hers. Was the fleeting expression that crossed his face concern? She grinned at him.

"Will you dance with me, Herr von Schroeder?" Trude asked, holding out her hand.

When they'd left the table, Tom looked pointedly at her half-empty glass. "Be careful," Tom said through tight lips.

She giggled, feeling as bubbly and light as the champagne. "Of Felix?"

"Of all of them," he said.

"Does that include you?" She tossed her head. "You are the most dangerous man I know."

She moved to pick up her glass, but he put his hand over hers. His skin was warm, and she felt a jolt of awareness flow up her arm to her chest, more potent than the champagne. "Let's dance instead."

He led her onto the floor. How well they fit together, how instinctively he moved to compensate for her bad leg, how safe she felt in his arms. Even here, in the heart of Berlin, in a tuxedo, he somehow smelled of tweed and home. "What are you doing?" he asked as she burrowed into his neck.

"Smelling you," she replied. "You remind me of England." She stumbled a little and he tightened his arm around her.

"I think you need some air," he said, and danced her right out the French doors that led to a wide balcony. Outside, the city was spread out before them, the landmarks lit by spotlights that illuminated swastika flags, made them glow like blood in the torchlight.

She realized that she hated Berlin. Tom stood beside her, silently staring at the view, and she wondered if he felt the same thing. Everything about the city overwhelmed her. The subterfuge and lies frightened her, made her certain that war was indeed coming, and it would be worse than the last. Her father's sacrifice, the sacrifice of so many, had been in vain. She didn't feel brave now. "It's all a lie," she murmured. "There is no festival of peace and joy."

"No," he agreed.

She shivered, and he mistook it for cold and took off his jacket and draped it around her shoulders. It reminded her of the day they'd met, when he pulled her out of the Channel like a flounder.

She drew it around her, burrowed into it. She didn't have to pretend with Tom. He knew her secrets, saw the person she was. He made her feel safe. "Are you rescuing me again, Mr. Graham?"

He turned his head to look at her, his face inches from her own.

"Do you need rescuing?" he asked.

"Not at the moment," she murmured, and rose on her toes, put her lips against his. His arms came around her body, pulled her into the heat of his own, and he deepened the kiss, made it perfect. She let her eyes drift shut, leaned in, and let go.

"There you are," a voice said, and they leaped apart. A tall man she didn't know stood in the doorway, regarding Tom. "Forgive the interruption, but I've been looking everywhere for you," he said, his eyes on her, not Tom, as he walked toward them, took her hand, and shook it. "I'm Alexander MacCann, and you must be Miss Alden. I've heard a great deal about you, but Tom did not say you were so pretty." The soft Scottish burr in his voice was hypnotic. He looked like Tom, very much like Tom, and she stared for a moment. He was still holding her hand, and she tugged gently. He let go at once. "Och, you're wondering about me, aren't you, and my resemblance to Tom. He's my nephew. May I say I admire your skills as a photographer?"

She looked at Tom, but his expression was as flat as a pond. Her heart was still pounding, her lips still buzzing from the interrupted kiss. Tom nodded almost imperceptibly. He looked almost embarrassed by his kinship to this man, and she wondered why.

"We developed the rolls you gave Tom and had a look. It appears you've had a very jolly holiday indeed."

"They're useful, then?" Tom asked. "Do you have enough?"

Alexander MacCann grinned. "Meaning are we done with Miss Alden? No, not quite." His eyes swung to Viviane. "In fact, we have a few other assignments for you if you'll take them. I won't lie. These will be more dangerous."

"She can say no," Tom said. He turned to her. "You should."

She looked between the two men, saw the sameness of their features. "What would I have to do?" she asked.

Tom groaned. "What do you want, Alex? Didn't you tell me I shouldn't have gotten her involved?"

Alex looked slightly rueful. "Ah, laddie, that was before I knew how good she is."

"No," Tom said sharply.

Viviane felt indignation replace the lingering effects of the champagne and the kiss. She drew herself up, still small between the two tall Scots. "You can't decide for me, Mr. Graham. I make my own choices."

"Mr. Graham?" Alexander MacCann said. "You're no' on a first-name basis?"

He meant the kiss, of course, and the fact that she was still wearing Tom's jacket. She took it off and handed it back to him, and instantly felt the night wind chilling her satin gown, pasting the slick fabric against her skin like cold water.

"I make my own choices," she said again.

"There you are, Viviane," Felix said, coming out onto the balcony. He pushed his glasses up his nose and looked at both her companions. "Tom Graham," he said. "And who is this?"

"Felix von Schroeder, this is Mr. MacCann," she said.

MacCann stepped up to shake Felix's hand, saw Felix frown at the similarity of his features to Tom's. "I'm his uncle," Alexander supplied before Felix could ask. "I thought we'd spend a wee bit of time together while we were both in Berlin."

"Are you here on business?" Felix asked.

"No, it's strictly a holiday—well, with a bit of research involved. I'm writing a novel."

Interest kindled in Felix's eyes. "A novel? What is it about?"

"Frederick the Great. I'm off to Potsdam tomorrow, and Tom and I were just trying to convince Miss Alden to join us."

"Potsdam?" Felix glanced at Viviane, who was thinking the same thing.

"Yes, the marvelous palaces, the gardens, the statues . . ." Alexander said.

"Oh, I know. I was there once," Felix said without enthusiasm.

"We thought we might steal Miss Alden away for the day tomorrow, show her the sights—"

"Tomorrow?" Felix gaped at Alexander. "My parents will need to be consulted. Viviane and her stepsister are in their care, and they'll wish to ensure she'll be safe."

"Safe?" Tom muttered, but Alexander put a hand on his sleeve.

"My own maiden aunt—Tom's great-aunt—is here in Berlin with me. She's the matron of a girls' school in Dundee, and she's very strict about propriety and proper manners. She is researching Potsdam herself, so she might add a class on German history to her curriculum, you see, and Sanssouci Palace is of particular interest to her. Miss Alden has just been telling us that she's quite handy with a camera, and Aunt Effie knows the girls at the school will benefit greatly from seeing photographs of what she's lecturing on. A picture is worth a thousand words, as they say."

Felix's eyes had glazed over with boredom. "Do you really want to go, Vee? It's very dull."

She hadn't even thought of going to Potsdam, but she looked him straight in the eyes and lied. "I have always wanted to see Frederick the Great's palace."

"Does she have your permission, Herr von Schroeder?" Alexander asked. "It would be a simple day trip, straight there and back again. My aunt is also a football fan, and she's especially keen to see the quarter-finals of the football match at the stadium on Saturday."

Felix looked startled. "*My* permission isn't required. If you're interested in palaces, then Charlottenburg is quite magnificent, and it's right here in Berlin."

Alexander ignored the suggestion and smiled at Viviane instead. It was Tom's smile, twenty years older. He'd be handsome all his life, then, she thought. "I'd be delighted to accompany you, and to meet your aunt," she said.

Alex grinned. "Thank you, Miss Alden. I shall inform Effie that you'll be joining us tomorrow. We'll collect you at your hotel in the morning. Until then, I hope you all enjoy the rest of the party." He bowed over her hand, kissed it in an old-world gesture, and squeezed her fingertips gently. "It was a pleasure to meet you. Aunt Effie will be delighted to have a young woman along, but she does chatter on, I warn you. She'll want pictures of every statue, every stone of the palace."

"I'll be sure to bring plenty of film," Viviane said, feeling Tom and Felix staring at her. She clenched her teeth, both against the chill wind and the questions that came to mind as Alex MacCann strode away.

"That wind is cold. Better go back inside where it's warm," Tom said.

Felix immediately grasped her arm. "Yes, of course. Mutti will be looking for you—for *us*," he said pointedly. "She'll want to hear all about your little trip tomorrow." He glanced at Tom and had to look up to meet his eyes. She felt Felix rise on his toes slightly to compensate for the height difference. "I believe Trude is looking for you, *Tommy*."

"I'll be in in a moment," Tom said, his eyes on Viviane, waiting for her to walk away with Felix. He leaned on the railing of the balcony, with the lights of the city glittering like rhinestones behind him. He was holding his jacket over his shoulder with easy grace, a slight breeze lifting his hair, his expression as placid and unreadable as a lake under cloudy skies.

But under it all, she could see the telltale tic in his jaw.

CHAPTER FORTY-ONE

"What's really in Potsdam?" Tom asked his uncle when he returned to the party and found Alex waiting at the bar.

"Palaces and statues, I suppose." He nodded to the dance floor, where Viviane danced with Felix von Schroeder. "You've got a fine eye, lad. I can see why you recruited Miss Alden."

"What's that supposed to mean?" Tom demanded.

"She's as quick and clever as she is pretty," Alex said. "She has that inestimably marvelous quality, grace under pressure. She barely even blinked when I told Felix von Schroeder we were all going to Potsdam, and after I startled her out of your embrace, too. Is that a regular thing between you, by the way?"

Tom's brows rose. "It isn't any of your business."

Alex reached into his breast pocket and took out a cigarette case. Light glinted on the Strathwood crest. He opened it and held it out. Tom shook his head and waited while Alex lit a cigarette. "I'm afraid everything you do is my business. You were recruited for a job, a very dangerous job. If you're caught, it will embarrass your country at best, and cost you your life at worst. This isn't a game, Tom, a bit of subterfuge and seduction. If you let your guard down, pick at the wrong scab, kick over the wrong stone, there's consequences. Don't underestimate Otto von Schroeder, or his brother. So I'll ask again—is there anything I should know about you and Miss Alden?"

He could smell the faint echo of her perfume on his jacket, feel the lingering tingle of her lips on his mouth. If she hadn't kissed him, he would have kissed her. He hadn't realized how badly he wanted to until their lips met, and she was in his arms. He swallowed. If anyone other than Alex had seen them, if Felix had arrived a few minutes sooner . . . He felt a sick guilt that a kiss could put her in danger.

"That's right, lad. I can see you take my meaning. It's not a game," Alexander said softly.

"What's in Potsdam?" Tom asked again.

Alex drew on his cigarette, and the tip glowed red. He leaned closer to Tom. "It's not Potsdam we want to see. It's a place near to it, in a village called Oranienburg. The Nazis are building a camp there, quite experimental, something beyond the usual compound for political prisoners, and just a stone's throw from all this." He indicated the glamorous guests and the glorious whirl of genteel merriment around them.

"It's called Sachsenhausen."

CHAPTER FORTY-TWO

"Ah, Potsdam, and the dear Sanssouci Palace!" the count said when Viviane mentioned—asked for permission, really—that she'd been invited to visit Potsdam with some friends from home. They were in the car on the way back to the hotel, the state reception over at last. "I was often there in my youth to visit the kaiser. The gardens are beautiful at this time of year. You shall enjoy it immensely."

"Who are these people you are going with?" the countess said distractedly.

"Oh, I know them. Well, I know Tom Graham," Julia said. "He's a friend of Margaret's. He was the best man at her wedding. He's quite safe. I've never seen him do anything the least bit interesting."

Viviane glanced at her, but her stepsister winked.

The count began to reminisce about the court parties and blissful summer days of his youth in Potsdam, and Viviane noticed the countess had closed her eyes and drifted off to sleep. She supposed permission had been granted.

The car pulled up at the Adlon, and the doorman opened the door with a smart bow. The count escorted them to the door of their suite, talking all the way about Potsdam, far more excited about it than Viviane was. *What was really in Potsdam?* She smiled and nodded without really listening. She'd kissed Tom Graham and, worse, she'd been *caught* kissing him. Would it make things awkward between them? It hadn't felt awkward. It had been—she mentally shook herself. It was too much champagne, a case of homesickness, a foolish whim of a moment.

In their suite, Julia kicked off her dancing shoes and rubbed her feet with a sigh. "I had such fun tonight!" she said. "Otto introduced me to everyone. Herr Göring is quite a charming rascal. Did you meet him?"

"Only long enough to nod when we were introduced," Viviane said. She had her camera out, was checking it over, loading it with a fresh roll of film, ready for tomorrow.

"Do you really want to go to Potsdam?" Julia asked, watching her.

"Of course," she said.

Julia yawned. "Sounds like *such* fun with Tom-Stick-in-the-Mud Graham. I remember him at Meg's wedding. He scarcely spoke to anyone."

"He spoke to me," Viviane said.

Julia sat up straight. "Oh? Do tell! Is there something between you and Mr. Graham?"

He kissed me—or I kissed him, she might have said, but instead she shrugged. "Of course not. He's simply shepherding his uncle and his great-aunt around while they're here. They were discussing it this evening when I came upon them at the party. I suppose they thought it was only polite to ask me to join them."

"You could have said no," Julia said.

"And spend another day shopping for gowns I don't need or sitting in the stadium watching pole-vaulting or discus throwing? No thank you. You heard the count—Potsdam is beautiful this time of year."

Julia rolled her eyes. "If you say so," she said. She got to her feet and came over to Viviane. "Unhook me, will you? I'm off to bed." Viviane undid the pearl buttons on the back of her stepsister's gown.

"You looked lovely tonight."

"I did, didn't I?" Julia replied smugly. "I had a marvelous time. It's so different from England, so . . ."

Viviane smiled at her gently. "We'll be going home soon."

Julia sighed. "Don't remind me. I don't want to think about it."

The telephone rang.

"Who could be calling at this hour?" Viviane asked, but Julia picked up the phone and carried it to her bedroom, unraveling the long cord as she went.

"It's just Otto. He promised to telephone to say good night."

Through the half-open door, Viviane heard her giggle, then sigh, and the conversation turned to whispers in the dark.

CHAPTER FORTY-THREE

VIVIANE PROMISED HERSELF she wouldn't let her heart leap or her body react when she saw Tom Graham the next morning. She would stick close to his elderly great-aunt, be polite to his uncle, and take photos.

But when she came out of the hotel and saw him leaning against a car with Alex MacCann, waiting for her, her heart melted. Tom stood with casual ease, his face shadowed by the brim of his hat. The sunlight still illuminated his mouth, and his lips rippled as he watched her coming toward him, and her knees weakened. She caught a sharp little breath, and his eyes narrowed, a warning.

She raised her chin. "Good morning," she said, her voice as steady and bland as if she were greeting a stranger.

Unlike his nephew, Alex smiled when he saw her. "Good morning, Miss Alden. I trust you slept well?"

"Yes, thank you," she said. He opened the rear door of the car, and she got in. Tom rounded the car without a word and climbed in beside her. The car was not as grand as the count's Daimlers, was something smaller and more modest, which meant Tom was inches from her. She kept her eyes on Alex in the front seat and held up a handful of brochures and maps about Potsdam. "Count von Schroeder had the concierge provide these this morning. I thought perhaps your aunt might like to have them. I'm looking forward to meeting her."

"That's very thoughtful of you—I'm sure they'll come in handy. Ah, here she is now." He was looking through the windscreen at a woman hurrying across the street, holding her hat against the wind. His elderly aunt looked surprisingly spry for her age. She made a beeline for the car and slid into the driver's seat.

"All set?" Alex asked her, and she nodded. She turned to look over the seat and Viviane stared. The woman was young, scarcely older than Julia. "This is Effie?" Tom asked in surprise.

"Actually, her name is Edda," Alexander said. "Edda Fleischer, meet Miss Viviane Alden and Tom Graham, my nephew. Edda will be our tour guide today."

The German girl didn't smile. Her expression was guarded as she looked at Viviane. "I am pleased to know you. Thank you for coming. Let's go." She pulled away from the curb and into traffic.

"Edda is a student at the university," Alex said as they drove. "She and her brother also do other things—like that clever brochure you got the other day, Tom."

"We are trying to expose the truth of what the Nazis are really doing to Germany," Edda said. "We are not all Nazis. There are a number of us in the resistance group I'm with. One of our members is a secretary in a government office. She recently saw a top secret memorandum that came straight from Hitler. While he is promoting peace and joy and brotherhood to the world, behind the scenes he is planning a very different future. The memo commands that the German army must be ready for deployment within four years, and the economy must be capable of supporting war." She glanced at Viviane and Tom in the rearview mirror. "War," she said again.

Viviane frowned as they drove on. Outside, a few drops of rain hit the windscreen with a sharp gunfire crack.

"How are you enjoying your holiday, Miss Alden?" Alex MacCann asked, trying to make conversation, but the mood was somber, everyone tense. Tom sat in silence beside her, his hands clenched on his knees.

The signs indicating the turning for Potsdam came up, but Edda didn't slow the vehicle. "Did we miss the turn?" Viviane asked.

Alexander MacCann turned in his seat. "We're not actually going to Potsdam. We're going to Oranienburg. The Nazis are building a concentration camp just outside the town. It's top secret, of course. There's a women's work camp close to it where the inmates make bricks for building the glorious new architectural wonders of the Reich—but the new camp is different. We've heard a variety of things about its purpose—that it's a training facility for guards for other camps, for one. But at Sachsenhausen, they're constructing workshops for some special purpose, new weapons, perhaps. We don't know yet. And so, we need pictures." He kept his eyes on Viviane. "I have seen a few of your photographs, Miss Alden, and I've been told you're very good at this. Are you?"

She felt Tom's eyes on her. The Leica sat in its case in her lap, and Viviane closed her hand over it. "Yes, I am." Alexander McCann grinned.

"It will be dangerous," Edda warned. "If we're caught, they won't go easy on you because you're a woman or a foreign tourist. You'll find yourself inside the fence of this camp, and a concentration camp is an unpleasant place to be. In truth, I do not know how we will even get close to the camp. It is hidden in the woods." She tilted her head. "How did you manage to get the other photographs?"

Viviane could feel Tom's eyes on her like a touch, as enigmatic as ever. Was his jaw twitching now? She didn't dare look. He didn't like her being here. Perhaps he didn't trust her. She raised her chin, concentrated on Edda instead.

"I'm a woman and a foreign tourist. Your countrymen have been told to be kind and friendly and helpful to visitors from abroad. They may wish to show us how peaceable and beautiful Germany is, but they cannot help but brag about how superior they are as well, to show off. That's what I have photographed."

"Is that how we'll proceed today?" Edda asked, surprising Viviane. "What are your instructions?"

She heard Tom's sharp intake of breath.

"Me?" She kept her eyes on Alex.

Alex grinned. "Don't be shocked, Miss Alden. How this goes today will be mostly up to you. Do you have any ideas?"

Viviane swallowed. She looked at Tom, read disapproval in his frown. He hoped she'd refuse, demand that they take her back to Berlin and safety. His face was inches from her own in the cramped back seat. Close enough to kiss. She turned her eyes toward Alex, saw the challenge in *his* eyes, so similar to Tom's, read the unspoken thought mirrored there, too. *Are you truly brave enough?*

Tense silence filled the car as they waited for her to reply. Viviane looked at Edda in the rearview mirror. Her blue eyes intent on the road, her knuckles white on the steering wheel. She was as lovely as Julia, and she should have been just as carefree. Instead, she lived a very different life. The sense of unease, of dangerous currents below the sunlit surface that Viviane felt in Germany, the secrets and the subterfuge, were things Edda faced every day. The young woman was here, on a clandestine mission, when she should be enjoying herself, flirting with boys, like Julia.

"What do men think of when they look at you, Edda, before they know you're smart or funny or brave?" Viviane asked. Edda frowned at her in the mirror.

"Why? What does that matter?"

"It's something my stepsister said once. She said she'd prefer that people think of her as pretty, rather than clever, when they first meet. Most people see what they expect. Only the interesting ones look deeper. The rest are easy to fool, and easy to dismiss."

In the mirror, Viviane saw understanding kindle in Edda's pretty blue eyes, and she smiled.

"Can you speak English?" Viviane asked.

"A little. What do I need to do?"

Viviane smiled. "Leave it to me."

They had reached the charming little town of Oranienburg, and Viviane pointed to a busy café on the main street. "First, we'll stop for a drink."

"What are you doing, Viviane?" Tom asked, frowning.

She glanced at him. "Precisely what you asked me to do. I'm a tourist with a camera."

He winced at that, as if he regretted it.

"You asked me to come," she reminded him.

"That was before I knew exactly how dangerous it would be," he said angrily. He looked at Alex. "She shouldn't be here at all."

"Now you think I can't do this, use my camera to stop a war," she said, raising her chin. "I've been doing it for weeks." She looked at Alex. "You said my photos were useful."

Even he looked dubious. "Yes, but this is supposed to be a clandestine mission, Miss Alden. The Schroeders aren't here to protect you now. Everyone in town will know we're here."

"I understand what she's doing," Edda said. "There are so many tourists in Germany. We've become used to seeing them. They're part of the scenery. Despite the official government orders, ordinary Germans have become bored with having to smile and be pleasant and pretend. The visitors remind people that this is indeed normal, or at least how it should be. Fun is unsettling now, unfamiliar. So, like everything else in Germany, we don't look too deeply at our foreign guests, or the sudden relaxing of the rules, or think too much. We might not like what we see. It's easier to be gay and bright, have a little fun ourselves. Is that not right, Fräulein Alden?"

Viviane smiled. "Yes."

Alex MacCann chuckled, looking at her with admiration. "I hadn't thought of that. We'll follow your lead, then."

Tom was stiff as a poker beside her, and she glanced at him, saw the uncertainty in his eyes. Did he doubt she could do this? She gave him a bright smile, the silly, dazzled, happy tourist grin she'd learned from Julia. It only made his frown deepen. "After our drink, we will purchase the things we'll need for a picnic," she said to everyone, looking away, checking the camera yet again, though she knew it was fully loaded, ready.

"First of all, we must look the part," she said. She took off her hat and loosened her curls into windswept abandon, then set the hat back at a jauntier angle. She nodded to Edda, who was watching her with interest in the rearview mirror. "How would you look if you were going hiking with your friends?" she asked.

Edda nodded without smiling and released the thick blond braids that were coiled under her hat, let them fall over her shoulders.

"Smile," Alex said, and Edda looked at him fiercely. "Smile, lass, or no one will believe you're having fun," he said more gently. Edda's grin looked more like a grimace.

"Loosen your ties a little, gentlemen. You're on holiday," Viviane said as she handed out the maps and the brochures. She slung the Leica over her shoulder, took a breath, and opened the car door, pasting a giddy grin on her own face. She raised the camera and snapped several photos of the charming little village, true tourist shots of flower boxes and quaint houses. The locals barely glanced at her. They nodded politely, then instantly forgot yet another carload of holidaymakers as they passed them. She watched Tom as he got out of the car, his eyes darting everywhere before they fixed on her. His tie was loose, his tweed jacket open, but he looked anything but relaxed.

"Stand over there by the flowers, everyone, and I'll take your picture."

Edda, Alex, and Tom dutifully lined up, and she took their photograph. They strolled along the street until they found a café and took seats at an outdoor table. The proprietor smiled broadly. "Welcome. Vere iz it you are frum?" he asked, as if he'd learned the few words by rote.

"England," Viviane said with a bright smile, using her best, plummiest, lady-of-the-manor tone. "Germany is simply lovely," she said. The man beamed and nodded, his eyes on Edda's cleavage, then on Viviane's. If he was asked to describe their faces later, she doubted he'd recall anything else. "Don't you agree, darling?" she said to Tom.

He raised one brow. "The mountains are magnificent."

"Oh, but the peaks here are quite small. The Alps are . . ." The proprietor blushed, realizing he'd switched to German. "Your pardon," he said. He made a steeple of his hands to indicate mountains and pointed toward the south. "You would like to dine?" he asked in English, miming the act of putting food into his mouth. "Iz good here." He rolled his hand over his broad belly.

Viviane smiled. "Oh, just a drink for now," she said. "Beer, perhaps?"

The man smiled and held up four fingers, and Alex nodded, confirming the order.

"Shall we take a walk in the woods? Perhaps a picnic?" Viviane asked her companions.

The waiter rubbed his hands on his apron. "Eet looks most like there will be rain," he said.

"Perhaps not, then," Viviane said, setting her lips in a disappointed pout, just the way Julia did when thwarted.

Alex leaned in. "Where's your sense of adventure, my dear girl? We're English—" His Scottish tongue caught on that for an instant. He raised his chin and regarded their host. "We're well used to a spot of rain, my good man. Can you pack us a picnic lunch or not?"

The man's eyes glazed over, though his smile remained bright. "*Ja*. I will pack a basket for you to take with you while you drink."

Alex grinned at Viviane as the man departed. "You're enjoying this, aren't you?"

She was. She glanced at Tom, who remained watchful and stone-faced. "Open the maps and the brochures, spread them out on the table, just as if we're looking for the perfect spot for our picnic."

"Which we are," Edda said, smiling for the first time.

"Where is the camp?" Alex asked Edda quietly.

"Northeast of town," Edda said, her smile fading once more. "There is a road, which we shall have to avoid. We must go through the woods and try to see it from the cover of the trees, but there will be patrols."

"Then we'll have to move quickly," Alex said.

"That will be difficult with four people," Viviane said. "Might I suggest—"

"No," Tom said, speaking for the first time. "I know what you're thinking, Viviane, but this isn't England. This is far more dangerous than riots or bar fights."

"What an interesting life you must lead, Miss Alden," Alex said, listening. He shifted his chair closer to hers. "I hope to get to know you better and hear some of these tantalizing tales when this is over."

"This could get her killed," Tom said, regarding his uncle coldly, leaning closer to Viviane himself.

"Two people died in that riot," Viviane reminded him.

"Yes, well, the chaps here aren't throwing rocks and bottles. They have guns, and they're trained to shoot to kill. They want to protect their secrets at all costs," Tom replied, looking at her sharply.

"And we want to expose them at all costs," Viviane said, staring into his eyes, glass on steel. "Surely you understand that, given the line of work you're in." They scowled at each other fiercely.

"This isn't a game. The only games are back in Berlin, in that stadium. Here the gloves are off, and the rapiers have no safety tips."

She turned toward him, did her best to look amused and easy. His eyes blazed into hers, and she held his stare boldly, refused to be the one to look away first.

"I think we'd better go before the pair of them set the café alight," Alex murmured to Edda, who was watching the argument with interest. Tom turned his glare on them.

"She can't—" he began, but the proprietor returned with their beer, and behind him a girl dipped a curtsy, set a heavy picnic basket down at Alex's feet, and walked away without a backward glance.

They drank their beer, paid the bill, tipped handsomely, and returned to the car.

Edda drove along a sheep track and pointed at the thick forest. "The camp is in these woods. About a mile in, I think."

Viviane nodded, looking around. Alex had his arm resting across the back of the front seat, at ease. Tom was tense, scanning the trees with a wary scowl. She couldn't resist teasing him, trying to lighten his mood, though her own belly was tight. "Just look at the lovely wildflowers in that meadow," Viviane said, leaning against Tom's shoulder and pointing past his nose, out the window. "Wouldn't you agree there's not a prettier spot for a picnic in all of Germany?" He didn't reply, but the muscle in his jaw ticked.

Edda stopped the car, and they walked up the slope to a likely spot under a tree, in plain sight of the road, in case anyone happened to see the car and wonder where the owners were.

"You and Tom set out the picnic," Viviane instructed Alex. "Edda and I will take a walk to stretch our legs and see what there is to take pictures of."

"I'm coming with you," Tom said.

"No, you're not," Alex said firmly. "Let her do the job you recruited her for," he said, and his gaze clashed with Tom's, glass on glass. He jerked his head at Viviane. "Off you go. We'll wait here. Tom, unpack the sandwiches. I hope it's not bloody liverwurst."

Instead Tom sat down with his back against the tree, his knees bent. His eyes flicked away to scan the view.

"Look, there'll be much less suspicion if we're seen, two lost female tourists wandering in the wood."

"Fine place for a stroll, with gun-toting Nazis behind every tree. Shall we keep the engine running, be prepared for a quick escape and a car chase?" Tom asked sarcastically.

Viviane tilted her head and gave him a saucy smile, not a Julia smile, but one all her own. "Just save us a slice of cake."

"I can't rescue you, Viviane. Not this time."

She raised her chin. "I don't need rescuing, Tom Graham. I never have." She picked up her hat, her camera, and a map. Edda pointed toward the dark fringe of trees. "It's that way," she said, and they set off.

Viviane glanced over her shoulder once. Tom was watching her. She considered grinning at him, waving. Instead, she stopped, raised her camera, and took his picture.

THE WOODS WERE quiet and fragrant, filled with birdsong and the soft rush of wind in the pines above them. Edda led the way, climbed over fallen logs, peering through the thick undergrowth. Viviane saw a patch of wildflowers and stopped to gather some, pushing them into the band of her hat.

"What are you doing?" Edda asked. "Is this some English custom?"

"Not at all. Were you ever a Girl Guide? A Girl Guide is always prepared."

"We have the League of German Girls here. They train us to be good little Nazis, ready and willing to grow up to marry Nazis and breed still more Nazis," Edda replied. "Do your Girl Guides teach that?"

"We learn to tie knots, give first aid, and do good deeds," Viviane murmured.

They walked on. Above the canopy of trees, thick clouds scudded in, paused, and massed in a surly huddle above them, threatening rain.

"There!" Edda said at last. Viviane could see a barbed wire fence snaking through the trees. They followed it until they heard the clatter of hammers, barking dogs, and shouted orders. They crept forward, crouching in the foliage, and peered down at the clearing below. Men in striped uniforms were working, guarded by soldiers with machine guns.

Viviane raised her camera and took pictures.

The prisoners were hauling massive loads of bricks or timber toward half-finished buildings. If they moved too slowly, a guard with a whip lashed out, tearing open a cheek or knocking the prisoner to the ground, savagely beating him as he struggled to pick up his load.

Viviane's throat closed as she photographed the terrible scene, her hands shaking, the shutter clicking furiously. This was not the rage and frustration of a riot for jobs and bread. This was calculated, cold-eyed hatred. The fury penetrated the very air, poisoned the forest. She shivered. Beside her, Edda gasped. "It is even worse than I'd heard," she whispered in German. "A friend of mine spent eight months in Dachau. And he returned a broken man. His stories were heart wrenching, but this . . ." She shook her head, flinched when a guard screamed as another man fell under his load and was beaten until blood spurted. Still, he struggled to rise, helpless terror on his face, only to be knocked down over and over again under more blows.

Viviane's heart hammered as she concentrated on framing each shot, trying not to scream at the brutality. This was the only way she could fight back. Her camera was her sword. Didn't Tom understand that? She wished she could show these pictures to Rutherford and Phillip, and push them into the smug faces of appeasers in England. Would they be so complacent then? Her stepfather would never have sent them here, to a country capable of *this*.

The guard with the whip stopped at the sound of a car horn. He shouted an order to open the gates and was instantly obeyed. The beaten prisoner crawled away.

"I wonder who that might be. It's someone important in a car like that," Edda whispered. "In Berlin, it would have Nazi flags on the front, carry someone like Heydrich or Himmler or even Hitler." Viviane stared at the vehicle, waiting for the gates to open, but the dapple of sunlight and shadows cast by the trees made it impossible to see inside.

They both jumped at the snap of a twig, the sound of someone walking through the foliage behind them. Edda grabbed Viviane's arm. "A patrol!"

Edda looked around frantically. "There's nowhere to hide. We'll have to make a run for it."

Viviane stopped her. "Wait," she said. "Open the map, hold it up."

She took off her hat and wrapped it around her camera, hiding it from sight, and tucked it under her arm. She turned away from the camp, waited for the patrol to reach them.

Behind her, Edda was still watching the camp. She gasped. "The man in the car. It's—"

"Halt!" Viviane heard the screamed command before Edda could finish, and three armed soldiers rushed up. The man in front raised his pistol and pointed it at Viviane's face. She heard the click of the safety mechanism on the trigger, loud in the silent woods, and for an instant her nerve left her. The other two raised their rifles, their eyes hard with suspicion.

Beside her, Edda turned and raised her hands, her breathing ragged. The sound of her fear made Viviane straighten her spine.

"Thank *gawd* you've found us. We're quite lost," she drawled in English. "Is there a telephone down there?"

The man with the pistol wasn't impressed. "This area is forbidden. What are you doing here?" the guard with the pistol shouted in German.

Viviane flinched. There was no need to feign fear now. Her knees shook. "Please don't shoot!" she said in English. "We're lost, that's all. We were picking flowers, and we wandered off the path. I am . . ." She gulped air into her tortured lungs, past her pounding heart. "I am very glad to see you. Show him the map, Effie," she said, using the name Alex had used the night before.

Edda's hands shook as she tried to unfold the map.

For a moment the soldier watched her, his frown deepening, the pistol in his hand still pointed at her face. "Give it here," he said impatiently, snatching it with his other hand. He looked at the flowers in Viviane's hat, crushed now but visible.

"Where have you come from?" the soldier demanded, lowering the gun a scant inch.

Viviane dared to point. "From that little village down there. We collect wildflowers, you see, press them in an album. We heard there was a little white flower in the mountains we simply must see . . ." She trailed off. "They told us the name of it, but I cannot think with that gun in my face. Are the blossoms protected by law or something? I assure you, we mean no harm at all. We heard voices, hoped *someone* might point the way out. We've been wandering around for an *age*."

The guard sighed and holstered his weapon. His men lowered their rifles as well but kept hard eyes on the two women. "Edelweiss is the flower you want. It grows higher in the mountains, not here," he said in English. He turned to his men. "Stand down," he ordered in guttural German. "We'll escort them back to the main road. Cursed tourists."

Two soldiers marched behind them, one in front. Edda clung to Viviane's arm, breathing fast.

"What's it is you are named?" one soldier asked, practicing his limited English. "Where do you from?"

Viviane gave him a dazzling smile. "I am Lady Victoria Pilchard-Smith of Little Withering-by-the-Sea. It's near Blithering. Do you know it?"

He looked baffled as he shook his head, not understanding a word. "And you?" he asked Edda.

"She's my cousin Effie," Viviane supplied, since Edda looked too terrified to speak.

The other soldier bent to pick a small yellow flower, the gun rattling against the straps on his uniform. He handed it to her with a smile, the universal language of flirtation. Edda took it from him. Viviane saw how badly her hand was shaking.

"Where is it you are stopping in Germany?" the soldier asked her.

"Leipzig," Viviane supplied for Edda, striving to keep her tone normal, though her heart was pounding against her ribs, where her camera was nestled, hidden in her hat. "Do you know the city?"

"Are you enjoying your visit to our fair fatherland?" he carried on, not answering the question, using a phrase every German was probably taught to use to charm visitors.

Not my fatherland, thought Viviane, but she smiled and nodded.

"Move along, Private. You aren't making a date," the soldier in charge said sharply in German. "I have heard English girls are frigid, and seeing how skinny these two are, I believe it."

Edda colored, and Viviane almost laughed. They came out onto the road. "Oranienburg is that way," the soldier said, pointing. "Ensure that you do not wander this way again." He barked an order, and the three soldiers marched away without a backward glance.

Viviane and Edda hurried back toward the place where they'd left Tom and Alex. Both men rose and waited for them, frowning. Edda collapsed on the picnic rug, her hand to her chest.

"What happened?" Tom asked at the same time Alex asked, "Did you get photographs?"

"We were almost caught," Edda gasped. "We *were* caught." She looked at Viviane. "If not for Miss Alden, we would have been put up against a tree and shot, I think, or worse. We saw . . ." She put her hand to her mouth and shook her head, her eyes wide pools of horror. Alex pressed a flask to her lips.

"It's over now, lass. You're safe."

"But others aren't. What did they do? What was their crime?" Edda asked.

Viviane concentrated on rewinding the film in the camera. Her fingers were shaking, and her knees were knocking so hard she was surprised they weren't clattering. She clenched her jaw so Tom wouldn't see, kept her eyes on the task of rewinding the film, though she knew he was watching her. What would he do? Would he sling his coat around her shoulders, stand close, hold her up if she swooned? For an instant she wanted the comfort of that.

She reached up to touch the gold coin around her neck, the one with King Arthur's face on one side and Excalibur on the other, drawing on the power of luck and magic. She saw Tom note the gesture. She tucked the coin back into her blouse and buttoned the collar over it.

She turned to Alex. "I believe we got what you wanted, Mr. Mac-Cann," she said, handing the roll over, refusing to let her fear show, not now, when it was all over—or perhaps it was just beginning.

He regarded her with surprise for a moment, mistook the flatness of her expression for courage. He clasped her fingers, enveloped the film and her whole hand, giving them a squeeze. "Bloody marvelous. I think ye'd better call me Alex."

"We'd best get back," Tom said, tossing the picnic things into the basket, then striding toward the car. Viviane followed him.

"No 'thank you,' no 'good job'?" she said, her heart still pounding.

He stopped so suddenly she bumped into him. He put his arm out to steady her as she stumbled, then let go. "Is that what you want to hear? From me?" he asked. "You're not going to get it."

"You take chances," she said.

"I do my bloody job," he said. He indicated the woods, or the whole country, with a wave of his hand. "This isn't journalism. This is all you, seeking a thrill, an adventure. You're just a bored aristocrat with a hobby. You'll give it up when you marry."

She folded her arms over her chest and looked at him with the full force of her birth and breeding. "No, this isn't journalism. It's spying. Yet isn't that the definition of journalism—seeking the truth by fair means or foul? Words lie, they hurt, and they mislead. Photographs don't."

He was silent for a moment. "Touché, Miss Alden. You can have that carved on your tomb when they shoot you—with a gun, not a camera." He opened the car's boot, threw the picnic basket in, and slammed it shut, dismissing her as he turned away to light a cigarette.

She glanced back at Edda and Alex. Their heads were together, and Alex was frowning as Edda spoke to him, his face as grim as hers now. He glanced up at Viviane, saw her watching, and clamped his mouth shut in a firm line. He stepped in front of Edda, said something else, put his arm around her and led her down the slope.

"We'd best get back," he said, echoing Tom, when they reached the car. The clouds chose that instant to open, and they hurriedly tumbled into the vehicle.

They drove out of the village in silence, the streets empty now that people had gone inside to escape the rain.

"I think we might have time to stop in Potsdam and take a few happier photos," Alex said soberly. "Just in case anyone asks to see them."

CHAPTER FORTY-FOUR

"Austria and Peru, playing football. How boring." Trude sighed, hanging on Tom's arm at the quarterfinal match.

Alexander, who'd tagged along with Tom, grinned at her. He was eating peanuts from a paper cone, a habit he'd picked up while attending baseball games in the United States. He offered her a peanut. "I'll make a bet with you, Trude. I'll wager that Peru wins hands down. No one expects a South American team to defeat one of Europe's best. What can Peruvians know about football—but what if they surprise everyone?"

Trude's eyes lit. "I'll take that bet. Austria will win."

They shook hands on it, Trude's small white manicured hand disappearing into Alex MacCann's big, tanned palm.

"Care to wager on the final score, Tom?" Alex said, leaning over to regard Tom. Tom was busy making notes on the event. He had hoped that Alex might have developed Viviane's photos, might tell him what she saw yesterday, but when he'd appeared this afternoon, he looked relaxed, well rested, and completely uninterested in anything besides flirting with Trude. Trude was certainly willing to flirt back.

Tom had paced the floor of his room all night, unable to sleep. He rang Alex's room at the Eden first thing this morning, but his uncle had already gone out and had left no word as to when he might be expected back. Tom called three more times, but Alex wasn't in, or did not wish to be disturbed. Tom wanted him to find a way to send Viviane home to England. Yesterday was a close call. While Edda had returned shaking, her face pale as milk, Viviane looked alive, exhilarated. He'd been terrified for her safety while she'd been having a lark in the woods with armed Nazi soldiers holding her at gunpoint. She'd risked arrest, even death. He'd known she took chances—swimming in the sea during storms, walking into riots and dangerous places no other lady would dare to go, but that was in England. This was Germany.

He wished that he hadn't encouraged her to come to Germany. Without his interference, she'd be home now, betrothed or married to the Duke of Bellshire, probably bored to tears, but safe.

He wondered what she was doing right now. She'd probably climbed into the lion's cage at the zoo and was tempting the beast with bits of bloody meat while she held her camera at the ready.

It was nearly four o'clock, and he was here to cover the quarterfinal football match for the *Herald*, a dull assignment but one that didn't require complex thought, and he was glad of that. He was only slightly surprised when Alex appeared at the stadium, arriving as if meeting him was entirely accidental. Trude had been delighted to see Alex, a welcome diversion to the game. Alex left Tom to his thoughts and his work as he charmed Trude, had her laughing and eating peanuts with him within minutes.

"Isn't that Jenny Jugo over there? The famous actress?" Alex asked. "Do you know her, Miss Unger? I suppose it makes sense that she's here, being Austrian."

"Where?" Trude exclaimed, following his point. "Oh, she's with Willi Forst!"

"Why don't you go and say hello?" Tom suggested. "I promise I'll stay right here."

Trude pinched her cheeks. "I couldn't possibly," she said, but she was already on her feet.

Tom waited until she was gone. "You were busy today. I tried to reach you at your hotel," he said to his uncle. "Having some film developed, were you?"

Alex kept his gaze on the match. The Peruvian team was doing remarkably well, though a goal was called back. The crowd roared, and the Peruvian players objected.

"Among other things," Alex said. "The photographs are excellent, by the way. She acquitted herself remarkably well. I can see why you like her."

Tom clenched the pencil in his hand so tight the wood cracked. "She shouldn't have done it at all."

"Maybe not, but she's very good at it," Alex said easily, breaking open another peanut. "You asked me to look into Felix von Schroeder. Why?"

"Just curious," Tom said, shrugging. He couldn't tell Alex that he strongly suspected that Felix knew what Viviane was up to. Tom wasn't sure if it was Felix's own politics that kept him from turning her in or animosity toward his older brother or even true affection for Viviane. Whatever his reason, it was because it suited him to help her or to turn a blind eye on her clandestine activities. Men like Felix von Schroeder always had aces up their sleeves, kept tabs on favors given and owed, and they liked to cause trouble when it suited them. They did it with a grin, of course, as if it were a joke.

"He's a brilliant chemist, a scion of one of Germany's premier Nazi families, though he doesn't seem as rabid about it as the rest of his kin," Alex reported. "Actually, his boss is much more intriguing than Felix is—Solomon Hitzig. Have you heard of him?"

"The Nobel Prize winner?"

Alex nodded. "That's him. He's working for the Nazis, although he's a Jew. He's been given special status. Felix von Schroeder is his direct assistant, his second-in-command, you might say." He glanced at Tom. "Isn't that interesting?"

"Otto von Schroeder's brother works for a Jew?" Tom asked. "Now that must make for fascinating conversations across the supper table."

"Indeed, but I doubt they discuss it. The work Hitzig is doing is top secret. Something to do with gases. We've been trying to find out what it might be for some time. Even inside the laboratory Hitzig works alone, assisted only by one chemist."

"Felix?"

Alex put a finger to the tip of his nose. "Exactly. I was going to assign—ask—you to interview Felix, or at least chat him up as a friend of your Miss Alden, see what information you might be able to winkle out of him." He frowned. "Actually, I was considering asking her to do it, but not now."

"Why not now?" Tom asked. Alex was quiet for a moment.

"You have a tendency to want to protect Viviane Alden. You brought her into this, and she's good at it. Yet you keep trying to get her out of it, warn her off. I understand why. Have you never been in love before, lad? You need to back off a little, give her some space, let her do the job."

Tom gritted his teeth and ignored Alex's personal opinion of the state of his affections. "What have you found out, Alex?" he asked. "There's something, isn't there?" He wondered if it meant asking Viviane to put herself into even deeper danger, take a bigger risk. Hard to imagine what that might be after yesterday's escapade.

"A car arrived in the camp yesterday while Edda and Viviane were there. Viviane's back was to the camp, and she was so busy talking their way out of trouble that she didn't see the man who got out of the vehicle.

Edda did. It would have been useful if Viviane had, and could've gotten a photograph of him, but perhaps it's better she didn't after all."

"What did Edda see?"

Alex rubbed his jaw and looked around carefully to be sure no one was listening, but the football match had become interesting. The Peruvians had managed to tie the score, and the Austrians were protesting. The crowd roared, waiting for the call, and Alex leaned close to Tom's ear. "One of the rumors we'd heard about Sachsenhausen is that it houses a laboratory for the development of gas weapons. We weren't sure if that was true. Now we are."

A chill ran up Tom's spine.

On the playing field, the Peruvian goal was disallowed. The Peruvians were protesting the call, and the spectators were on their feet, screaming their opinion.

"Who was it?" Tom asked. "Who got out of the car?"

Alex turned to look at him. "I'm telling you in strictest confidence, because I think you need to know. You can't tell Viviane or warn her. Not yet. I don't want to frighten her or keep her from doing what she's here for. I want you to find out—subtly—what she knows and if she can find out more."

Understanding hit Tom like a brick. "No," he murmured, but Alex nodded.

"Aye. The man in the car was Felix von Schroeder."

CHAPTER FORTY-FIVE

VIVIANE LOOKED AROUND the crowded little restaurant. It was old-fashioned and charming, dark wood and white tablecloths. The patrons were locals, with few tourists among their number. Her arrival with Felix and Professor Hitzig had halted conversation, made waiters pause and stare and smiles fade to blankness or animosity.

"This is a mistake," Hitzig murmured to Felix, his face sheened with sweat.

Felix grinned encouragingly. "Nonsense. It is still a free country, and you said this was your favorite restaurant."

"It was," the professor replied. "I have not been here in a very long while. The last time I came was nearly two years ago." He nodded toward the bar, his eyes on a blank space on the wall. "There was a sign posted there that said Jews were forbidden to eat here."

Felix led them to a table, and they sat down. The professor had his back to the wall, scanning the room anxiously. Still, he kept his posture dignified.

"They took the sign down for the Olympics," Felix said, mostly to Viviane. "For a few glorious days things are normal again."

Hitzig scanned the room sadly and nodded toward a table by the window. "I used to come here often, Miss Alden. That was my usual table. I proposed to my wife there. It's where I knew we were going to have a baby, because she could not eat the oysters, which had always been her favorite. We came here to celebrate my Nobel Prize with their best bottle of champagne. It's where I told her I had joined the army." He looked at Viviane. "It was also where we argued about my career and she begged me not to let them use my work to kill other human beings. I refused to listen."

He watched a young waiter hurry past, weaving between the crowded tables with lithe grace. "I don't know anyone here now, and I doubt they'd remember me. If they did, they would throw me out into the street."

Felix smiled at him. "No one will do that today, Professor. No one would dare, with Viviane by your side, and me, of course. They may not recognize you, but they know me. Otto dines here often."

The professor leaned in. "But he is a Nazi. Look around you. They are all Nazis. A plain suit and a false smile do not make them less so. Why did you bring me here, Felix?"

Felix glanced at Viviane. "I wanted Viviane to see the truth. Things will indeed return to normal next week—not the professor's normal, but Adolf Hitler's. Once the games are over, the last moments of freedom for Jews in this country will indeed end—this time forever."

Viviane regarded the old professor, noted the sweat on his brow, the way his hands shook. It wasn't a kindness to bring him here, she thought. It was torment. "Felix," she murmured, made it a plea to stop whatever game he was playing now.

He regarded her evenly. "I wanted you to understand what is happening," he said. "Do you see the truth now, Viviane?"

She thought of Sachsenhausen, of the beaten prisoners, the swaggering, malevolent guards. She swallowed and did not reply. Felix clasped her hand where it lay on the tablecloth, squeezed it.

"Your hand is cold. Are you nervous? As nervous as the professor? You will return to England soon, to safety and sanity, but it will be quite the opposite here. The professor's work is nearly finished. A few days more, a week, and once it is complete . . ." Felix let the comment trail away into a sigh. She glanced at Solomon Hitzig, read resignation in his eyes.

He was quiet as the waiter brought food, veal pounded thin and breaded, served with new potatoes. The man paused with the plate in midair as he glanced at Hitzig, his lips tightening, his eyes narrowing.

"Is there a problem?" Felix asked in German, his voice loud. The waiter's expression turned from hatred to surprise to resignation. He glanced at Viviane.

"Not at all," he replied in English, offering her the smile Germans reserved for tourists, polite, careful, and cool. Over the days of the Olympics, that universal smile, commanded by the Nazi government, had become more of an impatient grimace. He set the plates down and backed away. Viviane watched him sidle up to another waiter and whisper a comment. Felix glared at that waiter as well.

"Please don't draw attention," Hitzig whispered. "There's no point, and there will be reprisals."

"What sort of reprisals?" Viviane asked.

Felix shrugged. "A visit in the night, an arrest, and the professor will be allowed—forced—to continue his work in prison, or not at all."

Hitzig winced, blanching.

"Don't look so sorrowful, Viviane. People are watching. We are supposed to be enjoying ourselves. It is not so hopeless. You see, the professor has had a letter from his son in England." He smiled at his mentor. "Tell her, my friend."

Hitzig nodded, his face relaxing for a moment. "It's true. My son is willing to forgive me. He wants to see me." He looked away. "It's impos-

sible of course, but it is a gift after all these years, a blessing. I owe that
to Felix. He found my son, wrote to him, asked him to consider recon-
ciling with me. It is enough that he has forgiven me. He lives in Surrey
now. Do you know it?"

Before she could answer, two men entered the restaurant, and their
waiter hurried up, had a quiet word. Their eyes turned toward Hitzig
and Viviane and Felix. They took seats at the bar, watching.

Hitzig tensed. "Gestapo. We must go," he muttered. The pleasant
atmosphere in the room soured, and smiles turned to disdainful glares
and frowns. Viviane glared back. Her camera was in her bag under her
chair. Her fingers itched to take it out, capture the hatred, the suppressed fury that surrounded them, suffocating and devastating.

Felix glanced at the men and frowned. "Yes, I suppose we must," he
said. He looked at Viviane. "Have you considered what I asked you, to
take the professor with you when you go home to England?"

The reminder, here, now, shocked her. She glanced at the professor
and tried to imagine him being flogged and tortured in a place like
Sachsenhausen.

"We'll be here for several more weeks," Viviane said. "Your father is
most anxious that we attend the Bayreuth Festival with him. Julia
wants to stay until September."

Felix shook his head. "That would be impossible. If you wish to help
the professor, to save him, you must leave the moment the closing ceremonies end."

"But that's two days from now!" Viviane said.

"Two days," the professor said.

Felix turned to him. "Can you be finished by then, my friend?"

Hitzig shut his eyes. "There are still some final experiments to do, a
few calculations . . ."

"But it is essentially finished, is it not?" Felix insisted.

Hitzig nodded.

The bill was presented, and Felix handed it back to the waiter. "Put it on my brother's tab," he said. "Obersturmführer Otto von Schroeder." He smiled as the waiter's face changed to surprise, then respect. "I see you know him," Felix said.

"Yes, Herr von Schroeder," the man said, snapping to attention as if Felix was, by extension, Otto.

They rose, and Felix tipped his hat to the men at the bar on the way out. Outside, he took Viviane's arm. "Now you see why it must be right after the closing ceremonies. The games will end, and everything will be in chaos as the athletes and visitors depart, everyone hurrying through the train stations. It will be crowded, and that will make it easy for the professor to slip away unnoticed," Felix said. "Is it not a brilliant plan?"

"But Julia—" Viviane began.

Felix looked impatient. "Please, Viviane. I am asking for a favor, an important one, a man's life."

The two Gestapo agents had followed them out of the restaurant and stood watching them from a short distance away. They looked like leashed dogs waiting for an excuse, ready to spring at the slightest provocation. She swallowed hard.

"I must talk to Julia, make arrangements, speak to—" Her breath caught in her throat.

Tom. She needed Tom—or his contacts. They could help, surely.

"I've helped you, have I not?" Felix said, his expression fierce now. He leaned close to her ear. "Your photographs, the clever way you use your camera to expose so very much. Do you think I haven't noticed? What will you do with those charming snapshots, I wonder? Perhaps Otto might wish to have some of the ones of Julia, a souvenir to remember her by. The one in front of the aircraft works was quite a fetching pose. Have you had them developed? I know a good chemist who can do them for you if you like."

Viviane's throat closed, and she stared at the man she thought was a friend. She felt a chill go through her. His frown turned to a charming grin in an instant, and he caught her hand. "Your face, Viviane! Don't look so horrified. There's no need to worry, dearest girl. You know that I'm your friend and your greatest admirer. I would never betray you. I only meant to show you how easily innocent pleasures can be misunderstood."

She blinked at him, saw the warm, teasing light in his dark eyes, his earnest smile. "How I wish I could come to England with you. Perhaps I will. Would you like that?" She was speechless, her throat tight. He lifted her hand to his mouth, let his eyes drift shut as he kissed her knuckles, his mouth warm on her icy skin. "In time, of course. I have things to see to here first."

He turned to Hitzig. "What do you say, Professor? Should history repeat itself? Should I propose right here and now?"

"Felix," she murmured to deter him, to stop him from making a scene on the busy street, but he laughed out loud and waved a hand at the charming façade of the restaurant, the bow window, the hand-painted sign, the striped awning, the lace curtains, and the swastika flags that flanked the door.

"Would it not be a perfect way to end your final meal at this restaurant, this place that has meant so much to you, to see a new romance blossom?"

The professor blinked at his protégé. He looked frightened and confused, an old man pushed to his limits. Felix laughed as if it had all been a joke, but he didn't let go of Viviane's hand. Passersby were forced to step around them.

"Come, Professor. Let's be happy for a little while longer and ignore politics. Of course Viviane will help us. She is all that is good and kind and decent." He smiled at her as if she'd already agreed to help. How could she say no?

Behind them, the watchers were still watching. They'd exited the café to follow them.

The games were almost done, just two days left, and the pleasant holiday that had been so carefully staged was coming to an end with them.

Despite the warmth of the sun, Viviane shivered.

CHAPTER FORTY-SIX

JULIA WAS HUMMING a German lullaby as she dressed for the Goebbelses' party, the last and grandest party of the Olympic interlude. The closing ceremonies would take place tomorrow, and the games would be over.

Viviane stood in the doorway of her stepsister's room and watched as she dressed. Julia had yet another new gown, gauzy and pretty and utterly feminine. The pale green silk shimmered when she breathed, and embroidered flowers accented with tiny gemstones in a dozen different colors sprayed across the bodice and threw dazzling darts of light across the room. She looked beautiful.

"Julia, darling, I've had a letter from my mother. She hasn't been feeling well and she's asked us to come home at once," Viviane said, starting the subterfuge.

Julia turned away from the mirror, her face crumpling. "Oh, Vee—is it anything serious?"

"She didn't say, but she's always had those dreadful headaches."

Julia turned to pick up a tube of lipstick with a sigh. "Yes, and they've always been nothing at all," she said blandly. "I'm sure she's fine. We'll wire Father tomorrow morning and find out, shall we? Tonight isn't the time to worry."

"But I *am* worried," Viviane said, raising her chin. "Felix offered to book train tickets for us for tomorrow evening, and I accepted."

Julia spun again. "*Us*? Why do I have to go?"

Viviane stared at her stepsister. "I just thought you'd want to come. She's your stepmother."

Julia bit her lower lip. "Vee, I'm not going home. Otto has asked me to marry him, and I've said yes. I'm staying in Germany."

Viviane felt the blood drain from her face. "What? Julia, you can't. Has he spoken to Rutherford, asked for—"

Julia tossed her blond head. "Papa will insist I come home. He'll tell me I'm too young, and I'm being impetuous. Well, I'm not. I'm in love with Otto, and I don't want a long engagement. I want to make my life here. Germany is modern and bold and if England could see how efficient this country is, how fine and noble and—" She broke off and gave Viviane a tight little smile. "Oh, your face, Vee. Can you not be happy for me?"

"You're serious, then? How can you know he's the right man?"

Julia dabbed powder over the bridge of her nose. "I love him. I know what I want. Ilsa and Magda Goebbels have agreed to teach me all I need to know to be a suitable German wife. Otto has already applied to his superiors for the necessary permissions to marry me."

Viviane gaped at her. "If my mother was here, or Margaret, or anyone, they'd tell you to wait, to consider—"

"I don't want to wait. I want to be with Otto now. If you wish to go home, you'll have to go on your own. I'd love for you to stay, and stand with me at my wedding, of course. I was thinking September."

Just a few weeks away. Viviane felt numb and cold, and yet her skin burned as if she'd been swimming too long in cold water, as if her lungs were crying for air, for sanity.

There was a knock on the door. "Come," Julia called in German.

"This arrived for you, fräulein," said a maid, entering with a single flower and a note on a tray. "And the Countess von Schroeder asked me to say that the car is waiting downstairs when you are ready."

"Tell her we will be down directly," Julia said, and waited for the door to close. She snatched up the flower—a perfect pink rose—and held it to her nose as she opened the note. "It's from Otto—'An English rose becomes a German garden.'" Viviane winced at the tortured sentiment. "Isn't that the most romantic thing you've ever heard?" Julia asked. She clipped the stem short and held out the rose. "Help me pin it to my gown," she said, and Viviane came forward with shaking hands.

Julia grasped her shoulders and kissed her cheek. "Oh, Vee, do be happy for me. I am so much in love—with Otto, and Germany, and everything! Don't leave tomorrow. Stay. None of my sisters will be here to stand up with me at my wedding. I won't have anyone I know. Be my maid of honor. Well, no, Magda will insist on being that. My bridesmaid, then."

Viviane stared at the rose over her stepsister's heart and forced a smile. She gave Julia a quick nod, and her stepsister beamed. Julia glanced at the tiny pendant on the chain around Viviane's neck. "That old coin . . . you found it in that lake of yours, didn't you?" She brushed a fingertip over it. "I've never seen you without it. Perhaps you'll lend it to me, and it can be my 'something borrowed.'" Then she frowned. "Though I'm not sure Nazis follow that tradition. Oh, I truly do have so much to learn! I am so very, very happy."

Viviane imagined a wedding cake adorned with swastikas, the groom wearing polished jackboots as he strode to a pagan altar, but she forced a smile and nodded.

How could she leave now, without Julia? She had to stay, find a way to convince her stepsister to come home. She'd write to Rutherford, to her mother . . . but that would have to wait.

"Oh, look at the time," Julia said, and rushed to pick up her white fox fur wrap. "I hate to keep the Schroeders waiting." She linked her arm through Viviane's and headed for the door. "I don't want to wait, either. This party promises to be the grandest event of the year, and I want to dance the night away with Otto."

CHAPTER FORTY-SEVEN

ILSA VON SCHROEDER clasped the magnificent pearl and diamond collar around her throat. It had been in her husband's family for years, had been worn to countless grand balls and coronations, state dinners and operas. It was a trifle old fashioned, but it made up for that in the size and quality of the gems. Her gown was pale ivory, elegant and simple, bias cut to drape over every curve. She'd kept her figure, even after three children, and she looked younger than most women her age, even Magda, who was ten years younger. Poor Magda was worn out by the task of churning out four children for the glory of the Third Reich, and rumor had it that she was pregnant again. How tragic to have a husband with a roving eye who was surrounded by beautiful actresses every day.

Ilsa sighed as she put the final touches on her makeup. Georg had never strayed, never even looked at any woman besides her. He didn't approve of her politics, but he loved her, still found her beautiful.

But Georg had gotten old. He looked careworn and weary. The war had taken its toll on most of the men who served, however honorable and heroic they'd been. Georg had been at Verdun, though he never spoke of it. She'd heard other accounts. She didn't ask for personal details from her husband. She knew only that the Germans should have won. They were superior to the French, and the defeat had been a devastating humiliation. The German nation had been surprised by that loss, and by the terrible defeat at the end of that war. They'd endured privation and starvation for the four long years of the conflict, surviving on pride and the assurance of their leaders that Germany was winning. Then came the truth—defeat, surrender, and shame. Pride had collapsed along with the economy, and everything got even worse. Georg watched as his friend the kaiser was forced to abdicate, sent into exile in the Netherlands. The suffering, the degradation, the misery grew even worse.

Then Hitler rose to power, brought back hope and prosperity, honor and pride. Germany would not be kept down, he promised. The German people weren't to blame for the defeat. They were tricked by an international conspiracy, one that had existed for centuries, finally growing into a plague that wanted nothing more than to choke the life out of the German race. Jews, of course. If there was another war, this time they wouldn't lose.

She turned as the door opened and Georg entered. He wore a tuxedo. "Where is your Iron Cross?" she asked. "You promised you'd wear it."

He ignored her question. "How lovely you look, my dear."

He crossed to the small desk in the corner. A half-finished letter lay on the mahogany surface, and he picked it up, read it before looking at Isla in surprise.

"This is to Magda Goebbels," he said. "Otto wishes to marry Julia?"

Ilsa smiled, then crossed to straighten his tie, an intimate, wifely gesture to soothe his ruffled feathers. He would have been the very next one to know, of course. "Have you not noticed how they look at each other, how devoted they are? Are you truly surprised?"

The grin that lit his face made him look almost young again. "I'm delighted," he said. "I'll write to Lionel in England, tell him Otto will be returning to England with Julia to ask for her hand. Perhaps they'll settle there. Rutherford has set aside small estates for each of his daughters as part of their dowries."

Ilsa's own smile faded. "Otto go to England? Are you mad? His place is here, in Germany. She will stay here, become a proper German wife, take her place in our society. He cannot leave Germany."

"He must," Georg muttered, letting the letter flutter back to the desktop. "If he stays . . ." He looked at his wife, and there was sorrow in his eyes when there should have been joy. Ilsa drew herself up and stepped back, glaring at him.

"Your son—*sons*—are the future of a new Germany. We will rule the world because we deserve to do so, the fittest, purest race on the planet. Otto will be in the vanguard, a leader."

Georg's brow crumpled. "No, Ilsa. Our boys are Nazis. They have no pride, no honor. They do not think for themselves. They belong to a raving madman who will drag us into another war." He shook his head. "I fear—I *know*—that the next war will be far worse than the last, and that was terrible enough."

"You are a coward," she hissed at him, and saw him flinch.

"I am a father and a German. I do not want my country, or my family, torn apart by Adolf Hitler. I fought in the last war, saw the devastation it caused. I do not want to go back to war, and I don't wish it upon my children." He raised his chin. "Julia will go home. I insist on it. There will be no wedding." He picked up the letter again, crumpled it into a ball, and tossed it into the waste bin under the desk. He drew himself up to military stiffness. "It is time to go. Are you ready?"

Her mouth tasted bitter with suppressed fury, but she nodded, her eyes downcast, unable to look at him. Her husband was a traitor. He helped her on with her wrap, doing it silently, refraining from touching her, then opened the door for her.

She paused. "If it were Viviane, would you let her stay?"

She saw a flicker of surprise in his eyes before he frowned. "She is a far more sensible young woman than Julia. She hasn't been fooled by this Olympic charade."

The hair on the back of Ilsa's neck rose. "What do you mean?" she said. "How do you know what she thinks?"

He stabbed the button for the elevator. "She will return to England, and she will tell them what she saw—not what they wanted her to see, but what they did not. Don't you understand? The ones like her are the only true hope this country has. Someone must stop that man before—"

The door slid open, and the elevator operator smiled politely. "Going down?" he said, stepping back. They got in.

"Before what, Georg?" Ilsa said, goading him. "Before what?"

"Before it's too late," he said, staring straight ahead.

CHAPTER FORTY-EIGHT

THE GOEBBELSES' GUEST list included some 2,700 people. The party was being held on the propaganda minister's private island estate in the River Havel. Tonight, the former playground of German princes was an Italian-inspired fairyland choreographed by Germany's finest film set designers, who'd been given a lavish, almost unlimited budget. Among those invited were crowned heads, diplomats, and a glittering array of international artists and celebrities.

Felix and Otto were waiting when the count's car pulled up on the shore. Across the shining strip of river, Pfaueninsel island, named for the peacocks that roamed there, glowed in the darkness.

Julia had eyes only for Otto as he helped her out of the car. "You look gorgeous," he whispered, kissing her upturned cheek. He tucked her arm under his, and she leaned close to him, blushing prettily.

"Hello, dearest girl," Felix said with a jaunty grin as he offered Viviane his hand. "I have never beheld anything or anyone so beautiful, I swear it. You are a vision." He followed her distracted gaze to Julia and Otto. "Perhaps we should throw cold water on them?" he suggested. "Come on—the way to the festivities lies across a cleverly constructed pontoon bridge. We could tip my brother into the Havel, cool his ardor. What do you say?"

Viviane shook her head, her tongue stuck to the roof of her mouth, thinking of her conversation with Julia. Felix sobered and took her arm. "Come. There's nothing to worry about tonight. We have a grand party to attend, one designed to make everyone forget their troubles and simply . . . frolic. Isn't that a perfect word for it?"

They crossed the bridge and were greeted by elf-like pages on the other side, young women clad in white, with shimmering makeup that made their skin luminous in the light of the lanterns they carried. They led the way along a path through the woods. The trees were set with thousands of butterfly-shaped lights, and the effect was breathtaking. Julia grinned at Viviane. "How magical it looks!"

"How expensive it must be," Felix murmured.

The page bowed as they reached a wide clearing set with tables, a fountain, and what must have been every flower for a hundred miles. There was a stage and a dance floor, where a trio of professional dancers was performing, flitting through light and shadows like moths, their mesmerizing costumes designed to shimmer and swirl around them.

Magda and Joseph Goebbels, both dressed in white, stood waiting to greet their guests. Magda preened like a queen, and her husband's darkling eyes took in every detail—the jewels on Julia's gown, Ilsa's heirloom necklace, Georg's stiff spine. His gaze landed on Viviane and flicked away almost as fast. No one important. She felt a chill rush through her.

Otto broke the spell. "Heil Hitler!" he cried, snapping to attention and throwing his arm in the air. A number of guests turned to stare, some frowning.

"Heil Hitler," Goebbels replied more quietly, not bothering to salute.

"Please help yourselves to food and drink," Magda invited her guests. "There is champagne and schnapps, and plenty to eat. Do try the caviar." Magda beamed at them, her wide grin making up for her husband's lack of any kind of smile at all. Then her attention passed on to the guests coming behind them, and the audience was over.

"Look—that's the King of Greece, and there's the American ambassador," Julia said. "He looks very unhappy for someone attending a party. And there's our ambassador, Sir Eric Phipps, and the Vansittarts. I must say hello—they're old government colleagues of Papa's."

Viviane wondered what those gentlemen would make of Julia's attachment to Otto von Schroeder. Both diplomats were critical of Hitler's regime. She imagined the scandal Julia would cause, the daughter of a member of the cabinet marrying a Nazi officer. It would certainly knock her own broken betrothal out of the gossip circles. It would also likely destroy Lord Rutherford's career. She wondered if Julia had considered that. Would that convince her stepsister to wait? Perhaps seeing her father's English colleagues would make her think things through, use her head instead of her heart. Viviane had to try again, make Julia see sense, consider the consequences for others. She'd talk to her again after the party.

"Shall we find our table?" Georg asked, looking at the tableau as if he did not entirely approve.

Felix took Viviane's arm. "First I think we need a glass of champagne. I think that nymph flitting through the crowd has an entire tray of glasses. Shall we follow her or find the bar?" He grinned at his parents. "We'll join you later. Save me a slice of virgin if the waiter comes around."

The nymph flitted onward, and they moved through the crowd to the bar, set up by a pavilion that overlooked the river. Felix claimed two glasses of champagne, and they climbed the steps to look at the view.

Somewhere in the dark a peacock cried out, its voice remarkably human, full of woe and warning.

"Quite an accomplishment, isn't it? Like stepping through the door into another world," Felix said, not looking at the river but at her. "If only it could truly be like this, all happiness and pleasure and none of the conflict. Would you like that, a perfect world?"

She considered. "It is beautiful, but I think it would become dull after a time. Where's the adventure, the challenge, in such a world?"

He chuckled. "I suppose that *is* the challenge. To have Elysium and be satisfied with nothing but peace and harmony and endless pleasure."

A cool breeze blew in off the river, and Viviane pulled her wrap closer to her throat. "But Elysium is the land of the dead, not the living."

"Given by the gods as an eternal reward for a righteous life," he said. He reached out to touch her face, a gentle caress. "How lovely you are, how sweet and young and utterly perfect. And after tomorrow, you will be gone," he murmured. "I shall miss you. Did you bring that camera of yours? Perhaps I shall ask someone to take our photograph, just to prove this night was real and for a moment at least joy existed. Tomorrow we shall have to face reality again." He sipped his champagne.

"Camelot, then, instead of Elysium," she said. "A dream of peace that can only exist for a fleeting moment in time before it is gone."

"Don't say it. King Arthur was a warrior. He had to fight to carve out that perfect world of his, and yet his noble ideals came to nothing. The world he left was no better than the one he inherited. All the sins and the arrogance and the desire for power overwhelmed any good he did. He won a kingdom for a time, yes, but he lost the greater goal, a better world."

She shook her head. "I don't agree. If King Arthur didn't quite vanquish all the woes of the world, he conquered the worst ones. He was given a gift, a shining moment of promise, and he did his very best, fought for what he believed was right and true. He was only one man, one person." She thought of her father, another Arthur in a different time, another struggle for right over might.

"And do you believe that he will return, as the legend says, and take up his sword and fight for Britain?"

She looked out at the flowing water, saw a fish jump, catch the moonlight for a fleeting second, silver and shining, before disappearing again into the dark water, leaving only ripples to mark its passage. "Yes."

She turned to find him studying her, the shadows lying in the furrow between his brows and in the lines around his mouth. A chill went through her at the intensity of his gaze, and she felt a moment of surprise. The peacock called again, another warning, or a lament, nearer this time. Felix drew a breath, and his smile was back.

"Come, it's chilly so close to the river, and my glass is empty. Let's go and find some of that caviar our host recommended, and dance the night away, for tomorrow . . . Well, you know how the rest of the saying goes."

We die, she thought, filling in the blank, the quote a reminder of the inevitability of strife and death and the fleeting nature of pleasure and joy. The warriors and Valkyries of old—even King Arthur and his knights—would raise a similar toast on the eve of battle, drink to the hope for glory and the reward of an eternity in Elysium.

They strolled along the path, back into the light and the noise. A juggler wandered past, tossing lighted batons into the air and catching them deftly. A young woman was swallowing a sword for an appreciative audience. On the path, a peacock strutted, dropping one iridescent feather. Felix bent to pick it up and handed it to her. "How magical, how lovely it is—the all-seeing eye."

"Yes, it is lovely," she said. "Yet it also represents ill fate and death," she said. "In England it is considered bad luck to bring peacock feathers into your house." She glanced around, saw that the ever-watchful feathers had been worked into the floral displays in honor of the name of this place, Pfaueninsel, peacock island.

Felix took it from her. "Leave it, then," he said with a shrug, and tossed the iridescent feather away. "We must make our own luck."

CHAPTER FORTY-NINE

Tom crossed the pontoon bridge with Trude on his arm. She wore gold lamé tonight, a starlet's gown that shimmered and flashed in the torchlight as she moved. It was designed to attract attention. Appreciative eyes skimmed her lush curves, her golden curls, her lovely face as she passed. She looked back, taking note of who was looking, ignoring the ones she did not know and beaming at the people who could help her career. She may be on duty tonight, minding Tom for the people she truly worked for, but she was in her own world as well, and he was simply an accessory, a bangle on a charm bracelet, a favored foreign reporter who recognized and reported on the glory of the Nazi regime.

Goebbels smiled at Tom approvingly, thin lipped, narrow eyed, and reptilian, while his wife gauged her husband's interest in Trude. She relaxed when she realized Joseph was regarding Tom, not the dazzling actress. The propaganda minister's flesh was cold and dry when they shook hands. Tom resisted the urge to wipe his palm on his trousers.

Then the attention of their hosts shifted to the next guest behind them, and they moved on, led away by a girl in white satin knee breeches and soundless slippers, toward the sound of music and laughter.

"I do believe that's Oscar Joost's band," Trude enthused. "He plays at the Eden Hotel. I wonder how much it cost to hire *him*? Oh, we shall dance the night away, Tommy, and have such fun!"

They arrived at the clearing, and their elfin escort bowed and left them. For a moment they stood and stared, and even Trude was speechless at the sight before them. Then her grip on Tom's arm tightened.

"There's the actress Lída Baarová, and the great actor Gustav Fröhlich," she said. "And that's the King and Queen of Greece—I recognize them from their photographs in the newspapers! Oh, and look—"

But Tom stopped listening. Across the clearing, he saw Viviane with Felix von Schroeder, arm in arm, watching a pair of acrobats. She wore blue again, iridescent layers of some gauzy fabric that flowed around her like water, making her look as if she'd just risen from the sea. She said something to Schroeder, leaning her head close to his, that made him laugh. Tom felt his mouth dry. He took a step toward her, but Trude still held his arm, and she was tugging him in the opposite direction. A tray of champagne floated past them, and Trude let go to take a pair of glasses, pressing one into his hand. She touched her glass to his in a toast and laughed gaily. "How serious you look, Tommy. Tonight is for fun. You must relax, enjoy yourself. I doubt there has ever been a party like this one."

He forced a smile. "Isn't that Pola Negri over there?" he said, and she spun to look.

When he looked again at Viviane, she'd disappeared into the crowd.

He caught glimpses of her throughout the evening, always too far away for him to catch her attention. The crowd exposed her and swallowed her again like a rolling storm tide.

Trude carried him along from table to table, her eyes glazing with boredom or disapproval when he stopped to speak with his fellow journalists or the members of British society he knew from his days at Cambridge or had met as part of Geoffrey's set in London. They found a table, and someone introduced him to Unity Mitford, Diana Guinness's younger sister. She was a thin, languid creature with dreamy, half-focused eyes. She was wearing a gown embroidered with tiny swastikas, and a matching necklace. She offered him a Hitler salute and raised one sculpted English brow, daring him to return it. He grasped her raised hand and shook it instead. "I hear you're a friend of Medway's," she said, lighting a cigarette and draping herself over the back of her chair. "He's Ozzie's latest protégé," she said, referring to Oswald Mosley.

"Yes, I know him," Tom said. "We rowed on the same crew at university."

She looked bored, her eyes scanning the crowd. "How interesting," she said. "Did you know his former ladylove is here tonight? Miss Viviane Alden. She threw him over, the fool. D'you suppose she shares our convictions on Fascism?"

Our convictions. Tom gritted his teeth.

"And there she is." He followed the point of Unity's cigarette, saw Viviane again, still with Felix, their heads together on the dance floor.

"Ooh, she's caught herself a Schroeder. Perhaps she's smarter than I thought. She's pretty. I shall have to keep her away from Adolf, or she'll turn his head. He likes English girls. He says I have a special place in his heart." She smiled at Tom expectantly, waiting for him to be impressed, or to offer her a compliment. He held her gaze, kept his expression neutral, and she sighed and blew another plume of smoke into the air, then looked at the burning end of the cigarette. "He can't abide smoking, especially in women, but he isn't here—he never comes to parties—and I need a fag now and then or I'd go mad. He doesn't like women drinking, either. Will you be a dear and fetch me more champers?" Her pert expression once again dared him to comment. She giggled when he didn't. "Go on, then, if you don't wish to play. I might be forgiven having a drink or a cigarette, but there'd be questions asked if I was seen flirting with you. I'd come out all right, but I daresay it might be unpleasant for you."

He got to his feet. "Thank you for the warning. I'll send a waiter over with more champagne."

"Tell him to bring a whole bottle," Unity called after him.

ILSA FOUND HER hostess emerging from the ladies' retiring room, looking wan under her makeup. "Magda, darling, are you well?" She wondered if the shellfish had turned in the heat, or if Magda had drunk too much, but Magda pressed her hand and smiled.

"I'm fine. I'm—with child once again." Her hand fluttered for an instant over her stomach, confirming the rumor. Her eyes darted over her guests. "Please say nothing about it. I have not told the führer yet. He likes to be the first one to know. He is always so pleased . . ."

Magda pressed her handkerchief to her mouth for an instant. "The first few months are always the worst. Where's Joseph?" she asked, straightening, fixing her smile, and nodding in case anyone was watching. "The last I saw him he was speaking with that actress, Lída Baarová. She and her movie star fiancé have just moved in next door. Have you seen her? She's very beautiful." She couldn't quite keep the edge of scorn from her voice. "Joseph can't seem to keep his eyes off her." She regarded Ilsa, perhaps wondering if she'd said too much. "You look lovely tonight, Ilsa. Are you enjoying our little party?"

"It's an utter triumph," Ilsa said. She bit her lip, hesitated a moment. She needed Magda's advice, her help, the help of those higher up, and to reach them, she must go through Magda. "I have happy news of my own—Otto has proposed to Lady Julia Devellin."

A flicker of something dark passed through Magda's eyes even as she grasped Ilsa's hands in hers and kissed both her cheeks. "What happy news," she said. "She will have to be approved, but I doubt there'll be a problem with that. Her bloodlines go back to the German kings of England, and she is so charming. She is just the kind of English rose that the führer likes. He will be enchanted when he meets her. Is Georg pleased as well?"

Ilsa's smile faded slightly, and she sighed. "I suppose he is. I don't know, you see. He's . . ."

Magda was sympathetic. "Yes, I understand." She glanced at the people around them and drew Ilsa aside. "I must say his . . . reticence . . . has been noticed. He's never fully embraced the policies of our glorious new Reich. I daresay that's why Otto has not risen faster. Your son is popular, and very efficient, a man who can be relied upon to do his duty, but his father . . . well. To have a war hero, a member of the old nobility, lack the proper enthusiasm . . ." Her languid shrug spoke volumes. She regarded Ilsa sadly. "Does Georg oppose the marriage?"

"No," Ilsa said quickly. "But he wishes Otto to go to England, to throw off his great destiny and become a farmer."

Magda looked properly horrified. "Surely he understands Germany cannot lose her best and brightest, that young men like Otto are the future of this country, of the entire world." She sounded like one of her husband's propaganda speeches.

It was Ilsa's turn to shrug. "What can I do? Georg is the past, but it was a proud past. His family has served Germany for hundreds of years."

Magda tapped a lacquered fingernail against her lip. "Let me see what I can do. Perhaps a senior post in the Wehrmacht, something dignified but distant?"

Ilsa smiled. "I'm sure Georg would be very pleased to be called to serve his country once again, to fight, and even die if it is required."

Magda's slow smile spread across her face. "Yes. If it is required, we must all make the ultimate sacrifice." She patted Ilsa's hand. "Leave it with me."

GEORG VON SCHROEDER was enjoying a glass of beer with his old friend Wilhelm Canaris, once a sailor, now the head of the Abwehr, the Reich's military intelligence service. They stood on the fringes of the party, watching the festivities. Georg had never felt awkward around Canaris before. They had spent a great deal of time together over the years, swapping war stories, comparing wounds, and toasting the friends they'd lost in battle. "I wonder how much a party like this costs?" Wilhelm said now.

"Remarkable, isn't it?" Georg said.

One of the female pages shrieked with laughter at a comment whispered in her ear by a drunken guest. "In the old days, in the presence of crowned heads and international diplomats, we would have maintained our dignity," Canaris said. "I enjoy a party as much as the next man, but some decorum is called for. Still, it is the perfect finale to the Olympic Games, is it not? A grand fantasy to end a deception."

Georg looked at his old friend sharply. If anyone else had expressed such a sentiment, or been overheard, they might have expected a visit from Canaris's rival organization, the interior intelligence office of the Reich. SD officers like Otto would arrive in a long dark car, bang on the door, and demand an explanation. They saw treason behind every joke, every harmless remark. Georg wondered if there were agents listening even now. Perhaps Wilhelm read his thoughts, for he winked. "We're safe enough here, Georg."

Canaris nodded toward the dance floor, at Otto and Julia and Felix and Viviane. "Your English guests are very charming young ladies."

Georg regarded his eldest son. "Yes. Otto has expressed a wish to marry Lady Julia Devellin." He sipped his beer, which tasted bitter now. "I had hoped he'd follow her to England, or perhaps . . ."

Canaris's gaze was sharp. "Or perhaps temper his political views and ambitions for her?" He shook his head. "He's one of Reinhard Heydrich's lads, Hitler's most rabid fanatics. I do believe he'll make his führer—if not his father—proud. Your other guest is quite charming as well. She has also aroused some interest. She was observed having lunch with Felix and his boss, Professor Solomon Hitzig. Hitzig may be Jewish, but he's a useful Jew, indispensable, I've heard. His work is key to some of the darker plans of our government." Canaris tapped his forehead. "So far, Herr Hitzig has been clever enough to keep his formulas here, but there is no safe that cannot be cracked." He glanced at Georg. "Your son is his closest colleague."

Georg glanced at his old friend. "Oh, but Felix isn't a Nazi, Wilhelm."

Canaris smiled back. "Is he not, my friend? Then we have no need to worry. But what is he otherwise? What are his politics and loyalties? Will there be a double wedding, perhaps? He seems to enjoy the charming Miss Alden as much as she enjoys her camera. Did you know that there are people assigned to keep watch on what our visitors are taking pictures of? We—they—can't have visitors carrying away snapshots of things we don't want foreigners to see. Behind every eager photographer there is another eager photographer, a German one, keeping tabs, making notes. You should advise her—*warn* her—that everything in Germany, like everything here this evening, is an illusion. There is a dragon in every fairy tale. Have you by chance seen any of her photographs?"

Georg frowned. He had not. It had seemed harmless enough, capturing a few souvenirs of a glorious summer abroad. He recalled the places they'd been, the shots she might have taken. He glanced at her again, dancing with Felix, carefree and lovely, and his mouth dried. "Do you—do *they*—suspect she's a—"

Canaris clinked his glass hard against Georg's to shush him. "No one's said a word about that. At least not yet."

TOM WATCHED VIVIANE in Felix von Schroeder's arms on the dance floor, her gown shimmering and shifting around their ankles. Tom kept his eyes on her as he made his way through the crowd of dancers, half fearing she'd vanish again.

The party was growing louder as alcohol loosened inhibitions and the illusions of the decor and entertainment took hold, made guests feel they truly were in a magical place where nothing was forbidden or denied. Careful smiles turned to sloppy, lecherous grins as proper manners and good sense fell away.

Felix von Schroeder's eyes narrowed as he saw Tom coming, a warning glance that told him to stay away, but Tom ignored him and kept walking. "Mind if I cut in?" he said when he reached the couple.

Viviane looked over her shoulder, the jewels in her hair twinkling like drops of water. "Tom!" Her smile was glorious, and he felt it like sun on his skin. She stopped dancing, tried to turn fully, but Schroeder held her tight.

"Actually, I do mind, old chap. I am very much enjoying this dance— too much to give her up."

Viviane's smile faded slightly, and her eyes flicked between the two men.

"But I insist," Tom said.

"Go to—" An explosion cut off the rude command, and a bloom of color and light burst overhead. Guests screamed with surprise and delight as fireworks filled the sky, red, white, and gold, reflected in the river and in the dazzled eyes of the guests.

The dancing stopped, and everyone stood still, their eyes on the spectacle. The explosions echoed off the buildings and hills, and the smell of smoke and blasting powder filled the air. It looked and sounded and smelled like war. Smiles faded as the bombardment went on and on, and people began to flinch.

Viviane was staring skyward, her face white, her smile entirely gone now. Felix laughed aloud. "There you see it—chemistry in action!" he said gleefully. The flashes reflected in his spectacles.

Around them, the shrieks of delight turned to gasps of dismay. One of the torchbearers dropped her torch, and Tom saw a dark-clad arm snake around her white satin waist and drag her backward into the bushes. The next explosion drowned out her scream, if she made one. He looked around. The scene was being repeated all around him, girls carried off by male guests, couples locked in lewd embraces as the party slowly turned to a drunken orgy. Viviane watched the debauchery with horror on her face. Felix von Schroeder was still staring heavenward, gleefully applauding the grotesque fireworks show. It looked like an air raid.

"Come on," Tom said in Viviane's ear, and she bit her lip for an instant, then nodded, clasped his hand, and let him lead her through the crowd. They hurried along the path toward the bridge. A drunken guest lurched at Viviane, grabbed her arm, and Tom didn't hesitate—he punched him, watched him fall, and kept a tight grip on Viviane. Other fights broke out, and he could hear the sound of glass breaking, of curses and screams. Whistles blew, and orders were shouted to halt, but the chaos went on. Tom put his arm around Viviane, felt the heat of her body through the thin fabric of her gown, and half carried her, aware that her bad leg would slow them down. She tried to twist, to glance behind her, but he hurried her onward. "Stop! I can't leave Julia!" she said.

"She's with Otto von Schroeder. He'll keep her safe," Tom said.

"What about your Trude?"

He almost laughed. "She's not my Trude, Viviane."

They reached the land end of the pontoon bridge, and he looked back at the glittering little island, now a scene of mayhem. Others were following them, fleeing the riot.

Tom went to the nearest cab and opened the door. "Go," he ordered the driver.

"Where are we going?" Viviane asked, settling beside him, breathing hard. Her careful coiffure had lost a pin or two, and her red locks tumbled around her face. She was rosy from the run, her eyes wide and luminous. She was staring at him, her lips parted. He hadn't considered where he was taking her, just away from harm. He looked into her eyes. He was still holding her hand. He squeezed it, a silent question.

"Are you rescuing me again, Tom Graham?" She said it softly, a hopeful, husky whisper that undid any resolve he had, any sense of mission.

"Hotel am Zoo," he told the driver. He cupped her chin in his hand and lowered his mouth to hers.

CHAPTER FIFTY

HE PAID THE driver without letting go of her hand, as if he feared she'd disappear or run, or change her mind. She'd squeezed his hand as they endured the endless wait for the elevator, met his eyes, saw the vulnerability in his expression, the fierceness, the question, and knew her own face mirrored the same. Had every moment been leading up to this one, from the instant they'd met?

Alone in the elevator, they came together, kissing desperately. He'd pushed the doors open, drew her down the hall, her hand still in his. He fumbled for his key, as breathless as she was.

He dropped it. He swore in dockyard Scots, picked it up, and got the door open. He kicked it shut behind him as she reached for him, dragged him into her arms, found his lips in the darkness of the room, lit only by the lights of the city filtering through the curtains.

His eyes glittered in the dark. "Are you sure?" he asked, breaking the kiss, pausing with his big hands splayed on her waist.

"I'm sure," she whispered back, wondering when—or if—she'd ever been so sure of anything else in her whole life. He gasped with relief, or desire, or some deeper emotion. His mouth found her neck, her ear.

Clothes fluttered, fell away, and when he scooped her up and carried her to the bedroom, they were both naked. "You're beautiful," he murmured, laying her down. "I knew you would be."

"You thought about it? About this, about me?"

"Aye," he drawled. "Are you surprised?"

She considered what that meant.

"You're thinking, aren't you?" he said. "Don't. Not now."

He lowered his mouth to hers, and she let go, and everything felt safe and right and perfect.

Afterward, she lay in his arms, her body curled against his, his chin on her head, his hand idly caressing her arm, hers splayed against his chest, his heart still beating rapidly under her palm.

"It's nearly dawn. They'll be worried about you. We should get you back before they send a search party," he said, though he made no move to release her or get out of bed.

"I suppose so," she said. He lifted her chin, tilted her head enough so their eyes met. He was studying her, a frown gathering between his brows, the soft, sexy lines around his mouth deepening. She felt a shiver rush through her. Did he regret it? "Now who's thinking too much?" she asked, keeping her tone light, teasing. She shifted, moved out of his arms. Cool air touched her skin, and reality rushed in. She glanced at the window, saw the red glow of dawn. "Julia—" she murmured.

"She was with Otto von Schroeder. She's safe," he said again.

She glanced at him. "Still, I need to be sure. She's probably worried about me as well. And the Schroeders, Felix—"

"Felix," he murmured. His face took on that familiar guardedness, but he couldn't hide the acid in his voice. "That lad has nine lives. He'll survive. His kind always do."

She laughed. "Are you jealous of Felix? Don't be."

He frowned and looked away. "I'm not jealous. He's dangerous, Viviane, more than you know."

Her skin prickled at the warning. "Felix is . . ." She paused. What was he? A shape-shifter, a charmer, a true friend, or a liar? "He's harmless," she said aloud.

"He isn't what you think. He's more like his brother than you know," he said.

She tossed her head. "I can handle Felix—he's more like *my* stepbrother, Miles, than Otto."

"Don't be naive. He's not a schoolboy. He's—"

She didn't want to hear it. Not now. She rose from the bed, dragged the sheet with her, wrapped it around her body, and stood beside the bed, regarding him imperiously. "I don't need rescuing. Not from Felix. He's not a Nazi. He wants to stop a war from happening as much as I do. He's kind and he's funny, and he cares deeply about the future of this world, not just this country."

His mouth drew into a firm line, and he got up as well, stood before her, stark naked. That might be new, but the superior disapproval on his face wasn't. There was something else behind it, she thought, something unspoken that the camera would capture and illuminate. She scanned his face, but she couldn't penetrate his thoughts. "What is this really about?" she asked him.

The whole empty width of the bed lay between them, a barrier now. For a moment he continued to stare at her without replying. A secret, then—and a dark one, or a suspicion. He opened his mouth to speak, then closed it, swore softly. "Look, all I can say is that Felix von Schroeder is not what you think," he said again. "Be careful."

She felt her chest tighten at the warning, a tingle like a disturbance in a spider's web, a ripple on still water. "I don't need rescuing," she said again. "Have I not proven I can do this?"

"Sachsenhausen," he said, his lips twisting on the word.

"Yes," she said. "I got what you wanted, didn't I?"

He looked tormented. "Not what *I* wanted. What I want—" He stopped. "You bloody do need rescuing—from yourself. You're living in some kind of fantasy, a long-dead legend of knights and magic, where what's right and true trumps evil. It doesn't. Men are ambitious, and ambition trumps honor every time. Even your father—" He closed his mouth on the rest.

She frowned. "Even my father?" she prompted. "What does he have to do with this?"

He ran his hand through his hair. "He has everything to do with this. Don't you see? He's the reason why you rush in, try to fix all the ills of the world. You can't. His sins were his own, not yours."

Her mouth dried, and she drew the sheet more tightly around her body, like a royal robe. She lifted her chin, glaring down the length of her nose at him. "His sins? My father was a hero. He was brave and caring and chivalrous. How can that be a sin?"

"Everyone has a flaw, Viviane, a dark side."

She regarded him, noted the conviction in his gaze. "You truly believe that, don't you? You can't bring yourself to trust that there's good in the world, can you? What do you believe in?"

"Not a damned legend that isn't true. I think for myself."

She felt anger rise. "How dare you? Men like my father *are* legends. They make the world a better place, right the wrongs, are the examples of what we should be and must be. There are other men, even now, other people, like that. They aren't myths—they're flesh and blood."

"Please tell me you aren't speaking of Felix von Schroeder."

She felt a jolt of surprise. She hadn't been thinking of him at all. She'd been defending her father, herself. "Felix? What does he have to do—"

"Look, he's not what you think," he said again, cutting her off. He looked haunted, stood silent for a moment, still naked. "I can't say more than that. Just . . ." He trailed off.

She gaped at him. "Are you *jealous*? Do you imagine I'm in love with Felix, even now, after . . ."

He made a low sound in his throat, turned away, paced a few steps before he turned back to her. He shut his eyes and seemed to be considering a problem. "This isn't Camelot," he said finally.

She folded her arms over her chest, bunched her fists in the sheet, holding it against her body like armor. "No, it isn't," she said. "Not for you, at any rate. You don't believe in heroes, of the power of chivalry and honor and courage. I was raised to believe, to understand that I must continue those traditions, guard them, live them every day, do my best, even if it's dangerous."

His expression twisted, blooming to sudden anger. "Then you're a fool. Your father wasn't a hero. He wasn't bloody King Arthur. If anything, he was more like poor bloody Lancelot, the shining image of perfection on the outside but spoiled by envy and lust in his heart. Didn't he ever tell you the truth?"

She felt a chill invade her body, like being dropped into cold water, felt the cold move up her body. "Now what could you possibly mean by that?" He knew something she didn't, or thought he did. She knew then that it was what he hid behind his eyes when he looked at her, that wariness she'd always sensed in him. It was there now, raw in his eyes, in every line of his body, that smug certainty. She'd thought it was disdain for her class, but it was more than that, deeper. She braced herself, raised her chin, met the challenge, though it made her heart pound. "Come now. You can't say something like that and simply stop. You seem to think you know more than I do about everything. You look for imperfections in other people, and you peel back the layers until they're all exposed while you hold so tightly to your own secrets. Is it because you are a bastard, that you feel you have to prove over and over that you are worthy—no, not worthy—*superior* to everyone else?"

Anger sharpened to rage, and his eyes were sharp, dangerous, a stiletto suddenly bared. Her barb had gone deep, drawn blood.

"There are many ways a man can be a bastard, Viviane," he said, his voice dangerously soft, his jaw tight. He came around the bed toward her, and she waited until he reached her, unflinching. He stopped before her. He was taller than she was, and he loomed over her, but she held his gaze, refused to step back. "You think your father wasn't a bastard? It wasn't supposed to go the way it did at Sainte Courcelle. My uncle was there, remember? He came from HQ with orders for Major Kellyn. He saw your father read them, watched him crumple them into a ball, throw them into a corner. 'Get the men ready to attack, Sergeant,' he ordered. 'The objective must be taken.' It wasn't the command he'd expected, and Archie told me he'd been surprised. The men had heard rumors that there was a chance of gas being deployed. They expected the order would call for a retreat, not an attack."

"How is that my father's fault? The blame didn't lie with him, but with the commanders behind the lines who ordered the attack. My father acted honorably, saved the lives of twenty men that day," she said.

"Twenty men. And how many died? Yes, when things went wrong, when the first men over the top began to choke and die, Kellyn ran out on the field to save them. But that wasn't honor—it was fear. It was his fault."

She felt her bones turn to water. "That's not true," she said. "You're lying." He regarded her with smug pity, and with a curse she moved to slap him, but he caught her wrist, held her, made her listen.

"Archie saw the orders. He found the crumpled paper in the corner of the dugout after the attack went wrong. Kellyn had been ordered to stand down, to cancel the attack and hold the line."

She gaped at him. "No, that's not true. It can't be. He would never do such a thing! Why would he?" She tried to pull away, but Tom's grip tightened.

"He wanted a promotion, a chance to make colonel," Tom said baldly. "Archie saw something else that day, a letter your father had been writing when he came in with the orders. It was to your mother."

"My mother?" Her lips were so stiff she could barely form the words. She wanted him to stop, didn't want to know, but he wouldn't relent, and all she could do was listen. She recalled her mother receiving letters from her father during the war. She would read parts of them to Viviane, convey the messages of love and hope.

"The letter said that he was hoping for a promotion at last, that he'd make colonel after that day's attack if it was successful. He promised he'd do everything in his power to win the day, to prove to her family once and for all that she hadn't made a mistake in marrying him. He disobeyed an order for his own gain."

She let her hand go limp in his grip. She couldn't breathe, dared not draw breath for fear she'd fall, or cry. "No. That can't be true. No, my father wasn't ambitious. He didn't care what my mother's family thought of him," she said, even though she knew he must have. It explained so much. Her mother had felt her family's disapproval of her marriage keenly, and she spoke of her former life as a duke's daughter with wistful regret. She missed her siblings, her parents, her old friends. Arthur had promised her he'd make her proud of him, rise in the world, prove to her family that she'd made the right choice in marrying him. After the war, there'd been a distance between Estella and her husband, a hopelessness. Viviane had seen it, though she hadn't understood. She thought it was Papa who'd changed, grown sick and sad. It was guilt. He'd failed his wife, betrayed his men. The honor of a medal, the empty title of hero hadn't been enough. He'd tried to make amends, to mold his daughter into the person he couldn't be, to use her to expiate his sins.

She was numb. "My father was a hero. He saved the lives of twenty men, and he won a medal for bravery." She recited the familiar words like a spell against evil. This time it didn't work. The truth of Tom's version sank into her bones, bit deep, a counterspell that broke the enchantment. She clutched the sheet in her fist, held it over her shattered heart. That day at the lake, the day she'd found his body . . . it hadn't been an accident at all. She forced herself to breathe, drew a shaky gasp, felt it invade her lungs. Her stomach hurt.

Tom was still holding her wrist, but his grip had slackened, become gentle. She stared at his hand, then looked up at his face. The anger in his eyes was gone, replaced with regret and pity. Pity was worse than superiority. She had spent her whole life trying to live up to her father's legacy—his *legend*, the myth.

"Let me go," she said. He released her at once, and she turned away.

"Viviane," he said, calling her back, but she couldn't look at him. Her eyes blurred with tears she refused to shed. She saw her dress on the floor, retrieved it, and went into the bathroom and locked the door. She dressed with ruthless efficiency, used his comb to tame her wild hair into some semblance of sanity. She stared at herself in the mirror and took a breath, tried to squeeze it past the hard nub of anguish and betrayal that filled her chest. Who else knew the truth? Her mother? Rutherford? How many people pitied her, hid the truth from her? She'd spent her life trying to right the world, be a hero like her father, make sense of chaos and suffering. It had been a lie, a *mistake*. What was she now, who was she?

She wrapped her arms around her body. She couldn't let Tom see her like this. She was in his bathroom, and he was outside, waiting. She didn't want to face him. She couldn't let him see the way her heart lay torn to shreds in her breast, but there was no way out except through the bathroom door. She stared at herself in the mirror, at the glitter of tears in her eyes—her father's eyes. No, her own eyes, wide open.

What now? she wondered. What would he have done? The familiar question that had always given her strength and courage failed her now. She listened for his voice in her mind, his guidance—find the grail, wield the sword, save the kingdom, the whole bloody world. But there was only silence now, and she was on her own, Viviane Alden and her foolish pride.

She wiped away her tears before she opened the door.

Tom was sitting on the bed, dressed now, and he rose to his feet. "I shouldn't have told you. Not like that," he said. "I'm sorry."

She didn't answer.

"Look, I'll just wash my face and I'll take you back to the Adlon," he said, and went into the bathroom and shut the door.

She crossed the room and found her shoes. She opened the door of the suite and walked out.

CHAPTER FIFTY-ONE

"Ready?" Tom asked as he came out of the bathroom. "I'll lend you my coat again."

Viviane didn't answer, and he walked out into the sitting room. "Viviane?" he called, but the room was empty, and he knew she'd gone.

He swore and moved to go after her. Halfway to the door he stepped on something on the floor. He bent to retrieve it and found the Roman coin necklace she always wore. He'd never seen her without it. He stared at it, her talisman from Kellyn, her good luck charm, the cherished memory of a perfect day with her beloved father.

Guilt punched him in the gut. He'd destroyed that. He hadn't meant to, but he'd let his determination to save her, to prove he knew better than she did, ruin everything. He couldn't say what he'd wanted to, to tell her why she couldn't trust Felix. He wished he'd disregarded Alex's orders. He'd been careless and callous, and he'd torn her world apart.

He was so bloody good with words, so glib, so convincing. This time, though, they'd turned on him.

His uncle Archie had told Tom the story after one too many drinks, when memories of the war, the terrible shadows of all Sergeant Archie

Graham had seen and done and lost, crowded in to haunt him. Tom had carried him back from the pub and was putting him to bed when Archie began to talk. It was the anniversary of the battle, and Archie was remembering it, seeing it played out before his eyes in that little Glasgow kitchen. Major Sir Arthur Alden of Kellyn's name had come up, spoken through tears. He was a good officer, the kind that cared about his men, mourned every death and wounding, and always had a kind word for even the lowliest private as he passed through the trenches to buck 'em up. He'd wanted to save them all, and that was impossible. The war always won. It had been victorious over every good man, including the major. The façade of Major Alden's cheer, his stiff upper lip and encouraging smile, had been shaken by too many battles, too many casualties, too much horror and loss. Archie had said he wanted to hate him, after he knew what Alden had done, but how could he hate a man for wanting out? Every soldier wanted out. Alden was just fortunate enough to have friends in high places. "I would have hated him if he'd gone after that, gotten that promotion, taken a job at HQ, or at home in England, but he gave it all up, stuck with us lads in the field. His way of making amends, I suppose. You should have seen him when the gas hit us. He stood there, his face white as he watched the poor lads out on the field, writhing and clutching their throats. 'Sir, we must pull back,' I said, but he didn't hear. I tried to stop him when he climbed out of the trench, but he kicked me off. He crawled through the mud to get to 'em. It was a fool's errand. Some were already far gone when he got 'em back, but he kept going out there, under fire, with that terrible cloud coming closer. It crawled over the ground like a snake, slithered toward us on the wind. A hundred men drowned in that yellow smoke. That's the only way to describe it, lad. They sank into it and never came up again, and it was Alden's fault. They called him a hero and pinned a medal on him, but he accepted it with a guilty conscience." Archie had sat down heavily on the bed and rubbed his face. "I kept those crumpled orders and that damned letter for years after. I thought someday I'd face him, ask him why he'd done it, broken our trust in him, but I never did. It was the war, the goddamned awful war. It killed him, too, in the end. I went to his funeral to see how he died, and if he regretted it. I suppose he did, didn't he? His wife wasn't there, nor any kin other than his poor wee daughter. I burned them that very night, those bloody papers, threw them into the stove. Now no one will ever know but me." Archie had passed out then and didn't recall a word of the conversation the next day. Nor did he ever mention the battle again. He never said a word against Major Sir Arthur Alden of Kellyn. "Aye, I served with him," he'd say if asked, and nothing more. Tom wished he'd kept his own mouth shut. The hard, cold, ugly words that had spilled out had been cruel, and in the aftermath of love, of connection, of passion, it felt all the more hurtful.

He looked at the coin in his hand, King Arthur on one side, Excalibur on the other, and wondered if she'd tossed the coin aside when she left, or if the chain had snapped as they shed their clothes, lost to everything but passion.

He had to find her, try to make it right. He put the necklace in his breast pocket, felt his stomach knot. Even Viviane, strong and brave as she was, had her breaking point.

This was exactly the kind of thing that drove someone to utter despair. Or into the arms of another for comfort.

It wouldn't be Julia she ran to.

It would be Felix.

CHAPTER FIFTY-TWO

JULIA'S BEDROOM WAS empty when Viviane reached their shared suite. She felt a moment of concern and forced it away. Her stepsister was safe with Otto or breakfasting with the count and countess.

She ran a hot bath and sank into it. She wished she could swim in the cold sea for an hour instead, dive deep, purge her mind and soul.

She felt hollow. Everything she'd done in her life, all she'd grown up to become, had been in her father's image. She'd been brave for him, good for him, and she'd tried to fix the ills of the world for him because he was gone and no longer could. She was the last of the Aldens of Kellyn, the guardian and champion of a precious legend.

If it was all a lie, what did that make her now?

Tom had known all along, before they had ever even met. She remembered the day on the cliff, when she'd called him a social climber, played the daughter of a hero who wasn't a hero. He'd said nothing at all then. He probably thought her an arrogant fool, too stupid or class bound to admit the truth.

She hadn't seen any of that in the way he looked at her last night or felt it in the way he touched her. It wasn't a man using a convenient and willing woman. It was a sharing, a reverence, a joining of more than bodies. She hadn't felt that kind of connection with another person since her father died. This wasn't hero worship. It was the kind of love a woman had for a man, the *right* man. She realized that it was what she'd been searching for all along, why she'd stumbled into her betrothal to Phillip, and stumbled out of it, too. She wanted what she felt for Tom. Did she still feel it, even now? She searched her heart, and he was still there.

Loving him shocked her even as it settled into her mind and her heart. It wasn't joy that she felt, not like Julia's love for Otto, but vulnerability, and unbearable hurt.

She wasn't stupid, or naive. She truly believed that it was possible to make the world better by upholding nobility and honor and goodness. Light must triumph over darkness, and that required courage. Her father had taught her that, and whatever else he'd been, no matter how flawed, it was a good lesson, a true, shining sentiment.

If all Tom had said about him was true, then it only made it more important to take up that sword, to restore her legacy, to try to be the hero her father wanted to be, had raised her to be.

A knock at the door made her jump, and she slid under the bubbles. "Yes?" she asked breathlessly.

"It is the maid, fraülein. I have a letter for you. I shall leave it on the desk."

Viviane listened to her footsteps retreating across the floor and heard the door close. It was from Tom, no doubt—an apology perhaps. For *everything*.

She got out of the bath, pulled on her robe, and stood in the doorway staring at the small white packet on the desk, dreading what it might contain. Kind regrets, a farewell, or another warning.

She tightened the sash on her robe and steeled herself as she picked up the envelope and ran her thumb under the flap, holding her breath.

It wasn't from Tom. The envelope held three train tickets to Hamburg, departing tonight. *Our friend is ready to go. I have enclosed an extra ticket for Julia, if she's willing to leave,* the accompanying note read, signed only *F.*

She wondered what had happened to Felix last night, if he'd been worried when she'd gone. She considered what Tom had told her, that Felix was dangerous.

He was wrong about that. Felix was merely . . .

She couldn't find the word to describe him. He defied description, serious one minute, playful the next, sweet and charming, then cutting and cruel. Which was the real Felix? He personified everything about Germany.

She stared at the tickets. Escape lay in her palm, an ending and a new beginning. She'd been afraid of leaving too soon, but they'd arrived at the perfect time. There was no reason to stay in Germany now. The Berlin games were over, or they would be by the time she reached the station this evening. She'd help Solomon Hitzig escape, save his life, prevent the Nazis from using his poison gas as a weapon. It would be dangerous, and if they were caught . . . She put the tickets down and turned to get dressed.

She packed a small valise. She left her gowns and the clothes she wouldn't need.

She picked up Julia's battered Baedeker's, now well-thumbed, from the desk. How this holiday had changed them both, she marveled. She hoped Julia would come to her senses and return to England, think before she did something she might live to regret. But isn't that exactly what she was doing, rescuing a stranger she barely knew, risking everything she loved, even her very life? They were both taking terrible risks, but the rewards—and the cost of failure—were equally high.

Viviane tucked one of the rail tickets between the pages of the Baedeker's and left the room.

CHAPTER FIFTY-THREE

"I think we may have a problem," Felix said, pacing his mother's sitting room at the hotel, looking at her with the sheepish, contrite expression he'd practiced in the mirror. It was enough to melt the heart of any mother, even a Valkyrie like Ilsa.

He'd asked to see her alone before they left for the closing ceremonies with his father and Viviane, Julia and Otto, and even Klaus, a jolly, happy little family outing. It was going to be a very busy day. "I fear it may be my fault entirely."

She looked at him blandly, unimpressed. "What have you done, Felix? Did your flapping tongue get you into trouble again? Your jokes are not nearly as amusing as you think."

He couldn't resist. "Oh, it's not my *tongue* this time, not entirely at any rate. It's Viviane."

His mother colored. "Viviane? Have you come to tell me you wish to marry her?"

"Certainly not," he said, a moment of real surprise rushing up his spine. "I see her—I *saw* her—only as a charming visitor. I simply wished to be polite, good company, and to help her enjoy her holiday." He looked sorrowful. "It seems she had other ideas."

His mother's face hardened to stone. "What other ideas?"

"I think . . ." He paused for dramatic effect, then rushed on. "I think Viviane Alden may have misled all of us." She regarded him silently, waiting.

"Have you seen any of her snapshots by chance?" he asked.

Something flickered in her eyes, concern, perhaps, or was it fear? She lowered her gaze to her hands to hide it, pretended to examine her manicured fingertips. "No. What of them?"

Felix ran a hand through his hair. "Have you all been so busy that you haven't noticed *what* she has been photographing? Not just holiday snaps. The factories. The soldiers."

Her jaw dropped and her luminous blue eyes popped. "She's *spying* on us? *On Germany?* How do you know?

Felix sighed, a mighty gust of guilt and dejection, and spun the lie. "She asked what it was I do for a living. I showed her the lab, gave her a tour. I . . . I introduced her to Professor Hitzig. She insisted he must join us for lunch. She was very interested in his work, and she even suggested that he might enjoy visiting England."

"England?"

She didn't bother to hide the horror in her eyes now. He rubbed a hand over his own mouth to hide a smirk, making it look as if it pained him to speak, to admit what he was telling her, to ask for her help. "I *hoped* I was wrong about her, but she has an English friend, a member of the press corps, a man named Tom Graham."

"Graham?" She tasted the name, rolled it on her tongue, memorized it. "Does Otto know?"

He didn't reply. There it was. The trap was set. Ilsa would now take over, and make sure Otto knew. Felix wouldn't be sorry to see the last of Tom Graham.

"What are we to do?" Ilsa asked. "When the reports about Viviane come out, that she's a spy in our very nest, that we have trusted her, it will harm your brother's reputation. He could hardly marry Julia then, not without damage to his credibility."

As always, her concern was all for Otto.

"It's worse than that, even, I fear," Felix said. "I saw the professor this morning. He trusts me completely. He confided he'll be taking a trip, that Viviane had purchased train tickets for this evening. I fear she intends to take him out of the country."

"One less Jew," she muttered.

Did she understand nothing at all? Sometimes it was hard to be smarter than the rest of his family. He spoke slowly. "He is one of our leading scientists, so important that he has special status to continue his work. He's working on a new gas weapon, but he has not quite finished the final part of his formula."

She paused to look at him. "What if he leaves Germany, takes the formula with him?"

He stopped pacing and clasped his hands together. "That's exactly what I fear."

"But Julia—is she helping Viviane? Does she know?"

Felix gritted his teeth and didn't bother answering that. "I believe I have a solution. I can stop Hitzig from escaping, and foil Viviane's plan." He looked at his mother to see if she was listening. "The professor keeps his formula for the new gas in a small notebook he keeps hidden. He would certainly take it with him if he left the country. If we had that notebook, we wouldn't need the professor any longer. Do you understand?"

She nodded.

"I know what train they're taking, Hitzig and Viviane. They're planning to go tonight, while half the world is trying to leave the city."

"As soon as the games are over," Ilsa said. "She's clever."

"Yes, but I'm smarter," Felix said. "I will accompany her tonight, promise to escort her and the professor to safety. You will alert Otto. He can follow us and stop the train at some small station, perhaps, somewhere where it won't be noticed too much."

She looked at him with something akin to admiration for once. "You'll be a hero for capturing a fleeing Jew, for keeping his work in Germany."

"Better. Once I have the notebook, I can finish his work. I will be the director of the institute."

He saw the realization of that hit her. Her nostrils flared. "Yes," she breathed. "Yes, it would be an important role, a key part of the führer's plans."

He smiled at her.

"But Viviane?" Ilsa asked. "What will happen to her?"

He shrugged as if it didn't matter. "She'll have to disappear," he said quietly, coldly, with no regret.

For an instant she pursed her lips, shocked, perhaps, that he could be so ruthless, as cold as Otto was—as she herself was. Then she smiled. "Yes, of course. It is a good plan. Perhaps I have underestimated you, Felix."

He raised one eyebrow. "I am your son, dear Mutti, as much a product of your loins as Otto or Klaus. Are you truly so surprised?"

She patted his cheek. "I am pleased."

CHAPTER FIFTY-FOUR

GEORG VON SCHROEDER watched Julia as she used his field glasses to scan the crowded stadium on this, the final day of the Olympic Games. The equestrian finals were underway, with Germany favored to win. The closing ceremonies would take place late in the day, after the last medals were awarded. He was looking forward to the end, to leaving the city and returning to the peace and quiet of the mountains, and Glücksstern. In early September, the Nazi party's "Rally of Honor" would take place in Nuremburg, and Ilsa was already making plans to attend. Julia had looked nearly as avid as her hostess.

But now, the usually carefree young woman's brow was furrowed.

"What's wrong, my dear?" Georg asked.

"I expected Viviane to meet us here, but she's late," Julia replied. "Where could she be?"

"Felix and Ilsa are also late," he pointed out. "Perhaps she'll arrive with them."

"Vee and I had an argument before the party last night," Julia confided. "She doesn't think I should marry Otto without speaking to Papa. I know he'll say I'm too young, insist that I wait a year or two." She met Georg's eyes. "I have never disobeyed my father in my life."

"Then why do so now?" he asked her gently. "If you were my daughter, I would wish to meet any young man who claimed to have stolen your heart. I would wish to make certain I liked him before I let him take you from me."

"How silly you are," Julia said. "Otto is your son. Surely you know he'd make a fine husband." She tucked her arm through his. "And if I married him, I would indeed be your daughter."

He smiled at her. "I would like that very much, but things may change between your country and mine, dear girl. You have a duty to England, and to your parents."

"I'm not worried. I adore Germany, and I love Otto. What if I return home and Otto forgets me? I couldn't bear that."

He patted her hand. "No man could forget you."

He looked at the Baedeker's on her lap, battered now from constant use. "We shall talk more about this tomorrow, over coffee in a café, just the two of us. Where shall we go?" He picked up her travel guide and opened it.

A railway ticket fell into his lap. He frowned when he saw it was dated for tonight's Hamburg train, leaving after the closing ceremonies. He glanced at her in confusion. Was she eloping with Otto, going to England after all?

Before he could ask her about it, a fanfare sounded and Adolf Hitler and his entourage entered the stadium. The crowd rose, their arms and voices raised in devotion, Julia included, her face alight with the same fanatical joy.

Georg felt his heart drop. Julia was lost. His hopes that she would show Otto another way, a better way, and lure him to England were dashed.

He slipped the rail ticket into his pocket. He had to talk to Viviane.

Felix and Ilsa arrived at last and took their seats, and worry nagged at Georg. He recalled what Wilhelm Canaris had said about the risks Viviane had been taking, the danger she might now be in. He sat in the stadium without seeing the event below.

"Smile, Georg. We're being watched, you know," Ilsa murmured to him. Her face was a picture of placidity behind the binoculars.

"I'm worried about Viviane," he murmured.

She turned to look at him sharply. "Then you know that she's betrayed us?"

He felt a jolt of surprise. "What do you mean?"

"It appears Miss Alden is not what she seems after all."

He stared at her in dismay, but she pinched his arm, hard. "Don't frown. Your attitude is noticed. Everything you do is noticed, especially now. You should be more careful."

He felt a flare of anger. "Perhaps that's the problem. Do you want to live in a country where everyone is watched, where we cannot say what we think or object to the wrongs we see?"

Her eyes were flakes of ice. "If there is something wrong, it is you," she hissed.

Georg looked around at the happy crowds, the fools cheering a monster who postured and smirked at the adulation. Was it possible to love Germany and hate it at the same time? He felt his heart clench. Did no one see the terrible things the Nazis were doing, how they twisted and mocked all that Germans held dear? He felt sick.

"I'm going back to the hotel," he said to his wife. "Otto will escort you and Julia back later."

Isla looked at him with naked disdain. She wasn't his Ilsa anymore. She belonged to *him*, Adolf Hitler. "We are going to have drinks with friends after the closing to celebrate the führer's great triumph. I don't know when I'll be back, but it will be very late," she said, and turned away, picking up the binoculars again.

What was there to say? There were wrongs he could not right. He was too old, or too afraid of losing what he had, perhaps. Or not brave enough.

He simply nodded and left the stadium. There was only one thing he could protect now, one person.

CHAPTER FIFTY-FIVE

T<small>HERE WAS NO</small> answer when Tom called Viviane's room from the lobby, or when he knocked on her door, so he broke in.

They'd trained him to use a picklock as part of the preparation for this job. He'd thought it silly at the time, a skill he'd never need, but it was useful now, and surprisingly easy. In seconds he had the door open. He entered a well-appointed sitting room five times the size of his tiny room at the Hotel am Zoo and shut the door behind him. The room was dark, the curtains drawn against the heat of the afternoon. Two doors flanked the room, bedrooms, no doubt, one for Viviane, one for her stepsister.

He chose the half-open door on the right and pushed it open, caught the echo of her perfume and knew he had the right room. His body jolted with awareness and the memory of that scent on her skin and in his bed.

The room was empty. He thought she'd be here, curled in her bed, sleeping or angry or crushed by regrets and his callousness, but the bed was empty and neatly made up. Where was she?

He opened the door of the closet. Her clothes were there, including the gauzy blue gown she'd worn to the Goebbelses' party, wrinkled now. He lifted the sleeve, held it to his nose, and breathed in the fragrance of his shaving soap mixed with her perfume. He felt a surge of desire and regret and a need to see her so sharp it made him gasp.

He let go of the garment to shut the closet door.

He considered leaving the coin necklace on the dressing table, a kind of calling card so she'd know he'd been here looking for her. He reached into his pocket for it, felt the soft edges of the gold against his palm, but he left it where it was. He wanted to see her, to put it directly into her hand and apologize.

Alex be damned—he'd tell her the truth about Felix, get her away to safety. This time, rescuing her wasn't about chivalry—it was a matter of life and death. What if it was already too late? If Felix knew what she was up to, even suspected . . . Fear caught him by the throat, and he swallowed hard.

The door of the suite opened, and Tom felt a surge of relief go through him. "Viviane?" he called, exiting her bedroom.

But it wasn't Viviane or Julia.

Instead, he found himself face-to-face with Count Georg von Schroeder.

CHAPTER FIFTY-SIX

VIVIANE HURRIED THROUGH the street, her hat pulled low over her face, the collar of her raincoat around her chin, her small case bumping against her thigh, her camera slung around her neck. She was aware of eyes upon her from behind window curtains and in doorways, but no one tipped their hat or smiled. In this part of town, home to a once-vibrant Jewish community, it was safer not to look or see or hear.

She climbed the stairs of the building she'd visited with Felix and knocked softly on Professor Hitzig's door.

"*Ja?*" he said softly through the door after a pause.

"It's Miss Alden," she replied, and the door opened.

"Come inside." He looked at the empty hallway behind her. "Where is Felix?" he asked.

She shook her head. She had no idea where Felix might be. She hadn't seen him or heard from him. She could have telephoned him, but she needed time to think. She'd come to the person who'd been nearest to her father that day on the battlefield, his enemy.

"You are early, Miss Alden. Felix asked me to be ready to leave for the station precisely at ten minutes to five. It's barely past four." He shut the door and bolted it behind her. "Is there a problem, perhaps? Have you come to tell me you've changed your mind?"

Solomon Hitzig was the same age as Georg von Schroeder, the age her father would have been if he'd lived, and yet he looked a dozen years older. He was stooped, his body drawn in upon itself as if he was trapped within the cage of his own bones. Only his eyes were still fully alive, dark and shining as pebbles in clear water. He regarded her over his glasses, his expression carefully blank.

"Have you changed your mind?" he asked her again, his tone deliberately flat, as if he dared not hope.

"No," she said. "Felix sent me train tickets this morning."

He sighed and removed his spectacles to rub his eyes with thumb and forefinger. Without them, his eyes were blue, like deep water. "Thank you," he said with dignity. "I believe I know what this means to you, what it is costing you to do this for me of all people. Come and sit down. We will wait for Felix together."

He led the way to his sitting room, still crowded with books and papers. "I shall miss this place," he said. "And yet, I hope never to see it again. I am ready to go. Would you care for coffee? I suppose I must get used to drinking tea from now on."

"We have coffee in England, too," she said as she perched on the edge of a chair by a window. She moved to open the curtains, to let in light and air.

"Don't!" he said quickly, and her hand paused in midair. "They'll see you," he said.

He peered carefully around the edge of the faded lace panel. "They stand in the doorway across the street, watching me, waiting." She saw a man in a broad-brimmed hat leaning against the wall, smoking. A dozen cigarette butts littered the ground around him. Hitzig jumped back as the man glanced upward. "How will we get past them?" he muttered.

She had no idea. She was out of her depth now. "I'm sure Felix will know," she murmured.

She glanced at the dusty clock on the mantel. Julia and the Schroeders were probably at the stadium by now, no doubt wondering where she was. She still held on to the faint hope that Julia would find the ticket, see sense, follow Viviane to the station, and come home.

If nothing else, Julia would know Viviane had gone.

She'd left no word for Tom Graham. What would she say? She reached for the coin around her neck and felt empty flesh, felt her heart crack. It wasn't there.

"Is something wrong, fraülein?" Herr Hitzig asked.

"I've lost my—" She paused. It was more than a necklace. It was her last link to her father, to her past, to the lake, to who she was and where she'd come from. The professor was watching her, his expression concerned.

"We've all lost so very much," he murmured. "Again, I am sorry for the loss of your father. If it is of comfort, I have suffered for what I did."

She dropped her hand to her lap. "Did you see him that day? On the battlefield?"

He regarded her for a moment, his expression pregnant. Then he shook his head. "War is chaos. There is smoke and screaming and . . ." He wiped his hand across his mouth.

"And gas," she added.

He got to his feet, went to the crowded bookshelf, and picked up a small, framed photo. He ran his fingertips over the picture. "This is my wife and son. That chair you are sitting in was her favorite. She used to sit there by the window, where the light is good, and sew. She read to my son there, taught him his letters and told him fairy tales. I sat at my desk and wished they'd be silent and let me work." He said it softly, regretfully. "How often I have wanted them back again to fill my life with disruption, to keep me from my equations and formulations." He looked up at her. "Your life—your father's life—was not the only one shattered that day." He looked at the photograph again. "This photo was taken a year before my wife's death. We were happy then. Then I was given a new job, an important one, part of a group of scientists charged with developing new gas weapons to help us win the war. I thought it was a humane weapon, you see, swift, and without the terrible destruction, the shattering of bodies and livelihoods with bombs and bullets. I was so gleeful when I told my wife. She didn't applaud my brilliance. She was horrified. She pleaded with me to stop working on such a terrible thing." He looked up at Viviane with tears in his eyes. "I refused, and I was ordered to go to the front to observe the deployment of the gas at Sainte Courcelle, against the British." He paused and met her eyes, and she swallowed.

"My father was there," she said.

He nodded. "Did he speak of it?"

"Some of it. He was given a medal, you see, for saving the lives of twenty men who'd been overcome by the gas. I read the citations after he died, learned the story." She bit her lip and fell silent, unable to tell him what Tom had said, the true story. "Many others died," she said instead.

His eyes returned to the photograph in his hand. "When I returned home after that day, my son was here. He was only seventeen, but he'd been called up because they needed soldiers, even boys. He'd come to say goodbye to his mother, dressed in an ill-fitting uniform. It wasn't even a new uniform, but one taken from a dead soldier, cleaned and repaired as well as possible because there was no more new cloth at that point in the war." He blinked rapidly, pointing to the carpet. "My son was on the floor with his mother in his arms. At first, I didn't understand what had happened. I thought she'd fainted at the sight of him in uniform. Then he looked up at me with such terrible hatred in his eyes that it stole the breath from my lungs, and I understood. I stood there as my son lifted his mother's body and carried her to the bed. I watched him fold her slashed wrists over her chest and tenderly cover her with a blanket. He walked out of the apartment without a word. He didn't go to the front. He went to Switzerland instead, then to England. He has not spoken to me since that day."

Viviane swallowed, her own eyes misting with tears.

"A battlefield is chaos," he said again. "That is the nature of war. Soldiers know this. Not even the ones who sent them into battle, or the ones who love them most, can comprehend war as they do. That is why men do not speak of it. You are incapable of understanding."

"Then tell me. I want to understand," Viviane said. "My father was the person he was because of that battle. It changed his life, destroyed it, and he was never the same. I grew up believing he was a hero, that he was a good officer and a good man. I'm not sure I can bear to believe that he was not."

"Who is it that has made you doubt it?" he asked.

She studied her hands. "A friend. Well, someone I believed was a friend. His uncle was there that day, but his story is different from the one I know, or thought I knew."

"And so you have come to ask his enemy."

She looked up at him. "Yes."

He was quiet for a moment, and the ticking of the clock was the only sound. "If I can tell you nothing, will you walk away now, leave me to my fate?"

She thought about what that would mean, recalled the abused prisoners she'd seen at Sachsenhausen. "No. Not if it means making certain that it will not happen again. Can you promise me that?"

His eyes narrowed behind his glasses, sharpened to hard points. "You do not want me to hand over my formulas to your countrymen so they can use it to take revenge?"

She winced. "I very much wanted revenge, once. More than anything. I hated Germany and Germans for starting the war that killed my father. I came to Germany . . ." She paused. "I came to help stop another war. I was so sure I could make a difference, that it would be easy to see what lay behind the façade they erected for the tourists. Now I know I cannot stop a war on my own, but perhaps if I can help one person, they will help one more . . . so I am choosing to help you."

"But what is the price of your help, fraülein? What if I cannot pay it? What if I want revenge of my own on the Nazis?"

He crossed to the desk, opened the drawer, and held up a small notebook. "What if I told you my formulas are all here, in this little book, a recipe for the kind of gas that will unfailingly kill, not merely wound? Would you take it from me, give it to your people?"

She stared at the little pocket notebook with a blue cover, so similar to the kind Tom used, and yet this one held the power of life and death, war and destruction. "I would much prefer that such weapons are never used again, not by anyone, ever."

"I could burn it, throw it into the fire, destroy it forever," he said. "I will, if you wish it. Do you?"

Before she could reply, there was another knock at the door. Hitzig jumped in surprise and knocked the framed photograph off the edge of his desk. The glass shattered, and he regarded it in dismay.

"Professor? It's Felix," came a muffled call, followed by a second knock. Viviane rose from her chair, but Hitzig stayed her with a wave of his hand. He crossed and opened the door, and Felix came in.

He saw Viviane and grinned at her. "You're here! Mutti was quite concerned when you weren't at the closing ceremonies. I believe she sent a note to Magda Goebbels, asking her to check the shrubbery on the island for you, in case you met with disaster at the party. But here you are, safe and sound with the professor. Where did you go last night?"

She managed a tight smile but offered no explanation. She didn't want to think of Tom now, or the events of last night. She didn't have the time or the strength to analyze her turbulent feelings. "Julia is also worried," Felix prompted.

"I will explain when I see her," she said.

Felix shrugged. "As you wish." He glanced at his watch. "We haven't time now at any rate. He crossed to pour three glasses of schnapps and passed them out. "The equestrian event was marvelous, a fitting end to our grand and glorious games. Germany won the gold medal, of course. The British took the bronze. It's a pity you missed it." He raised his glass. "Here's to the next games, in Tokyo, another government that wants nothing but peace and harmony." He sipped, and Viviane met the professor's eyes. The notebook had disappeared from view. Hitzig set the tiny glass on the desk, the drink untouched, and bent to retrieve the photograph from amid the broken glass. He grunted when he cut his finger.

"What have you done, my friend?" Felix asked, crossing to look. "Viviane, we need a bandage."

Viviane retrieved her handkerchief from her pocketbook to wrap Hitzig's injury. His hand shook slightly in hers, but his voice was steady as he turned to Felix. "How will this work? How will we get past the men outside?" Hitzig asked.

"Are you afraid you'll be shot?" Felix asked. Viviane looked at him sharply, but he laughed. "Just a little joke to lighten the mood. Leave it to me. By the time they realize you're gone, you'll be taking tea with your son in Kent."

Viviane could have sworn he'd told her that Hitzig's son lived in Surrey.

"This is no time for levity. What is your plan?" Hitzig asked impatiently, a stern teacher to an unruly pupil, and a momentary flash of annoyance crossed Felix's jovial face.

"Why, a disguise, Herr Professor. Something they'll never expect. Why should we not have a little fun?" He grinned at Viviane. "I got the idea from your own English history, a book of stories my father read to me as a child, all about heroic escapes from the dread Tower of London. Do you recall the tale of the accused traitor who received a visit from his wife and her ladies-in-waiting on the eve of his execution? They brought an extra set of women's clothes, which he put on. He walked out among the crying women, right past the guards. Brilliant, don't you think?"

The professor glared at him. "You expect me to dress as a woman?"

"Isn't it a wonderful jest?" Felix said brightly. "You will be able to walk right past the agents outside, and they'll simply tip their hats politely and wish you a good day, *meine gute Frau*." He sketched an exaggerated bow.

Hitzig drew himself up. "No. I prefer to keep my dignity."

Felix's smile faded, and he rolled his eyes. "Suit yourself, then. We'll leave through the cellar door. I just thought we might have a little fun creating subterfuge, leaving them wondering how you managed to simply vanish. Very well then." He looked around the room. "How many happy hours I spent in this room, learning from you. I shall miss coming here. Do you have what you need? You have not forgotten your notes, I trust?"

"I have them," the professor assured him without revealing the notebook he'd shown to Viviane. He looked around the room as if memorizing it, taking in the belongings that had made up his life—his books, his wife's chair, the glitter of the delicate schnapps glasses in the light that snuck around the edge of the drawn curtains. Viviane bent to retrieve the photograph from the broken glass. The corner was marked with a spot of blood now. She handed it to him, and he nodded his thanks and put it into the pocket of his jacket.

Felix beamed at him and glanced at the clock. "It's getting late, and the traffic will be dreadful. We mustn't delay. Let's go."

CHAPTER FIFTY-SEVEN

Tom's heart pounded as he regarded Georg von Schroeder across the width of the sitting room at the Adlon. For a moment neither of them moved. If the Count von Schroeder was surprised to find a man in Viviane's room, he hid it well. He set the key he used to enter the room on a side table. "I trust you're a friend of Viviane's. I saw you with her at the party last night."

"Tom Graham," Tom said by way of confirmation.

He watched the count glance at the bedroom door, half ajar behind Tom. "Is she here?"

Tom shook his head.

The count was tall, his hair gray at the temples, his eyes keen. He looked like a man who'd been, first and foremost, a soldier for most of his life, had been raised to that life as much as to the privileged aristocracy. He took off his gloves and regarded Tom with bland disapproval and a touch of bafflement. It was the way his father looked at him, Tom thought. But this man had the power to have him arrested, or worse.

"Have you come to take her back to England?" the count asked, going to the desk, looking almost casually at the papers there—sightseeing brochures, fashion magazines, and a copy of *Mein Kampf*. He opened the cover, winced at the sight of Julia's name written inside. He closed the book again and turned back to Tom, his brows raised, waiting for his reply.

"Do you know where I can find her?" Tom asked, answering the question with one of his own.

The count tapped a long finger on the cover of the book, and Tom saw a scar on his hand, a silver line that snaked under the monogrammed cuffs of his shirt and coat, an old war wound, perhaps. "Unfortunately, I do not. That's why I'm here. She was not at the closing ceremonies, and I wanted to make certain she's safe."

The count looked again at the half-open door of Viviane's bedroom and then passed another assessing look over Tom. Tom knew what he saw—a plain man in a plain suit, tall and lean, his bearing every bit as proud as his own, out of habit if not breeding. Tom waited until the count had finished taking his measure and made his decision as to what to do next.

"I follow the English newspapers, and I've read your work. Do you truly believe what you write?"

Tom held his eyes, though his heart kicked his ribs, urging caution. "Why would I not?"

"You don't look like a fool."

The count reached into his coat, and Tom's mouth dried, but instead of a gun, the count held out a railway ticket. Tom took it. It bore today's date, a boarding time of seven o'clock, traveling to Hamburg. The boat train to England departed from there. Tom looked at Georg von Schroeder in surprise. "Do you expect me to leave?"

"Viviane left it for Julia. I assume she has one of her own. She has not said goodbye to me or my wife, and I came to see if she was perhaps here, packing, or if she'd left a note."

"Her clothes are here," Tom said.

"But her camera is gone, I trust."

Tom held his breath.

"She would not leave without that," Georg said, the comment pointed, his eyes sharp. Tom held his tongue, and the count sighed. "You have nothing to fear from me, Mr. Graham. I have developed a great affection for Viviane during her stay. She is—quite brave, but if she remains in Germany much longer, she will not find it so welcoming, and my protection will not be enough to keep her safe. My son is a dangerous man for all that he loves Julia. Do you understand?"

He meant Otto, Tom realized. Did he know about Felix's activities? "I believe I understand," he said, his jaw tight. He wanted to ask where Felix was, but the count spoke first.

"I won't ask how you know that. I don't wish to know." He shook his head, his expression careworn and haunted. "We are not all Nazis in Germany, you know. Please, go and find Viviane before it's too late. Take her home to England and keep her safe."

Tom felt a lump in his chest. If she'd let him, if she didn't reject his help. If she wasn't with Felix even now, in danger, or on her way to Sachsenhausen or some other prison. He tightened his grip on the train ticket and felt sweat trickle between his shoulder blades. He didn't have time to call Alex, to tell him he was leaving, and Trude had no doubt alerted her superiors that he was missing. Were they looking for him even now, Gestapo agents fanning out across the city, watching the train stations, the bus stops, even the airport?

"I'll find Viviane," he said. He had to. He put the train ticket into his pocket with her necklace, hoped it would bring him luck.

The count closed his eyes for a moment, out of relief or resignation, forced to leave the matter in the hands of a stranger. "Thank you," he said slowly. For a moment Georg von Schroeder stood where he was, blocking the way to the door. "If I might ask a favor of you, Mr. Graham. Would you please send me word that she's safe? That's all I want."

"I will."

The count glanced at his watch. "You'd better hurry. The traffic will be terrible, and German trains are very prompt."

CHAPTER FIFTY-EIGHT

THE RAILWAY STATION bustled with tourists heading homeward, the games done, their holiday over. Trains were full, and laden porters dodged through the crowds.

"Did you know there were more than three hundred and eighty thousand tourists registered in Berlin over the past month?" Felix asked as they hurried along the platform. "What a triumph for the führer. Look, that's his special train there on the siding. I hear he's leaving Berlin himself tonight, heading for a holiday at Berchtesgaden. Did you know it's very near Glücksstern? We're practically neighbors." He looked calm, jovial even, while Viviane's heart pounded in her chest. She held tight to the professor's arm, guided him through the crowds so he could keep his head down. He startled at every whistle, every shout. She could feel the tremors coursing through his body, noted the sweat that dampened the collar of his shirt. Her own knees shook, and she scanned the crowd for Julia, still hopeful she'd come. There was no sign of her stepsister, though, and Viviane's heart ached. There were still a few minutes before the train would depart. Perhaps Julia was already at the platform or on the train.

She scanned the departures board. "The train to Hamburg is leaving from track eight," she said, but Felix shook his head.

"*Nein*. I have a surprise—I changed the tickets. We want track five, going to Hanover instead, toward the Dutch border. You will cross at one of the smaller towns where you're less likely to be noticed. It will be safer for the professor." He grinned. "Isn't that a brilliant plan? Better still, I am going with you—at least as far as the border, where we will, alas, have to say goodbye."

Viviane glanced over her shoulder. "But Julia won't know we've changed trains."

"Don't be a fool. Do you honestly think she'll leave Otto?" he asked impatiently.

Viviane glanced around, still hopeful, but there was no sign of her stepsister. "I'll leave a message for her, just in case," she said, looking for a conductor, a porter, anyone, but Felix grabbed her arm. "Don't be ridiculous. There isn't time. We'll miss the train." She looked at him in surprise. "You can write her a note once we've boarded, and I'll deliver it as soon as I get back to Berlin." He smiled, but this time it didn't quite meet his eyes. "This is the professor's only chance, Viviane. Will you abandon him now?" Solomon Hitzig was watching her, his expression guarded. "Isn't this what you wanted, a chance to stop the war, avenge your father's death? Why hesitate now? I thought you were braver than this. Shall I take you back to my mother? Or is there someone else you regret leaving?"

Tom. He meant Tom. She saw the crackle of something dark and unfamiliar in his eyes—jealousy, perhaps, or spite. "Just your parents," she murmured. "They've been so kind to me."

He led her toward the train, firmly gripping her elbow. "I'll tell them you had an emergency at home and had to go at once. You can write to them from England."

They settled into their private compartment, a luxurious amount of space on the crowded train, but the reservation was under the powerful name of Schroeder. Just the sound of it spoken aloud was a magic charm that opened doors, granted access to anything money or power could buy. She made note of the route. The train would take them from Berlin, through Hanover, and on to Aachen and the Dutch border. Viviane stared out the window, scanning the crowds, but there was still no sign of Julia. Her heart sank. She heard the whistle sound and the conductor's call for the last passengers to board.

Steam rose, blocking the last view of the platform as the train jolted and began to move. Viviane felt tears sting her eyes for all she was leaving behind, but the games were over, and it was time to go home. She thought of Julia, and Tom, and turned her attention to Solomon Hitzig.

THE TRAFFIC WAS a hopeless snarl, and Tom abandoned the cab halfway to the train station and ran the rest of the way.

He was sweating like a long-distance runner when he ran up the steps and shoved the ticket under the nose of a porter, too breathless to speak.

"You want track eight, but you'd better hurry. The Hamburg train is leaving in precisely four minutes."

Tom looked at the clock, noted the time, and pushed past a family of tourists consulting a timetable in the middle of the platform. If he hadn't glanced up, he would have missed the glimpse of red curls, half hidden under a familiar broad-brimmed hat, in the window of a train. He skidded to a stop and looked up at the track number. This was track five, the train to Hanover, not Hamburg. Was she on the wrong train? Then he saw Felix von Schroeder take a seat beside her. He felt his pounding heart jolt, kick harder. "What the hell are you doing?" he gasped, though she couldn't possibly hear him. People looked at him. There was another passenger he didn't know in the compartment, a man bundled thickly in an overcoat with the collar turned up despite the summer heat. Viviane was listening to Felix, turned away from the window, so she couldn't see him. He rushed toward the open door, only to find his way blocked by a conductor.

"Are you taking this train?" the official demanded. "Do you have a ticket?"

"I—" He hesitated. What if she realized her mistake? He looked down the length of the train. A few latecomers were rushing to climb aboard, but no one got off.

"Suit yourself," the conductor said. "Get on or step back, if you please. We have a schedule to keep." He blew his whistle.

Tom didn't hesitate any longer. He jumped aboard the train.

CHAPTER FIFTY-NINE

VIVIANE SAW TEARS in Solomon Hitzig's eyes as the train moved forward. He scanned the retreating platform. He caught her gaze and shook his head. "I have not left Germany since the war, and now I shall not return. I am as German as any one of those people on that platform. I was born here, fought for this land, gave everything I had to making it a great nation, and in return . . ." His mouth twisted bitterly.

"But in just a few days you shall be with your son, and all will be well," Felix said. "Tell him about the English countryside, Viviane. My father spent time there as a young man, Professor, and loved it."

Hitzig regarded his protégé. "Young men have their lives ahead of them, everything to look forward to. For old men there is only longing for what once was, for the better, happier times they knew. Old men understand the world and the way of things better than people think."

Felix's smile held. "You have a lifetime of great work to look back on, a Nobel Prize, many admirers."

"And yet not one person in my native land will regret that I've gone."

"They will understand your worth soon enough, old friend. Did you bring your notebook, your formulas?"

The professor regarded him soberly. "Of course. My work goes with me always. How long is our journey?" he asked. "When will we reach the border?"

"Several hours," Felix said vaguely, his tone soothing. "Don't worry about anything. Just rest and leave everything to me." He smiled at Viviane and sat back.

"What made you decide to come with us today? It's a long trip," she said to him.

He raised one eyebrow. "My mother raised me to be a gentleman. She would be most displeased if I let you go unescorted. Besides, I wanted to spend more time with you, even if it is just a few hours on a train." He scanned her face. "How I wish . . ." He paused.

"What?" she asked.

"How I wish I'd kissed you when I had the chance. I wanted to, you know, last night at the Goebbelses' party, but things did not go as planned for anyone, did they?" He tilted his head. "So where did you disappear to? How did you get back to town? I was frantic when I couldn't find you. I looked for you everywhere."

His eyes were sharper now behind his spectacles, boring into her skull, and she felt a frisson of fear run up her spine. There was something different about Felix today, an intensity she'd never seen before. His gaiety was forced, his smile brittle. *He's dangerous*, she recalled Tom saying. She swallowed her fear and forced a laugh.

"Oh, I found a ride back with a friend. He . . ." She studied her hands. "He rescued me, I suppose."

"Mr. Graham," he murmured. She looked at him in surprise, and he barked a laugh. "He is the reason why I did not kiss you. He took you from me on the dance floor, bore you away. Perhaps I should have fought harder for you, punched him in the nose for his audacity. Would you have liked that? Do not all ladies like to be fought over? Did *he* kiss you?"

She looked away. What would Felix do if he knew? She thought of the journalist run down in the street. "He's a friend of my brother-in-law, just an acquaintance, really. I barely know him. Geoffrey asked him to keep an eye on us," she lied, reciting the familiar explanation.

Felix laughed. "You are such a coquette, Viviane. You are as deep as the sea, brave and cowardly at the same time. You will take on the whole Reich, lay it bare, expose sins and deceptions with your clever photographs, but your thoughts, your heart, are an enigma. Does Graham see behind your Mona Lisa smile, understand what lies inside that heart of yours?"

"Stop it," she said, feeling hot blood filling her cheeks.

"I can tell when you are lying, you know. Do you love him?"

She sent him a quelling glare without replying.

"Even when you say nothing, you speak volumes. You do, don't you? Love him, I mean. Does he know where you are now, that you've fled?" he persisted. "I could take him a note for you on my return, but perhaps you prefer to remain mysterious, to make your admirers swoon and pant for you, only to abandon them. It makes their desire for you all the sharper, I imagine." He put a hand over his heart. "I know I shall dream of you for a long time to come, dearest Viviane. I shall never forget you, and always regret that I didn't kiss you. Of course, there's still time, hours of it. What else is there to do? What if I were to kiss you now?" He leaned toward her, his lips puckered.

"Tell me again about England," Hitzig said, interrupting.

Felix shot him a sharp glance, then relaxed and sat back. "What would you like to know?"

"Where does he live? I've forgotten."

"Sussex," Felix said.

Viviane glanced at him. "Not Surrey?" she asked, and saw his smile slip.

"Yes, that was it. English place names confuse me, and when the professor showed me the letter, I read it so quickly." He grinned. "I do recall the part that said how happy he would be to be reunited with his dear papa again, which is what truly matters, *nein*?"

The professor studied Felix's face but said nothing. He turned to the window, watching the city slip past and fall away as the train gathered speed.

The train came to a stop at a small station, the first of many. The sun was setting now, and the sky was red, the shadows long. Hitzig shrank away from the window as a detachment of brown-shirted soldiers marched past.

Viviane slid a sideways glance at Felix, waiting for him to reassure his dear old friend, but his face was intense as he scanned the crowds on the platform. He looked as if he were watching for someone he knew. Did he fear pursuit? Her skin prickled.

The train resumed its journey and she glanced at him again. Felix von Schroeder smiled at her, boyishly charming once more, and made some silly joke. She wondered if a trick of the light had fooled her into imagining something that wasn't there at all.

CHAPTER SIXTY

"WILL YOU SHOW me your notebook, Professor?" Felix asked later, as darkness fell and there was nothing to see of the passing countryside but shapes and shadows. "Perhaps we could discuss the formula. I will miss our intellectual discussions."

Hitzig regarded his protégé. "I, too, will miss collaborating with a brilliant student who has such a full understanding of the importance of my life's work." He turned to Viviane. "He is quite brilliant, you know. His mind works in ways I never expected."

"I don't deserve such great praise," Felix said, though he didn't look humble. He was staring at the professor the way a dog eyes a bone.

Hitzig looked out the window. "Where did you say my son lives?" he asked again.

"I told you, Essex."

Viviane glanced at Felix. He wasn't smiling now. His eyes were narrowed on the professor.

"Tell me again. Tell me how he will be waiting at the station to meet me when I get to England," Hitzig insisted, his eyes burning into Felix.

"Just so. It will be a joyous reunion," Felix said, his voice colored by a slight edge of annoyance. "Please show me your notes, Professor.

You're worrying me. Did you truly remember to bring them? Where have you hidden them? Will they be safe if they search you at the border?"

Hitzig glanced at him. "This train has stopped in several places. No one has even come to check our tickets. We have empty seats here in our compartment, and yet this train must be very full."

"It is one of the perks of being wealthy, and a Schroeder," Felix said.

Hitzig studied his hands, looked at the wedding band that he still wore. "I am looking forward to being free at last," he said softly. "This is no way to live, with fear and guilt." He looked up at Viviane. "I am not sorry to go, you know, Miss Alden. I understand now that there is truly nothing left in Germany for me. What time is it, please?"

"It's getting late," Felix answered before she could, his irritation barely concealed. "Where is your notebook?"

The professor scanned his friend's face for a moment before he reached into his coat and pulled out the battered blue notebook he'd shown her at the apartment. He held it up, and Felix grabbed it eagerly. He flipped through the pages, scanning each one. He looked up at Hitzig with a horrified expression.

"What's the matter, Felix? Is it not what you wanted? You told me I must bring only what is most important to me, my best work."

Felix glared at him, the book still in his hand.

"These aren't formulas—there are grocery lists written here, appointments, dates."

"Yes, but if you look, you'll see a drawing done by my son when he was very small. There's a small speck of blood on another page from the day when my wife cut herself while she was cooking my favorite meal. We'd only been married a year. She came running to me at my desk for comfort, in tears over such a little cut, interrupting my work. The blood dripped on the page, and I was cross with her. Then it came tumbling out that she was pregnant. Suddenly, it didn't matter what else was on that page, just that it was her blood and the blood of my unborn son, my whole world. I might have thrown the notebook away, bought a new one, but I kept this one, because that drop of blood, that testament of life, reminded me what was most important. There's also a lock of her hair between the pages, and a photograph . . ."

Felix swore and threw the book on the floor. "Fool! This is not what we agreed, not what you promised me!"

"I didn't promise you anything," Hitzig said calmly.

With a sharp cry, Felix slapped the professor across the face, and Hitzig fell back against the seat, his lip bleeding.

"Felix!" Viviane cried, and switched seats so she could tend to the old man.

"You lied to me!" Felix raged at the professor.

Viviane pressed a handkerchief to the cut on Hitzig's mouth, but he pushed her hand away and faced Felix fiercely. "I promised I would bring the formula with me, keep it safe." He tapped a finger to the side of his head. "It is safe."

Felix swore again and reached into his coat. Viviane recoiled when she saw the gun in his hand. "Felix, what are you doing?"

He kept his eyes on Hitzig. "Do you have a pencil, Viviane? Give it to him. There's still time. He will write down the formula from memory."

But Hitzig shook his head. "No." He glanced at the gun, then back at Felix. "I knew it would come to this. I said you were like me, did I not? I was in earnest when I said I had never had a more brilliant pupil. You are every bit as arrogant as I was, as focused on glory and recognition and prizes. You have learned a great deal from me over the past few years, but you have failed to understand the most important lesson of all. What matters most is how your work is perceived by the world, how others will make use of it. Now we have come to the end, just as you planned it, and I am still smarter than you are." He grinned triumphantly at Felix.

Felix's face reddened. "I gave you what you wanted most, to get out of Germany, to see your son again."

Hitzig sighed. The blood oozed from his split lip. "Yes, I would have liked to see my son once more, but that's impossible, isn't it, Felix?" He looked at Viviane. "He's dead, you see. He died in a car accident in *Somerset* three years ago. Felix wrote the letter, and he has been playing a little game with me. This is the last gambit, getting me to flee. Is that not correct, Felix?"

Felix was blinking hard, his face contorted in desperate fury. "I saved you, you old fool. You were in danger, and I saved you," Felix said, the gun still pointed at Hitzig. He raised his chin. "You owe me everything."

But the professor smiled sadly. "I owe you nothing at all. I went along with your game to see where it would lead, to what lengths you'd go to betray me. Is it because I am a Jew after all?"

"It's because you are in my way," Felix said. "*I* should be running the institute, not working under you, a worthless—" He paused. "If not for me, you would have been locked in a cell, beaten and tortured until you gave up every drop of useful information."

"Yes, I know," Hitzig said quietly. "I also know I will never leave Germany alive. You cannot allow that. It would mean your own doom to let me go. I just wanted one last taste of freedom, to see honesty in your eyes at last, to make you admit what you've done and to know you finally understand that you cannot fool me or best me. You will never be anything but an assistant, a—"

The gun went off, and Hitzig fell to the floor. The train's whistle shrieked, covering Viviane's scream. She dropped beside the old man, saw the blood blooming through the white linen of his shirt. "Oh no, no," she cried. Hitzig gasped at the pain, gripped her hand and held it tight. The train was slowing, coming into a station.

"Don't fret, my dear. I don't regret dying," Hitzig said. "I am only sorry you are involved in this. You have been truly noble, truly kind, but he fooled you, too."

"Hold on, Professor. We are coming to a station, we will get you help," she said. There was so much blood—too much.

The door of the compartment opened behind her. "Felix, get help—" she began, and stopped.

It wasn't Felix standing behind her. It was Otto, in full uniform. He didn't greet her or smile. His eyes narrowed as he looked at her on the floor, kneeling in the professor's blood. His lip curled in disgust.

He turned to Felix. "What the hell have you done?"

CHAPTER SIXTY-ONE

"You are on the wrong train," the conductor said when Tom handed over his ticket.

"I'll buy a new ticket, then," Tom said.

"But the train is full. There is no seat for you."

"I'll stand," he said, but the conductor frowned.

"*Nein.* You will have to get off at the next station and purchase a ticket there for the next train." He pulled his watch from his pocket with an irritated tsk, checked the time, and replaced the watch. "We will be there in precisely six minutes."

"I am willing to pay for a ticket now," Tom said. "I have a friend on this train."

The conductor looked down his nose at Tom. "This is not England, *mein* Herr. We prefer a more orderly, efficient system. You must do things the proper way here, the *German* way. The Olympics are over now."

The train slowed, and the whistle sounded as they reached the station, and once again the watch appeared. "We have arrived early," he said with a frown. When the train stopped, he indicated with a sweep of his hand that Tom should move toward the exit. The conductor watched him step off the train and pointed. "The ticket office is that way," he said, and turned away.

But there was a queue at the ticket office and the train would depart again before he reached the front.

Tom ran down the length of the train, dodging passengers, peering into windows until he found Viviane. She was in a first-class compartment, alone.

There was blood on her face.

Tom called out, but she didn't look up. He saw a phalanx of Gestapo officers on the platform. Tom's belly tightened. Why were they here? Was it just a routine check of passports and papers before the train reached the border? They ignored the scant handful of people in the small station as they approached the conductor. The man instantly snapped to attention and raised his arm in salute.

The officer returned the salute, and in the light from the ticket office, Tom saw the flash of the SD insignia on his sleeve, the secret police.

This wasn't just a passport check. Someone was about to be arrested.

Viviane.

Tom felt the breath leave his body in a rush of fear for her.

The conductor stepped aside, and they began to board.

When the train lurched forward, Tom threw himself at the nearest doorway and slipped. He held tight, and his feet dragged along the pavement as he fought to pull himself up onto the moving train. They were coming to the end of the platform and the barrier. He was going to be knocked off, and Viviane would be arrested.

He couldn't let that happen.

He swore as he reached the handle, gripped it tight, and swung his body upward. The barrier grabbed the back of his coat, tore it, but he landed on the step as the train gathered speed, plunging out of the station and into the darkness once more.

CHAPTER SIXTY-TWO

OTTO VON SCHROEDER flicked an expressionless glance around the compartment. He took in the man on the floor, the blood, and Viviane, kneeling beside him. He looked down at her, his blue eyes icy, as if they were strangers or enemies. "He needs a doctor—" she began, but he silenced her with the abrupt motion of one black-gloved hand before turning to Felix. "What the hell have you done?" he asked again when Felix didn't answer.

He grabbed Felix by the collar and dragged him into the corridor, shutting the door behind them. Viviane heard the sound of raised voices, but she had more important things to worry about.

She knelt beside Solomon Hitzig, doing her best to stop the blood seeping from the hole in his chest. He caught her hand, held it. "Leave it, please. There is no pain. I thought it would hurt, but there is nothing at all. It really is better this way. I will be free, and they will get nothing from me." He smiled faintly. "You have been kind to me, though you have every reason to hate me. More reason than *they* have." He swallowed. "I have something to tell you, fraülein. I was not entirely honest about what I know of the events at Sainte Courcelle. I told you I didn't see your father, but I lied. He was there, on the field, in full view, risking his life to save his men. We could easily have shot him, but we were—impressed—by such courage, and baffled as well. He could have retreated, but he bravely risked his own life for his men. It was a test, you see, a trial to see if the gas would work. At best, it would kill a few enemy soldiers. The rest would retreat, but the fear of that weapon would remain. They would refuse to fight, and the men in charge would be forced to sue for peace. But that's not what happened, of course. It was the first time we'd tested that type of gas on humans, a new formulation, stronger and more deadly than anything we'd used before. I was a scientist. I worked in a laboratory, developed theories and ideas and formulas. I'd never been to the front before." He coughed, and a bubble of blood appeared on his lips. He shut his eyes for a moment, then forced them open again. "It was a terrible thing to see, men in agony, choking to death, and all around them a cloud of the gas I'd invented, swirling in the dawn light. It settled into the ground, poisoning that, as well. Even the water in the shell holes was yellow, and it stuck to the men when they fell, burned them . . . It looked like a vision of hell. The fog rolled over the enemy, crushed the breath from their lungs, blistered and burned their skin." Viviane saw a tear roll down his cheek. "Our officer was horrified. As I told you, he ordered his men to shoot, to end the terrible suffering as quickly as they could.

"Then an officer climbed out of the trench, a major. He crawled to the men lying on the field, dragged them back. He kept coming back, again and again, dragging more men away, a pointless exercise. The gas was killing them anyway. He saved many men that day, but we thought him a fool. He might have saved hundreds more if he'd only just retreated. How I wished he would. I prayed for it. I remember his face, fräulein. The terrible mistakes we both made, that English major and I, have haunted me since that day. I didn't know who he was. Not until I met you. Did he pay for his sin?"

Viviane nodded, unable to speak. She didn't even know she was crying until Hitzig reached up to swipe a tear away with the pad of his thumb. "You loved him. I'm sorry for your loss, and for my own. We all make terrible choices we must live with, and I hope you will forgive your father, remember the good he did." He shuddered and sighed. "I hope that my work will die with me, that it will never be used again against humans, but I fear—I *know*—what they will do. I have signed the death warrant for tens of thousands, millions. I sought to make something for good, but they will twist it and use it for evil. The formula doesn't matter. I have left it unfinished, but Felix will figure out the last steps, or someone else will." He looked up at her. "But perhaps there are more people out there like you. You are brave, fraülein. Promise me you will do what you can to stop another war. When you get home to England, tell your government, tell the soldiers who remember what it was like the last time, make them listen."

"I will. Rest, Professor. Save your strength," she said softly.

Hitzig squeezed her hand weakly, both their fingers slippery with his blood. "Plenty of time for that," he said. He drew a gasp of air, and his lungs rattled. "Do you think they'll be waiting for me after all, my wife and son?"

"Yes," she said, feeling tears spill, rolling down her cheeks.

"What time is it? Are we still in Germany?"

"Yes," she said.

He managed a smile. "Ha. Then I have won. They have not succeeded in getting rid of me. I am free. They've lost the game, and I am . . . free." His hand went slack in hers, and a long sigh left him as he died.

Outside, Otto and Felix still squabbled. She wondered if they'd let her go, for Julia's sake, or if she'd be taken away to disappear in the night, and the train would simply arrive at its destination without her. No one would know what happened to her. She hadn't told anyone she was leaving. Not Julia, or the count, or Tom Graham.

He'd been right about Felix. She regretted not saying goodbye, not telling him she loved him.

She didn't want to die. She glanced out the window at the platform. A man was racing the train, a latecomer, trying to catch it as it left the station. She saw him grab on and stumble, but he didn't let go. He was being dragged along as the train picked up speed. She couldn't see his face, but some hopeful part of her thought it must be Tom, come to rescue her yet again.

But that was impossible. He had no idea she was here. It was a figment of her imagination, an illusion. The man disappeared as the train slid into the darkness.

She felt a wave of loss wash over her, threatening to drown her in regret and fear. Tom was in Berlin, and there was no rescue coming. She shut her eyes, drew steel into her spine, and refused to give in. She'd fight if she had to, but she would not go quietly.

CHAPTER SIXTY-THREE

"I TRIED TO stop her—I had no idea she even had a gun," Felix said, facing his brother. He glanced through the window of the compartment, saw Viviane on the floor with Hitzig. The professor was babbling, his lips moving, bloody bubbles forming. There was blood on her hands and her face and her dress, and Felix felt his stomach turn.

Otto was inches from him, taller than Felix by a head and twice as wide. He was still the arrogant bully he'd always been, the favored first-born son. He was dumb as a block of wood, Felix thought, a follower, not a leader. Felix had learned to outsmart him when they were boys, run away laughing, leaving Otto baffled.

But his brother didn't look baffled now. He didn't even look like his brother. He was a pitiless marble monument to Nazi perfection, and he was glaring down at Felix with icy fury in his eyes—their mother's eyes—without a shred of emotion. Felix felt fear rise in his chest, and he pushed it down, forced himself to smile. Otto had the power to arrest him, and Felix knew it wouldn't bother him any more than it would concern him to swat a fly. At least he was smarter than his older brother, quicker, cleverer, more agile. He could think and talk rings around Otto.

"She shot him, not I," Felix said quickly, and Otto's eyes narrowed.

"*Viviane* shot Hitzig?" Otto said.

"I should have known," Felix said. "Her father died of gas in the war. She blamed Hitzig, lured him away by promising him sanctuary in England. She wanted to use him, use his secrets against Germany. I came to stop her. Once we were on the train, she accused the professor of terrible crimes, talked of revenge and justice." Otto still hadn't so much as blinked. Felix felt a prickle of fear, and he swallowed, ran his finger under his collar, suddenly too tight. "She—" he said, and swallowed hard. Could Otto tell he was lying? "She demanded he give her the notebook," he rushed on. "He refused, of course. She pulled a gun and said she would kill him if he didn't give her the formula, and so she has—or nearly, anyway." He glanced into the compartment, looking away from his brother's all-seeing gaze. Viviane was still on the floor, and the old professor wasn't moving. The train was, though. They were close to the Dutch border now. He'd expected Otto sooner.

"So Viviane had a gun," Otto said thoughtfully. "Did she keep it in the case with her camera? I wonder. You say she bore the Jew such hatred, yet she is on the floor beside him, tending to him."

Felix swallowed and glanced along the corridor. One of Otto's associates stood guard at the end of the passage. There was one at the opposite end as well. "Did Mutti not tell you that this whole thing was my idea, that I planned to stop her, to save the professor's life, to bring his notebook and his formula back to Berlin?" He was surprised by the reediness of his own voice, the panic he couldn't quite hide under his brother's glare.

"And do you have the notebook?" Otto asked calmly.

Felix blinked rapidly, looking into the compartment again. Perhaps it wasn't too late, perhaps he could still make the old man talk—or Otto could. Right now, he was whispering urgently to Viviane. What the devil was he saying?

"There was no notebook," Felix said, looking boldly into his brother's eyes. "Hitzig feared this might happen, that she would try to steal it. He . . . he told me the formula a few days ago." He tapped his forehead just the way the professor had done. "I have it all right here."

If Otto was impressed, or fooled, he gave no sign of it. His expression didn't change. The flat, terrifying coldness in his brother's eyes was enough to cause frostbite, if one didn't die of sheer terror. Felix wondered if they'd taught Otto that in some dark SS classroom, or if he'd learned it through more direct experience with intimidation and interrogation. "Then why bother to help him escape?" Otto asked blandly.

Felix's glasses slipped down his nose, and he pushed them back up with one finger. "I—I wanted to help Hitzig. Perhaps I am too sentimental, and I wished to expose her plot, prove that she is an enemy of Germany. Would Mutti and Papa have simply taken me at my word if I'd told them their pretty little visitor was plotting the downfall of our great nation?"

Otto's mouth twisted. "You are an even bigger idiot than I thought you were."

Felix felt hot blood fill his face. "What harm has been done? Hitzig's as good as dead, and her hateful plot against our fatherland has failed."

"There is no hatred in her eyes now, no vengeance. There are tears on her face."

"She's a woman, an Englishwoman, weak and foolish," Felix said, trying to appeal to his brother's belief in the utter masculine superiority of the pure-blooded German.

Otto pushed open the door and looked down at her dispassionately. "Viviane, did you shoot this Jew?"

Felix didn't hesitate. Before she could answer, he pushed past Otto and reached for her arm, dragged her away from the body. "What did Hitzig tell you?" he screamed at her.

There were splotches of blood on her face and clothes, like roses in bloom. Even so, her eyes were alive, her cheeks flushed, and she met his eyes coldly, unafraid.

"Do you intend to shoot me as well?" she asked calmly, detaching his hand from her arm, leaving a smear of Hitzig's blood on his skin. Instinctively, Felix wiped it on his trousers. She glanced at Otto. "Am I under arrest?"

"Tell me what really happened," Otto said, almost gently.

But Felix couldn't have that, not now. He leaped forward again and slapped her before she could speak. "What did he tell you? Did he give you the formula?" he demanded. "Tell me now, or—"

She put a hand to her cheek, and when she looked at him, Felix saw controlled anger in her eyes, banked fury, a Valkyrie held in check by the merest of threads. "Or what?" she asked through clenched teeth.

Felix drew his hand back to hit her again, but Otto caught it in one black-gloved fist.

"Sit down, Felix," Otto said tiredly, but Felix shook him off. He was sweating again, and it stung his eyes, made him blink. Who would have thought she'd be so fierce, so bloody courageous? He almost admired her for it, but then she smiled. A smirk really, full of condescension, as if she'd won, bested him at his own game. He couldn't have that, couldn't lose now, in front of Otto.

Felix lunged for the gun on the seat beside him, left where he'd dropped it when Otto burst in. His brother recognized it, of course. It was their father's pistol, the sidearm Georg had carried in the Great War. Would it remind Otto of family loyalty? Felix pointed it at Viviane. Still, her expression didn't change. She held his gaze, and he was *sure* Hitzig had told her everything. She had the formula. He felt the breath leave his body for an instant, leaving him hollow and empty and burning. The gun shook in his hand.

"Felix." Otto's terse warning sounded bored.

"No," Felix said. "No, I won't kill you. I won't have to." He glanced at Otto. "We won't have to. She'll tell us what we want to know because we have Julia." He saw a flicker of fear in her eyes now, felt a thrill of power go through him. He had her. She'd tell him anything now. But that damnable aristocratic little chin of hers came up, all British arrogance and assumed superiority.

"What will you do to Julia? Will you put us both in Sachsenhausen, or a place like it?"

Felix felt his guts contract against his spine. "How do you—"

Otto's head snapped around to look at him, his body rigid. Felix felt his brother's gaze burn into him like acid. "She knows about Sachsenhausen?" he asked tightly. "It's top secret. How can she know unless you told her?"

"I was there," she said.

Felix gaped at her. "You followed me?"

Surprise widened her eyes, and Felix clamped his teeth together. She hadn't known about his involvement. He'd given himself away, and worse, made Otto think he'd told others. He heard Otto's indrawn breath, harsh and angry. His fists tightened until the black leather gloves squeaked.

Felix didn't dare to glance at his brother now. Kinship no longer mattered. He was an SD officer on duty, ruthless and cold. Nothing mattered but devotion to the führer. Otto had recommended Felix for the post of chief scientist at the new camp, the top secret camp. He'd promised that his brother knew secrets that could speed up the process of developing new weapons. He wouldn't like looking like a fool in front of his superiors. Felix felt his knees turn to jelly.

"What does it matter what she knows? She can't tell anyone if she's dead."

"What am I to tell Julia?" Otto asked, his voice flat and calm. Too calm.

"Tell her that her stepsister went home and somehow met with a misadventure along the way and disappeared. Tell her she was a spy. People disappear all the time in Germany. We're almost as famous for that as we are for strudel," he said sarcastically.

Otto didn't laugh. His eyes glittered dangerously. "You have betrayed us all, Felix—your family, your country, and even your friend," he said, glancing at Hitzig's body. "You are a worm," he said, his tone almost pleasant.

Otto looked at Viviane. "What did the professor tell you before he died?" he asked in a mild tone.

"What will happen to Julia?" she asked. Holding her secret in desperation.

"Torture, death," Felix dared, and Otto turned on him.

"Shut your mouth, Felix. You've done enough," he said, the guttural growl as sharp as a slap. "What did he tell you?" He gentled his tone as he asked Viviane again.

The door opened. "Obersturmführer von Schroeder? This man demands to see you. He says he has information."

Felix looked at the man they held by the collar. "No, it can't be. Not you again," he muttered.

"Tom!" Viviane cried, struggling to rise from the floor beside the professor's body, but Otto pointed his finger at her like a bayonet.

"Sit down, Viviane," he ordered. He turned to Tom Graham. "I know you. We met at the Quartier Latin. Julia said you were a friend of the family. You are Trude Unger's . . . companion."

"He's a journalist and a *spy*," Felix said, spitting the word. He looked at Tom, but Tom's eyes were on Viviane, and hers on him. "Oh, this is perfect. We won't need to harm Julia after all—or not right away." He put the gun against Tom Graham's temple. "How much does she care about you, old chap?" he said in English.

Tom shrugged. "We're barely acquainted. An old friend of mine married her stepsister. We were both in the wedding party."

"Barely acquainted?" Felix said. "And yet you have come to rescue her?"

The bastard smiled as if the gun wasn't there. "From what I know of her, Viviane Alden doesn't like to be rescued."

"Why did you wish to see me?" Otto asked him.

"I wanted to interview you."

"Interview me? Whatever for?"

"About your upcoming wedding to the Earl of Rutherford's daughter, of course, for the British papers."

Otto looked at Viviane.

"Julia told you this?" he asked. "Your stepsister has not yet said yes. May I assume she is going to?"

Felix rolled his eyes. "This is very touching, but we're nearing the border. Shouldn't you stop the train and take them into custody? She knows the formula. Hitzig must have told her before he died."

Otto looked at his brother. "You said he'd already told you, that you had it."

Felix felt his face heat at the mistake. He saw the smirk on Tom Graham's face, pity for a bested fool.

"Did he really tell you?" Otto asked Viviane. She remained silent, defiant, and Felix waited for Otto to slap her, to make her talk. Instead, he smiled. "I love Julia, you know. I would not let any harm come to her. I shall cherish her."

"Then why harm her countrymen?" Viviane asked. "Why help create a weapon that will kill the people she loves, her brother perhaps, her friends?"

"War is—" He paused.

Viviane raised her chin. "What, Otto? Inevitable? Unavoidable? Yes, I've seen that, even behind the dazzling façade of the games. But honorable war, war for the right reasons," she said.

"I believe we know the right reasons," Otto murmured, raising his chin. "It is our destiny."

"Then if the cause is noble, should not the means be noble as well?" she asked.

Felix jumped in. "War advances science. Battle is just a catalyst, a release valve for the tensions in the world. Why should we not use our discoveries? We are the master race, destined to triumph, to rule the world." He'd hoped to impress Otto, but his brother frowned at him.

"I told you to be silent, Felix. You have done a great deal of harm today. Professor Hitzig was necessary to a good many things, and you have ruined plans well beyond your knowledge."

Otto looked at Viviane. "What were the professor's final words?"

"He asked if I thought he'd see his son and wife, if they'd be waiting for him." She looked at Tom Graham. "He told me what really happened at Sainte Courcelle."

"Yes, yes, but did he speak about his work?" Otto asked.

"No. Why would he? I'm not a chemist."

Felix felt the gun shake in his hand. Hitzig would never go to the grave with his life's work unfulfilled. It was his legacy, his only legacy. He would want the world to know, to see his genius. He knew the professor better than anyone. "He must have said something! She's lying. We must force her to tell the truth—" He jabbed the gun into Tom Graham's temple, but the train lurched, and he stumbled on Hitzig's body, and the gun went off. The shot hit Otto and he fell, dragging Felix down with him. The next bullet hit Tom Graham. Felix heard Viviane scream, and she climbed over Hitzig and Otto and Felix, trying to reach the Englishman. She was clumsy with her bad leg, and Felix grabbed her ankle and twisted it. She uttered the kind of oath that would make a sailor blush, a gutter curse, and kicked out. Her heel connected with his nose. Blood spattered and he felt the sickening crunch as the bone and his glasses shattered. He raised the gun again, but Otto grabbed his arm, knocked the gun away. He heard footsteps in the passage, a conductor's whistle, shouts. "They're coming," Felix screamed. "They're coming. Tell me what he truly said to you!"

But she had her arm around Tom Graham. "Can you run?" she asked.

The reporter forced himself to his feet. "Just watch me," he said.

Felix struggled to get up, but Otto grabbed him, hauled him back down, and Felix reached for the gun, tried to tear it from Otto's hand.

The shot was muffled, and for a moment he stared into Otto's eyes, Mutti's eyes, surprised. Then the pain came, hot and searing and immediate, stealing his breath. "No," Felix muttered. "No, not like this." He tasted blood. He gripped Otto's collar, tried to hold on, but it was too late. He'd lost after all.

As he drifted into the darkness, he heard Solomon Hitzig laugh.

CHAPTER SIXTY-FOUR

Tom was losing consciousness. Pain radiated through his left arm, and he could feel blood dripping over his hand. He could smell Viviane's perfume, feel her arm around him as she dragged him along the corridor of the train. "Help me," she ordered. He realized she didn't want him to rescue her. She was trying to rescue him. He smiled at that.

"I'm here," he said, fighting the lure of darkness, staggering forward, putting one foot in front of the other. He heard shouts behind him. She glanced over his shoulder, her gasp fanning his cheek. They were close, then, he thought.

"We have to get off the train. Can you jump?" she asked. *Jump?* He could barely walk, but he nodded.

The train lurched and slowed. "Dutch border, have your papers ready," he heard the conductor call. Viviane let him go, and he sagged against a wall as she dragged the door open. He felt a gust of cool air, gulped it down. She gripped his lapels and pulled him into her body. "Hold on to me," she whispered.

Then they were flying through the air, out into the dark. He landed hard on the ground, and the pain was agonizing. He felt himself sliding into oblivion, but her hands bunched in his clothing, shaking him, hauling him upright, giving him no respite. He forced himself to his feet, leaned on her, and she pointed along the tracks to a red, white, and blue flag flying above a lighted gate. "That's the Dutch border." It was only a hundred yards or so, just across a rail bridge over the river, but it might as well have been a thousand miles away. His shoulder ached, and the blood had soaked his sleeve. He was dizzy, and the world was spinning before his eyes. There were voices behind them, orders to halt shouted in German, the crunch of boots on the gravel and the wooden sleepers of the railway tracks. "Run," Viviane said. "We have to run," she repeated, trying to make him move.

"Stop," he muttered. They stood on the edge of the bridge, and he heard the rush of the water below. "We'll be exposed out there. We'll never make it. Leave me here."

"No," she said, her voice fierce, calm. She looked back, then looked down. "Can you swim?"

"No," he said. "I row and I sail, but I hate being in the water."

"Take a deep breath," she commanded as she shoved him, hard, and he felt himself falling through space.

The water closed around him. The sudden icy chill brought him fully back to his senses, numbed the pain, and gave him something new to worry about. It was dark, and he sank like a stone, had no idea which way was up. His lungs began to burn, desperate for air. He was drowning, and that was decidedly not the way he wanted to die.

He felt something brush against his face, then hands gripped him, locked on to him, and he fought, sure he was being dragged under. He screamed and felt bubbles rush out of his throat, the last vestiges of life departing. He felt a body wrap around him, surround him, pull him close. He felt her mouth on his, and a breath of air filled his beleaguered lungs. *Viviane.* He let go, stopped fighting, and let her carry him.

He clung to her as they broke the surface, dragged in a long breath of air, then another. Her strong, supple limbs moved beneath him, her limp invisible, irrelevant, in the water.

He heard the voices on the bridge above them, saw torchlight circles swirling around them, but she kept swimming. His heels scraped gravel, and she let go, held his hand, helped him crawl out of the water.

He lay on the shore, sweet breath singing in his lungs and his heart still thundering in his chest, alive. He didn't feel any pain from the hole in his arm. He lay back, exhausted. "No, not yet," she said, nudging him, slapping his cheek, keeping him conscious. A bullet hit the bank beside him, and sharp shards of gravel sprayed his face. Viviane scrambled to her feet, reaching down for him. He grabbed her hand and looked over his shoulder as they climbed the bank. Lights swept the river and the banks, searching for them, finding them; more bullets ricocheted around them. Viviane held Tom's hand in a fierce grip, and he was awake now, adrenaline keeping him moving, fighting to survive. They made it up the slope. Ahead of them lay the border, mere yards away now. "Hurry!" she cried.

Ahead, he could see the Dutch guards at the border post. Behind them, the Germans were screaming, ordering them to halt. They were close, so close. He didn't waste the time to look back, but kept on running, his hand in Viviane's.

"Help!" Viviane screamed in English at the Dutch guards, but they could not leave their post or venture across the border onto German soil. Still, they beckoned, holding out their hands, waiting for them. When she was near enough, someone caught Viviane's hand, pulled her over the line, and she held tight to Tom, dragging him with her.

Tom turned, saw Otto von Schroeder standing on the bridge, watching them. He waved his hand, ordering his men to stop shooting.

They were hustled into the small border post and they fell to the floor, panting. A man in a railway uniform leaned over them. "Did you come from the train? Do you have tickets?"

Tom began to laugh, and Viviane stared at him, her wide hazel eyes luminous, her lashes wet, her hair streaming water over him.

He pulled her into his arms and kissed her.

CHAPTER SIXTY-FIVE

Holland

TOM WAS SITTING in a chair by the bed when she woke the next morning, reading a newspaper with his shirt off, the thick bandage around his upper arm white and antiseptic against his skin. The small Dutch inn was quiet, with only the sound of birds outside, so unlike the constant roar of traffic she'd grown used to in Berlin.

She stayed in bed, leaned on her elbow to watch him. He glanced up at her, and for a moment they stared at each other in silence.

"Shall I call down for breakfast?" he asked. "Not on the phone. There isn't one. The woman at the desk said to lean over the stair rail and tell her when we were ready to eat."

"That's kind of her," Viviane said. "Your arm—how are you?"

"Hurts like the devil, but I'm alive." He folded the newspaper and set it aside, rising and coming to sit on the bed beside her. He caressed her face and tucked an errant curl behind her ear. "Thanks to you."

She put her hand on his. "You came to rescue me," she said.

"I think you were the one who rescued me," he said.

He lay down beside her, pulled her against him, and looked into her eyes. There was so much to say, so much between them, but they each seemed to be waiting for the other to start. "What happens now?" she asked him. "What will you do? We both left people behind, Alex and Julia, and they need—" He stiffened in her arms and frowned.

"Do you ever stop thinking about everyone else? Things might have gone very differently last night. We were lucky, Viviane."

"Otto let us go," she said softly.

"Yes. He's not a man known for kindness. There's no going back to Berlin."

"Perhaps he did it for Julia's sake. Perhaps he really does love her. I think—" She touched his face, the words hovering on her lips, that she loved him, too, but something in his eyes stopped her, a wariness, a distance. "You're not coming home to England, are you?" she asked. "Where will you go? You can't mean to go back to Germany!"

He scanned her face. "After the Winter Olympics, Hitler invaded the Rhineland, and no one stopped him. I can't help but wonder what he'll do to follow up the Summer Games. There's a civil war in Spain, and I understand the Germans have been shipping airplanes and pilots to the Fascists. I've decided to go to Spain, to report on it." He kept his features deliberately flat as he said it, waiting for her reaction, bracing for objections or tears or pleas. Would it matter? She knew him well enough to know that he was as stubborn as she was, and when he made up his mind, nothing could change it.

"They're bombing civilians, supporting the Fascists. The Communists are doing the same for the other side. Ordinary people are suffering. It's a practice run for another, bigger war."

"There's more to it than that, isn't there?" she asked. "For you, I mean. It's not just a story." She put her hand on his chest, felt his heart beating under her palm.

He looked away, focused on the wall behind her. "I spent months in Germany, writing lies. I hated it. Do you remember the day you arrived in Berlin, the journalist who was run down in the street?"

"Yes." She remembered how she'd feared it was Tom.

"It was a Canadian reporter named Charlie Ellis. Ellis reported what he saw, what was happening behind the illusions, made sure the world understood what the Nazis were really doing. He took daft chances, put himself in danger every day, but he got the job done." He put his hand over hers. "Does that remind you of anyone?"

For a moment she stared at him, and he raised his brows and laughed. "Come now, Viviane. Don't be modest."

"Me?" she asked.

"Yes, you. You wield your camera the way Charlie used his reports, to reveal the truth." He shut his eyes. "I feared you'd meet the same fate as Charlie did, or worse. I also resented that you found a way to keep your honor, that you never took the easy way out, or lied."

"You had a job to do, a mission," she said. "That wasn't you."

"But no one knows that. My family and friends don't know that it was all pretense, all to get close to monsters in their lair and expose them. I can't go home again, face them, knowing they believe I've betrayed them. Not yet. Oh, I tried to make it work, to get the truth out. I told Charlie what I really saw, fed him facts and figures and reports while I wrote lies. We both thought we were being clever, I suppose, fooling everyone. I nearly got him killed. And then I dragged you into it, recruited you." He swallowed. "It might have gone badly, you might have—" She put a finger to his lips.

"It didn't happen," she said.

"It's a miscalculation, underestimating them. There *will* be another war, and it will be terrible. We'll be caught up in it."

"So you're going to Spain to tell the truth," she said.

"I can't do otherwise," he said. "Do you understand?"

She nodded, felt the lump in her throat thicken. She recognized that it was also to make amends for telling her the truth about her father the way he had. Penance. It was for himself, not her, but she accepted it. They wouldn't speak of it again. It was in the past, and there was the present—and an uncertain future—still to face. She turned away before she gave in to tears, sat up, her back to him. "Yes," she managed. "Will you come home eventually?" She looked for the answer in his eyes, but they were shuttered, cautious.

"In time," he said.

She got up, found the clothes their host had provided—plain things, unfamiliar, slightly worn, but clean—and began to dress. "If you're not killed." Her hands were shaking.

"There is that, I suppose. I haven't thought about it."

She turned on him. "Of course you have. How could you not? If you die, how will I—" She faltered, stopped.

He got up, took the skirt from her hands, and tossed it aside. He pulled her into his arms and held her close, and she pressed her face into his shoulder. "Then I will die an honest man, with the truth on my lips, not lies and subterfuge." He looked at her. "You may have enjoyed playing the spy, Viviane, but I didn't. I hated it, and it soiled me. I'm hoping this will help me feel clean again. Did you think about dying? On that train, or in the woods at Sachsenhausen? What *did* you think about?"

He had her. Her mind was on the next photograph, capturing the instant of truth before her, revealing it, preserving it. "I regretted not saying goodbye to you in Berlin," she said instead. Was that really only yesterday? It felt like a lifetime ago. "That's what I thought about on the train."

He pulled back and looked into her eyes, but he didn't let her go. He was thinking the same thing, remembering. "That's why I followed you."

She read the emotions—love and regret—in his eyes, knew it was reflected in her own. "Where does that leave us? Is this goodbye, then?" she asked.

"For now," he said. "Just—for now. We both need time—*I* need time."

She swallowed and nodded.

He kissed her. "What will you do now?"

She looked up, half hopeful. "I could come with you, take pictures."

He looked away, his brow furrowing. "You'd be a distraction. A sweet distraction, but a distraction nonetheless. You'd rush in, and I'd want to keep you safe. You'd resent that, Viviane, being protected, rescued."

He was right, but she felt tears prick her eyes anyway. She let him go, crossed to the washbasin, and examined her face in the flyblown little mirror above it. She had a faint bruise on her cheek where Felix had hit her, and her hair was a jumble.

"I should send a telegram to Julia, let her know I'm safe, and perhaps one to Reggie to ask him to meet me in London."

"What will you tell them?"

She clasped her arms around her body. "That the games are over, and I'm coming home."

"I suppose I'd better send word to Alex so he doesn't tell my poor mother I'm dead," he said. They looked at each other across the width of the small room, a few steps that suddenly felt like miles. "Once we're done at the telegraph office, I'll see you to Ostend."

They finished dressing and took another train to the coast, and a cab to the ferry terminal, where he escorted her to the boat, the last leg of her journey home.

"I'll write," he said, and she knew he wouldn't.

She kissed his cheek, then caressed the spot with her thumb, smoothing away the tic in his jaw. "I intend to carry a torch for you, Tom Graham," she said, striving for a jaunty tone, but it fell flat, betrayed by the wobble in her voice. "Perhaps when you're ready . . ." She let it trail away. She stood on her toes to kiss his cheek again, and he turned his head at the last second, met her lips, and kissed her properly. She saw in his eyes what he wouldn't say, didn't dare admit, knowing she'd never get on the ferry if he said it aloud, or she did. He wouldn't go to Spain, and he'd regret it if he stayed with her now. And it would kill the love in his eyes, his pride and determination, and all that she loved best about him.

"What will you do with yourself?" he asked her again. "The *Herald* could always use a good photographer."

"I left my camera on the train," she said. The future yawned before her, uncertain. She made herself step back. "Be safe," she whispered. She turned and walked up the gangplank. When she reached the deck and looked back, he was gone.

PART IV

Endgame

CHAPTER SIXTY-SIX

Wrenwood
May 1940

THE WIRELESS CRACKLED in the sitting room at Wrenwood, the muffled voice of Winston Churchill, now prime minster, filling the room, imparting the gloomy news that the Germans were advancing through Europe. The Low Countries had fallen, and France was on the brink of collapse. The British Expeditionary Force, some three hundred thousand soldiers, the entire army, was trapped between the relentless German army and the Channel, facing annihilation.

"What will happen to Miles and Geoffrey?" Grace murmured with tears in her eyes.

And Tom, Viviane thought. She had no idea where he was.

"And what about Julia?" Grace asked.

Julia was still in Germany, married to Otto, who was now the equivalent of a major. They had two small children, a boy and a girl. Both Rutherford and Estella had accepted Julia's plan to marry the eldest son of Rutherford's dear old friend in the fall of 1936, ignoring Viviane's pleas to encourage Julia to wait, that things in Germany were not at all the way they thought. Rutherford believed money and class would fix everything. When war was declared, Rutherford tried to use his influence to bring his daughter out of Germany, but it was far too late. The war made them enemies, at least in name, and letters and telephone calls became impossible. Julia had written to Viviane after their German holiday. She returned Viviane's camera, the film removed—a warning from Otto, she supposed, and an acknowledgment that he knew about her activities in Germany during the Olympics. It was a kind of truce between them, she suspected. Julia said that the Leica had been found on the train and turned in to authorities before eventually finding its way into Otto's hands. She also broke the news that Felix had been killed in a road accident the day after the games ended, and she hoped Viviane wasn't too upset by such terrible news.

"Julia will be okay," Viviane said to Grace now, her lips tight, and hoped it was true.

The door of the sitting room opened, and a maid stepped aside to let Reggie in. He was home on leave from the Royal Navy and wobbled into the room with a cane, having broken his leg in a training exercise. The servant waited for his raincoat and hat, listening to the ill news on the wireless for a moment, her face crumpling. "Terrible news," she said. "We've got it on in the kitchen. Three of our footmen are over there and dozens of village lads." Viviane had taken photos of those boys before they left, gave the pictures to their mothers and wives and sweethearts to keep close while their boys were away. What were they doing now, on the other side of the Channel, staring across at the distant shores of home, less than fifty miles away? It might as well be a million.

"Tell them we're all hoping for the best," Reggie said, and came to sit down. "Dreadful, isn't it?"

Grace pressed her hand to her lips. "I can't bear to think of it."

"There must be something we can do," Viviane said, regarding her old friend. Reggie hadn't married after all. Lady Susan had married the Duke of Bellshire instead. Geoffrey and Margaret had two fine sons, and it had taken the pressure off Reggie to marry and produce heirs.

THAT SUMMER IN BERLIN · 425

Geoffrey had joined up, taken a post as a captain, serving under his boss, Major Duncan Chapman. He'd sent his wife and children north to stay with Lady Janet, Tom's half sister, at Strathwood House in Scotland, her father's estate.

"Shouldn't you be in London?" Reggie asked Viviane. "Not that I'm not glad to see you, of course."

"I have a few days off. My mother is having one of her spells. She cannot bear the thought of war. She remembers the last one, losing two of her brothers and so many friends. And Papa. Rutherford asked me to come down and see her."

The trip to Germany had strained her relationship with her mother. Estella saw only that another of Viviane's stepsisters was to be married to a man with a title, while Viviane remained single and evasive about what had happened to her in Germany. "You're different now, Viviane. The trip changed you, made you even more stubborn than you were before. What do you intend to do with yourself? It's quite impossible to do a third Season in the spring, you know."

Impossible indeed, especially when the scandal of Julia's wedding to a Nazi officer broke, and it was all anyone could talk about. Rutherford found himself shunned by some of his government colleagues and esteemed by others who hoped to use his German connections to forge closer ties and treaties. All the Rutherford girls became infamous, and even when Felicity and Grace made their debuts three years later, they were popular and intriguing as dance partners, but no one wanted to marry them.

Worst for Estella was the day in early October, just a few weeks after Viviane's return from Germany, when she announced that she'd spoken to her father's old friend, Sir Maudesley Grainger, and had taken a job as a staff photographer at the London *Herald*. Her mother didn't speak to her for weeks.

Alexander MacCann had come to see Viviane in London nearly a year after she'd come home, and Viviane had feared he was bringing bad news about Tom. Instead, he had come to lure her away from the *Herald*—*recruit* her, she supposed was the right word—inviting her to join him in a new and secret venture to train other photographers who would be sent into Germany. She accepted. "Don't you wish to ask me for news of Tom?" he'd asked. "I thought the two of you were quite close."

She'd bitten her lip, and a thousand questions sprang to mind, but she shook her head. Tom had wanted time and privacy. There'd be time to ask when—if—he returned to England and to her. She read his published reports from Spain, syndicated in newspapers around the world, all of them well written, brutally honest, and daring. When the Spanish cause was lost, he went to Paris and reported from there. He had not, as far as she knew, returned to England. She thought of him often and wondered if he thought of her. He wrote thousands of words, but not a single letter to her. The threat of war had grown more inevitable by the month, then the week, and then came down to days and hours when Germany invaded Poland and Britain was forced to declare war.

Men joined up by the thousands—Geoffrey and Reggie and Miles, and most of the other men she knew. They took posts in the Royal Air Force or the Royal Navy or the army and went to France, just as they had in 1914.

At home, they'd taped windows, filled sandbags, and hung blackout curtains. They'd practiced air-raid drills, stocked Anderson shelters, learned first aid and how to use a gas mask. Felicity joined the Wrens, and Grace helped monitor coastal defenses.

But the bombs hadn't fallen. Christmas came and went, the winter snows fell and melted, and the spring flowers and warm breezes made everyone feel complacent.

Then in just weeks, the Germans rolled over Norway and the Netherlands and Belgium, then bypassed the "unbreakable" French defenses of the Maginot Line and swept across France.

Now the world held its breath, waited for the clash of armies, for the brave soldiers of France and England to make a stand and stop the terrible German onslaught. Instead, the tanks rolled over the defenders like broken dolls, pushing them back and back and back until the English army stood with its back to the sea. The Luftwaffe owned the skies and rained down destruction.

The wireless was on day and night, and no one strayed far from it as they waited for news.

"I've heard there's a plan afoot," Reggie said now. "The navy has begun commandeering civilian vessels along the south coast—fishing boats, launches, yachts, anything with a motor that might cross the Channel and take soldiers off the beach at Dunkirk and bring them home."

Viviane looked at him. "Reggie, does your father still have the launch?"

He peered at her. "Yes, but you can't be thinking what I think you are. It's much too dangerous, Vee."

Grace gaped at her, her wide blue eyes so much like Julia's.

"That boat is big enough to hold at least a dozen men," Viviane said. "One of them might be Geoff or Miles."

Reggie shut his eyes for a long moment, and when he opened them again, she knew he'd given in. "It's a fool's errand, a dangerous one. How much use do you think I'll be like this?" he asked, indicating his leg cast.

She grinned at him. "I'll drive. You navigate. I can't do both. They said they wanted the boats to be crewed by naval personnel. You qualify."

He rolled his eyes and looked at her with affection. "I never could deny you anything you wanted." He still joked about marrying Viviane someday. "Look, if we pull this off, I intend to propose again, and this time I'll be entirely serious. How's that sound? Don't answer now, just think about it."

"Golly," Grace said. "What can I do?"

"Gather flasks of tea and biscuits and blankets. We'll take them with us." She looked at the row of gas masks that hung by the door.

"Don't forget your camera," Reggie said, getting awkwardly to his feet. He glanced at his watch with the sober precision of a proper naval officer. "We'll leave within the hour."

CHAPTER SIXTY-SEVEN

Dunkirk

"ALL THESE BLOODY days, sitting on this damned beach, waiting for our turn to go. How long have we been here? How many lads have they taken off now? How many more boats can there be? There's still thousands waiting," Lieutenant Matthew Jamieson complained. "I'm so thirsty, I could drink the bloody Channel dry if it wasn't salt water, and then we could walk home."

Tom had listened to Jamieson's complaints for days, and he'd stopped answering his pointless questions. Tom had joined up last fall, was a war correspondent and a lieutenant. Jamieson was the photographer they'd assigned him. Tom had never had much luck with the photographers they gave him.

Except Viviane Alden. He still judged every picture against the quality of what she might have taken if she'd been here. He thanked heaven at the moment that she was far from this beach and safe at home. It was beginning to look likely that he was going to die here or be taken prisoner by the Germans. Given his reputation for criticizing the Nazi regime, he doubted they'd be merciful now.

A sergeant ran up to where they lay in the sand. "Your turn to go. There are four small boats coming in, lads. You'll have to swim out to them." He raced on.

Tom's heart sank. The boats were at least a hundred yards offshore, and it got deep fast.

Jamieson was already on his feet. He dumped his pack and his cameras in the sand. He looked at Tom. "Aren't you coming?"

"Can't swim," Tom murmured.

Jamieson's eyes popped. "You can't swim? All those bloody tales of rowing at Oxford and you can't swim?"

"Cambridge," Tom murmured. Jamieson stared at him, then held out his hand.

"Come on. I'll help you. We'll go together."

Tom's throat closed as he looked at the Channel, but it was a chance, his only chance. He rose and followed his comrade into the surf, felt the water rise over his ankles, then his knees. He felt his belly tense. "Don't fret—you'll float like a cork," Jamieson said when the waves reached his chest. "I'll just hold on to you, move you in the right direction. You can kick your feet, can't you? Are you ready?"

Tom nodded and let Jamieson take hold of him, swim beside him. He kept his eyes on the boat ahead of him, a red hull, jaunty against the gray of the sea. He saw other men moving in the water around them, grunting, calling out, splashing, swimming for their lives.

Then he heard another sound, a buzz that became a whine, then a roar. A black shape bore down on them from the sky. He saw the bullets stitch the water with plumes of white spray, saw one of those dotted lines heading straight for him.

Jamieson screamed and let go, and Tom was on his own.

THE CHANNEL WAS choppy, the wind against them, and it had been a rough crossing, but they were now within sight of Dunkirk. Viviane saw the devastation, the smoking vehicles that lay on their sides on the sands, and black lines of waiting men straggling along the water's edge and on the mole, the breakwater, where larger ships were coming in to pick them up. "Get as close to the beach as you can. The men will swim out," a naval officer with a bullhorn called to them. "Pick them up fast and turn for home. Don't linger."

"You don't have to tell us twice, mate," Reggie murmured, seated in the bow of the boat with his injured leg stretched before him. He was scanning the sky through binoculars, his face grim. "No one's going to hang around and watch the German dive-bombers swoop in like vultures."

Viviane was at the wheel, and she guided the launch in toward the beach, getting as close as she dared.

She could see men wading into the water, plunging, swimming toward them with desperate strokes.

"Come on, lads," Reggie called, his hand over the side, ready to grab hold, pull the soldiers to safety.

Viviane saw them first, a pair of dark shapes crossing the sky like fast-moving gulls. They were coming straight at the launch, at her. She saw the bright flash of the bullets as the pilot fired, saw the shots hit the water, heard the screams of the men, saw blood bloom red in the water. She dragged the wheel hard over, felt the tired launch respond.

But not fast enough. A bullet hit the wheelhouse next to her face, spraying splinters against her cheek. There wasn't time to think about that now. She looked for Reggie, saw that he was crouched in the bow, unhurt, but looking upward in horrified surprise. Hard on the tail of the first plane came another, but this one was a Spitfire, one of their own. Reggie scrambled up, cheering as the British pilot chased the German Stukas away.

In the water, it was chaos. Bodies floated, and men were twice as desperate. The ones who reached the boat tried to haul themselves to safety, threatening to capsize it. "Stop, one at a time," Reggie said vainly. He pulled one man aboard, told him to help others, then leaned out again himself. Viviane kept count . . . nine men, then ten. They had space for another two, perhaps five, but no more than that.

She saw a soldier struggling to stay afloat, his face white with pain, the water red around him. The man in the water beside him was pushing him toward the launch. "Reggie!" she called, and pointed, but Reggie was busy.

She went to the railing and waited. They were a dozen yards out, floundering. They couldn't wait for another boat. They wouldn't make it.

"Come on," she called, holding her hand out, reaching for them. She wondered if there were more planes, more danger, but she didn't dare look up now.

They reached the boat. "He's hurt, take him first," one said, the slight Scottish burr hitting her ear, reminding her of—

Tom.

With a cry, she grabbed hold of a floating flap of khaki and pulled with all her might. Someone reached over the side to help her, and a big body tumbled over the side, soaking her. It wasn't Tom, she knew without looking. He was too broad, too short.

She looked for the second man and saw a hand in the water, sinking fast. She reached down, grabbed for it, and caught hold.

The white fingers clasped hers, held tight, and she pulled with all her might. He came up beside the boat, gasping for air, and she looked down into his face, knew those gray eyes. She felt a sob gather in her throat, and she pulled harder. He braced his foot against the hull, helped her pull him in. She knew the shape of his head, the lean body under the wet khaki uniform. He fell to his knees on the deck, and she dropped beside him, her hands on his face, trying to lift his head and look into his eyes.

"Tom," she whispered. "Tom."

His hand shook as it reached for hers. He was out of breath, and he looked up at her. "You appear in the damndest places, Miss Alden," he said, and she threw herself at him, not caring if he was wet and cold, the water seeping into her own clothes. He was in her arms, real and solid. He held her tight for a moment before he pulled back. "Jamieson?" he muttered, looking at the wet, hollow-eyed men around him.

"Here, Graham," Jamieson said, grimacing. "Took one in the shoulder. Not sure who rescued who, but I'm grateful you got me here." He looked at Viviane. "Thank you for coming, miss."

"Vee?" Reggie called. "We're full up. Get us out of here." He waved his finger in the air and pointed back toward England. "Good God, is that Tom Graham?" he asked, gaping at Tom. Then he looked at Viviane, took note of the way she held tight to Tom's hand. The merriment in his eyes faded slightly, and he forced a jaunty grin. "All right, lads, let's go home to dear old Blighty."

CHAPTER SIXTY-EIGHT

Wrenwood

TWO MORNINGS LATER Viviane met Tom at the fence that marked the border between Halliwell and Wrenwood. It was summer again, and the meadow was in bloom, filled with wildflowers and bees.

The news on the wireless said that more than three hundred thousand men had been rescued from Dunkirk. They were reported to be in good spirits, glad to be home, and ready to fight on.

Viviane had guided the valiant little launch into the cove at Halliwell, where Grace had organized helping hands to provide hot tea, warm beds, and medical care. Reggie had telephoned HQ in London to report that there were fifteen men alive and well at Halliwell. It was considered a great local triumph, and Reggie was lauded as a hero.

"You acquitted yourself well, darling girl. You are a marvel," Reggie had said to Viviane when they arrived back. He followed her gaze to where Tom was helping his friend Jamieson off the boat. "And fancy finding Tom Graham over there."

She glanced at Reggie when he said Tom's name. "Yes," she replied.

"I always liked him, you know," Reggie said. He stepped back. "I know I promised I'd propose to you when we got back, but I'm all in. I need some rest, and so do you. Mind if we wait on that? I'll get someone to drive you and Grace back to Wrenwood."

And now, as the sun rose, she walked across the meadow. They hadn't spoken, she and Tom, but she knew all the same that he'd be at the familiar spot, waiting for her.

Her heart leaped as she saw him, looking out toward the sea, and France, where the war raged. They had a moment of reprieve here in England, a chance to catch their breath, but not for long. He turned and watched her walk toward him, his face unreadable.

She hauled herself up on the fence beside him. Her heart was pounding in her chest, but she kept her smile guarded. "How are you?" she asked.

"Ready to fight another day, thanks to you."

"Well, it was my turn to rescue you." She paused. "Is that what you intend to do? Fight another day?"

He looked at her, let his gaze roam over her face for a long moment. "I think I must, don't you?"

She looked away, scanned the meadow without seeing it, bereft at the idea of losing him yet again.

"I have something for you." He put his hand in his pocket, and she saw the glint of something gold. He picked up her hand and dropped it into her palm. She stared down at the small gold coin.

"My coin! I thought I'd lost it, that I'd never see it again."

"I found it the morning after the party, in my hotel room."

She felt herself blush at the memory. "You kept it all this time?"

"It gave me a reason to find you again, so I could return it."

She scanned his face. "I wish you hadn't waited so long."

It was on the tip of her tongue to say it, *I love you, don't go*, but instead she looked away, braced herself. "What happens now?"

"We're at war," he said simply.

They watched a crowd of larks fly overhead, an exultation, as a flock was called, a celebration of an English summer. She thought of the planes over Dunkirk, of the dark days that would surely come. She could see by Tom's grim expression that he was thinking the same.

He reached out and took her hand. "When I was on that beach, there was only one thing I regretted. Well, two things, if you include not learning how to swim."

"What else did you regret?" she asked.

"Leaving you. I wanted to come back to you a hundred times. I wished I'd told you I loved you when I had the chance." He squeezed her hand. "Reggie asked me last night what my intentions are toward you. Have the two of you come to an agreement at last?"

"He said he would propose when—if—we got back safely from Dunkirk."

"Will you say yes?"

She shook her head. "It wouldn't be fair. Not when I'm in love with someone else. I'd be Guinevere in truth, then."

He scanned her face, and she held her breath and waited for him to speak.

"Would you consider . . ." He paused and looked away, and she saw the familiar telltale tic in his jaw, the one that told her he was nervous. She resisted the urge to kiss the spot. "Look, I thought I'd go up and see my mother in Glasgow before I'm reassigned. If you're not busy, perhaps you'd like to come with me? My uncle Archie would like to meet you as well. It's a daft time to ask, of course, and I considered waiting, but I think this has waited long enough. One thing I've learned in the past few years is to seize the moment while you can. There's no way to know if . . ."

"Is this a proposition, Mr. Graham?"

He blinked. "Yes. But it's the other kind of proposition this time, the romantic kind."

"Good," she said. "Then, yes, I'll go to Scotland with you, meet your family."

"I was actually going to ask you . . . well, that is . . . damn it. I'm a journalist. I'm never lost for words. Not until now. I've practiced how I'd say it if I got the chance, how I'd ask you to marry me, tell you I love you, that I loved you in Berlin, and it hasn't faded with time. I don't even have a ring."

She picked up his hand and put the coin back into his palm. "Will this do?" she said. He put it around her neck and fastened the clasp. The coin rested against her heart once again. "I was wondering, Miss Viviane Alden, if you'd like to marry me?"

She threw herself into his arms, knocking them both off the fence into the long soft grass. "Yes, Tom Graham, I'll marry you. One thing, though."

He kissed her. "What's that?"

"Before we go anywhere, I'm going to teach you how to swim."

ACKNOWLEDGMENTS
AND NOTES

THANK YOU FOR reading *That Summer in Berlin*. I'd like to thank my wonderful editor at Berkley, Sarah Blumenstock, and my fabulous agent, Kevan Lyon, for all their patience while I worked on this story. I owe a huge debt of gratitude to all the people who turn a manuscript into a beautiful book, including the copyeditors and proofreaders, the cover designers, and the publicity team. It truly takes a village—or a roundtable—of brilliant minds to create a book!

Sometimes (and writers know this), a story comes into your heart and mind almost fully formed, and all you have to do is write it down.

This wasn't one of those books.

That Summer in Berlin was a very different book from any of the stories I've written before. It came in little pieces, a giant game of connect the dots during a pandemic, which made writing infinitely harder.

The seed for this story was sown when I came across an article about young English debutantes who were sent off to Germany between the wars, right up until the summer of 1939, just weeks before the Second World War began. In part, it was believed that if the upper classes of the two former enemies intermarried, then there simply couldn't be another war. The chance to experience German society also gave the young ladies a spot of continental polish, an appreciation of another culture. Many believed that England would do better to ally itself with Germany if another war came and avoid another French connection. The idea of titled English debs dancing with young Nazi officers as the threat of war loomed became the first dot in the story, a pin in the map, so to speak.

The second dot appeared when I started reading about the 1936 Olympic Games. Americans will know those games as the ones in which Jesse Owens won four gold medals and became the most famous Olympic athlete of all time.

When Adolf Hitler came to power in 1933, he planned to cancel Germany's offer to host the 1936 games. Others convinced him that the Olympics would provide a wonderful way to use propaganda to impress the world and show off Aryan culture and superiority. For those games, the Germans designed many of the Olympic rituals we still use today in order to tie themselves to the noblest traditions of ancient Greece. The Olympic flame was actually invented by the Germans, for example, and today it's hard to imagine the Olympics without that symbol.

For the duration of the games, the Nazis were on their best behavior. They presented an image of peace, brotherhood, and goodwill to the world. They hid anti-Semitism, repression, and violence. But behind the scenes, preparations for war were already in progress—conscription, training programs for soldiers and future soldiers through the Hitler Youth. New and more powerful weapons were already being developed, despite the fact that Germany was forbidden from doing so by the treaty that ended the First World War.

The next dot appeared when I began researching English society in the 1930s. I loved reading about the flamboyant Mitford sisters, the belles of society. Diana Mitford divorced her first husband to marry

British Fascist Oswald Mosley. Unity Mitford was a dear friend of Adolf Hitler. Other members of the British upper classes admired Hitler's Germany in the 1930s. Ladies swooned over the dashing uniforms of the SS, created by high fashion designers to make the man inside bigger, his legs longer, his shoulders wider. They admired the efficiency of how Germany rose from the ashes of defeat in the war faster than any other nation and became the leading world power in steel and chemistry. Britain was in the grip of the Depression, suffering violence, hunger, and unemployment. Many believed that England would eventually be forced to choose between Communism and Fascism to restore order and prosperity.

In creating the main characters in the story, I turned to areas where new social developments were unfolding. In the 1930s, female photographers like Dorothea Lange and Margaret Bourke-White were making the world sit up and take notice with powerful, daring photographic images, stories told in pictures from a female perspective. I made Viviane Alden a photographer and let her use her camera to tell the truth others tried to hide. True story: I once dreamed of growing up to be a *National Geographic* photojournalist. I bought my first camera at age seventeen, an Olympus OM-1. A few years ago I passed it on to my son, Griffin, who takes wonderful old-school film photographs. In doing the research for this book, I was also fortunate to meet Dave Marshall at Prairie Light Gallery in Longview, Alberta. Dave is a film camera and photography guru. I'd like to thank him for his advice on Leica cameras of the 1930s and how they worked. In response to my awkward question about what kind of camera Viviane might have used, he took the very model out of the case and showed me everything about the Leica III. "There's her camera," he said with a grin, and so it was. Someday I'm going to buy that camera!

When I read Canadian journalist David Halton's 2014 biography of his father, *Dispatches from the Front: The Life of Matthew Halton, Canada's Voice at War*, I knew my hero had to be a journalist. Matthew Halton was from Alberta, Canada, and he was one of the most prolific, outspoken, and well-regarded reporters in the world during the 1930s and 1940s. Tom Graham is my way of saluting Matthew Halton.

A big part of writing this book was, of course, the elephant in the room—the rise of the Nazis and the terrible crimes against humanity that took place even long before the war began. I've always wanted to understand how ordinary people could think such things, do such things, and create highly efficient systems of such incredible evil. It's the most brutal, terrifying horror story in history, and sadly it's all true.

I've always had a soft spot for the King Arthur legend. I love the idea that when England's need is greatest, the Once and Future King will return to defend the land. You must admit that the incredible events of World War II, the way plucky little Britain stood alone against the Nazis, seem almost miraculous, magical, brave, and worthy of legend. Viviane is named for the Lady of the Lake. Felix von Schroeder is my interpretation of Mordred, the wicked trickster who brings down a kingdom. Alex MacCann is Merlin, and Arthur—well, I'll leave it up to you, dear reader. Is he Arthur Alden or Tom Graham? I like to think that there is a bit of King Arthur in all of us—the ideals of courage, might for right, and a belief in magic, miracles, and our own powers to change the world for the better.

Thank you to my in-house tech expert on all things Mac, my son, Griffin. There were two computer disasters during this project, one that required a whole new hard drive. Then, on the very day I finished the first draft, wrote the last few words, the worst possible thing happened: the computer blinked, and the whole manuscript disappeared into the ether. After much gnashing of teeth and wailing from me, Griffin did some Merlin-like magic and saved the day.

Last, and certainly not least, I'd like to thank my daughter, Olivia Cotton Cornwall, historian, editor, and adviser, who waded through the early drafts of *That Summer in Berlin*, pointed out flaws and goofups, and helped me create a strong, brave, wonderful heroine who is just like her.

THAT
SUMMER
IN BERLIN

LECIA CORNWALL

THAT
SUMMER
IN BERLIN

LECIA CORNWALL

DISCUSSION QUESTIONS

1. Despite the fact that women were excluded from politics in Germany under the Nazis, Ilsa von Schroeder believes that women are the true power behind the scenes. How did women influence policies in history? How do women influence the action of the novel?

2. Tom walks a fine line in his role as a foreign journalist in Berlin, posting the kinds of stories that wouldn't offend his hosts in order to gain their trust. Do you think this ultimately does more harm than good? Why or why not?

3. It was the practice of the upper classes in Britain to send their debutantes to Germany during the 1930s in hopes of forming social connections that would make war impossible. Was this a legitimate possibility, a naive hope, or a form of appeasement? How does this play out in the novel?

4. Propaganda was successfully used by the Germans to create a false impression of Germany under Nazi rule. Why were tourists so willing to believe what they saw? How do messages portrayed in movies, books, music, and art in the past and the present shape political opinion?

5. Viviane takes photographs because she believes the camera cannot lie. Does a camera truly reveal truth or simply reflect the photographer's beliefs and opinions, another form of propaganda?

6. Julia falls in love not only with the façade of the Olympic Games but also with a man striving to rise in the new Germany. What must she give up in order to be happy in Germany?

7. While Georg von Schroeder does not consider himself a Nazi, he does little to prevent the rise of the Nazis or the fact that his own sons enthusiastically follow Hitler. How does he passively try to thwart Nazi power?

8. In the story, Viviane symbolizes the Lady of the Lake, guardian of the magical sword of King Arthur. In what Arthurian roles do other story characters fit best? How does the story compare to the legends of Camelot?

9. Is Viviane naive to believe the stories her father told her about King Arthur, or do the stories lend her strength and make her more resilient?

10. Could the actions of ordinary people like Viviane or Tom have truly had an impact on stopping another war? Can ordinary people have an impact in modern society?

PHOTO BY LAURIE MACBROWN

Lecia Cornwall, acclaimed author of *The Woman at the Front* and numerous historical romance novels, lives and writes in the beautiful foothills of the Canadian Rockies with four cats and a wild and crazy ninety-pound chocolate Lab named Andy. She has two grown children and one very patient husband. When she is not writing, Lecia is a dedicated volunteer at the Museum of the Highwood in High River, Alberta.

CONNECT ONLINE

LeciaCornwall.com
🐦 LeciaCornwall
📷 LeciaCornwall
ⓕ Lecia.Cornwall

Ready to find
your next great read?

Let us help.

Visit prh.com/nextread